Until...

Until...

TIMMOTHY B. McCANN

AVON BOOKS NEW YORK

In memory of my father.

This is a work of fiction. Names, characters, places, and incidents either are the product of the author's imagination or are used fictitiously. Any resemblance to actual events, locales, organizations, or persons, living or dead, is entirely coincidental and beyond the intent of either the author or the publisher.

Avon Books, Inc.
1350 Avenue of the Americas
New York, New York 10019

Copyright © 1999 by Timmothy B. McCann
Cover photography by Rob Lewine/The Stock Market and
Maria Taglienti/The Image Bank
Interior design by Kellan Peck
Back cover author photo by Mike Shea Photography
Published by arrangement with the author
Library of Congress Catalog Card Number: 99-94860
ISBN: 0-380-80579-0
www.avonbooks.com

First Avon Books Trade Paperback Printing: June 1999

AVON TRADEMARK REG. U.S. PAT. OFF. AND IN OTHER COUNTRIES, MARCA REGISTRADA, HECHO EN U.S.A.

Printed in the U.S.A.

OPM 10 9 8 7 6 5 4

Acknowledgments

I must start by acknowledging God for first giving me a level of talent and then allowing me to share it with you.

Whenever I speak publicly, I always introduce you as My Heart and My Soul. To my daughter Anna Janay McCann and son Timmothy B. (Jake) McCann II, my love for you is ForAlways.

To my mother Annie Mae McCann, thank you for teaching me the true meaning of faith. In more ways than one if there were no you, there would be no me.

Thank you to all of the book clubs nationwide and in particular Circle of Friends II in Atlanta and Juliet Harrison, as well as Minds In Motion Book Club in Columbus, Ohio, and its founder, Dorothy Malone Daniel. I also would like to take a moment to mention the numerous bookstores who welcomed me on my first tour. Most notably Felicia A. Wintons and Books for Thought, Inc., in Tampa and Shondoalon and RaMin of RaMin Books in New Bruswick, New Jersey.

It is said that no man is an island unto himself, so with that in mind I would like to thank three special women. Victoria Sanders for putting it together, Cynthia Johnson in Dallas for the encouragement, and Jennifer Sawyer Fisher in New York City for the focus. I would also like to thank the women readers across the country who said, "Tim . . . you have something here," even when the words were raw. You can never ever know how much that meant to me then and now.

Thank you to the thousands who hit our web page at www.DLastRomeo.com. I appreciate the sharing of your thoughts and you give Phillippians 1:3 a new meaning.

Last, but not least, to my family and fellow writers. Euripides said, "Life has no blessing like a prudent friend." I am honored to consider you a friend and now I trust you will enjoy the ride . . . Until . . .

With a search of his backseat, the sheriff found his coffee cup. "Here, sugar, drink this," he said, and offered the hastily poured cocoa from his thermos to the little girl who was still wet, shaking, and scared. The muscular gentleman with fingers as thick as a roll of quarters was the first highway patrolman at the scene that rainy afternoon, and the one to rescue her from the vehicle. Her forehead bled from the impact, but more than anything, she was in shock.

CHAPTER 1

‡

Thursday morning

Betty flung her childhood comforter to the floor, flipped her pillow to the cool side, and lay quietly on her bed as she gazed at the ceiling fan. In darkness, the cream-colored room turned to shades of blue. Her pillowcase was damp, but not with tears. From within the silence of the room, it seemed each sound outside her home was magnified. She heard the sweeping thrash of her neighbor's sprinkler system against her wall. She heard the soft sigh of the pine tree next door moving in the breeze. On this morning, even the chirps of the crickets were more audible. The time was 4:17, and in three hours she would face the most important day of her career. She had been tossing in bed for over an hour. Neither the taste of warm milk nor the counting of yawns had worked, so she closed her eyes and whispered, "God, please let me go to sleep." The ghost in the shadows of her mind had made a return visit.

With a shallow inhale of the peach-hyacinth-scented air in her bedroom, she said out loud, "I need to relax." She thought about Jacqui and smiled as she remembered their last conversation and the story about a certain police officer in town. Her thoughts went to Evander and how much she missed sleeping beside him, especially on a night like this one. Betty thought of the courtroom that smelled like an old textbook and the look on the sequestered jurors' faces. And then she noticed the clock. It was 4:18. She curled around her pillow with the sheet tucked over her shoulders and closed her eyes with the knowledge that once again, for her, sleep would not come easy.

"We the people of the state of Florida, in the matter of Lopez versus Midway Railroad United, case number 98-170C, rule in favor of the plaintiff."

As the foreman of the jury read from the index card, the widowed mother of two children wept. A couple of individuals in the gallery screamed, "Yes!" as the judge brought the court back to order with a swift pounding of the gavel. As a tear slid down Mrs. Lopez's face and under her chin, her lawyer reached over and covered her quivering hand. With a peripheral glance, the attorney closed her eyes while anticipation evaporated in her throat. Years of litigation were over, and the two ladies waited to hear the amount awarded to the family.

"Count one, in the charge of wrongful death and reckless endangerment of Mr. José Roberto Federico Lopez, the people award in the amount of one million dollars," the double-chinned brunette juror read from the card. After they heard the award amount, the spectators in the court again displayed their approval.

"This is my *final* warning," the judge said, and opted not to pound the gavel but to point its handle toward the disrupters.

"Count two, in the charge of wrongful death and reckless endangerment of Lorenzo José Roberto Lopez, the people award in the amount of five hundred thousand dollars." After saying these words, the jury foreman allowed a smile to appear, but never looked up from her card. Spectators in the gallery were again ecstatic, but restrained, as they squirmed with excitement.

The people had spoken and Betty Anne Robinson had won the case no one in her firm wanted to take. She looked across the courtroom at the long table of attorneys and the CEO of the railroad company as they huddled together. Their appeal process had no doubt begun, but it didn't matter to Betty. Once again she had reached into nothingness and pulled out a victory.

Mrs. Lopez, the thirty-three-year-old Mexican fruit picker who always wore a stroke too much makeup, sat placid as the eyes of the courtroom fell upon her. In the months prior to the trial, she and Betty had worked closely in preparation of the case. While they'd had numerous meetings in the conference room of Murphy, Renfro and Collins, there were often times Betty felt she sat in the room alone. And then one day she pushed her chair away from the dark mahogany table and turned to face her client. She knew their chances of winning the case were minimal if she did not get full cooperation from Mrs. Lopez, so she asked her point-blank what was wrong.

As she cleaned her glasses with the hem of her floral dress, Mrs. Lopez looked at Betty with eyes rimmed in red and then told of how she'd been working in her garden on a chilly, overcast afternoon. How she'd been putting a protective covering over her tomatoes and squash when she heard the phone ring and ran into the house. The first thing she'd looked at was the Caller ID box and noticed the call was from the Gainesville Police Department. Since Federico, who had had a pet peeve about punctuality, was more than two hours late from his run to the store, she'd refused to answer it. She recounted how she'd walked into the living room and taken her rosary beads from the mantel over the fireplace and held them to her heart. She'd murmured a prayer to herself as the phone rang because all was well until it was answered. And then her twelve-year-old daughter had lifted the receiver, said "Hello?" and changed her life forever.

"Miss Robinson, I don't know if you have ever lost anyone you've loved, but it's a feeling that I can't describe," she said as she gazed back and forth at the shelves of the conference room lined with gold-trimmed law books. "The best way to describe the way I felt is that I was dead too. But still breathing. No mother should ever bury her child and husband." With a shaky voice she continued, "A hundred times I've thought about dropping this suit. It seems every time I tell the story, a little part of me dies all over again and I don't know if I can go through it in court."

"Consuela?" Betty said softly.

"Ma'am?"

"Consuela, you've come too far."

"Excuse me?"

"You've come too far to allow them to get away. But it's not about them anymore. They were wrong, and they were petty. But then many companies do terrible things every day to people and they will continue to do so whether we win or lose. No, this is no longer just about who's right or wrong. This is about Federico now. This is about your baby and making what happened to them, for whatever reason it happened, mean something."

Mrs. Lopez had looked at Betty and, with tears in her eyes, had for the first time opened up and answered the questions she was asked in depth.

Now, months later, the Honorable Peter Travsky thanked the jury as questions formed in Betty's mind. *Should I have brought in another witness from Midway to testify about their lack of maintenance of the railroad crossing arms in Little Havana? Maybe I could have gotten three million for her.*

"Mrs. Lopez," Betty said quietly so as to not draw the judge's ire, "I know no amount will replace what you've lost, but I am hopeful this will save someone else's life." Consuela Lopez shook her head once, wiped her weary eyes, and blew her nose into the wadded tissue in her hand.

When the case was finally brought to a close, a smattering of applause was heard in the half-full courtroom. Betty turned, and the first face she saw was that of her mentor and senior partner of the firm, Jack Murphy.

"Wonderful job, Betty, wonderful job," Jack said, while he displayed a wide smile and extended his large palm. For the first two years Betty was with the firm she only did grunt work and felt like a glorified paralegal, until Jack stepped in and demanded she receive more of a challenge. Since then she had not let him down.

"Thank you," she said as she shook his hand and exhaled a sigh of relief. "I'm just glad it's over."

Jack bore cinematic features, was perpetually tanned, and smelled of Polo cologne. He was an angular man in his seventies, but looked in better shape than someone twenty years his junior. His suits were tailored in the garment district of Manhattan and shipped to him every season and the Italian shoes he wore in a week's time cost more than the firm paid administrative assistants in a month. "Listen," he said. "I must return upstairs for that civil case with Patterson. He's having a mess of a time up there. But I would love for you and Evander to join us for dinner tonight at the house. That is, of course, if you didn't have anything planned."

"I'll have to see if Evander can make it, but as far as I am concerned, I would love to."

"Great, great. Let's say, eightish?"

"Eight would be fine. Thank you, sir."

"No, Betty, thank you," Jack replied, and gave her a thumbs-up sign. Before he left, he added in his part Irish, part North Florida drawl, "We'll see y'awll round eight."

Surrounded by family and friends, old and new, Mrs. Lopez stood in the midst of the courtroom as her two daughters fought to get closer to her. Betty decided not to muscle through the crowd. Instead she gathered her files and allowed her client to enjoy the moment as much as she could. She reached for her attaché, then walked through the low saloon-style doors toward the courtroom exit. Betty sighed, shook her head, and looked back on the scrambling attorneys, the courtroom support staff, and Mrs. Lopez encircled by her mob of admirers. Her work that day was complete.

As she walked out of the elevator, Betty hit the speed dial on her cellular phone to call Jacqui.

Betty and Jacqui had been a pair since Betty's freshman year at the University of Florida. They'd met in Drop-Add when Betty was being harassed by a jock who happened to be the star receiver on the football team. As he'd begun to get more obnoxious in front of the other football players, Jacqui Jordan had come to her aid. She'd stepped between the two with her five-eleven, size-twelve frame and let him know in no uncertain terms that what he'd done was un-called-for. She had come to Betty's aid in one way or another ever since. The word *sister* could only begin to describe the relationship the two had formed.

With skin and eyes as dark as a raven and hair she always wore pulled back in a single ponytail, Jacqui was Cleopatra beautiful. She wore dark auburn lipstick and natural-toned makeup. Her teeth were pefectly straight, her build perfectly symmetrical, and her style was completely ebony. Jacqui was a lady unafraid to say what she felt in any situation. She harvested a natural energy, a smoldering fire to succeed in spite of the odds. In the tenth grade Jacqui had gotten pregnant but lost the baby after the second trimester. Her grades were not the same afterward, so she'd dropped out of school and gotten a job with a plumbing supply company. But at twenty-one she'd started attending night school, re-ceived her GED, and continued her education until she grad-uated with an MBA from the University of Florida.

Jacqui had opened Jacquetta's three years out of college. She'd left a position with a brokerage firm because she had grown tired of working twice as hard as her colleagues and not progressing half as far as they did. After she listened to a Les Brown speech, she decided if she was going to be a success, she would need to find her own bootstraps. She'd chosen the restaurant business because she'd always wanted to employ family, and most of them worked in the food industry in one capacity or another. But Jacqui was the straw that stirred the drink.

"Hey," Betty said into the cell phone. "What are you doing?"

"Nothing special, girl. Just reviewing a couple of menu changes and the receipts from last night. So what's up? What happened? Is the verdict in this fast?"

"Yes! One five!"

"Million?" Jacqui whispered although no one could hear her in her office.

"Yes, girl. One point five million. Can you believe it?"

"But you were thinking three fifty *tops* last night!"

"I know," Betty said, as a couple of well-dressed Wall Street types looked up from their papers as she passed. "I totally misread them. I figured they would award two fifty for Lopez because he was *slightly* inebriated and a hundred for their son, but the jury felt she deserved more. Go figure. What can I say?"

As the young attorney, in her early thirties, walked through the courtyard, heads turned. Even as a demure child, Betty moved with confidence as she walked. In no way was she vain, but at times when she passed a mirror she would smile at what she saw. Her appearance was delicate, and the curves of her body now accentuated by an olive pin-striped suit were graceful. Her hair was pulled up in a French twist, her supple lips were heart shaped, and her eyebrows arched above smoked-almond eyes like the wings of an angel.

"Well, that's great. What did old Consuela do when they announced it? I would have been on the floor. You know how I am about a dollar. Right now, if I'd won that kinda money, somebody would be asking me, how many fingers do you see?" Jacqui laughed.

"You know, that was the strangest part. But when I think about it, it makes sense. I watched her the whole while, and her face never changed. It was more than the money for her."

"Really?"

"Yeah. I mean, this woman worshiped her husband. You know, he was the only one she had ever *been* with. And still, to this day, she can't say her son's name without crying. I asked her to complete a document one time and she cried for a half hour after just writing their names. I couldn't imagine losing my husband *and* a child in one accident. Then today, to top it all off, all these people who were never even in the courtroom for the trial show up yelling like fools as the foreman was reading the verdict. It was so embarrassing. As soon as it was over, they were all over her like flies. I wanted to speak with her yesterday about talking to a financial planner or something before the family could get to her purse. They don't realize that money could be held up for years." As she spoke, Betty leaned her cell phone on her shoulder while searching for her car keys. "But I didn't want to put the cart before the horse. I'll give her a call tonight or in the morning."

"That's good. You know how people are when they smell a few dollars."

"Tell me about it," Betty replied, and clicked off the alarm as she opened the door to her navy BMW convertible.

"Damn shame you're still on salary and don't get to share in any of that."

"The money really wasn't that important to me."

"Whatever," Jacqui said over a sigh.

"No, seriously. I just wanted them to pay for what they did to this woman's family and to that community. Just because it was a Hispanic neighborhood, they thought they could get away with not maintaining those crossing arms. They also figured since our firm was based out of little old Gainesville, they could bring in all of those big-city attorneys. Get real," Betty said with a twist of the neck as if they spoke face-to-face. "No, no, no, this one went deep. You know how teachers always say they're compensated in a way other than money? Well, they couldn't give me enough money for the way I felt when the verdict was read. Midway didn't even have the decency to send that woman a bouquet of flowers. They had the audacity to say if he and the baby were buckled up, they would have survived the crash. Girl, I would have done it for free."

"Well, I don't know about all that free stuff, but guess who I finally got a chance to meet? Evander!"

"You mean my Evander?" Betty said with a smile in her voice.

"Oh, so it's 'my Evander' now, huh? Excuse me. I haven't heard you say that since you were strung out over Donnell. Two grown folks playing you-hang-up-first on the phone, but I ain't gonna go there."

"Jac, this man has got me wearing blinders. I don't wanna even talk about another man, he's so sweet. You know our office manager, Lisa? She keeps telling me about this football player she knows who has a financial consulting firm or something here in town. But I really don't want to—"

"Tell her to give him my number. Now, as I was going to say, Evander wanted to get the restaurant's business for his bakery. He'd called me a few months ago and I told him to phone after the holidays, so I give him credit for following up. I like that. I told him about the problem I had with the other bread man f'ing up my bill, and he said he would handle our account personally if I gave my business to Ferguson. But I don't know. Their prices are still a little higher than what we were paying before."

"So what are you going to do?"

"I guess I'll help a brother out, but don't tell him that. I'm still trying to get him to come down a little."

"How much do you need him to drop?" Betty asked as she steered her car through midmorning traffic.

"About three percent, at least."

"Jacqui, did you say *three* percent?"

"Hell yeah. Every penny counts in business." And then her voice lowered and Betty imagined her using her mental calculator. "If I could save three percent . . . on my bread cost . . . do you know what that would add up to . . . over a year? Just guess. Come on, guess."

"I don't know," Betty said, and slowed for the yellow light. "But I bet you got it down to the penny, don'tcha?"

"Two hundred and seventy-five dollars, thank you very much. That's enough to cover a week's pay for a waiter. Okay?"

"You're a trip."

"No, sweetie, I'm a *tour.* I don't pay retail for anything. I negotiated down the price for a pair of black pumps in the mall just last Saturday night."

"I'm glad you don't do that when I'm around."

"Please. I asked if they would be going on sale in the future. The clerk said in three weeks. So I told her I'd buy three pairs if she'd give me the sale price now."

"And she did it?"

"Child, please? I talked to the manager and got fifty percent off no less, and I only ended up buying two pairs. I just can't bring myself to pay full price since the time I heard that old Jewish lady my momma worked for say only niggers pay retail."

"You need help," Betty whispered with a half smile as she thought about the irony of the last comment. "Hey, I got a joke for you. I heard it during deliberation. You ready? This lawyer fails the bar examination because he thought an *antitrust* was a chastity belt! Get it? Anti . . . aw, never mind."

After a pause Jacqui laughed. "Child, you wouldn't know a good lawyer joke if you tripped over it. How about this one. A man is walking through a graveyard. He sees this headstone that says, 'Here lies a lawyer and a decent man,' and the man says, 'Dayumb! They got two men buried in the same hole'!"

"Okay, okay, you got me," Betty laughed. "That was pretty good. So tell me, what did you think about *Vander*?"

"He's cute! I didn't know he was that big, though. How tall is he anyway?"

"I think he said six four," Betty said, and blushed like a teenager "I'm not sure, though. Six three or six four."

"Girl, it doesn't matter. Six foot four? My, my, my. Driving a pearl white Land Cruiser no less? Tell me, how does it feel to rub your fingers through all of that curly hair?"

"See, now you acting silly."

"Bump that! I couldn't tell, does he still have all of his hair?"

"He's losing a little in the middle, but—"

"Let me tell you something. On a man as fine as him, it doesn't really matter. And I usually don't get into light-skinned brothers. I noticed he has some big hands and thick fingers. Like softball mitts or something. Does he have big feet?"

"Jacqui!" Betty said, in an embarrassed tone, knowing where her friend was going with the question.

"What? You better tell me something! I want de-tails. You know what they say about men with big hands and feet."

"Okay, okay. His feet are big too. I don't know what shoe size he wears, but they're big. And guess what," Betty added in an attempt to change the direction of the conversation. "When we were watching *Soul Food* the other night, I noticed the hair on his chest is shaped like a giant curly valentine. I just love running my fingers—"

"Please. He could have a toupee stapled to his chest for all I care. Be glad he got big feet. I dated this guy named

Morris?" she said, raising her voice at the end of each sentence in a questioning tone. "I think he was a Sigma? Brother was six feet three? Two hundred pounds, I think? Wore a size-eight shoe. Swear ta God, I kid you not! I ain't never dated a man who got a package of M&M's and a Rugrats coloring book when he bought new shoes. Homeboy was Buster Browned down to the ground," Jacqui said to Betty. "And on top of that I think he was gay or at least bi."

"Noooo. Really?"

"Yeah. I always thought he had a little sugar in his tank, but I sent him to the video store to get a movie and he came back and handed me the box. So I looked at it quick thinking it was Forrest Gump."

"And it wasn't?"

"Please," Jacqui said with a cluck of her tongue. "It was a gay movie from Greece. Title of it was, Soros Rumps! And then he tried to act like he made a mistake. Girl can I pick'um or what? But tell me. Getting back to your man, does he have hair on his back?"

"Oh God, no! I hate that."

"Well, I think it's kinda sexy. But yes," she said in a you-go-girl voice, "he looks . . . good. I wish I could find me a brother like that."

"Girl, please. Don't even go there. Clarke was all that and you chased him away. He was cute."

"Let's not even get started on Officer Smith. The man had the intellect of a wet spiderweb. And aggravating? Brother always wanted to fuss about something. He didn't have ulcers, but he damn sure knew how to give them. I mean, I just can't go out like that. I'm thirty-four, soon to be thirty-five and—"

"Jac, you're thirty-six."

"Who asked you anything?"

"Jacqui, you're thirty-six. Repeat after me. Thirty?"

"Like I was going to say, I've waited this long. You know?"

"Well, I thought you kinda liked him. Freda Mae was crazy about him."

"Listen. Freda Mae Jordan just wants some grandchildren.

She doesn't care where they come from. The stork could bring them or they could come out of the cabbage patch for real. Okay? She told me she didn't care if I wasn't even married, just get her some gaddamn grandkids. But seriously, I'm saving myself." As Betty started to giggle, Jacqui said, "Stop laughing! I'm serious! Can I finish? Damn! I'm saving myself emotionally. I'm just not gonna give myself to all these sweet dick Negroes anymore. Don't get me wrong, I enjoy a good piece of—"

"Jacqui!"

"Let me finish, please. When you start saying you love men now'days, they start acting a fool. So I'm just not gonna be as liberal with my love. When the right man comes, I wanna have something left for him, emotionally."

"I know how you feel." As the words passed, for a moment each woman reflected on all of the Evanders who had walked in and out of their lives. "I see a lot I like in him. I really do. But you know how that can be when you first start dating. I don't want to get in too deep too fast. You know how I was raised. But," Betty said, and released a puff of air, "I'm glad you finally met Vander. How long since he left there anyway?"

"About a half hour or so, I guess. Why?"

"Get this," Betty said, and politely waved on a gentleman who had slowed his car to get her attention. "Jack Murphy, Mr. Jack Murphy himself, invited Evander and me to his house for dinner tonight. And you know what? He remembered Vander's name from that office function a couple of weeks ago. I mean, I always noticed he remembered everybody's spouse's name, but Vander and I are just dating."

"Damn, really?"

"Yeah. Jack's all right. He was in the courtroom most days during the trial, you know. He's helped me a lot."

"Umm. Well, I'm happy you won. Can you imagine if you had won that case in private practice?"

"Don't start again. I'm just trying to play the game," Betty replied as she tried to wave off the guy who was beginning to be a pest. "Jack has been watching me closely, and the executive board may be getting ready to make an offer. Rumor has it they're going to offer a partnership within the next sixty to ninety days. I noticed on a memorandum for the partners that my billable hours were about thirty percent higher then the next associate on the list. With this verdict and my record, I look good, so we'll see. But in regards to going solo, if I wasn't with this firm, I may have never seen a case like this, so there are two sides to it."

"Maybe you wouldn't, maybe you would. But four hundred and fifty thousand dollars is a lot of money to 'maybe' about. You understand me?" Jacqui said in a parental tone. "I mean, one case like that and, girl, you set. Let's say they put you on the letterhead. You'll still have that idiot Renfro as managing partner. He'll still be calling the shots around there. If you hang a shingle, you can pick and choose which cases make you happy. Just think. Four hundred and fifty—"

"I know, I know, I know," Betty said, and gave the guy in the other car a sneer that prompted him to give up and drive away. "But sometimes it has to be more than just the money. Hey, I gotta call Evander to see if he's free tonight. Are you going to be around later on?"

"More than likely. I'm short a waitress since Kathleen is off again. She went to visit that fool in prison, so I'm filling in where they need me."

"Okay. Well, if I don't call back, I'll just drop by later, okay?"

"So if you have time to drop by here, you must be all moved in, huh?"

"Yeah. I got a few boxes to open still, but everything is at least in the right room now. Thanks for the help last night. I just never thought buying a house would be this involved."

"Tell me about it. Well, I will be here when you get here. Oh yeah," Jacqui said before Betty hung up, "again, girl, congratulations. I know those MFs over there thought you couldn't do it, but you did."

"Thanks. I appreciate that," Betty replied as she said good-bye, heard the dial tone and laid the phone to rest on the passenger seat.

CHAPTER 2

‡

Betty used the speed dial to call Evander. She had known him for some time, but they had only started dating recently. While she'd noticed he was always courteous to the other shoppers in the bakery she stopped at in the mornings, he would never so much as make eye contact with her. Not only had it not bothered her that he didn't look at her, she'd preferred it. She was focused on the brass ring in her career and didn't need diversions. Then, out of nowhere, he'd sent flowers to her office. When she'd called to thank him for the gesture, he'd made some conversations, which had come as a complete surprise to Betty. He was gregarious when he made jokes with customers and was often loud in the mornings when she came in for her pumpernickel bagel schmear. Evander was also more than ten years older than she, so the shy routine did not add up. But two weeks later he'd called back, and since then, when she was not at work on the Lopez case, the two were inseparable.

On their first date Evander explained to Betty that before he had become a baker, he'd worked in the construction field. He'd worked construction because he'd dropped out of college after the birth of his son. Evander and his son, whom everyone called Junior, had been constantly together on weekends. While Evander and his child's mother were never close, he'd looked forward to taking him to the movies, the playground, and even miniature golf. But one night Junior's mother had called and told him she had been offered a promotion and would be moving to Los Angeles. Now, outside of one summer his son had spent in Florida, his only contact was a weekly phone call.

After losing Junior, Evander had decided to improve himself and had taken the job in the bakery because he had gotten tired of the cyclical drywall business. Since the owner of the business was a friend of the family and needed a manager, it was an easy solution to his career dilemma.

"Hello, Eastside Bakery. Would you like to try our new chocolate twirlers today?"

"Hi. Is Evander in?"

"Yes. Is this Betty?"

"Yes, it is, Mr. Ferguson. How are you today?"

"I'm fine. Evander's been on pins and needles all day worrying about that case."

Betty smiled. "Really?"

"Yep. Let me get him. One second, okay?"

"What happened? Did you win?" Evander asked as soon as he got on the phone, his dark voice filled with youthful excitement.

"Yes, sweetie, I won."

"Damn! That's great," he said with pride. "One second, okay? Hey, everybody, she won. Again! Oh . . . damn, I forgot to ask her. One second."

"Tell them one point five million," Betty replied in anticipation of the question.

"Dollars? One point . . . five million . . . dollars? Are you serious? But he was drunk and didn't have a seat belt on the baby in the front seat."

"Hey, the jury listened. They looked at the facts and did what they felt was right."

Betty could hear a voice in the background that screamed, "Did you say one point five *million* dollars?"

"Yeah," Evander said. "My baby tough."

"Hey, Evander? I need to ask you a favor."

"Anything, dear, but before I forget, could you come over tonight, about nine o'clock? I special-ordered the rack of lamb you like so much, and I have a few other surprises as well. That wouldn't interfere with anything you had planned for this evening, I hope? All those night meetings regarding the case are over now, right?''

Damn, Betty thought. She hadn't spent any quality time with Evander in weeks. Between the case and moving into the house, she'd had little free time. And now she was going to spoil his special evening with another Murphy, Renfro and Collins commitment. "Did you say nine?" Betty said, thinking fast.

"Yes. Is that a problem? I know you still have a lot of unpacking to do in the house. If you like, we could have dinner a little earlier?"

"No. No, honey, nine o'clock is fine."

"Good. I can't wait to see you, and if you like, I'll follow you home to help. Oh yeah, what did you want to ask me?"

"Oh, umm, it's so funny. I was gonna invite you out to dinner with me." Betty had never put personal affairs before business in her six years with the firm, but she felt no guilt for doing so tonight. She had devoted all of her time to the firm since she had become an associate, but on this night Betty just wanted a little time to herself and this man in her life. She would call and cancel with Murphy, although she knew that politically, with a partnership in the offing, it would not be the wisest move. But tonight she did not feel like being Betty Anne Robinson, Esquire. Being congratulated and reviewing all of the steps that had brought in the large civil award was the last thing she needed this evening. She just wanted to be Evander's Betty. As she drove into the parking lot of Murphy, Renfro and Collins she said, "I miss spending time with you too."

"So nine o'clock it is. I hate to hang up, sweetheart, but we're in rush hour here for some reason. Can I call you back a little later?"

"Ah, yeah," Betty said. "Try me at Jacqui's or at home. I just got to the firm, but I didn't get much sleep last night, so I think I'm going to check on my messages and then head out for the rest of the day. I should be out of here no later than two o'clock."

"Okay, I'll call you then. Also, Ferguson told me a great lawyer joke today. I bet this one is better than Jacqui's."

With a smile Betty replied, "Thanks. I could use it." As she pressed the off button on her flip phone and returned it to her purse, Betty leaned back into her taupe leather seat and turned on the radio. She was not ready to go inside the firm. Once there, she knew she would be beset by congratulations, some insincere, from the partners, associates, and support staff. News like this traveled through the firm in the wink of an eye. Although she wanted to feel their adulation, for now, she wanted to savor this time alone. The moment she had worked so hard to attain had arrived. The moment she had sacrificed and disciplined herself for had come. Since the day she'd enrolled in law school, she had envisioned walking into a courtroom with the odds against her and leaving the room abuzz. She had dreamed a victory would feel special, but she still felt the same.

All aspects of Betty's life were where she wanted them to be. She was not married, but she had convinced herself that she was not looking for matrimony. So why couldn't she smile inside? Why did she feel empty? Why didn't she feel as delighted as Jacqui, Evander, or even Jack Murphy at her accomplishment? Why, after she'd received the verdict, had she not been able to enjoy it before critiquing herself? At one time she'd thought she would be happy when she graduated from college. Then her happiness had been delayed until she'd graduated from law school. She'd thought she would feel fulfilled when she was accepted by a prestigious firm, but she was not. And then she'd felt she would not feel ultimately satisfied until she won a case in which all the odds were stacked against her. Now, as she sat in her car, she released her tight grip on her steering wheel and pondered what her next "until" would be.

CHAPTER 3

‡

Friday morning

Betty sat up in her bed in a cold sweat as she heard the faint yelp of a dog in the distance. She had enjoyed a delectable dinner with Evander, and afterward they'd sat in front of the fireplace, played footsy as they told childhood stories, and then made love. Since he had to be in the bakery before the morning rush, he'd quietly left before dawn without waking her. But for Betty, this morning was to be another one of those mornings. The small prickly goose bumps on her arms had come again. She'd had the same vision she'd had too often in the past. It had occurred during the summer of seventy-nine, which seemed like a long time ago, but only if one measured in years. Whenever she had the nightmare, it felt like yesterday.

She glanced at the green digital numbers on her clock and noticed it was once again 4:17. *Not again,* Betty thought as the heels of her palms pressed firmly into her satin-covered mattress, with her chin touching her chest. In frustration she kicked her comforter off her feet. She wanted to cry so badly it felt as though her lungs would burst, but she could not. If only the silent grief of her heart could manifest itself in her eyes, she knew she would feel better. *Maybe I could finally get over it,* she thought as she looked at her white antique rocker in the corner. The rocker she had sat in so many nights when she feared sleep itself. But on this night, just like many nights before, her tears flowed inside.

For over a decade, two dreams had haunted her. One was of a dark figure who handed her a piece of paper, while she stood naked and unashamed before it. She could never tell if the figure was a man or woman, or someone from her past or present, and she would always awaken before she could read the words on the paper. She always wondered why she was disrobed and yet felt no sense of shame. But while one dream remained a mystery, she clearly understood the other. It was based on reality, which was why it gave her the shivers. And it was always the same vision. She was lying in bed as a child, with a pillow secured over her head by her elbow, sucking her thumb and trying to block out her parents' voices. Her stepfather was screaming so loud it seemed her Foster Sylvers poster would shake off the wall. Betty's mother responded in kind with an embittered roar.

With the images of her parents' fight freshly inscribed in her mind, Betty got out of bed and maneuvered her hands in front of her, attempting to find the bathroom. As she sat on the porcelain chair to relieve herself, she clasped her fingers around both arms and bent until her chin and knees met, thinking, *Why can't I shake this? Why is it, the more I accomplish, the more I think about it?* Those thoughts had bounced in Betty's mind like a Ping-Pong ball since she was a teenager and started having the dream. There had been no answers for her then, nor were there any tonight.

With her return to bed, Betty lost the battle to sleep, and the movie that played in her mind took over. She was twelve years old again, preparing to go with her parents on a vacation to visit relatives in Massapequa Park, New York. The morning of their drive, she lay in bed, flinching with every scream that radiated throughout the house. Her stepfather seemed more enraged than usual that morning. He and her mother fought about anything. A lost receipt, a cold supper, a wrinkled shirt. Anything was sure to cause an eruption in the Ryans' household.

It was hard for Betty to figure out what her stepfather said that morning because he talked so fast. Whatever it was, it made him madder than usual. When he was calm, he was genteel, noble, one might even say charming. But when he was mad, he became barbaric.

First there would be the thud of her stepfather's oversized feet double-stepping down the hallway as his voice diminished in volume. Then came her mother's voice like a siren in hot pursuit screaming, "Don't you turn your back on me, gaddammit!"

With his large fist he would pound the wall from time to time, which made Betty cringe beneath her comforter. She could hear her mother scream back with equal intensity. While she was a small woman, she could stare men down with eyes that pierced like fire, and she never gave an inch in an argument.

As the arguments esclated, Betty sucked her thumb harder. She'd sucked a pacifier until she was of school age, but sucked her thumb whenever she was afraid. She sucked it for safety. To feel secure. Betty sucked it so she would not cry, and it seemed to dampen her fears.

There were mornings when Betty would awaken before the sun, tiptoe downstairs, and sneak a breakfast of cake and Kool-Aid before her parents got up. But such mornings were rare. In their little town of Langston, Oklahoma, most kids could depend on their alarm clock before school. Betty could often depend on a fight. They were more predictable than any alarm clock or rooster on their small midwestern farm. Every now and then, alarm clocks lost power in the middle of the night. Sometimes even roosters would sleep in. But Betty rarely had cake and Kool-Aid for breakfast and the fights rarely slept in, not in the Ryans' household.

"Gaddamn you, woman! I ain't telling you no more!"

"Bring yo ass right back here! You ain't no man. Won't you act like a real fucking man for a change!"

All the words Betty felt wrong to even think of were being yelled loud enough for the neighbors to hear. *I can't wait till I grow up,* she thought. *I ain't never getting married. Never!*

It didn't matter to Betty who was right or wrong. She just wanted it to stop like it would on TV. James and Florida Evans argued, but never like this. George and Wheezy Jefferson always had differences, but with time they would subside. Yet the fights in her home seemed to go on and on and on as Betty squeezed her pillow closer to her ear and pressed her thumb against the roof of her mouth.

In her dream, Betty got out of bed in her high-water pajamas and began to play with her toys. She tried to play with Barbie and Ken, but for some reason they had no appeal on that morning. They looked so beautiful. So white. So blond. They looked like they were headed to a Malibu beach party or another ball and not to the screams she would face when she walked down the hallway for her cereal and milk.

Betty's biological father had lost contact with her mother long ago. He'd moved to Detroit with thousands of other Negroes with processed hair in the late sixties to stake his claim in the world of soul music. For some reason, he'd felt if he walked the streets of Detroit, he would hit the notes he could never touch in their bathroom. The plan was for him to move to Michigan for six months with the family's savings, and if the music did not work out, he would return to Betty and her mother. The plan did not include getting a backup singer pregnant and starting another family. After two years of continuous lies, Betty and her mother never heard from him again.

In her dream, Betty watched herself put on her seat belt and look for her crossword puzzle for the long trip to New York. After she helped her mother prepare for the trip, the little Afro-puff-wearing girl felt better because the screams had stopped—for now. But Betty was still upset. Although her parents were speaking to each other for the time being, the fight that morning had been especially scary.

Reaching back, her mother handed Betty her favorite snack. She could eat bologna and cheese sandwiches every day of the week and never get enough. She liked the way the mustard and mayonnaise smelled spread evenly on the pink, thick-sliced meat. The way her fingers would leave prints in the soft bread. How the cellophane crackled when her mother let her take it off the individual slices of cheese. Betty Anne simply loved everything about a bologna and cheese sandwich. "No, ma'am," she said to the offer of the snack as her mother eyed her suspiciously.

Betty's eyes opened as her nightmare ended with a thump

of the morning newspaper on her door. It was now 5:33; maybe she could just stay up. At least she would get a jump on her day's work. Breathing heavily, she wiped the small beads of sweat from her brow and got out of bed. As she walked into her kitchen she found the box marked "Pots and Pans Only." Opening it, she took out her kettle and filled it with water for a cup of Earl Grey.

This was Betty's first home. No more first and last month's rent and no pet rules, so she could finally get a cat. No more noisy neighbors to keep her awake at night banging on the walls while they engaged in loud sex. This was a place where Betty could start the herb garden she saw in *Southern Living* magazine. This was home. In this neighborhood, every family had a dogwood tree in the yard, a basketball net over the two-car garage, and a dog named Spot or King.

Betty poured herself a half cup of tea and leaned against a wall, staring outside through her bay window. As she cradled the warm, smooth, porcelain mug in her hands, she brought it to her nose and allowed the aroma to soothe her.

What a beautiful morning, she thought. It seemed the stars themselves spelled words, as a yellow and orange ball cast shards of light against the horizon. On this morning everything it graced turned into shades of crimson as Betty cracked a window and was welcomed by a wisp of warm air greeting her exposed midriff. And then the feathery pink clouds above began to turn white, and a despondent smile formed on her lips.

She sat in the breakfast nook and noticed a faded, yellowed picture on the floor. Ironically, it was the last picture taken of her with her mom and stepfather outside of Deliverance Temple. Her mother wore a bright yellow hat which she held in place with her lace-gloved hand that Sunday while her stepfather wore the only suit he owned. As always, he looked spectacular. Their child looked somewhat distant in the photograph. While her face did not look sad, it did not resemble Betty. She looked like what she was in many ways, a child caught in the cross fire.

As Betty looked at the photo, she thought of Mrs. Lopez, because every nightmare brought with it a small taste of death. She vividly remembered the highway that day twenty years ago, when her mother and stepfather joked nonstop, although the weather was horrific. It was strange to Betty how they could be at each other's throats one minute and laughing the next.

The rain fell thick that afternoon and landed with rhythm on the car, like the beat of a snare drum playing taps.

In spite of the elements, the couple in the front seat seemed cheerful. At least for now they were civil. Despite the storms in their relationship, there were times when they would act like two teenagers on a date.

The rest of what happened on the trip was carved in Betty's mind. She'd just awakened to the lighthearted melodies of the Fifth Dimension on the radio and looked out her window in an attempt to see if they were there yet when it happened. She had no idea by the time the last note of "Beautiful Balloon" was played that her life would be changed forever. *Crash!* A truck had careened across the median of the interstate and broadsided the Ryans' Lincoln on the driver's side. Betty's first thought as she woke up was, *Why is the car spinning like the teacup ride?* The car whirled so fast she was pinned to the seat, yet it felt everything moved in slow motion. Then she heard her mother scream, "Henry, watch out!" but to no avail, as the automobile was hit again by an oncoming truck that tossed it into the grassy median as if it were litter. And then it was quiet. From the angle at which his head was lying, Betty could tell immediately that her stepfather was dead. She looked at her mother and knew she was still alive because of her moans and faint gasps for air. She made a gurgling sound, and Betty knew she was in pain.

"Momma, Momma!" Betty cried out. "You okay, Ma? Are you okay?" As she tried to release her seat belt, she felt blood dripping from her forehead and then she looked up to see the window was cracked where her head had made contact. Secured in the seat, she could not move due to the damage done to her side of the car. Betty screamed, "Momma, Momma," again at the top of her lungs, but her cries were met with no response. In time she no longer heard the moans, the gurgles, or the fight for another breath of air. Soon all she heard was silence, and the silence was numbing.

Out in the marshy median on Interstate 71, in the cool of the night, with the blood on her face and the rain continuing to fall, lightning struck, and Betty sat trapped in the car with her thumb pressed against the roof of her mouth, crying, all alone.

Within the hour a highway patrolman pulled apart the door with a crowbar after he called for medical assistance. As Betty got into the patrol car, soaked to the skin, he gave her a towel and a hot cup of cocoa.

Betty sat in her canary yellow dinette chair and returned the photo to the album from which it had dropped. She had mentioned how it had felt to watch car after car pass, with the blood of her parents on her, to only one other person. Jacqui. She had told her best friend how it had felt to have the other officers make jokes about a card game the previous night as the paramedics loaded the bodies into the ambulance as if it were just another day at the office. As an adult, her analytical side begged her to get counseling. But the emotional side of her did not wish to relive the pain. With a gaze at the newly applied wallpaper, she lightly touched her bergamot-scented tea with the tip of her ring finger, and pensively reviewed all of the whys that trampled her mind like a lost herd of elephants. *What do you do when it hurts too much to cry?* she wondered as she took a small sip of the hot brew.

Years later she could pinpoint the moment she shed her last tear. It was at the burial when her uncle, thinking it would bring her closure, made her sit and watch as they lowered and put dirt on her mother's pink casket. As an adult, Betty realized that some wounds are never meant to heal. She rubbed the scar on her forehead as she thought about the conversation with Mrs. Lopez. Slouched in her dinette chair, she murmured, "No twelve-year-old should ever have to bury her mom." With a look up at the ceiling, her eyes closed as the memories continued to play. After winning the case, buying the home, and having Evander in her life, she still could not sleep. And on this morning, unlike at the graveside, there would be no tears.

CHAPTER 4

‡

Friday, three weeks later

"Hello," he said. And then he changed the tone of his voice. "Hello," he said again, this time with a softer smile than before. "Hi, Mr. Renfro," he repeated with a courteous southern pitch. He tried it with a gentle, confident arch to his brow, while he gazed at his reflection in the mirror.

"My name is Andrew. No. Andrew Patrick Staley of Andrew Staley and Associates." He rehearsed the lines as he had done for what felt like a million times before. His credo was simple. Practice does not make perfect. Perfect practice makes perfect, and he could ill afford to leave anything to chance. Again and again he repeated the introduction until it was perfect, or at least it felt as such.

"Andrew, will you ever come out of that bathroom?" Grace, the office secretary, asked as she stood in front of the open door. "You're going to do just fine."

"I know, I just need to make sure everything is right," he replied, never breaking eye contact with his reflection.

Grace smiled and shook her head. "Is that a new suit you're wearing?"

"Yeah," he said as he brushed invisible lint off the forearm of the jacket with the back of his hand. "I bought it . . ." And then his smile blew away like a candle in the wind. "I bought it for the funeral."

Grace looked away and said, "Oh," then walked back to

her desk in the reception area. As she left, Drew shot the cuffs of his navy suit and adjusted the silver cuff links as he held up his chin, but it soon gave way to a quiet lean against the wall. It had been two weeks since the funeral, and the pain still throbbed like salt on an exposed wound.

After standing in the hallway momentarily, Peggy walked into the tiny unisex rest room, rubbed between Drew's shoulders, and said in a soothing tone, "Are you okay, baby?"

With his eyes still closed, he attempted to relax the thump of the heart he could hear in his ear and said, "Yeah, I'm fine."

Peggy Randal was the only member of the firm over forty and the wife of a prosperous advertising executive twenty-two years her senior. Although she had been in the firm less than a year, she had a take-charge attitude that Drew admired.

"Look at me," she said, forcing him to open his eyes. "We can always cancel the appointment. I mean Lisa is easy to work with and she'll get you back on the schedule to see him. I'm not worried about that."

After he opened his eyes, he looked at Peggy and shook his head. "No. No, I need to do this one way or the other."

"Are you sure?"

Drew stood to attention, nodded his head yes, and checked himself one last time in the mirror as Peggy nodded her head, too, and walked back into the reception area.

"Drew," he whispered to himself. "We have got to do this. We've got too much riding on this one. We have to pull this off," he said, looking at his clean-shaven face from both angles in the mirror. As he did, he asked aloud, "Hey, does anyone have any—"

"Visine?" Grace said, and stood in the doorway with the small clear bottle.

As he took the solution, his smile thanked her. "I need everything I can to knock this good old boy off his feet today."

"And you will. He's gonna love that proposal. I saw one of the ladies who works there in the secretarial pool at church, and she said they have not had a decent employee benefits plan in years."

"I know. I've been trying to get in the door about a year now," Drew said as he rubbed the tension lines in his forehead. "Peggy and I worked on the proposal until midnight last night."

"And don't forget those three nights last week," Peggy said as she walked rapidly past the door of the rest room.

"You're gonna do fine, Drew," Grace repeated. "But you better hurry up, it's almost time."

Handing her back the bottle, he gave a faint smile and asked, "Better?"

"Yeah, you look great," she said as she looked in his weary bloodshot eyes.

Grabbing her briefcase and the folder for the appointment off Grace's desk, Peggy said, "You wanna take my car or yours?"

"Ah, where are you going?" Drew asked as his eyes followed her to the door.

"Where else? You wanna take my car or yours?"

"But you got an appointment in an hour."

"Canceled," she said in a matter-of-fact manner as she folded her arms over her thick waist. "I asked you to cancel yours, but you were too stubborn, so I canceled mine. Now, let me try this again. You wanna—"

With an appreciative smile Drew said, "I'll drive. Come on."

As he drove down the highway just above the speed limit so as not to get a ticket from most police officers, Drew asked, "Now, how you wanna do this today?"

"Simple. When you walk into his office, just tell Renfro I'm your assistant who worked with you on the deal. And if you need any help, I will be there for you."

Drew did not say a word. He didn't smile or blink, just looked straight ahead as he drove. The last couple of weeks had been tough on the entire staff as everyone walked on eggshells not knowing what to say. For the first time since establishing his consulting firm, Drew had taken several days off, and they'd had no idea where he'd gone. When he'd returned from his unexpected mini vacation, he'd said he felt better, but his dazed expression told another story.

"I never got a chance to say good-bye, you know," he said suddenly.

Peggy was shocked he would mention Felicia. He had not spoken of her since the funeral, and the unwritten code in the office was never to mention the subject until he was ready. For some reason, that time was now. "Really?" she said, and gazed ahead, not wanting to interrupt his flow while she checked for patrol cars.

Before responding, it occurred to Drew that he was no longer awakened in the morning by his alarm clock or the ray of sunlight through the curtains he always left open at night. Since her death, he was awakened each morning by the remembrance of the scent of her hair and the brush of her cheek on his chest. "Yeah," he whispered, and looked in his rearview mirror and then blindly ahead. "When we met, for the first three years we never ever said good-bye. We just always said I love you." Drew looked at the road ahead of him as he was taken to the painful space in his past. "But then for some reason, somehow we changed. Maybe it was the illness. Maybe it was the . . ." And then he massaged his temple with his thumb and said, "I don't know."

Peggy was hanging on every word he spoke, when she saw a police car ahead. "Ah, Drew?"

He continued to speak as they passed the officer, who chatted with his partner and did not see them. "I've never been able to accept death, I guess. When I was seven, this man got shot on our carport, and I saw it. I saw him running down the road. I saw the woman take aim and I saw the look in his eyes when he died. Trust me when I say it's nothing like it looks on television. I've watched thousands of people die in the movies, but no actor I've noticed has made the sound a person makes after they take their last breath. I saw when they covered his face with the sheet. My daddy went out and scrubbed down the concrete while my mom tried to explain to me the concept of death. I remember her asking me to close my eyes and hold my breath. And then she said, when people do that and fall asleep, that was how it felt to be dead. She told me that so I could understand that the man was not really in pain. But for weeks I was afraid to go to sleep at night."

And then Drew's voice and eyes lowered together. "You know, it's nothing like getting that call. When the phone rang three weeks ago, it was 4:17 in the morning. I looked right at the clock. If I live to be a hundred, I'll never forget the time I got that call, because I knew. I knew she was gone. The nurse, or whoever, said, 'Is this Mr. Staley,' and that's the last thing I heard."

"Well, Drew, if it's any consolation, Felicia is—"

"Yeah, I know. I know, but you still hate losing someone you love. I mean we knew she had cancer, and we knew she was going to leave, but I never expected—" And then Drew looked in the rearview mirror, and for a moment at Peggy. "Listen to me," he said, relaxing his shoulders, and his foot on the gas pedal. "We got work to do." Drew sat straight and said, "We've got business to handle."

Peggy gazed ahead and nodded her head yes.

As they drove into the parking lot of the Olsen Building, a tall dark sister with a long flowing ponytail walked by with a smaller lady in a sweat suit. As they opened the door to the building, the smaller woman looked back at Drew, but noticing he had company in the passenger seat, she continued inside the building.

Such looks from women were not uncommon since Drew was well over six feet and had a body that screamed linebacker. The thick arms and thighs and broad shoulders were a throwback to his days on the gridiron. His face featured distinctive cheekbones, deep-set oval eyes, and a distinguished chin. Drew had a shy blush when his real smile appeared, and his teeth were toothpaste-commercial straight. He also had a melodic baritone voice made for soft midnight conversations over candlelight or private whispers in the ear. Unlike many men his age, he wore no facial hair, and his Denzel brown complexion was void of razor bumps. Drew's wavy, sable black hair had a conservative part on the side, and although he was in his midthirties, he did not have the over-thirty midsection paunch. Even under the tailored wool pants, his thighs looked massive and muscular, and his legs were bowed just enough to get attention when he wore shorts.

Drew had worked for the past eight years for this hour, when he could swim with the big boys. He tried to block out all that had happened and thought, *It's all come down to this. Everything we've worked for has come down to the next two hours.* He looked over at Peggy as his confidence bloomed like a flower kissing the sun, and said with his first true smile of the day, "This man is in trouble."

Peggy noticed the change in his demeanor. He walked through the doors of the building as if he were ten feet tall and bulletproof, and the only reason Murphy, Renfro and Collins had decided to start a firm was to one day do business with Staley and Associates.

Murphy, Renfro and Collins was one of the top law firms in the Southeast. They specialized in medical malpractice cases and had won three of the fifty largest verdicts awarded in the United States. Since bringing in a former state senator as a partner, they were venturing into other types of litigation as well.

As they stepped inside the Olsen Building, Drew was focused as the lobby receptionist asked, "May I help you?"

Peggy, who walked in behind him, replied, "We're headed up to Murphy, Renfro and Collins on seventeen." Drew pushed the up button and waited at the elevator door, clearly in his zone. "I've never been in here before," Peggy said. "This is nice. Really nice."

Drew smiled as the doors opened and allowed Peggy to enter first. "I've been here a couple of times. I had an appointment," he said as the door whispered closed, "with an accounting firm here back in November. There's also a great restaurant in the basement called The Sovereign." And then as the elevator began its ascent, their eyes focused on the number above the doors as they listened to The Police's "Every Breath You Take" on the Muzak.

When the doors opened, Drew stood face-to-face with the young lady who had just entered the building with the woman wearing the ponytail. Their eyes met as Drew allowed her and her friend, who was talking about a date the previous night, to get on the elevator before he and Peggy made an exit. And then, wanting to be polite, he turned to smile and made eye contact with her as the doors closed.

Turning back around, he paused with Peggy to take in the opulent environment. The stairwells in the reception area of the firm were dark gray marble and higlighted with imported ivory. The foyer and atrium featured a forty-foot ceiling and deep mahogany borders which accented its arched windows and doors. The jasmine potpourri scented the air so heavily, one could almost taste it.

The firm occupied the top two floors of the tallest building in the north central Florida town of Gainesville. Murphy, Renfro and Collins looked over the city as the figurative big fish in a small pond. Most firms would rather settle than face the firm's litigators, who had a reputation for being ruthless and extremely effective in the courtroom. Jack Murphy led the firm, and his litigation skills were nothing short of folklore.

As he walked toward the reception desk, Drew noticed Lisa. She was the office manager and had been an employee of the firm longer than anyone else. By virtue of this, everyone knew she carried a tremendous amount of weight and influence with Jack Murphy.

Drew looked at the clock, which indicated he was two minutes early, and cleared his throat to get Lisa's attention. She turned toward him and motioned with a finger, saying she would be there momentarily, then returned to the other female employees who had gathered around her.

As he waited, he looked back and noticed Peggy, who sat in the waiting area. "Listen," he said after he walked over to her. "I appreciate you coming with me. But I think I better handle this alone."

With relief in her tone, she asked, "Are you sure? I don't mind."

"I know. And that's sweet. But I need to do this myself."

From her place on the imported leather sofa, she looked up at him. "You're gonna do good, Drew, I just know it."

"Thanks," he said, and reached for the business section

of the newspaper that was sitting on a lamp stand. Someone had drawn a circle around a picture of a ravishing young lady and an older gentleman. As he noticed the name in the caption, he realized that this Betty Anne Robinson person was the young lady he'd seen earlier. She had dark sultry eyes and beautiful white teeth, with an attractive mole over her lips. The body in the photo looked just as attractive as the one he'd noticed moments earlier, and she looked much too young and attractive to be an attorney in this conservative firm. Drew laid down the newspaper and looked again at his watch as his thoughts went back to Felicia, who looked similar to the attorney in stature, and her onetime dream of being a corporate litigator.

Both Drew and Peggy had built a warm relationship with Lisa since they had tried to get on Franklin Renfro's calendar. Lisa was a graceful, albeit overweight, well-dressed woman in her early fifties. Renfro, who handled the employee pension and benefits programs personally, had put him off for several months, but Drew had locked in on his goal and had never given up. In late November Renfro's secretary had called and said the absolute best she could do was to schedule him two hours the first week of February, to which Drew said, "I'll take it."

Now Lisa walked toward Drew, and it was obvious her mascara had run. As he looked at the other ladies, he noticed one of them holding a box of tissues, and said, "Umm, hello, Lisa?"

"I guess you haven't heard yet," she replied.

"Heard what?"

"Mr. Murphy had a heart attack last night and he's in intensive care. It's not looking good for him," Lisa blurted out.

"Oh my goodness. No, I hadn't heard. I'm so sorry."

"We—we've been in tears all morning. That man is the salt of the earth and, and I just . . ." Lisa stopped speaking, unable to finish her sentence. She placed a damp tissue to her round face and gingerly rubbed her nose. "You have an appointment today, don't you?" she half asked, as she gathered herself and cleared her throat.

"Ah, yes, at eleven forty-five. Is Mr. Renfro available today?"

"Hon, he might have forgotten about you. He just walked in from the hospital, and none of us have even looked at the schedules all day. Let me buzz Kathy to see if he's up there and whether he can meet with you," Lisa said, and blew her nose.

While Lisa turned her back and picked up the phone, a man who fit the description of Renfro given to Peggy walked toward the water cooler. As he did, she stood, cleared her throat, and half pointed in his direction after she got Drew's attention.

"Ah, Lisa," Drew said, and tapped the desk so as not to be heard by the gentleman. She turned to Drew and then noticed Renfro.

"Oh, Frank; this is your eleven forty-five, Andrew Staley. He's here to discuss our company benefits."

"This is Andrew Patrick Staley?" Renfro asked in surprise as he wiped water droplets from his chin.

"Yes, sir," Drew said as he produced his business card like a six-shooter after he shook the partner's hand, just as he was taught in college.

With breath that came from the pit of his belly, Renfro replied, dragging out every syllable of the name, "Mr. Staaaley, you have caught us at a very bad time." He then gazed at Lisa as if to say, *Why did you schedule me for this?* Lisa turned around with grace and walked back to the other women.

Franklin Clay Renfro was a man of middle age with a receding M-shaped hairline who lived in the shadow of Jack Murphy. Drew was surprised by his informal appearance in the prestigious firm. He wore a short-sleeve shirt which displayed blue veins in his arms, and wrinkled black pants. He had a rangy frame, moved with a slight limp, and wore his blond hair in a crew cut. The collar of his light blue shirt was loosened, and Drew noticed the stitches from a tracheotomy above the large knot in his polyester tie.

"I understand, sir, and under the circumstances, I would be happy to reschedule a more convenient time with your secretary to meet with you."

After he noticed Peggy, who stood in the background watching him as well, Renfro studied the business card thoroughly. He took an irate breath and exhaled. "No. No, come on up," he muttered.

Four years of college. Two years working for other firms. Eight years building his own business. Sweating to make payroll. Working vampirelike hours deep into the night. Being at his desk before dawn, out the door well past dusk. It had all come down to show time for Andrew Patrick Staley and Associates, and he winked at Peggy before he headed into the elevator shaft with Renfro.

"I love the decor in the lobby," Drew said to break the tension." It seems you've redecorated since I was last here."

"No, it's the same. Been the same for years."

"Umm. So do you follow Gator football? I heard that top recruit from Ohio has committed. I think he's going to—"

"I don't watch sports." And then the silence in the elevator became oppressive as both men watched the number ascend to the next floor.

Drew knew he had to find common ground with Renfro and was not willing to give up. This was obviously not going to be what was known as a "lay down" sale. It would be tough, but the tough ones always brought out the best in him. "I just heard about Mr. Murphy," Drew said in yet another attempt to engage Renfro in conversation. "He and I played in a charity golf function a couple of years ago. We were not paired together, but I did get a chance to meet him. I've always heard nothing but good things about him."

"Umm."

After an inflated pause, Drew cut the silence once again. "When did you find out about it?"

After the elevator door slid open, Renfro made a Patton-like march down the hallway and said in an irritated tone, "This morning." Without taking a breath, he walked toward his secretary. "Kathy what time is that appointment with Donna Geekler and her son Edward?"

"It's at two, sir."

"See if you can move them up to twelve-thirty, because I'm gonna have to get out of here early today."

"But," Kathy said with fear in her tone, "it's—eleven-fifty now, sir."

"Just call them."

Renfro's comments were a way of saying, *Kid, you better do what you got to do, because the meter is running.* After a glance at a few pieces of unopened mail on Kathy's desk, Renfro looked over his glasses at Drew. Just like a college professor, with a grunt he motioned for him to have a seat in his office. He then went into a tirade with his administrative assistant about a motion that had not been filed by an associate earlier that morning and a file he could not locate for a meeting with Burt Collins.

Drew entered Renfro's office and said to himself, *I'm in trouble now.* He was aware of Renfro's racist views, but nothing he had heard had prepared him for this. The first thing he saw was a print that read, "I Have a Dream," and underneath it were the stars and bars of the Confederate flag. Drew glanced around the room at the collection of rebel flags and the signed photograph taken with David Duke, and smiled confidently. *Wait'll he gets a load of me.*

An hour and a half later, Drew emerged from the mirrored elevator and entered the reception area of the law firm. As he walked through the thick sliding doors, he felt numb. He walked mummylike as he looked at Peggy, who had dropped her *Cosmopolitan* magazine on the floor in her haste to meet him in the lobby. When she approached with a *Well, what happened?* look on her brow, he reached inside the manila folder cinched under his arm and pulled out a six-figure draft. As he looked at Peggy, he mouthed the words without a smile, "Mission accomplished."

"Oh my God," she said in a faint voice, and allowed her emotion to show only in her eyes as she waved good-bye to Lisa and the rest of the ladies behind the reception desk.

As they got outside, Peggy exclaimed, "Drew, you pulled it off! We did it! I knew you could do it. He went for the entire plan? Even the ancillary coverage we added? Hook, line, and sinker?"

Feeling empty, Drew still could not enjoy the moment as he clicked the alarm to the car and opened the doors while Peggy stared at the draft. He wanted to share her joy, but inside he knew what he had done to get the signature, and the more he thought about it, the more he was not sure who had just won and just lost on the eighteenth floor of the Olsen Building.

CHAPTER 5

‡

After treating his staff to a celebratory lunch earlier that day, Drew passed the country club he was a member of but rarely used. Since it was Friday, he considered stopping for a round of golf, but changed his mind as he slowed for a red light. And then he noticed a navy convertible BMW driven by the attorney he had seen earlier in Murphy, Renfro and Collins, headed in the opposite direction. As he watched her taillights diminish in his rearview mirror, his fingers found the radio's volume knob and turned up the sound to block out the memory of Felicia. And then he looked across the street and noticed Harper and Sons Appliances. The spot held a special place for him because it was his first sale after opening his firm.

Drew had started his company with little cash. In college he hadn't known what he wanted to do when he graduated, but he'd always known it would not entail employment by someone else. So after he'd graduated, he'd worked for E.F. Hutton and then Prudential for a brief period of time to learn as much as he could about the investment and insurance arena. After he'd put together a program for a wealthy photographer in Boca Raton, he'd taken his profits and invested them in his dream. Andrew Patrick Staley and Associates. When he'd done so, there had been no Associates. Just him, a 386 computer, a coffeemaker, and a dream. His dark, dank studio office had had a single desk and a bad echo, and he'd done everything from vacuuming the carpet to designing the pension programs for his clients. But since he met most of his prospects in their offices, it had never posed a problem.

Feeling drained after the Renfro debacle, Drew did not feel up to returning to the office. So as the light turned green, he turned in to the mall parking lot, went inside the cinemaplex, and watched a matinee for the first time in years, alone.

Arriving home with his dinner in a Boston Market bag, Drew turned on the television and, after surfing the channels, called Peggy.

"Hello?"

"Hey, what are you up to?"

"Sweet pea, how you doing!" Peggy asked. "Thanks for lunch. That was nice of you."

"Is Walt there?"

"Yes, sweetie my husband is here. You trying to flirt, Mr. Staaaley?" she asked with a laugh.

"You better let him know it wasn't just me and you."

"Ah, I don't know if we can do that, Mr. Staley. I do happen to be married, you know."

"Listen at you. Always instigating something."

"You know me," she said. "He knows I'm crazy about him. So are you feeling better about the deal?"

Drew relaxed on his couch with his head on the armrest and toes buried between the thick cushions. "What do you mean?"

"I know something went down in there today. I just haven't figured out what happened. I mean that was the biggest sale you ever made. By far. And you would hardly talk to us during lunch."

Drew clicked off the TV and laid the remote on the oak table, never taking his eyes off a graduation portrait of Felicia on his mantel. Since he could not imagine another woman entering his home or his life at this juncture, it looked perfectly in place. Their love was tender and sweet. He would never forget the day or the time she first told him that she loved him. Because after she uttered the words, she added softly, "Drew, I must admit that I am a little selfish. You see, I know in my heart that I would like to die before you. Because I could never imagine being in a world without you here." After her death the irony of those words settled over his mind like a dark cloud that would not blow away and would always produce a tear.

He and Peggy had known each other for more than ten years, and since she was a few years older than he, she was the big sister he'd never had.

"Hello? Drew, are you there?"

As he cleared his throat Drew said, "I had to sell out to make the damn deal."

"What do you mean?"

With a deep breath Drew replied, "Renfro is the most racist person I have ever met, and I wanted to set him straight a couple of times, but I didn't. I should have . . . but I didn't."

"What do you mean, racist? Did he call you a name or something?"

"No. Of course not. But the man has these rebel flags displayed all over his office and even has, get this, a letter framed on his wall from Jerry Falwell. I'm not kidding."

"Well, actually, Drew, a letter from Falwell does not *exactly* make one a racist."

"Yeah, and neither does wearing a white sheet. What I mean is this. Things like that show no respect for black people. What if he was Jewish and walked into my office and I had German swastikas all over the place."

"Tell me something, Drew. Did you get the check?"

"Yeah, I know where you're going with—"

"Then you did a good job. Sleep well tonight. It's none of your business what he has in his office or his heart. There are people like him out there. They are nasty, crazy, stupid, dumb, whatever you wanna call them. But they are out there and we know it. Now that we know it, what do we do? Is it your job to educate him? Do we pitch our tents, give up, and not do business with them? Hell no! We deal with it. We get over it. We move on."

"I know, but I think I should have said something. You

didn't see his office. I should have shown a little backbone in there."

"Yeah, losing the sale would have taught him a lot. Don't get me wrong Andrew, I understand where you are coming from. But I—"

"Exactly! I mean, there are hardly any blacks employed in that place. I looked at the portraits of the partners and there's not one black face. Outside of the sister I saw who is an attorney there and a couple of custodians, I bet there aren't any blacks at all. I should have let him know he was talking to his worst nightmare. A black man with an education."

"No," Peggy replied. "See, you already did that because he bought the program. What you should have done was to ask that redneck for ten references and sold plans to ten of his Klan friends. That's what you *should* have done. Listen to me. Don't get mad Drew; get everything. See, you're talking to a child of the sixties. I graduated from old Lincoln High. I remember when they made us leave our school and sent the troops in and everything. I even remember my cousin Pam being brought home with her eyes swollen shut from the tear gas. But what a lot of us misunderstand in business today is that it's not our job to be martyrs. Okay? Your job was accomplished today and we got the draft to prove it. Murphy, Renfro and Collins, done deal, case closed. Next."

After finishing his conversation with Peggy, Drew noticed the time and put on his Topsiders and Knicks cap to do something he had done the previous weekend. He decided that he would do this on Friday nights because that was their date night. Each week they would alternate doing something special for each other. One time it had been as simple as when she'd made up words to "Song Bird," by Kenny G; another time, as elaborate as the surprise trip Drew had arranged to Paradise Island for the weekend.

As he got closer to his destination, rain started to fall, and Drew remembered he did not have a jacket or umbrella. *Damn, I wonder if Momma's okay tonight,* he thought as he drove down the highway. Drew's father had died four years earlier from plain old age. He'd been a good-natured gentle-man who'd spent what little free time he'd had helping in his community with political campaigns. Drew could re-member him pulling his red Chevy truck off the road and spending as much as an hour assisting a stranded driver. To Drew, his father was the definition of a man. His mother was in her late seventies and continued to chain-smoke, play cards every week, drink hard, and cry loudly about the death of her husband. They had been married more than fifty years and had lived in the same area in Gainesville for most of that time.

Drew, who was an only child, thought back to when he would come home from school and see his mother in the yard with their next-door neighbor, Mr. Douglass. His father had been an auto parts salesman and would at times be on the road for over a month. Drew had never noticed Mr. Douglass at the house when his dad was home, only when he was away. Far away. Mr. Douglass never came over for cookouts, to watch baseball, or anything else. But as soon as the coast was clear, he would appear.

One night after his father's retirement party, Drew had asked his mom point-blank for the real story in regards to her neighbor. Her answer was, "Oscar Douglass and I are just friends. And even if that was not true, I would tell you that anyway." Drew had never felt the need to ask her again.

One day shortly after his father passed, Drew, who was at this point a well-respected businessman in the commu-nity, drove up to the house and noticed Mr. Douglass sitting on their front step alone. He looked at Drew with fear in his eyes since he knew Drew's mother had in essence told her son of their bond. Drew glared at the slender dark man and wondered why he sat outside.

"She's inside, son. She does this every day almost, nowa-days. At lease three, fo' times a week."

"Does what?"

"Starts talking foolishness. Listen at her."

Drew walked closer, turned the knob, and noticed she had locked the bottom and likely the top lock as well. But he could hear her grievous rants inside.

"Oh my God, Jerry. Why did you have to leave me like this? Why did you have to go? You know I can't raise that boy on my own. How am I gonna send him to college, Jerry? How am I gonna pay for this big ole house? Jerry, you know I don't know how to work. You shouldn'a did me like this, Jerry. Jerry, I'm sorry for what I did to you all those years. I'm so sorry, Jerry," she wailed with a voice full of remorse and pain. "Just please come back."

Drew glanced at Mr. Douglass as he rubbed his trembling callused hands together like a raccoon and looked at the ground.

"How long has she been doing this?"

"Almost every day since your dad died. I always come by here to see if she needs me to run by the store or anything, and sometimes she'll let me in and everything is fine. And then other times . . . well, she is like this," he whispered, and looked up at Drew.

Time and a bimonthly visit with a counselor had dampened the loss of Jerry Staley. Time and the bimonthly visit had made it bearable for Judith to learn to live without him and get over the guilt. She had not married for love. She had married for security. Once, as a teenager, Drew had walked in and heard her say on the phone, "How do you leave a good man? If a man is sorry, it's easy. But what do you do when he's good?" Drew had never fully understood what she was talking about until as an adult he saw how she looked at Mr. Douglass.

At her advanced age, Judith Staley took a driving course to learn how to drive her husband's emerald Buick Electra and also put together a card-playing group, which rotated houses each Thursday and Saturday night. And every afternoon, after she watched "General Hospital" and "All My Children" back to back she and Mr. Douglass would drive, sing old Motown hits, and talk about yesterday. While she felt guilty because she had never been true to Jerry Staley, the pain lessened when she learned for the first time in her life it was all right to be true to herself.

Drew parked in front of the fresh-cut headstone with Felicia's name as the rain blew sideways. He turned off his motor and thought back to the first time he saw her. There was no magic. Not even a spark. He had walked downstairs from an appointment with an accountant on Valentine's Day. It was a few minutes before five, and as he'd walked through the secretarial pool toward the door, he'd noticed that every woman had a bouquet of flowers or a box of candy from her lover—except for the lady in the thigh-high yellow skirt. She'd had a picture of her man, but no gifts. "Child, you all know how Zack is. I bet you anything he sent them to my old department. He's so absentminded." Drew could hear her from across the room, and as he passed her desk he could see the hurt in her eyes as he and the accountant headed out the door.

Shaking his head to dust away the memory, Drew noticed the rain was falling in thick splats and he reached in the backseat to pull out the weekly gift to his beloved. Gazing at it, he was again pulled back to that fateful Valentine's Day. He'd decided that night that he would not spend the evening alone, so he'd gone out and by chance he'd seen Felicia again. That night had proven to be their first date. After they'd left the club, Drew had parked in front of her home and they had talked about everything imaginable deep into the night. And then the topic of the conversation had switched to eternal love and she'd mentioned how Paul and Linda McCartney had never slept in separate beds in over twenty years of marriage. She also mentioned how Joe Di Maggio had continued to have flowers sent to the tomb of Marilyn Monroe years after her death.

"Can you imagine loving someone that much? So much you want to give them flowers every day . . . forever?" And then she'd looked at him and said, "Drew, that's how much I want to be in love with someone one day. For just once, I'd like to be in love so much it hurt. Until it didn't make any sense. Know what I mean?"

It was then that he'd said, "This may sound crazy, and I can't believe I'm even saying it myself. I have never said this in my life to anyone, but one day I'm going to marry you."

That cold and wet February night seemed so long ago as Drew opened his car door and sloshed through the mud to her headstone. After stopping for a moment, he bent down and left that week's single unopened white rose.

*   *   *

Drew arrived home and, instead of turning on the TV, sat down at his computer. Several months earlier he'd been given a copy of Compu-Line, which allowed him to access the information superhighway. Drew had been on-line for several months, but mostly used Compu-Line for business, although every now and then he did give in to the urge to explore the chat areas. In the chat rooms, he could enter into conversations with individuals from all over the country on a variety of topics, from the comfort of his own home, via computer. There was a Whitepower room and a White-Males-Seek-Straight-Black-Males room. Drew could enter political debates or the Jean-Claude Van Damn-I-Can't-Act room, where anti-fans would come together to trash the actor's most recent work.

When he just wanted to relax on the Net, most of Drew's time was spent in the Ebony Over Thirty room. In this area he would chat with African-Americans from all over the world. He could discuss social issues with brothers and sisters in Miami and Mali simultaneously.

Everyone on the Net had a moniker. Each individual's name was in a way an extension of his or her personality. Drew's name was DLastRomeo. He'd been given the name Romeo in college by several of the guys he played football with. While at Florida A&M, he'd left a letter to his girlfriend on his dresser. After his roommate read it, he asked Drew to write one for him, and within months he was writing love letters for half the team. After the news had spread all over the small campus, he'd become the university's resident Romeo.

The chat on-line that night got deep, as usual.

TRICKDADDY: Well if you are looking for a GOOD black man I think you should consider some of us brothers who don't make a zillion dollars per year. We all can't be doctors.
RUDIEPOO2: Why sisters gotta always lower their standards? I get so tired of hearing that tired excuse. When do brothers ever lower their standards? (with a black woman that is) Why can't we have it

all? Most of the brothers I deal with are intimidated
because I refuse to dummy down. Now I'm aware that
when I'm seventy years old, it may be just me and my
dog, but believe me, me and Fido will be chilling
on the south of France.

DELTADREAM: What do you mean when you say lowering standards, Rudie? Are you referring solely to a man
that makes less money?

RUDIEPOO2: Well I hope it does not ostracize me but . . .
YES! That's exactly what I mean. I want a man I can
be proud to walk into hospital functions with or take
to social gatherings and he not be intimidated.

DELTADREAM: Then answer one question for me. Would you be
happier as a millionaire alone with no man in your
life or in section eight housing with a man who loved
you more than anything else in this world?

RUDIEPOO2: See for me that's a stupid question, Delta, so
I'll give someone else a crack at it.

DIBOYZ: Well, fellas, we may not all agree with the sister, but Rudie is just saying what a lot of other
females are thinking.

DLASTROMEO: Sup room.

NOIRLAZE: Hi, Romeo!

SHADIYA117: Romeo, Romeo, Romeo! Wherefore art thou
Romeo!

DELTADREAM: DiBoyz, some ladies think like that. Not all.
My man ain't hardly loaded, but it's not about
all that.

DLASTROMEO: Hi, Rudie, Shadiya. What's the conversation
about tonight?

The conversation continued on about African-American
male and female relationships, and after a few minutes of
the discussion, Drew got bored. He decided to review the
list of names in the room and noticed one that was new to
him. Drew typed her a note and sent it via an instant message, which was a way for him to chat with her in private.

DLASTROMEO: Hello. I am not trying to hit on you, I just
noticed the new name. Are you new to Compu-Line?

DELTADREAM: Basically.
DLASTROMEO: So what do you think of this twenty-first-century technology?
DELTADREAM: It's okay. But I do believe it's redefining the word perverse for the new millennium.
DLASTROMEO: LOL I guess that's true. I guess we men as a whole can be a little perverse. I guess it kinda comes naturally to us on Mars. But also remember we have not evolved as much as women. We're a little closer to primates I guess. LOL

LOL was the Internet shorthand for "laughing out loud."

DELTADREAM: That's funny, but I wouldn't go that far. I don't bash men. So why did you say you were not trying to hit on me? With such an interesting screen name, are you sure you are not using reverse psychology?
DLASTROMEO: No, not hardly. I don't like to use the service for that sorta thing and I've never believed in long distance relationships. With this screen name, I know, women often expect it and people often use the service for that, but to me it's just a way to meet people. And remember, Romeo had only one love.
DELTADREAM: Well that's a relief. I'm presently in a relationship and I am very happy. I get so tired of men—and women no less—sending me instant messages and asking me how large my breasts are or what size dress I wear. LOL
DLASTROMEO: Yeah I guess it can get a little raw. Well if I ever ask you anything you feel uncomfortable answering, just tell me, ''none of your business,'' okay?
DELTADREAM: Thanks. You know what they say about you people on the Internet.
DLASTROMEO: So I have heard. May I ask you about the relationship?
DELTADREAM: None of your business! Just joking. To call him the man of my dreams is an understatement. I

mean he is so considerate, so gentle, so kind, so
good-looking, so fine, so sweet, so manly . . . do
you need any more so's? LOL

DLastRomeo: No, no. I think I get the picture.

DeltaDream: Seriously. I feel fortunate to have him in my
life right now.

DLastRomeo: That's important and I'm glad to hear it. You
always hear about people who are not happy with
their relationship. I must say that I don't have a
person in my life like that at this time and I
really miss it. I just lost someone very dear and
there is definitely a void there.

DeltaDream: What do you miss the most about being in a
relationship?

DLastRomeo: I miss having someone in my life who knows how
to make me smile. Sounds simple, huh? I'm not
looking for fireworks. I'm not looking for magic. At
this point in my life, a nice body is great. A
touch would be nice as well. But to have someone who
could find my smile. I can't think of words to describe how that would feel.

DeltaDream: I can relate to it. I was single (not in a relationship) for the past five years. It seemed I
worked my butt off to be the best, and then I looked
around at my material possessions and realized I
had no one to share them with, and I confess, it hurt.

DLastRomeo: Damn, love. You making me feel bad. LOL Sounds
too much like me.

DeltaDream: I'm sorry. That's not my intention. I just
want you to know that she's out there somewhere.

DLastRomeo: Thank you. So tell me. What does this prince
of yours do to make you smile?

DeltaDream: It'll only make you feel worse. Let's not go
there. LOL

DLastRomeo: I agree . . . but give me a shot anyway.

DeltaDream: Well, where do I start? A couple of weeks ago
I was working on this huge project at work. I
worked on it for more than two years in fact. Well,
the results from my work were positive and when I
called him to tell him about it, he had this incredi-

ble date planned for me. First he invited me to
his house and welcomed me with seventeen yellow
long-stemmed roses. One for each week we had been
a couple.

DLastRomeo: Now that was suave. You like yellow roses,
huh?

DeltaDream: Are you kidding? They're my favorite. No of-
fense, but a man who gives cop-out red roses knows
nothing about romance or the meaning of flowers.

DLastRomeo: Interesting.

DeltaDream: After that he served my favorite dinner,
played my favorite CD softly (which I did not even
know he knew), and prepared this bath for me. Then,
well let's say I am a lady so we'll leave the rest
to your imagination.

DLastRomeo: Damn. A brother like that might make me change
my screen name.

DeltaDream: LOL. Maybe you are DLastRomeo . . . on-line.

CHAPTER 6

✝

"Baby? Are you coming to bed?"

"Oh, sweetie," Betty called to Evander, and turned down the classical music in her home office. "I didn't know you were awake. Let me sign off."

"No, don't. Just finish what you're doing and if I'm asleep when you come to bed, wake me up, okay?"

"Are you sure? I don't mind," she said as she typed words onto the screen of her monitor in the darkened room. "I'm just chatting."

"Positive," he said with a yawn. "Just wake me."

"Okay. I'll be in there in a minute," she replied as she continued to type to her new acquaintance.

DELTADREAM: I work long hours. Sometimes thirteen-hour
  days, and when I come home, I always get a phone
  call from him. And when he asks how my day has been,
  you know what? He really wants to know.
DLASTROMEO: I didn't want to say it, because I don't like
  talking about it, but I lost my lady a month ago.
DELTADREAM: I remember you said that earlier. Did she just
  decide to leave one day? Was there another guy?
  Or did you get caught with your hand in the cookie
  jar, Romeo? Listen to me, all up in your business.
DLASTROMEO: No, that's okay. I guess I started the per-

sonal questions anyway. For some reason it's eas-
ier to talk to you about this, with this computer
screen between us, than it is to talk to friends.
They just say I should get over it. But anyway . . .
she died last month.

DELTADREAM: Oh I'm so sorry. I had no idea.

DLASTROMEO: We'd dated three years, but we weren't engaged or anything. In fact the last few months of
our relationship were rough. But we stayed together.
The night before she died she got nasty with me.
I mean unusually nasty, and to this day I have no idea
as to why. She started crying and even pulled out
one of the tubes and tried to yell at me, but she was
too weak. She told me never to come to the hospital
again, so eventually I went downstairs and paced in
the MICU waiting room for about three or four
hours. I didn't want to go back up to the room, but I
couldn't leave. So I sat on the couch and fell
asleep. About one o'clock that morning, I went back
up to see her thinking she would be asleep, but
the nurse would not allow me back in the ward.

DELTADREAM: That's so sad. Once again, I'm sorry. I had
no idea.

DLASTROMEO: Please. Don't be. Really that's not why I told
you what happened, and as I read what I just typed
I'm sorry I got so deep so fast. I've never shared
that with anyone, but I just wanted to say, so
often I don't think we value love. I don't think we
ever really sit back and just enjoy the moment.
Now I do. Now I can see how I took her love for granted
at times, and although the pain of doing that does
not hurt as much as physically losing her . . . it's
running a close second.

DELTADREAM: You are in my prayers, Romeo.

DLASTROMEO: Thanks, love.

Love? Betty thought. How sweet.

DELTADREAM: Oh yeah. I guess I should tell you, I am only
DeltaDream on-line. I rarely tell anyone on the

Net my name, but you seem safe enough. My real name
is Betty. I don't believe I got yours.
DLastRomeo: Oh. My real name is Romeo. But please feel
free to call me Drew. :)
DeltaDream: Cute. Well, Mr. Drew, it's been nice chatting
with you and I would love to chat again sometime.
You are without a doubt one of the kindest men I've
met on the Internet. I feel a little guilty to be
in here typing with my friend in the bedroom. I hope
I'm not ending our conversation too abruptly.
DLastRomeo: Hey I'm sorry I kept you so long. It was nice
chatting with you as well. And I'm sorry for wearing out that shoulder with my love life. If you ever
need it, you can borrow mine sometime.

Betty signed off of the computer and headed to the bedroom. She felt very fortunate to have Evander in her life.
He was the one man she had met who seemed to understand her. He asked for nothing but her happiness. He gave
her everything, including his love.

Evander offered her moral support when she worked long
and hard on a case and listened to her talk when she got
depressed about problems at the firm. He could hold her
like a child when she wanted to be a baby or wine her and
dine her when she felt the need to be his lady.

Her feelings for him were strong. Betty felt deep inside
she loved Evander, but she had never said the L word out
loud. She had never felt as strong about another man in her
life, but for some reason, she knew once the word was uttered, her defenses would be down and she would be
vulnerable.

Betty's foster parents, while they loved each other, were
different from her mother and stepfather. She had never
seen her foster parents show emotion toward each other.
She never saw as much as a kiss or a gentle gesture shared
between the two. One night she called her foster mother
from law school and asked her about the affectionless union.
She confided in Betty that although she felt they would always love each other, in twenty-eight years of marriage they
had yet to say the words "I Love you." Not even when they

were dating or on the night of their wedding. "But then again, we never had to. We just knew it," she added. "And I'll tell you something else, Betty Anne. People now'days toss that word around too much—so much I don't think they even know what it means. *Love* is a powerful word. But if you love someone, you don't have to say it to them. They'll feel it. They'll know. Always remember that. Never *ever* say 'I love you,' then you will know what I mean."

"Your feet cold, baby," Evander mumbled as she snuggled closer to him in bed.

"I know. I couldn't find my slippers."

Evander eased out from the covers, took her childhood comforter from the antique oak chest at the foot of the bed, and placed it at her feet. He then went into the living room to turn on her Vivaldi CD, before he returned to their spooning position.

"Thank you, boo."

"You feel comfy?" Evander asked in the midst of a fatigued yawn.

"I do now," she said, and snuggled closer to him. After a pregnant pause, Betty looked up at her ceiling fan and said, "Vander?"

"Yes, honey?"

"Will it *always* be this good?"

"I hope so, baby," he said with sleep blanketing his tired voice. "I hope so." Evander kissed her behind the ear, gave her a teddy-bear hug to draw her even closer to his warmth, and then returned to sleep.

Saturday

Seven A.M. came earlier than it used to, or at least it seemed as such to Betty. As she pulled the cover from over her head, she looked at the clock with disdain. *I got a whole five hours' sleep?* she thought as she hit the snooze button.

As she lay in bed, she thought about her hair. This was without question a hot-curl morning. Although she knew Evander well, she did not know him well enough to sleep with him in curlers. Just at that moment he walked in the room and said, "Time to get up, Beeper." Beeper was one

of the pet names he called her because she had told him a
story of her father singing "Jeepers Creepers" to her as a
baby. Since she could not say "jeepers," she would end up
just singing "beepers, beepers."

She looked at Evander standing there, all six feet three
inches and 210 bronzed pounds of him. He wore a black
terry cloth robe tied loosely, which gave her a peek at his
swelling white bikini briefs. As he stood before her holding
a tray with an apple Danish, quarter slice of grapefruit, and
tea, Betty sighed to herself. "Get up, Beep. Remember, you
have to work on that lawsuit you mentioned last night."

Betty stretched and her toes separated under the satin
sheets as she replied, "I know, I know." And then with a
smile she said, "Thank you, honey. This is too sweet."

"After staying up so late, I knew you'd be tired this morning, so I got up and made you some tea. Did you sleep
well?" her prince asked.

"Yeah, I slept well, until that *thing* went off."

Evander smiled, put down the tray, and held out his large
hand to her. "It's time, Beep, come on." As she sat up in
her king-size bed, he secured her breakfast with care in front
of her, along with a copy of the Saturday morning paper.

"I take it you like Earl Grey. That's all I saw in there. I
hope it's not too strong."

"No, it's fine, I'm sure," she said, unable to wipe the smile
from her lips.

"Well, I made a little too much, so if you like it, I'll pour
some in a thermos for later today."

"Thanks," was all she could say.

Betty savored her breakfast while Evander tuned the radio
to "Tom Joyner Moving On" and headed for the shower.
She noticed her attaché was, as always, next to the bed, and
she reached inside for her favorite tattered article, "Midway
Railroad Loses Civil Case." As she ran her fingers over the
story, which she could recite verbatim, her smile reappeared
while she leaned back into her goose-down pillow.

Moments later, Evander turned off the shower and walked
back into the room with a black towel cinched around his
muscular waist. When she saw him, Betty leaped from the

bed to greet him with a kiss and a warm hug that said thanks.

"You know I love you like crazy, girl," he said as he dried his short silky locks with a hand towel.

"You're just too good to be true. Do you know that? How did I become so lucky?"

With a smiling gaze into her eyes, Evander softly kissed her on the tip of the nose. As she released the embrace, he walked to the bureau to dress for work. Betty felt guilty for not saying "I love you" back. She wanted to say it so badly. But not like this. When she said those three words, she wanted him to know they were heartfelt.

As she entered the bathroom, she noticed a heart drawn on the foggy mirror, which made her feel more ashamed that she could not share what she felt. With a step into the shower stall, Betty leaned against the smooth onyx tile, deep in thought. *When will we reach the end of the rainbow? Will it always be this good?* How long would she be able to keep this guy in her life, without uttering those three simple words? But most of all, Betty searched her soul for the answer as to why she felt uneasy about him. In so many ways he was everything she had dreamed of. So was it the old joke being personified? Did she not want to join any club that would have her as a member? She wasn't sure. But she did know what her heart felt for him, and debated whether she should just say those three little words so he would not walk away.

As Betty dried herself, Evander knocked on the door to the bathroom, which was ajar, instead of just walking in on her. "Come in," she said with a smile.

"I'm getting ready to go, Beep. I poured the rest of the tea in the thermos, and it's by the door. You'll probably need it to stay awake today. Can I bring you something for lunch?"

"No, sweetie, I'll be fine, but thanks anyway."

"Okay," he said, and reached out his arms to embrace her. As he did, Betty dropped her towel and pressed her nude body against his. His kiss met her lips with sweetness as he caressed her bottom and said, "You know something? I already miss you, and I haven't even left."

"I wish you didn't have to go *so* early," she said, with suggestion in her tone.

"So do I, but Ferguson is on vacation this week, and I need to make sure they got those orders out this morning on time. I mean," he said, pulling away and looking her in the eye, "I could spare ten or fifteen minutes, but I *never* want to spend just fifteen minutes with you."

The words *Evander? Do you know how much I love you?* burst from her heart, came up her throat, and sat heavy on her tongue, but she would not allow them to pass her lips as she smiled.

"Baby, have a nice day, okay?" He kissed her on both cheeks and then on the top of the head. As he backed away, he looked at her body, which glistened and begged for his. "I have to go, Beeper. I really do. Otherwise you know I would stay. Pick up that towel, honey, before you catch a cold, okay?"

Betty stood, wet, motionless, and nude, as he backed up to the door and slowly pointed with a single finger to his eye. He then made the shape of a heart with both thumbs and index fingers and pointed toward her. As the door closed behind him, Betty knew for the first time that her foster mother was right. At that moment there was no need to say the words. She could feel it all over her body.

In the steam of the bathroom, with the heart now fading from the mirror. With the tea he got up to make just for her on the edge of the countertop. With the memories of the seconds they'd just spent together and the towel nestled at her feet. She mouthed "I love you," so quietly she couldn't even hear the words. No man had moved her like this one. No man had made her shake and shiver without a single touch. No man had done so much just to bring her joy. While her foster mother would, or could, never understand, she felt her lips wrap around the words once again. "Evander, I love you so much."

After she backed out of the garage, Betty released the convertible top of her car and picked up her cellular to check her messages. The workday, although it was the weekend, had begun. Behind the gates of Royalton Oaks, most families pulled out their fishing boats, started searching for antiques, or put up their garage-sale signs on this sunny morning. The smell of dew in the air would soon be replaced with the scent of fresh-cut grass. But enjoying the leisure of the weekend was not a privilege she would allow herself to indulge. As she drove, she glanced at her organizer and her fingertips slid down the to-do section. Betty then pulled out her favorite cassette, Stevie Wonder's *Songs in the Key of Life*, and fast-forwarded the tape to the song "As."

The sun gave hints of a beautiful day as the temperature was well above the average for the season. While the calendar said it was winter, it was in the low seventies that morning in spite of torrential rains the previous night. The nesting birds let loose in song as Betty drove through the gates of the neighborhood, headed toward the firm.

When the track began, she put on her shades and burst out in song off-key.

The lyrics were special to Betty because she hoped to find that type of love. Unconditional love. The kind of love she could feel comfortable with just as if it were her favorite childhood comforter or a cozy sweater. A love in which she could roll up and rest after a long day. She would feel warm and sheltered from storms in this love, no matter how cold it became outside. The kind of love she would know in her heart would last forever. She had not reached that point with Evander, but she could feel herself getting closer to it each day. With every "I love you" from him, her heart tapped a little harder. With every flower, the words came closer to his ear.

The most difficult aspect in regards to Betty's relationship with Evander was that she lacked a frame of reference. The men who'd preceded him had little or no redeeming qualities to speak of. Her first lover had taken her money and much of her respect for men in general.

Then there was Derrick, who looked like a black Marlboro man and drove a thirty-thousand-dollar automobile. Betty met him at a bookstore one Saturday afternoon in the ancient history section. Her thought was, *Wow. A brother interested in ancient Egypt. One cool point.* He introduced himself without any of the nonsense men often used to mask their fear when they spoke to ladies. *Two cool points.* He could converse and he had an obvious command of the English language, which was due in part to the fact that he was an English teacher in a high school. *Three points.* Helping with the books, wearing her favorite men's cologne, and walking her out to the car were simply the cherry on top.

Derrick, after a little intelligent banter, asked for her phone number. Betty was not the type of woman who gave out such information, nor was she impressed by most men. Usually she asked men for their numbers if they asked for hers, and said she would call them. But if an exception was to be made to her rule, this would be the man. Derrick was a cocoa-fine brother in more ways than one, with an athletic chest, an L-shaped chin, and sculpted arms. *And after all, he did earn three cool points,* she thought, saying, "555-1831," as he wrote it in his palm. She even liked the fact he wrote it on his hand, because it showed her he was not there on a mission to pick up women.

As he walked backward, he smiled and opened his hand to show her he had the number, and headed off. *That was cute,* she thought. Then he took out his keys and opened the door to the cherry red SC300, making sure she saw him do so. The personalized, gold-framed vanity plates read SLIC RIC.

The attorney came out in Betty as she thought, *Now, I know teachers only make about twenty-six to twenty-eight when they start.* He had told Betty he had been a teacher for three years and received a coaching stipend. *So how could he afford a car like that? Well, maybe he's just a penny-pincher. Maybe his family is affluent. After all, he did appear to be cultured. Or maybe he's selling . . . Well, I'll give him the benefit of the doubt.*

Later that night she received the call she'd been waiting for. "Hello . . . this is Derrick," he said in a deep, sweet, slow-sex voice. "Is, ahh, Betty there?"

"This is Betty. How are you?" she replied as an electrical current of anticipation inched down her spine.

"I'm okay. You remembered my voice?"

"You have a nice voice."

With a smile in his tone he said, "Thank you. How did the rest of your day turn out?"

"It was okay. Got to run a few errands and rode my bike

for a couple of miles. Then I started reading the book I bought earlier by Tolstoy, *Resurrection*. Good book so far. How about you?" As she finished her sentence, she could hear him muffle the phone with his hand over the receiver and say something to someone else.

"Yeah, umm. I'm sorry, what did you say?"

"I said my day was fine. What about yours?"

"It was okay. Kids are kids, you know. It's always something different with them. Especially when you're trying to get them to practice on the weekends."

"I'd imagine. It takes a lot of courage to both coach and teach nowadays." And then she paused and tried to decide if she would go for it now or later. *What the hell. Why not try him now.* "When they pay you guys such meager wages and all."

"Yeah, you're right."

She continued like the skilled litigator she was, attempting to extract the truth from a key witness. "I admire you guys, because you have to put up with a lot from kids. They are so different from our generation. It's unfortunate so many teachers have to work a *second* job, just to make a decent living."

There was a pause, then he said, "Yeah, I know. So tell me, I don't think I ever asked, where do you work?"

I gotta do better. "Murphy, Renfro and Collins."

"Oh. Are you a secretary or a paralegal? I used to date a paralegal with Farris and Hall. Or is it Farris and Washington?"

"Ah, no. It's Blount and Farris, and I'm an attorney." That comment had cost SLIC Lexus-Driving, Ancient-Egypt-Reading, Syrupy Barry White–Sounding RIC all three *cool* points.

"Damn, that's impressive. Do you like it?"

"It pays the bills." She wanted to ask, *So tell me, what pays yours?* but she decided to let it die since she'd only spoken to him for all of three minutes.

"I'm sorry, Betty," he said, and took his hand once again away from the phone's receiver. "What did you say?"

"I said it's okay, nothing special."

"Damn, one second," he said. "I have a call coming through."

Tired of the interruptions, Betty tried to say, *You can call me when it's more convenient for you,* but he switched over before she could get it out. It was obvious he had company. *So if he was with his friends, why would he call me, and why wouldn't they respect him on the phone?*

"It's for you," she heard him say as he clicked over. "Betty, are you there? Betty? Betty!"

"Yeah, I'm here," she said, and tried to figure out what was going on.

"Can I call you back? An important call just came through."

"Sure, no problem," she said as she thought she now knew what was happening. Then she heard the nail in the coffin.

"Derrick, is that Pastor Camps on the phone?" an elderly lady's voice asked in the background.

She heard Derrick's muffled and aggravated voice saying, "Yeah! Damn! One second! Betty, ah, I'll call you in about thirty minutes, okay?" As he spoke to her, he obviously tried to take the agitated edge out of his voice, with little success.

"That's fine," she replied with a smile, and then hung up before he could say good-bye. "So that's it." *Homeboy fronting in a Lexus and living off his momma. How trifling,* she thought, and laughed to herself. *Brother drives an expensive car like that and walks around his momma's house in his drawers eating out of the fridge every day?* "And had the nerve to catch an attitude with his momma—about her phone no less!" she said out loud. For the next two weeks Betty checked the Caller ID box before she answered the phone until SLIC RIC stopped leaving messages.

And then there was Abdul, an ultra black man who always said *salam alaikum* to everybody and everything. Unfortunately, everything he knew about Islam he learned from Spike Lee's movie about Malcolm X. Abdul, who never changed his name legally from Reggie Carter, worked as a loan officer in the university credit union and did some computer programming on the side.

He wasn't the cutest brother on the block, but he had a confidence in himself that made him attractive. He knew what he wanted, and nothing, absolutely nothing, could stop him from getting it. Or so he thought.

After he took her to a film festival, they enjoyed dinner at The Sovereign, which happened to be in the basement of her firm's building and featured a spectacular view of the lake lit in a red sunset. Afterward he escorted Betty to her apartment and walked in as if he'd been invited. The conversation at dinner had been okay. A little long on rhetoric and he was a bit too self-aggrandizing, but that was all right when she considered the alternative.

Betty enjoyed it when a man took control. She was old-fashioned in that regard. But everything had a limit. She chose not to change clothes or even remove her high heels because she didn't wish to send the wrong message. Picking up the remote, Betty turned on "BET Tonight." As she sat on the couch, she placed it beside her because there was a feature on African-American superstar attorneys, so there was no need to channel-surf. Abdul stood and looked at her sitting and then looked at Tavis Smiley as if he wondered, *Why are we watching this?*

"You're welcome to sit if you like," Betty said, and moved a pillow aside.

He looked at the TV and then, without taking his eyes off it, he sat beside her. Abdul reached across her for the remote as she thought, *I know this is a take-charge brother and all, but I hope he is not about to do what I think he is going to do. I know he is not going to change stations during Tavis.* And to her surprise, he didn't. He turned the TV off. As Tavis's face disappeared, the click bounced around the room, or at least it sounded that way to Betty. *Ooo-kayy,* she thought, *now I gotta hurt this fool's feelings.*

Abdul lunged into the kiss and did not say a word. It was obvious he had watched a lot of cable TV or daytime soaps. Unfortunately for him, he was not nearly as successful as the actors he emulated. Betty's forearm went up and caught him between his chin and Adam's apple. She saw his eyes bulge as he let out a sharp grunt. The look was similar to the Three Stooges routine when Moe would slap Curly and Larry with one swat, but Abdul looked funnier.

"Heyyy, li'l bit, what's wrong?" he said in a perplexed voice as he rubbed his throat.

I know he didn't call me li'l bit. "Nothing. I just think this is moving a little fast."

"Too fast for a kiss?"

"Well," she said in an attempt to be diplomatic, "who knows what a kiss could lead to? I just don't think—"

Wrong words. Abdul smiled with one of those *your lips are saying no, no, no, but your eyes are saying yes, yes, yes* smiles. "Baby, it's time for you to exhale, because a kiss can't take *you* anywhere *you* don't wanna go."

Is that the best line you could come up with? "I'm not ready for this, *Abdul*," she reasserted as he continued to press his body against hers. Abdul was a small man, and since she was just a hair shorter, it was not a physical match made in heaven. If he were larger, she may have been a little more intimidated. But since she could look him in the eye in her stocking feet and spent the entire evening glancing over his head in her heels, she thought, *If push comes to shove, I'll just slap the hell out of him and send him home.* Since things had gone on a little longer in the touchy-grabby phase of the date, she'd been left with no choice. She'd had to hurt more than just his feelings.

Thinking back on it all, Betty, who had decided not to hot-curl her hair after all, smiled as her fingers tugged on the brim of her baseball cap. As she swiped her employee parking card to raise the guardrail, she noticed the normally empty parking lot was uncommonly full of cars.

CHAPTER 7

‡

"What!" Betty said in shock as she dropped her attaché and thermos on her desk. "When?"

"That's what I said when I heard about it. Mr. Murphy had a massive heart attack," Carol, a secretary Betty shared at the firm, said. "We got the news yesterday. I saw the files I left on your desk were missing and could tell you had been by. I knew you were working from home and tried to call you, but actually, I wasn't at my best. None of us were. Can you imagine what that penny-pinching weasel Renfro will do to this place? You remember how he tried to fire half of the clerical pool a couple of years ago. Yesterday most of the paralegals and secretaries were updating their résumés, for Pete's sakes."

"Oh my God," Betty said, unable to close her mouth as she blocked out Carol's last comment regarding job security. "I can't believe this. I wondered why no one was at the reception desk when we walked in yesterday. When we were leaving, I saw Lisa in the back with the secretaries, but it never dawned on me it could have been something like this."

"It's true!" Carol said. Her red, medium-length hair was gathered in a bun with a number-two pencil, and her burgundy freckles stood away from her white complexion. "This place has been an absolute zoo ever since."

"What do you mean?"

"You know how those assholish partners are. It's all about money with them. They're trying to get a senior partnership or a place on the executive board. And the associates? They're just as bad. You can see it on their faces."

Betty couldn't stop thinking about Jack Murphy. He was of Irish ancestry and was always willing to share the latest joke he had heard. He would set his appointments around attorneys' birthday parties and demanded everyone attend, including the partners. His wife, Agnes, even sent cards to all employees and their spouses on their birthdays and wedding anniversaries.

He took pride in calling the members of the firm "family." Each year the annual Christmas party was celebrated at one of the Murphy homes, either the one in the city or the one on nearby Amelia Island. While everyone in the firm would draw names, Jack and Agnes always bought gifts for each of the more than 125 employees and their spouses.

While Jack Murphy could be generous, he was a calculating and at times ruthless attorney. He was the lead litigator in each of the three largest cases awarded the firm. Unlike most senior partners, he enjoyed the fire of the courtroom. He would get as excited while practicing in his fifth decade as if he were preparing to deliver his first summation. He would always litigate with his toothy smile and familiar charisma. His favorite expression was "Kill them with kindness." Now he fought with every breath in his body for his life.

"So the vultures are lining up in formation already?" Betty asked as she sat behind her desk.

"Yeah, and we were just out of it yesterday. I came in today to work on a few things O'Shaughnessy gave me as well as to find the files you needed for the Henderson Electric case."

"I can't believe this! He was the picture of health. Poor Agnes."

"Yes, Mrs. Murphy has always been good to all of us, you know."

"Have any of you been out to see him yet?" Betty asked as she handed Carol a tissue from the box on her desk to wipe her eyes. "Except I guess he's still in ICU, so we can't, right?"

"Yeah. We took up a collection for flowers, but Lisa thought about it and told us we couldn't even send them yet. She even tried to call last night and find out if they had upgraded his condition, but they wouldn't tell her anything since she wasn't family."

"So what are you doing here, on a Saturday, at eight o'clock no less?"

"Like I said, we didn't do anything yesterday. It's sad to say it, but people were either praying the man would live so they could keep their job or hoping things would happen so they could get a promotion. I feel bad even thinking that, but it's true. I've got almost twenty years invested in this place and I know Renfro would love to get rid of me and hire someone for half as much. Lisa just said we should all try to ignore it, pray for Mr. Murphy, and come in early today to catch up on our work so we could get out before noon."

"Well, that would explain why there are so many cars out there today."

"Darling, they tell me they really are already discussing his replacement, and it's a domino effect for the other partners and associates, you know. Shush," Carol said with her finger to her lips as she turned to look into the hallway. "Hello, Mr. Patterson. How are you today, sir?" she said to the middle-aged balding attorney wearing Docker shorts and carrying his six iron.

"Fine, ladies, fine," he said as he looked at Betty. "So, are you as shocked about this as I am?" Patterson was considered a loner and rarely spoke to the other employees. Rumor had it he'd transferred to the firm from Stamford, Connecticut, with a partnership as bait, but four years later he was still an associate.

"I just heard about it this morning," Betty said between sips of tea. "Do you know if anyone has spoken with Agnes?"

"I'm told she and the boys are doing well, considering. Renfro has been out to the hospital several times, and Burt Collins will be there this morning with Cee Cee, and then possibly Danny and Beatrice Lake this evening. Muffy and I sent Agnes and the boys a fruit basket to the house, but outside of that, there's just not much we can do but wait. Jack's secretary, umm, umm . . . What's her name?" he asked, looking at Betty.

"Paula," Carol said in monotone.

"Ah, yeah," he said with a brief glance at Carol. "She told me there were telegrams and faxes from the governor's office and even one from Senator Graham." And then R. Raymond Patterson added with faux sincerity as he leaned his stubby body against the door, "That man was an institution in this state. In this country, in fact. Everybody loved Jack Murphy."

"That's true," Betty said.

Jack Murphy had been instrumental in Betty's recruitment and subsequent hiring. It was rumored that two of the partners, one of whom was Renfro, had been against the first African-American female associate joining the firm. Ten years earlier, an African-American male who had barely passed the bar had been brought into the fold. When Renfro caught him at his desk asleep, he was forever used as the excuse not to integrate. But Murphy, in his delicate and yet effective way, got what he wanted like a velvet bulldozer.

"Yep. He's one heck of a man," Patterson said, and then there was dead silence. Betty and Carol glanced at each other with looks that said, *Why is he still in here?* as Patterson glanced around Betty's office.

With a glimpse at her watch Betty said, "Well, I better get to work, guys. If you hear anything else, Ray, please let me know."

"You betcha, Betsy." And then he glanced at her nameplate on the door. "I mean, ahh, Betty."

Betty and Carol gave each other weak smiles, and then Carol followed him out the door after saying 'bye with a wink.

Betty looked at the pile of work in her in-box and prepared to catch up from the day missed as she noticed a note from George O'Shaughnessy.

To: Betty
From: George

If you have an opening @ 12:30 for lunch on Monday,
Sampkins and I would like to run something by you.
Please let me know.

O'Shaughnessy was the oldest associate in the firm and
was connected in the political arena from having served as
a bodyguard for former governor Claude Kirk and Vice
President Nelson Rockefeller. He was a husky man, which
bespoke his previous profession. If he had not ended up as
an attorney, he could have used his six-foot-eight-inch rock
truck of a frame as a bouncer. O'Shaughnessy was in his
midsixties and had spent thirty of those years in law en-
forcement with the state of Florida.

He'd had the tenacity to attend and receive a law degree
from a diploma mill and had taken the bar five times before
he'd received the letter in the mail stating he had passed.
Content with his position in the firm, O'Shaughnessy never
played the office politics game. He was satisfied with just
being an associate. This made him popular with the other
attorneys and the clerical staff as well, because he was free
to say what he felt.

O'Shaughnessy had an adequate win percentage, and his
billable hours were in league with the other associates. His
goal was to stay above the normal office jockeying for position and to enjoy his employment with Murphy, Renfro and
Collins before he retired with his wife and camping equip-
ment to Flagstaff.

Betty, on the other hand, was a cash register to the firm.
Her billable hours were thirty percent higher than the second highest associate, who happened to be R. Raymond Patterson. She was a rainmaker to the concern, not because Jack
Murphy was her mentor, but because she did as she'd been
instructed as a child. She always worked twice as hard as
the next person.

An hour after the departure of R. Raymond, George O'-
Shaughnessy tapped on the door. Betty, who was dressed

in her sorority red and white sweat suit, had her white Keds
perched on top of the desk. As she reviewed the Henderson
Electric file, she was not in the mood for company.

"How are you doing, Betty?"

"Fine," she said, and peered over the top of the reading
glasses she wore as a result of studying for hours in badly
lit dormitories and coffeehouses. "And yourself?"

"I can't complain, can't complain," he said, and looked at
a chair with her attaché on it. "May I?"

"Sure."

"So what do you think about what's going on in this
place?"

After she took a breath, Betty put her feet on the floor,
rested her elbows on her desk, and tugged softly at the brim
of her cap. "I just hope he pulls through," she said, trying
to camouflage her pain.

"Hey, don't you worry, little darling. Jack Murphy is one
of the toughest kids on the block," he said, with his Brook-
lyn accent somehow preserved after all the years in the sun
belt. "I've known da man twenty, thirty years, and it'll take
more than a li'l cramp in his ticker to take him out, believe
you me."

"I hope so," she said, and made eye contact with him.
"The only reason I came to this firm and decided to stay in
this godforsaken town was because of Murphy. He wasn't
like the others who talked to me. I could have done better
with several firms in Atlanta, Dallas, or New York. In fact,
I even had a firm here in town offer me more. It was never
just about money with Jack. I guess—" her voice lowered—
"that's why he has so much of it now. He once told me that
money was a great servant but a terrible master. He spoke
of the honor of this profession. About something called *eth-
ics.* Even after I graduated, I debated if one could be ethical
and still be a successful attorney. I found out the answer to
that question by watching Jack Murphy. No one else, and I
mean no one I spoke to, talked like that. Those were the
reasons I initially wanted to practice instead of going into
medicine," she said as she stared through George O'Shaughnessy. "He spoke of the law in such, I don't know, in such
eloquent terms. He has such a passion for what we do."

And then she added in a whisper as she thought about the words she'd said, "Mr. Murphy is what I wanted, I mean, would like to be."

"Well," O'Shaughnessy said in a consoling tone, "he'll be okay, darling. You know," he said, and tried to change the subject with the tact of a hungry pit bull in a butcher shop, "I was talking to Pete Sampkins last night about a case he's preparing a motion of dismissal on and it reminded me of you."

Betty, who'd taken another tissue from her box for her nose, looked at O'Shaughnessy.

"It appears this *African-American* kid is being denied a promotion with a Subaru distribution center and he's saying it's because of racism. He has no evidence as such. They have no other legal precedence for making the claim, yet because he is black, I mean *African-American,* it's discriminatory. He wants a promotion based solely on affirmative action, and that's just not right. Call me crazy, but I just don't understand it," he said with a smile and shake of his Nixonion jowls. "I hate it when people use racism as an excuse for anything and everything that happens. When you cry wolf like that, the next time someone comes with a valid claim, they'll be ignored. I mean, don't get me wrong, I've been around. My father couldn't get work in the union because of our last name. So I understand where you're coming from with the racism thing there. But you can't always blame it on race." As he spoke, Betty sat poker-faced. "Which is why I thought about you. Because you are the perfect example of what is *wrong* with affirmative action."

Betty tilted forward in her chair and removed her glasses. "Oh really?"

"Hell yeah!" he replied with a raised voice. "Look at you! You're black, I mean *African-American,* as well as a woman. I've worked with you on a couple of cases and you're a pretty good lawyer. I don't know what type of upbringing you've had, but you have had every reason in the world to give up. Every time I see Jesse Jackson or that Fair-a-con, yelling about quotas and affirmative action—I tell you, I think about you. Because," he said, and thumped his fist on the edge of her desk, causing Betty to look at the ripples in her tea, "it's people like you who show black folk that you *can* pull yourself up by your bootstraps in this country. In America," he finished, and thumped his fist with every syllable, "the opportunity is there for anybody if they want it, by golly. But some people—and I'm not just talking about the black people, there's some sorry-assed white folks out there too—would starve to death with a ham under each arm."

Betty was insulted, but almost laughed as he made the ludicrous comments and ended with the words "by golly."

O'Shaughnessy added, with a cock of the head and a gap-toothed grin, "You see, darling, the only thing America owes any of us is an opportunity. This is the land of opportunity. If you work hard in America, you can accomplish anything you want. I'm living proof of that. I never noticed that plaque over there. Did you just get it?"

"No. I mean yes," Betty said. "It's the Charlotte Rae award given each year by BALSA."

"I know her. She's from New York, I think. Queens to be exact. She used to play in that sitcom with the cute little col—I mean *African-American* kid. 'Diff'rent Strokes' or something. Did she give them some money or something?"

With a quiet sigh Betty said, "No. She's the first female African-American attorney in the United States. She was a corporate litigator and had to close her doors because she could not get work, but I want to go back to what you said earlier." Betty had to decide quickly, *Do I rip his heart out and leave him for dead or do I take out a scalpel and delicately remove his organs, one by one?* She chose the latter as the waves dissipated in her tea. O'Shaughnessy leaned back and crossed his long legs with a condescending smile on his lips.

Betty leaned to the side in her chair, swiveled silently between the ten- and two-o'clock positions, and said, "You know, I really do appreciate the compliment you gave me, George." Her mind moved quickly for the words, the right words.

O'Shaughnessy smiled and tipped his head as if to say *thank you*, but unbeknownst to him, he had walked into the abyss.

"But I can't believe you could sit here, with a straight face, and tell me you do not see the need for affirmative action. You're an educated man, George." She rose from her chair, turned her back on him, and looked down on the city below. "Do you know about the forty-acres-and-a-mule agreement made with the former *so-called* slaves after they were freed? It was referred to at the time as 'special order fifteen.' "

"Now, Betty, with all due respect, that stuff happened— what—two, three hundred years ago by people—"

"So you are aware of it?" She turned to look at him. "You know that a parcel of land which extended from South Carolina down to Jacksonville was given to the freed slaves and that *President* Andrew Johnson not only took it away from them, he gave it back to the Confederacy? The same army who months earlier killed his sons in battle? He gave it back to the army he had just defeated. And I am sure, George, you would say since it happened so long ago by people who have long since left this earth, we should forget about it, correct?"

"No, I was just—"

"But," she said, and cut him off again with a thrust of her hand into the air, "allow me to tell you, there are some things people should *never* forget. Imagine, if you would, a marathon. Now, imagine the gun going off and one runner being set free to run, while the other is held back. Imagine the runner running seven, eight, or nine miles before the other runner is set free. He is already behind nine miles. Don't you think it would be easy for this runner to just give up? Would you look at this race at the halfway mark and say, oh well, he was held back, but that is out of our hands now? We have no responsibility for the injustices he experienced at the starting gate? Of course you wouldn't, George, because I know you, and I know you to be both a fair and learned man."

O'Shaughnessy smiled and sunk lower in his chair.

"So you see, *African-Americans* will catch up, don't get me wrong. And *African-Americans* will not quit. We are too strong a people for that. The race is not over for us. It will take time, George, but African-Americans, as a whole, *will* catch up. And you know something else?" she continued with a slight twinkle in her eye as she smiled. "There are just some things we will never forget."

"I follow. But look at you, Betty," O'Shaughnessy said as he sat forward with his arms folded tight across his barrel chest. "You are a perfect example, because with your background, whatever it is, and with me and where I come from, we are both associates in one of the top firms in the country. Look at Clay Bancroft, or better yet, Raymond. Everybody knows that R. Raymond Patterson's family has more money than God Almighty, and yet we are all equals. We make practically the same money. You're Black, I mean an *African-American* girl, and R. Raymond and I are white. So obviously," he said with his palms held open to Betty, "it *can* be done without quotas and with good old-fashioned American hard work. See where I'm coming from? Did you need a quota to get into the law school at UF?"

"George," she said, and stood in front of her chair as she ignored yet another sexist and obtuse comment delivered with a chuckle. "First of all, like I said, African-Americans *as a whole* will catch up." And then she paused, as if to shift gears, and continued, "Secondly, George, if all things were fair and equal, no, I wouldn't be here."

A question mark appeared on O'Shaughnessy's wrinkled brow.

"With my education and dollars generated to this firm, I'd be a partner now and on my way to the governor's mansion." She plopped down in her chair on the word *mansion,* to drive home the point with a smile.

After a thorny silence, O'Shaughnessy flashed his toothy grin. "Point taken. Well," he said as he stood and brushed the wrinkles from his jeans before he reached for the doorknob, "I think I'll leave a note in Sampkins's box. We need to get started on that Subaru case."

"Ahh, George? Is that why you wanted to get together for lunch Monday?"

"Oh. Oh no," he said as he looked at the pink slip of paper between her fingers. "No, no, we were going to ask you a couple of questions about a civil case that was similar to that Biradial Foods case you worked on a few years ago.

That's all. But Phillip Sheridan answered our questions last night."

Betty crumpled the memo, put on her glasses, and skipped the opportunity to corner him with a lie.

"I'll tell Sampkins to thank his lucky stars he's not going to go against you in court, sugar," O'Shaughnessy said, and laughed as he closed her door.

Betty thought as she shook her head, *So you wanted me to be the token Negro attorney in the Subaru case, huh? Oh, you tried my natural soul that time.*

Betty and Carol searched for files and related documents for an hour to prepare for a large lawsuit filed against a hardware store by the parents of a kid who'd been hit by a truck driven by one of their delivery men who had been drinking on the job. After she located all of the files, Betty got a fresh cup of cocoa and settled in to finally get some work done. Fifteen minutes into her reading of a motion appeal filed by the company's attorney, there was yet another knock on her door.

"Yes!" she said in her driest, most frustrated voice. This time she removed her spectacles and leaned back on the desk she sat in front of Indian style.

"It's me, girl; calm down," Jacqui said as she opened the door and dropped her bag on Betty's antique oak desk.

"Thank goodness."

"Why? What the hell's going on here today? I've never seen that many cars outside this place on the weekend."

"Child, let me tell you; this place has been beyond crazy. Murphy is in the hospital, apparently with a heart attack. You know he was always in perfect health."

"I know," Jacqui replied with her mouth open. "I used to see him jogging every Saturday morning when I came by here from Books for Thought. As a matter of fact, I looked for him this morning. Where is he?"

"North Florida General. Apparently he's still in ICU and they're only allowing his immediate family to see him. I just found out about it this morning."

"Oh, snap. It happened yesterday? But we were in here. You mean to tell me these jerks didn't tell you?"

"No, no. Remember, we were in and out so fast we didn't see anyone. There was no one at the reception counter when we came in or when we left."

"Oh yeah. That's right."

"Carol tried to call me, but what with the move, the answering machine didn't pick up. But this morning," Betty said as she cupped her mouth and spoke lower, "she told me that the vultures are already circling for position."

Jacqui got up to close the door so they could speak without being overheard and sat on the edge of Betty's desk. "So what does this do to the partnership opportunities here for you?"

"Well, really, Jac, I haven't thought about it. I mean, I'm just hoping the man survives."

"Yada, yada, yada. Whatever, whatever. I understand all that, girl, but you better watch out for yourself in a place like this. I don't trust none of them here. You're working in a den of straight-up thieves. I bet you there're more than a few of these assholes praying the man—"

"Jacqui!"

"Well, it's true, girl. You got a good heart and all, and I admire you for that. I couldn't put up with them. A job like this is like spandex, it's just not for everybody. But Jack Murphy, God bless him and all, got your head all full of this money-as-a-servant stuff, and that's nice. But this is the real deal. Welcome to reality. You better watch your back before one of them starts greasing the skids for you."

"But, Jac, Murphy is one of the top attorneys in the country. And this man has taken me under his wing. I know his wife, his kids, and you can't put a value on that. I mean, I know Renfro has his issues to deal with, and believe me, that whole good-ole-boy system they play here gets old. But there is a method to my madness."

Picking at her fingernails, Jacqui said, "As Billie Holiday said, 'Mother may have and *Murphy* may have, but God bless the child that has his own, and I am through with that.'"

"Oh well," Betty said as she got up and sat on the edge of her desk beside Jacqui's Fendi purse. "You make a good point. Trust me, I understand where you are coming from, especially with what happened yesterday."

"Got an idea for you. Let's eat."

"I thought you'd never ask," Betty said, happy to end the conversation. As she dropped her files, cut off her reading lamp, and grabbed her purse, she said, "Maybe getting away awhile will clear my head a little. Oh yeah, child, don't let me forget to tell you about the discussion I just had with O'Shaughnessy. That fool is a trip."

CHAPTER 8

╪

As they walked into Jacquetta's, Betty waved and spoke to the family members she knew. Jacqui was greeted at the door by her cousin with a handful of receipts and messages from the night before. Apparently the cash drawer was off, and Jacqui had informed them that if the register was over or under by even one cent, she wanted to know about it. While it was a family business, she drove home the point that this was a business first and foremost. It was not personal. She'd even had to fire a cousin who she *thought* was on drugs, which made an uncle upset, but she'd felt that was a price she would have to pay in such an undertaking.

Jacqui finally joined Betty, who was seated at a booth stirring a beverage and watching people come in and out of the restaurant. "They were off again last night."

"How much?"

"That's not important. The receipts should *always* balance. What are you drinking?"

"Iced tea."

"Willie Mae," Jacqui shouted, and looked over her shoulder. "Bring me some tea, sweetheart." Willie Mae was another cousin of Jacqui's and about ten years older then she, but she jumped to attention as if she were a child at the beck and call of a parent.

"Let's go in my office where we can talk," Jacqui said,

getting out of the booth. "Willie Mae, bring it in the office honey, okay?"

"Awright."

After she closed the door, Betty took off her shoes, sank into her usual spot on the sofa, and buried her toes in the cushions. "When you gonna hire somebody in this place unrelated to you? You know Isaac is still with the state's attorney's office. One call from me and he'll bring you up on discriminatory hiring practices. Make you hire some white folk up in here."

"Please. I don't need any problems. I'll hire some white folk when those Chinese food joints on every corner in this neighborhood hire some black or white folk. Besides, I started to hire one little sister, but she had too many gotsnos," Jacqui said, looking through her mail.

"As in gotsno man and gotsno car? You told me that jacked-up joke two weeks ago."

"Shuddup. So you still stay in contact with Isaac?"

"Yeah, he's cool. He even sent me a few clients. He got married about a year ago, you know. Has a little girl named Rain."

"Damn," Jacqui said as she looked down at the paperwork on her desk. "Isaac married a white girl, huh."

"Is it that obvious? Child named Rain Kadesah Holmes. Now, that's jacked up. But guess who tried to talk to me in the grocery store last week. Billy Jefferson."

"Really. What does he look like now'days? I remember in college he used to look kinda rough. Ain't never combed his hair. Always used to look tired. Like a runaway slave or something."

"He ain't changed a bit," Betty said, and shook her head in disgust as she slipped a peppermint candy from the nearby dish into her mouth. "Girl, he looked broker than the Ten Commandments, and believe it or not, remember how he used to smell kinda gamey? Well, he smells worse now. And he looked just as rusty as ever, like he needed a Jurgeons IV. Hey, I got a joke for you. Evander told me this one a couple of weeks ago. What do you have when you have twenty thousand attorneys at the bottom of the ocean?"

Laughing at Betty, Jacqui said, "A damn good start! That's from the Denzel movie. Umm, *Philadelphia*. Let me hit you with this one. A woman asks this young attorney if he's honest. So the kid says, yes ma'am. I am *so* honest, in fact, I borrowed ten thousand dollars from my dad for law school and paid him back right after my first big case. So the woman said, that's impressive. What kinda case was it? And the kid said, well ahh, umm, my dad kinda sued me for ten thousand dollars."

"Okay, okay, you got me again," Betty said with a laugh.

"Girl, you never could tell a joke. I don't know why you even try. Thanks, honey," Jacqui said to Willie Mae, who walked in with her tea. "Are we getting busy out there?"

"A little. Not too much for us to handle, though."

"If it gets too busy, call me. Oh yeah," she said before Willie Mae left, "bring us back a couple of cheeseburgers and some fries. Kenny knows how to cook them."

"Okay. Oh, Jacqui? There's a guy out here named John. Said he wanted to talk to you when you got a minute?"

"Is it John Rivers? Big, tall dude? About six six?"

"I don't know what his last name is, but he is tall," Willie Mae answered.

Jacqui turned away and looked at Betty. With a twist of her lip she said to Willie Mae, "Tell him I left out the back."

"Okay," Willie Mae said, and shuffled back into the dining area.

"So tell me, what's up with you and *Vander*? That's what you calling him, right? You subscribing to *Brides* magazine yet?"

"Is that good-looking John *Superman* Rivers? Who used to play basketball for Grambling or something?"

"Please. If John even looked up the word *fine* in a dictionary it would say 'NOT YOU.' I guess you haven't seen him recently. Instead of calling him Superman, they ought to call him Breakfast, Lunch, and *Supper* Man."

"Put on a few pounds, huh? I thought you liked him. Works for FedEx or something, doesn't he?"

"Betty, Supper Man has not worked at FedEx in over a year. He's working as a sales rep or something at WGNE, the radio station that's always going out of business."

"Really? Other than the weight, is he as cute as he was when we watched him shooting ball at the park?"

Jacqui folded her arms, breathing deeply. "Yeah, he's cute, but he's still looking for himself. The whole while we were together, he talking about what he *gonna do.* Sound like a big ole kid talking about what he *gonna be* when he grows up. I mean this brother is thirty-four years old and still talking bout being a millionaire. Ain't got plan one to do it. And if he tells me one more time about that catch he made or basket he shot in high school to win the state championship, I'll puke. Swear to God! That stuff happened, what? Twenty years ago? And he still talking about it like I'm supposed to be impressed."

"Jacqui, to be honest, that's not a bad quality to have— the dream part, that is. At least he hasn't lost his ability to have a dream. So many black men today don't give a damn. Many of them don't know how to—"

"Dream, my ass!" Jacqui exclaimed. "I used to dream of being Cat Woman, but there comes a time when you have to look at reality."

"But brothers do have it hard out there, Jac. You must admit." Jacqui held her palm up six inches from Betty's nose as if to say, *spare me.* "Have you seen what the unemployment rates are for African-American men in this country?" Betty continued as she moved Jacqui's hand. "I mean, if a brother is out there trying, with all they come up against, I would be more than willing to help push him. Today we have fewer brothers in college than in—"

"Bullshit!"

"Excuse me?" Betty said, and wiped a drop of tea from her lip.

"That's bull, with a *capital* shit. I get tired of hearing sisters buying in to it," Jacqui said as her voice went up an octave. "I know more brothers are in the penetentiary than in college, but did we put them there? And in regards to the ones who are out, do they think we're getting jobs from the job fairy or something? Like there's a conspiracy by the *white* man, of course, to give jobs to us in an attempt to keep them down? Hell, we have to deal with the black thing and the female thing and we still get ours!"

"Well, I guess I'm from the old school, because I think the black men out there have it harder in society and need our support."

Jacqui smiled and shook her head in weary frustration. "Yeah. But when they get a dime, who do they run to? Who do *they* support? White women. Who runs to us, Betty? Have you ever asked yourself that question? Who on this earth do we as Black women have to run to?" Then Jacqui, seeing they were not going to agree on the issue, said, "Forget that. I'm tired of singing that song, I wanna hear about this Evander guy. How thick is it? Is he legit?"

Betty took off her baseball cap and combed out her hair with her fingers. "Let's just say we are not talking marriage, but I must admit, I do like what I see in him so far."

"Yeah? So tell me, what's up?"

"Not a lot to tell. I mean he's good to me and he's good for me. What more can you ask for?"

"How long y'all been together now?"

"We've been going out casually for about three months, but things have only gotten serious the last couple of weeks."

"What? You slept with him?"

"Have I slept with him? Umm," Betty said sheepishly.

"Wait a minute. I thought you were my girl. You been riding this nigga and ain't told me? See how wrong you are?" Jacqui said with a wide-eyed smile. "I thought you've been acting different. I knew it! How was it? Did he know how to work it?"

"Jac, listen to me. He's better then anything I could ever imagine. So soft, so gentle, so in control, so firm. I didn't know how much I missed it until I got some. And now—"

"And now you addicted. Or should I say a-dick-tad!" Jacqui laughed. "That's how it is. You go months and months without it and then you get a little and BAM, you hooked. I believe that damn penis is more addictive than crack. One hit, that's all it takes, and you strung-out like Pookie in *New Jack City*. You gotta have it! Well, it's about time. How long has it been since you slept with that jerk from college?"

"I don't know, and frankly, I do not care. All I do know," Betty said, "is this man makes me happy. And you know what? He seems to have a mission to do just that. He makes me smile and it feels good for a change. I like that about him."

"What about the age thing? Has anyone ever asked if he's your daddy?"

"Now, see, you wrong. That's why I can't tell you anything. You know he doesn't look that much older than me. I never thought I would be attracted to an older man, but I kinda like that in him. He is so mature as far as what he wants. I think he's sown all his wild oats and just wants to find happiness."

"Well, you my girl. I'm just watching out for a sister. I'm happy for you. You needed that," Jacqui said, and sipped her iced tea. "The last guy I had like that was great every damn where *but* in bed. Damn shame I had to drop him."

"Was he that bad?"

"Was he! His name was Chauncy and I dropped his ass like a New Year's resolution. He had to hit the bricks, the pavement, the concrete or whatever! Please," Jacqui said, and got annoyed all over again as she picked her nails. "I would be just laying there, counting ceiling tiles, thinking about what I had to do here at work, thinking about going shopping, any damn thing. He wasn't hitting on nothing." Jacqui said with a smile, "The brother was just an *aggravating* screw. He tried hard. I will give him credit for that. Almost broke *his* back actually. I'll let you in on a little secret about men. If you want a man to go that extra mile for you? Before you go to bed with him, just casually tell him, you know, I've *never* had an orgasm. He'll be smelling like Ben-Gay for two weeks afterwards.

But back to my boy, Chauncy. I've had flu-shot needles inside me longer—*and* deeper, I might add. One time, girl, he came so damn fast, when he finished, I gave his ass that look." Jacqui looked at Betty like a deer caught in the headlights. "I haven't seen his butt since. Now, you know a brother weak when a *look* will chase his ass off. I'm not talking about leaving bridal magazines around or talking to him about children's names. Those are old games. If you want a brother to evaporate? When he pulls down his pants, give his ass that deer look just like this," she said, and gazed at Betty with her lips apart and tongue showing, "and I swear the next time you see him will be on a milk carton. But as I was saying, Chauncy was just sickening. Just thinking about him makes me sick. I can feel my throat swelling right now. No lie. Hey, Willie Mae, bring me some cough drops," she shouted as they laughed.

"Damn, that's pretty bad," Betty said as Jacqui rubbed her throat.

"At one time I would fake it a little for him, like you the man, you the man, when all the while I would be thinking about a shoe sale at Burdine's. Now, you know a man has gotta go when he is having an orgasm and I am thinking about suede pumps."

"Well, fortunately Evander has that covered. He wants me to be happy. And listen to this," Betty said, and leaned forward on the couch. "The brother got up at six o'clock this morning and made *me* breakfast, at *my* place. Can you believe that?"

"No, I can't. If I can get my men to just get up and get the hell out in the morning, I feel fortunate."

"I tell you, when we did it, I felt like I was on cloud nine. Everything just flowed so naturally. And he says the sexiest things when we make love. None of that *whose is it* stuff."

"Well, ahh, I kinda like that, but I know what you getting at."

"I'm serious. He leaves me love songs on my cell phone and at home. Boy can't sing a lick to save his life, but just the thought gives me chills. Not a week has passed that I have not received a bouquet of yellow roses. I just don't know if I can handle it."

"Well, good. At least it will keep you off that damn computer chatting with them freaks and perverts."

"I use the Internet for research, *Ms. Lady*."

"Yeah, and my vibrator is for my back."

"Well, actually I was on last night and I met a really nice guy," she replied, knowing Jacqui's opinion of cyberspace and cyberpeople.

"Girl, I done told you about that stuff. Those people online are all crazy, you know. Don't you watch Mother Love?"

"No," Betty said, "I do not, and I don't read the *Enquirer* or the *Globe* either."

"Well, you should. Don't say I didn't try to warn you. Forget that; tell me this. How serious is this guy? Evander, I mean."

"What do you mean?"

"I mean, has he mentioned the word *marriage* or *love* or anything?"

Willie Mae walked in with their lunch and put it on Jacqui's desk. "Y'all need any mo tea?" she asked.

"Naw, we're cool. Thanks, darling," Jacqui said, and munched on a fry as Willie Mae headed for the door.

"Oh yeah," Willie Mae, said and turned around. "Brenda found that eighteen cents."

"Damn! Honey, you made my day! Thank you! Thank you!" Betty shook her head with a sarcastic smile as Jacqui shot her a look across the room. "Don't you start over there!"

As the door closed Betty replied, "Hey, I didn't say a word."

"You didn't have to. If it's a penny today, it's a dollar tomorrow, ten dollars next week, and a missing bank bag in a month."

"Jacqui? You talking to yourself. I didn't say a word."

"Thank you. That's how you gotta do it when you working with family. Now, tell me more about Evander! I get so tired of hearing females talk about sorry, good-for-nothing men. I need to hear about a good brother every now and then."

"So far everything is great. But now we are going through that transition phase. You know, when you don't exactly date but you become more of a couple? And you know how I am. I just don't want to chase him off."

"Chase him off how?"

"Well, you know how it is to live alone for so long. You get set in your ways, and it'll be an adjustment having a man around all the time. When I walk in the door, first thing I want to do is get my stockings off, and they may end up anywhere. In the sink, on the toaster, on the couch. And you know how I am about my baths."

"Oh yeah, I almost forgot. You take those two-hour marinade sessions. You should just drop a few onions and carrots in there and prepare dinner while you're at it."

"Well, not so much that. You know, he's never seen me without my hair done except in the morning. And I don't think I've ever been around him without perfume. I even wear it before I go to bed with him. And tell me something about men. Why do they always flush a few seconds before they stop peeing? You ever noticed that? They always get pee in the new water."

"Honey, you got just a little too much time on your hands if you're noticing that. But he can't be perfect either. Does he pass gas in his sleep or have bad breath or something?"

"Naw, he's not like most men at all, which is what's so damn scary about him. But to answer your other question," Betty said, looking down at her feet, "he has said he loved me a couple of times, but I just can't tell him that yet. I mean, I care for him. I really do. But I just don't wanna show that card."

"Well, if he's saying it, how are you going to be able to keep him interested without you saying it? Do you feel it?"

"I don't know. But I won't say it until I know for sure it feels right."

"I wish I had a man like that. I always end up with a brother without a job or living with his mammy or on drugs. And sometimes," she laughed, "they have all three qualities."

"Was Harry like that?"

"Harry was a freak! Girl! I thought I told you about that fool!" she said, waving her hand in front of her mouth as she tried to swallow her hot food quickly. "We went over to his house after the party at Kevin and Rachel's. I ain't gonna sit here and lie. I wanted him probably worse than he wanted me. He was dressed head to toe in black. Black pants. Black vest. Black jacket. Do you know how good triple black looks on a double-black man? Girl, he even wore Noir cologne, okay? So anyway, we kissed in the doorway as soon as he opened the door to his town house, and then boom, it was on."

"Don't tell me. Not in the doorway, Jacqui!"

"Child, I don't know what hit the floor first, my bag or my bra."

Laughing to the point of choking, Betty said, "You know you can get help for that sickness of yours, don't you?"

"As I was saying," Jacqui continued, "he went over and put on that Isley Brothers album, umm, you know, that old one?"

"Girl, all the Isley Brothers albums old!" Betty replied, unable to resist the temptation. "When is the last time you saw a *new* Isley Brothers album?" she asked, and grabbed her stomach as she bent over in laughter.

"Okay, you got me on that one. You know the one I'm talking about."

"Between the Sheets?"

"Yeah," she replied, and leaned back. "That's it. So we were just dancing there in his living room and then he says to me, baby, I'm a freak."

"He's a what?"

"Yeah, that's what I thought to myself. So I'm thinking, hey, that's cool with me, sorta thinking he was trying to tell me he liked oral sex or something."

"And . . . wait a minute. You didn't do *him*, did you?"

"Girl, please, I didn't *even* know that fool like that, but let me finish. So we were dancing to *Between the Sheets*. Then I feel it get bigger and bigger and bigger. And I'm saying to myself, damn, I hope this nigga don't split me in half. And he's grinding it harder and harder and I am praying these old fools singing on the CD would shut up, right? So as soon as it finishes, he takes my hand and I start playing the role."

"What role?"

"You know," Jacqui said, and counted off on her fingers in monotone. "Excuse me, I'm not that kinda girl, you don't know me like that yet, I can't go there with you, I don't know if we should do this yet, do you think we are ready for this, do you have protection, et cetera, et cetera."

"Girl—"

"So anyway," Jacqui said with a forefinger extended, and rolled her eyes upward, "we lay on the bed and started kissing. And I must admit, the brother's tongue was wicked, child. Wick-kid. I'm sure his tongue's double-jointed or something now that I think about it."

"No way!"

"This man damn near made me come with a kiss! And oh yes, there's a way. So we're kissing on the bed and then he lays me back and starts doing his thing, right? Well, then he asked, can I freak you. And I think to myself, oh, he's going to ask if he can take the southern route or something, right? Little did I know *how* far south the brother wanted to travel."

"What do you mean?"

"Brother wanted to go to *South America*. All past *Cuba*. I was just laying there *staring* at him."

"He did what?" Betty said, her eyes wide.

"Yeah! Child, I still spit when I think about that fool's tongue in my mouth."

"You did send him home, right."

"Girl, of course I did. You know me," Jacqui said as she leaned back in her chair.

"Did you give him some Jac?" Betty asked, and tried to look her friend in the eyes as if she were her mother.

"Hey, what did I say? I sent him home."

"Jacqui, did you do him?"

"No, I did not *fuck* him, Ms. Lady."

"Jacqui!" Betty said without a hint of a smile. "Tell the truth and make the devil shame."

"I told you! No!" And then she looked at Betty and smiled, unable to keep her serious face. "Okay, I *fucked* him. But I didn't come . . . more than once . . . or twice . . . in the first hour."

There was a moment of silence before they both burst into laughter. "Heifer, you are crazy."

"Shyeet, that brother swung like a horse, child," Jacqui said, and rolled her chair closer to Betty on the couch to whisper. "He came out of the bathroom, and all I could see was his silhouette. He turned toward the dresser to find something for me to sleep in, and when he turned sideways, Lord, it looked like the map of Florida . . . upside down!" As she raised her right hand, Jacqui said with a laugh, "I tell no lie. If you cut that damn thing in half, you'd know his age! Child, when I saw it, all I could do was make that face."

"What face?" Betty replied through her laughter.

"You know what face. That face you make when 'Let's Get It On' comes on. That ugly face? That was me."

Wiping her eyes with both hands, Betty said, "Damn, *that* face. Girl, you know you need Jesus! So it was good?"

"Yeah, it was good. But I couldn't keep a brother like that around for too long."

"Why you say that?"

"Big as he is? He'd have me wearing Pull-Ups and Depends by the time I'm fifty. Does the word *incontinence* mean anything to you? But I must admit, even that tongue thing felt good. But I wouldn't kiss him for all the tea in China. He tried to kiss me and I had my mouth all up by his ears. I wanted to say, you eat ass, not me."

Betty jerked with laughter and threw a wadded-up napkin at Jacqui. "Girl, I don't know why I fool with you."

Jacqui sat still and gave Betty a serious look for the first time since they had been in the room. "Girl, let me tell you something. You know I would never steer you wrong. I love you like a sister. In fact, I love you better than my sister, and you know that 'cause I can't stand her lazy butt. But if this brother loves you, and he's good for you, don't let him get away. Sisters out here would jump out a window for a brother like that."

"I know. Don't get me wrong, I enjoy being with Evander and I do care for him. But I just don't know for sure if it's love, at least not yet," she said, and stared at her friend and then into space as she recombed her fingers through her hair and laced them behind her head. "I just don't know. But damn, girl," she said, and looked back at Jacqui, "*Damn,* it feels good."

CHAPTER 9

‡

Tuesday night

It was late, it was hot, and Betty was lonely. "I wonder what Jacqui's up to," she said to herself as she listened to the phone ring on the other end, looked at the clock, and noticed it was well past midnight.

"Hello," Jacqui said after she clicked over from the other line.

"You on an important call?"

"Yeah, right. At midnight? No, just aggravating Bruce on the other line, *begging*, as usual."

"You want me to call you back later?"

"Are you serious? One second, let me get rid of his ass."

As Jacqui clicked over, Betty lay in the midst of several stuffed animals from her childhood which she kept on her bed, but always got rid of whenever Evander came over. Her favorite was one her dad had sent her which she'd named Tuddley.

She felt like going out, but since it was so late in the small town, most of the nicer jazz clubs would be closed. Evander had to get up so early in the mornings, so she could not imagine a call to him. As she'd watched TV, she'd realized it was a perfect time to talk to Jacqui.

On the screen there was a scene of the wide-open plains of Oklahoma. As the actors spoke, in the background there was a long, black, slippery oil drill that went up and down in the well. On a night like tonight, this was not something she needed to see and she turned off the TV.

"Back."

"Hey, what took you so long to get rid of him?"

"Child, he's pitiful. Just plain old pitiful. I'm glad you called," Jacqui said.

"Why?"

"I didn't want to hurt his feelings, but damn, he's boring as hell. I talk to him for fifteen minutes and it feels like we've been on the phone for an hour!"

"Bruce. Isn't that the guy who is a professor at the university or something?"

"Yeah, I thought I liked educated men, but after talking to him, the stupid brothers look kinda good."

Betty laughed as she cuddled closer to Tuddley. "Well, I know what I got with Evander. I got so tired of the same thing. But I keep watching him too, waiting for him to trip."

"Damn, one second. Who is this," Jacqui said in a falsetto tone, "calling me at twelve forty-five?"

Jacqui clicked over to the other line and then clicked back. "Girl, I gotta go. You gonna be up later on tonight?"

Betty smiled and said, "No, darling, as we speak, I'm running water for my bath and then I'm going to sleep."

"Okay. Good night."

"Girl, you're too through," Betty said, dropping the cordless on the bed, and walking into the bathroom to add oil and bubbles to her bath.

The bathroom was her special place, her haven where she could release all of her pressure from the day. The walls were white and accented by black tiles on the floor and trim. All of the fixtures were onyx; assorted greenery and uniquely shaped bottles of oils from around the world were scattered about, and the air was kissed with a wisp of perfume. Betty looked forward to relaxing with just her bubbles. Moments when she had time to sit in a tub until the water was lukewarm and run hot water again and again were rare. Moments when she could play Will Downing in complete darkness, light scented candles, pour herself two fingers of Bailey's, and sit it on the edge of her tub were few and far between. But this was such a moment.

She sat on the edge of the tub because the water was too hot to sit in. As she slowly put the tip of her toe in, she felt it was safe enough to stand in the fiery water. The hot water brought beads of sweat to her brow, and as they formed, she allowed herself to sit, reached for the bar of soap and started to lather herself. Betty washed her stomach and under her arms and allowed her hand to move over to her breasts. As she bathed herself, she felt this was the perfect time to check herself, as she'd been taught in high school, but the touch became a lot more than anything Coach Hopper had taught in sex ed.

After a few minutes, she decided she'd had about as much of this as she could stand on a night when she was going to be alone, and pulled the string that allowed the tub to drain. "Damn, I wish it wasn't so late," she said, and thought of Evander. Before the tub drained, Betty put the stopper back in and sat in the sudsy water. It felt good to her for some reason. She was still covered with tiny bubbles as she gradually slid back and forth in the tub, feeling the cool air from the vent blow on top of her and the hot water caress her bottom. She rubbed the lather over her neck and shoulders with both hands. It felt amorous and erotic. She guided the slippery bar around her nipples and under her breasts as she closed her eyes and took short, evenly spaced breaths of air. Her eyes became slits as both of her hands touched the center of her chest and slid down her stomach, past her navel, toward her V.

"No, no!" she said as she shook her head. She had made a pact with herself not to do that again since she met Evander. *Damn, damn, damn, why does it have to be so late?*

Betty stepped out of the bathroom with a towel wrapped around her and sat on the bed to curl her hair. She lay back to catch her breath and get over the emotions she had experienced earlier. Lying still, she allowed the top of the towel to come free and her hands returned to her nipples, which experienced a hard-on few men could bring on. As she lay exposed, allowing her body to air-dry, her hands did something she promised herself she would not do. Before she could stop them, they had dialed the last digit.

"Yeah," the sleepy voice on the other end said.

Betty was coy for a split second and wanted to hang up, but knew she had reached the point beyond which she could not back out. "I'm sorry, baby. I didn't want to wake you."

"No, I wasn't asleep," Evander lied. "I was just sitting here watching, ahh, television."

"Really," Betty said as she attempted to avoid being too direct. But reality had set in for the first time, revealing just how addicted to him she had become. "What are you watching?"

"Nothing really. Why are you up so late?"

"I, I, ahh, I just couldn't sleep."

"Umm. Well . . . would you like some company?"

Betty jumped from her bed, unable to believe what she had done. She paced as her new cat, Tickey, watched her with his head swiveling back and forth and then scurried from the room. She had never called a man in the middle of the night for attention. It went against everything she believed in. It was something Jacqui would do, not her. As she stood, she removed the two curlers from her hair and paced back and forth. Should she put on music, candles, and lingerie to set the mood? Or would it be more romantic if she just put on a pair of revealing silk jogging shorts and a tank top, turned on the television, and allowed nature to take its course? She walked into her living room naked and put on Teddy. There was something in his voice that was similar to Evander's. It was earnest yet passionate. Rough, yet sexy and sensual. After she listened to two bars of "Turn Off the Lights," she decided that tonight nature needed a little assistance.

It was not long until Evander parked his SUV and knocked on the door. Betty sat in her bedroom wearing the scarlet negligee she'd bought three years earlier for a special occasion. She kept it on the top shelf in the original bag with an imaginary ribbon around it that read "Break only in the event of an emergency." Tonight was such an emergency, and she looked forward to the seal being broken. As she stood with only the three-inch door between them, she looked through the peephole and saw his smile beneath his

evenly trimmed mustache and full lips. With her fist up to
her mouth, she closed her eyes and opened the door. Standing in the doorway, she did not know what to say. *What
took you so long? Hello, big boy? Damn, I'm glad you came?* No
words seemed right at this moment.

"Damn, Beep. God, you look beautiful."

"Thanks," Betty replied, and looked down to avoid his
engulfing eyes. As he walked in, she noticed he wore the
black basketball shorts that were so sheer she could tell what
religion he was. And it was obvious from the jiggle below,
there was nothing between him and her but mesh.

"I'm glad you called," he said as he stood in the foyer.
"It seems I just can't get you outta my mind. Beep, I'm
strung out on you."

With a newfound strength Betty said, "I know the feeling.
I was just—" and then Evander tilted her face upward with
his thumb and index finger and softly kissed her before she
could finish the thought. For a large man he could be amaz-
ingly gentle as his lips embraced and seized hers and his
arms held her close enough to feel his excitement.

As their lips separated, Evander looked at Betty, smiled,
and whispered, "Close your eyes."

"Why?"

"Because I said so."

Betty followed his wishes and closed her eyes with a smile
of anticipation as she felt Evander take her hand and place
a piece of metal in it. Opening her eyes, she looked down
at the key as Evander said again, "Beep, close your eyes."
And then he brought his lips inches from her ear, so close
her goose bumps returned. "Front door," he whispered, and
then handed her another key and said, "Back door," and
with the third key he said, "Garage door."

Opening her eyes, Betty looked down and asked,
"Evander? Are you sure you want to do this?"

"I have never been so sure about anything in my life. I
swear, if there is a better feeling than the one I get when
you look at me and smile, God must have kept it in heaven."
And then he brought her close and said, "Honey, if you
would just let me . . . I would love you more than you could
ever know."

Betty took a stiff swallow and still looked at the keys as she said, "Evander I—"

With a finger to her lips, he continued, "Betty? If you would just *let* me love you, baby, I would love you more than you would ever know." Betty felt weak as Evander once again pierced the air with his bass voice. "Beep, if you would just let *me,* I will love *you.*" Evander brought his lips back to hers. As they kissed, he removed his shirt and somehow relieved himself of the shoes and shorts while never diminishing the moment they shared.

Betty pulled back and lowered her head to his chest. She wanted to kiss his nipple, but Evander pulled away and whispered in her hair, "This night is for you, baby. It's all about you." He stood still and seemed to breathe Betty into himself. With his eyes he traced the shape of her lips and then her eyebrows and cheekbones. Although he had seen her face a hundred times, he seemed to look at her for the very first time as he lifted her, without effort, from the floor and walked into the bedroom.

As he lowered her to the bed, Betty felt like a leaf that had fallen on a soft lawn. His body was strong and hard. He knew what to do with her body, and how to do it so well. As she lay there, he pulled the string on her lingerie that exposed her breasts. Betty was embarrassed for a second because she had always been self-conscious about their size and shape, but those fears dissipated. He stood over her exposed, with only the light of the moon shining off his passion. And then he ran his hands featherlike across her breasts, barely teasing the surface. With his thumb he brushed the outer edges of the nipple and took his time as if nothing in the world were as important as making her feel safe in his arms. "I wish I had a nicer or more romantic way of saying this, baby," he whispered, "but you have the sexiest, most beautiful breasts I have ever seen. I sometimes lay in bed just thinking about them. No joke." He smiled.

Evander slid his tongue deep into the soft area of flesh above Betty's collarbone, which caused her to quiver. She loved his attention to detail. He allowed his kiss to tease the outer area of her breast, then brought it to the black-brown rim and toward its center. As he moved slowly, he felt every bump, and it seemed to only excite him more. Evander journeyed further and deeper with her into the valley of pleasure, and then she reached for his exposed fire and noticed it was moistened. He held her hand firm. "Not yet," he said. The message that night was clear. On that night she only had to open her heart, close her eyes, and enjoy the ride.

On previous nights they had shared passion, but never like this. There were nights they'd perspired together, but never made the windows fog. As they made love, the intensity changed like the seasons. There were moments when she held on to the thick muscles of his lower back and tried her best not to leave a scratch. And then the mood would swing as he would softly but firmly hold both of her wrists and take her places she had never been. Betty opened her eyes to look at Evander covered in sweat, which would occasionally drip onto her breasts. Breathing heavily, she wanted to watch him with his eyes closed, because she feared staring into them would leave her as defenseless as saying those three words. The satin sheet that had once covered her mattress was wrinkled at the foot of the bed. The top sheet and comforter were only a distant memory. And then she said with a tear in her throat to the rhythm of the love they were making, "Evander? You know how . . . I feel. If you truly love me . . . then you know how hard this is for me." Evander covered her lips with a kiss and then looked in her eyes with a blank expression.

As the CD changed to the O'Jays' "Let Me Make Love to You," Evander suddenly froze. "What's wrong?" Betty asked, fearing with her inexperience she had done something wrong.

But he just said softly, "I want to look at you." Catching her breath, Betty blushed and closed her eyes as Evander said, "Look at me." Betty did so with reluctance. To the beat of the music Evander moved again as she closed her eyes and then he said, "Betty. Look at me." Never had doing so been so difficult for her. As her fingers turned into fists he said once again to the rhythms in the air, "Betty . . . look . . . at . . . me!" And Betty opened her eyes and a little more of her heart to Evander as he mouthed the words slowly, *I love you.*

It was 3:30 A.M. and Betty was awake. As Evander slept, she eased out of bed to go to the bathroom. By far it was the most special night the two had shared. It was, in a way, frightening how good this man could be when he wanted to. As she walked toward the kitchen for a cup of tea, she turned off the CD changer with Teddy in the middle of "Come on Go with Me." Teddy never sounded as good as he sounded tonight.

After she returned to the room, Betty pulled her white antique rocking chair closer to the bed to sit and rock, and watch her *Vander*. He slept so peacefully. Like a forty-four-year-old baby. The face that made a passionate scowl while they made love was now at rest atop her pillow. The body that made her vibrate with a liquid fire lay innocently in a fetal position.

Being mischievous, Betty pulled off the remnants of satin that were still on him, leaving him totally exposed. As he lay there, her eyes rested on his chest as she wondered what kind of heart pumped inside of it. Was it cold or sincere? Could it walk away and leave or call out a name in an argument? Could it have been broken and in need of healing or was it as warm inside as it appeared from the outside?

The door cracked and Betty was startled until she heard the furry bundle of love meow and walk toward her. As she rocked, Tickey jumped in her lap and she held him close. After the hours she had just spent with this special man, her cat tingled and it felt good. Evander reached for the sheet to cover himself while he slept, and Betty rocked and sipped her tea. She had done things with him she had never heard Jacqui mention doing before. This was a night that exceeded her wildest dreams. Was it because she was lonely? Was it because she could truly admit to herself that she had fallen in love with this man deeper and faster than she ever wanted to admit? Or was it because of the fullness of the moon against the black velvet sky? Whatever it was, it had worked. "If it was because of the moonbeams, it's a damn shame you can't bottle them," she whispered and then yawned. Then Betty quietly put her cup on the dresser and picked up the key to Evander's front door. As she rocked and stared at it, Tickey curled into a tight ball on her lap and went to sleep.

CHAPTER 10

‡

Saturday, one month later

As the March winds blew, Betty and Evander traveled the interstate south. It was a weekend Betty had decided not to work because Evander had asked her to meet his mother. In spite of the increased caseload at the firm, being with him was something she looked forward to. Evander's family lived in Freemont, which at one time had been a prosperous black suburb of Orlando. It now stood as just another red-light district. A part of the city where no one jogged the streets, but people constantly ran them.

Her life had changed drastically since Evander had walked into it. There were times when, if she was not in the midst of a case, she would walk in her door after work, pull off her shoes, and chat with people on the Internet for hours—even at times eating her dinner while gazing into the screen. Many guys would proposition her, but none piqued her interest except for the one with the DLastRomeo moniker. But finding anything more than a friendship on the Net was the last thing she was looking for, because already Evander had made so many of her dreams come true.

The invitation from Evander came as a surprise and flattered Betty because it was a major step in their young relationship. She wanted to see another side of this man she had become so enamored of. They had made love almost every night for the past several weeks and each time it seemed he attempted to stretch the envelope. If she wanted to take this relationship to the next level, meeting the tree from which her mighty oak had fallen was essential.

The trip to the magic city could not come at a better time for Betty. Each day the tension and office politics intensified at the firm. It had been a little over a month since Mr. Murphy's heart attack, and although his condition had improved, the word was he would relinquish his interest in Murphy, Renfro and Collins. Since Renfro was running the concern single-handedly, everyone depended on rumors to determine in what direction the firm would travel. By most accounts, the feeling was that the following week a partnership would be extended.

After losing several contracts based on their exclusive white middle-aged brotherhood at the top, Bert Collins had spearheaded a nationwide task force to recruit a top minority candidate into the fold as a partner. But after reviewing the list of candidates who would consider the position, Agnes Murphy had informed Betty over coffee that she had both superior credentials and growth potential. She'd also added, "This is one time when your being a double minority will make you a shoo-in. Dear, I'm not at liberty to tell you where that came from, and you *didn't* hear it from me."

Two days after she'd spoken with Mrs. Murphy, five associates had been invited to interview over a three-day period, and according to Lisa, who'd sat in on the panel, Betty was by far the top partnership candidate. On the eve of what could potentially be the most important week of her career, Betty rode down the interstate with the wind in her face, holding Evander's hand and listening to Coltrane's "A Love Supreme" ooze from the speakers.

As they arrived in the old neighborhood, Evander made a point of identifying for Betty each significant landmark, or at least the ones important to him. "See that boulder over there?" Before Betty could answer Evander said, "That's where I use to catch the school bus when I was in middle school. One time when we were standing there in the rain," he reminisced with a faint smile, "a couple of white boys drove by in a red Mustang with their asses out the window.

And over there at that intersection, I was driving my first car, a 1978 Camaro Berlinetta mind you, and this lady ran a stop sign and broadsided me. She was driving an Olds Ninety-eight and I doubt she scratched the bumper."

Each street had its own story, its own special memory for Evander, and Betty was taken by the sound of his voice. These places, which would mean nothing to the average observer, meant so much to him. She was honored he wanted to reminisce with her.

"Hey, Beep, I forgot to tell you. Mom invited a few of the family members over for lunch. I hope you don't mind. I just found out about it last night."

"No," Betty replied with a heartfelt smile. "I don't mind at all."

As they drove up to his mother's house, they were beset by a couple of children who shouted, "Vander! Vander's here!" He jumped out of the SUV and swept both of them off their feet as if he were their father who had returned from a long day at the office. Betty checked her face in the rearview and applied a touch of lipstick before she exited the truck. There were a few people already in the house, and from behind it music blasted from a car trunk so loud it vibrated the metal with its thump.

"Who tat is?" the little boy asked Evander, staring at Betty.

"This is my friend. Betty."

Friend? Friend, huh? Betty thought, and tried not to read too much into the words.

"Tell Betty what your name is," he continued, while he attempted to get the little boy to stand in front of him. With a smile void of a tooth, the little boy shook his head no and ducked behind Evander with his face in between Evander's legs.

The little girl said, "My name is Anna Janay."

The little boy, now not wanting his sister to one-up him, lost his fear and said, "My name is Jake and I'm four years old."

Evander took the kids by the hand, and he and Betty walked toward the house. As Betty got closer, she noticed a tall, imposing woman at the door. She looked to be in her late sixties, stood at least six two, and had a distinctive streak of gray in the center of her hair. She had a small trace of a mustache, the kind people never notice, and large forearms a little out of proportion even for her.

"Well, look at my baby," she said, and walked out to Evander, who was at the base of the steps. Betty was in awe at the sight of the two large individuals embracing. "Why didn't you call, boy," she said with a raspy voice, "to let me know you were on the road? Had me worried sick. I tried to call you three or four times this morning and didn't know where you were." Evander gave his mother a boyish smile, not unnoticed by Betty. It was obvious he loved her, and she could see the love was returned. One of Jacqui's rules was "The way a man treats his momma is the way he will treat you," so the sight brought comfort.

Mrs. Jones looked at Betty, who smiled up at her. "So how are you? Evander's told me so much about you." And she spread her arms wide enough to give Betty a hug. Betty, who was several inches shorter, stepped up to accept the embrace. In spite of her size and slightly masculine features, Mrs. Jones had a warm, feminine, motherlike feel, with just a hint of Skin-So-Soft to her scent.

As she embraced Mrs. Jones, Betty thought, *I could feel comfortable calling her Mom. Oh my God, I know I did not think that. I did not consider how it would feel to call this lady . . . Mom?* But after they parted, she smiled, because it felt right. It would feel right to find out from her what Evander liked to eat and how he'd learned to ride a bike and why he was such a decent man in a sea of dogs.

"Y'all come on in here," she said, and headed up the steps as she retied her apron. "Let me introduce you to everybody. We got some more coming soon."

Evander looked at Betty and smiled as he reached for her hand. "Are you ready for this?" Betty nodded her head yes as they entered the home.

The semifull house at the end of the cul-de-sac was like most houses in the neighborhood. Constructed three decades earlier, it had a skirt around its frame structure and was painted a mustard color with black trim around the doorway and on the shutters. The ceiling was stucco with bright accents that looked like glitter, and roach bates were evident in the corners. On the living room walls there were stiff, browned, Olan Millsesque shots of family and friends of family, from at least four generations of Joneses. In the corner Betty saw a dusty picture of MLK, JFK, and RFK with the words "Freedom Fighters" inscribed beneath it, and a large fish tank with one lonely fish. The house was cooled with an underpowered AC unit in the eastern window. The ice blue shag carpet matched nothing in the house, yet it all fit together perfectly. In modern interior decorating magazines the look would best be described as eclectic. The Joneses just called it home.

"Let me introduce you to everybody, sugar," Mrs. Jones said to Betty. "This is Uncle Elmo. This is Alexandria and her little sister Araxá. Now, this is the newest member of the family over here. Her name is Bre—Bre—BreNushia, I think is how you say it. I don't know why that child momma named her that crazy mess in the first place." And then she looked at Betty and said, "Why is it people naming babies such foolish names? If I see another baby named Jordan or Kenya or Shenequasetta, I don't know what I'll do. What happened to names like Robert or Percy or Dorothy? You know what I mean?"

Although Betty could see a look on her face requesting a response such as *No ma'am, I would never name our child a name like that*, she opted to just nod in agreement.

"Now, that's my nephew Eric over there. His wife, Ling or Ding or something, couldn't make it." And then she whispered, "She's Vietnamese, you know."

"She ain't Vietnamese, Auntie!" Eric said in a huffy tone.

"Then what is she?"

After a pause and a glance at the family members who stared at him, he said in a muffled tone, "She Chinese."

"This is my sister Gladys and her husband, Ben," Mrs. Jones said as she ignored the comment. "Gladys!" she said, and kicked Gladys, who was half asleep, in the foot. "Evander got himself a li'l cute girl, doesn't he?"

"Yeah, Evander's got a cute one, all right," Gladys said, and rocked back and forth while she fanned herself with the back of the phone-book cover she had ripped off to stay awake.

With a look around the room, Mrs. Jones said with her hands on her narrow hips, "I guess that's just about everybody. There's a few fools in the backyard, but you don't need to know them yet," she laughed.

In the La-Z-Boy in the den was one last family member who stared at the TV without acknowledging the houseguest. As he watched TV, he fiddled with the beaded twists of hair on top of his head while talking on the phone.

"What's going on, Shawn?" Evander said, and gave him a playful smack on the back of the head as he pushed in the cordless phone's antenna.

Shawn ducked late and said as cool as a fan, "Yo! My name Red Dog now. You better recognize!"

"Red Dog? Oh . . . I'm sorry . . . Red Dog. Boy, please," Evander said, and palmed his head with his large hands. "How old you now—Shhhaaawwnnnn!"

"Yo," he said, "you can chill with that Shawn stuff," and then he noticed Betty and said, "Unk, I feel you trying to front for your honey and all. But if you don't know, you besta ask somebody. I'm seventeen."

"Seventeen what?" Evander asked in fake astonishment. "Seventeen what, Shawn? Not years old."

"Yep, my birthday is June twenty-eighth, 1980!"

"Boy, you lying. That would make you nineteen!"

"I mean eighty-one. I mean eighty-two! You didn't let me finish, I was gonna say eighty-two!"

Evander and Betty laughed as Mrs. Jones shouted from the kitchen, from which floated the aromas of grilled onions and pure calories, "Y'all come on in here!" As they walked in, she said "Bobby Jo will be over here soon, Evander, with them bad-ass churns of hers."

"How's Jo doing nowadays?" he asked, and hopped up on the kitchen counter. As he grabbed a bag of Crunch 'N Munch out of the cupboard, Betty sat at the dinette table. Bobby Jo was his youngest sister, and more than thirty years later, the umbilical cord was still attached.

"She's fine. Just crazy as a bag of dirt and worried about that good-for-nutin' husband of hers who will-not-work-to-save-his-life, and is still beating her in front of dem churn. I'm getting sick and tired of her running over here all time of night," she said, and stirred a pot of mustard greens full of fat ham hocks, okra, and dumplings. The aroma itself made Betty's mouth water.

"That's messed up, her getting you involved," Evander said.

"Oh, I'm not worried about that fool husband of hers coming over here starting anything," Mrs. Jones said, and looked Evander in the eye. "I *still* keep my little friend in the dresser." Although the words did not come from her lips, the assumption was clear. Mom had firepower in the bedroom. "Besides, Bobby Jo ought to clean up that nasty house of hers." And then Mrs. Jones lowered her voice so the others in the house would not hear. "She's the only person I know that had that Sears once-a-year pest-control treatment, and they gave her money back."

"What?"

"Child, dem folks were spraying that nasty-ass house every three, fo' weeks. They finally just said the hell with it, gave her a full refund, and said don't call us no more."

They continued to chat while Mrs. Jones put the finishing touches on the enormous lunch. It was easy to see that the Joneses' house was *the* house in the neighborhood, the house where everybody dropped by. A house where one could come just to use the phone or catch up on all the latest gossip in the neighborhood. People would walk in without knocking, speak, and walk out as if the house were publicly held property.

Evander's mother caught him up on the local news, such as his best friend from high school who was now in the marines but had come out of the closet, as well as the twins up the street who both got pregnant by the same kid down the block. She talked about the pastor who preached more on tithing after he bought a Navigator. "If God gave him that damn thing he's driving," she whispered with her hand cupping her mouth, "let him give God the payment book."

Then in the distance they could hear the rumbling sound of a lady hollering at her children. The sound was so loud, it could be heard over the conversation inside the house.

"Put that down, ya bastid! Okay, I done told you about that, Chandra, you li'l hooker. I'm gon slap the shit out chu. Jamale! Jamale! Stay outta my purse, you li'l-ass thief! You ain't gon be shit just like your daddy!" Betty and the rest of the guests looked out the window as the commotion drew closer to the house and then Bobby Jo came in with all her children. She had one on her hip and another still in a diaper, which begged to be changed. The other children scattered, looking for toys, paper to write on, or anything else they could get into.

Shawn sought refuge in his bedroom as he shouted at one of the little boys, "Yo! Don't come in here!" and locked the door.

Bobby Jo walked into the kitchen, fussed about how her husband was or was not doing something for the kids, spoke to a few relatives, then gave Evander a peck on the cheek. "You must be Betty," she said. Since she knew Evander was not close to his sister, Betty was surprised she knew her name at all. The gang, disguised as children, were on a rampage and hit the house like looters after a verdict. Evander's mom looked at Betty and Evander with her lips as straight as an arrow and an expression that said, *See what I have to put up with?*

"Damn, Momma," Bobby Jo laughed, "it's so hot in the living room, I saw the devil himself sitting by Aunt Gladys wearing hot pants. The air ain't working again? You know Freddy Lee got kicked out of school again, don'tcha?" She then sat at the dinette next to Betty with her legs spread like a construction worker on lunch break and checked the baby's diaper to verify what everyone in the room knew.

"No," her mother said with little expression.

"Yeah, that boy steal so much it's a shame. He kept stealing my money, so I told him that food stamps was the *new* kinda money. At least if he stole them, I could get some more at the end of the month. I know I shouldn't have lied to him like that, but, child," she said, and looked at Betty, "y'all just don't know! So he out to the school throwing dice for food stamps! Damn fool."

Betty widened her eyes and wanted to laugh, but noticed no one else was, so she muted the sound. Mrs. Jones's lips were as straight as the Statue of Liberty as she looked at her son, speechless.

After the kids were sent outside, the adults sat around the living room on the plastic-covered furniture to chat before the meal. Bobby Jo continued to talk about her favorite subject, and thirty minutes later Betty felt she still had not even begun to uncover just how sorry she felt this man was. This went on until Mrs. Jones served the meal and raised her palm to Bobby Jo as if to say, *Enough.*

Once Mrs. Jones summoned the children inside, everyone ran for their place at the table. Evander protected the seat at the head of the table for himself and the one to its right for Betty.

"Evander, say the prayer, son," his mother said as she showed her proud smile. As Evander began to pray, Betty felt a smile inside that forced its way to the surface. She smiled because in her mind she had been transported to another place. A place where it was late November and there was a slight chill outside. Where she had prepared her first full holiday dinner and where Evander's mom and Shawn were now guests in their home. Her foster parents were there, as well as a couple of children who favored her and Evander. At a special place at the opposite end of the table were her natural mother and stepfather, who had not aged or changed clothes since she last saw them as a child. In this place, Evander was grayer as he said grace, and she was just as proud to be with him then as she was at that very moment. *Stop thinking like that,* she scolded herself. But she could not resist and continued to smile. As Evander finished the prayer, she watched him, and as his eyes opened, he looked at her as if he had entertained similar thoughts to hers. *Betty Anne Robinson-Jones,* she thought. *Naw, that still sounds too cumbersome. Betty Jones. I just can't get use to that. Betty . . . Anne . . . Jones? That is so plain. But I guess . . . umm, not too bad. Not too bad at all. Attorney Betty Anne Jones, Esquire. I could work with that.*

Then the hands started to flail as each person maneuvered for dish position. Evander interceded for Betty since he was a veteran of such wars. They enjoyed smothered pork chops, greens, sweet potato pie, southern fried chicken, and Mrs.

Jones's own made-from-scratch biscuits. There was no doubt they were made from scratch, because they tasted delicious and she repeated to anyone who would listen, "These were made from scratch, you know. These were made from scratch."

After the late lunch, the women staggered onto the front porch for light gossip, the kids pulled out board games, and the men went through the back door to the yard.

"Baby, I need to go to the store for Momma to pick up something for dessert. Would you like to ride with me or hang out here?" Evander asked Betty.

"I don't know," Betty said with a shrug of indifference and a smile. "I guess I could stay here and meet everybody."

"Are you sure?"

Walking toward the bedroom, Mrs. Jones said with a smile in passing, "Boy, you can leave. Won't nobody eat her!"

As family members went either to the backyard or the front porch, Betty was unsure as to which way she should go until she heard Mrs. Jones call out, "Betty? Come here a second." Betty walked into the back room toward Mrs. Jones, who sat in the dent of her four-poster double-mattress bed. "Close the door, sugar, and have a seat." *Okay, what's this all about? Why is she sending him off and calling me back here?*

"Betty, I just wanted to say I am so happy you came today."

"Oh. Well, the pleasure is all mine. I've wanted to meet you and the rest of the family for some time now."

"Good," she said with a smile. "Evander's a good boy. You know that? And the reason I called you back here is because I know he's serious about you. He may not have let you know that yet, and the reason I got rid of him is because he would get upset with me for dipping into his business, but I know he has feelings for you."

Betty was unsure as to what to say. She wanted to reveal her heart to someone, but now was not the time, nor was this the place.

"If he has called me once in the past week, he has called me ten times to talk about you," Mrs. Jones continued. "He's proud of everything you've done. Actually, he would call me up every day you worked on that case just to tell me what was happening with it. I know more about Mrs. Lopez than I know about Kato Kaelin."

With a laugh Betty replied, "Really?"

"Like I said, he'd get upset if he knew I told you this, but he cares for you. He cares for you a lot. Momma can tell."

Betty smiled but could not come up with a reply.

"I guess the reason I am telling you this is because he was in a bad relationship. A very bad relationship," Mrs. Jones said, and looked away. "You know about his little boy, don't you?"

"Yes, ma'am. He's mentioned him. I spoke to Junior on the phone a couple of times also."

"He's a cute kid. Looks just like his daddy. I always knew the boy's mother wasn't worth a cold glass of spit, but how do you tell that to someone in love? This heifer used him about ten years ago, and I don't think he ever recovered." And then she looked at Betty and said, "Until now. It was the first time I saw him cry as a grown man. I mean," she continued with her mouth curled and her hand rubbing the sheet of her bed, "break right down and cry in this room. The heifer took all the money out of the savings, took the baby, took everything and left him with nothing. He was in construction at that time. Did drywalling. But he couldn't work for three weeks. They were engaged and she slept with his neighbor. He respected this old hooker so much he would get mad if I said anything about her. But I knew something was up with her. She could sweet-talk him. She couldn't sweet-talk Momma," she added with a tongue cluck. "But you see, I raised a good boy. A decent boy. He walked in on them one Sunday morning with her on her knees and him watching ESPN. I did try to tell him a couple of times she wasn't any good, but you know how y'all are when you get something stuck in your mind. So I went along with it. But now I wish I had stepped in to do more."

"I'm so sorry to hear that. He's never really talked about her to me, but I know he misses his son."

"Yeah, it was rough all the way round," she said, and looked out the window at the men who played dominoes and laughed out loud in her backyard. "It was rough on both of us. September the eleventh was the day he caught them. I'll never forget that day because every year on that date he would be messed up something awful. I would either have to drive to Gainesville to be with him or have him drive home for a couple of days."

And then the air stilled in the room as Mrs. Jones looked into her palms as if she spoke only to them and said, "He once even talked about killing himself. Went through counseling for about a year or so. When I was your age, Betty," she continued as her voice creaked like an unoiled door "I hurt when I broke up with a guy. But I *never* imagined men hurt when they had breakups. Not real men like Evander. I just thought they were like 'Oh well, off to the next one.' But going through that with him changed me. I could sorta see for the first time why *some* men treat women like they do. Sometimes they don't know how to deal with the pain."

Outside there was laughter as a child's knock on the door was ignored. "I guess that's true. I never really thought about it like that," Betty whispered. "But I must say, Mrs. Jones, Evander has been the best thing that ever happened to me, and I could never imagine hurting him." As she spoke, Mrs. Jones sat up and gave her her undivided attention. "I mean he's attentive and thoughtful and has gone out of his way to be supportive."

"Well, I'm glad to hear that. That's what I wanted to know. He's a good boy deep down inside. He had a couple of other girlfriends since Yolanda, but since he wasn't over her, they didn't work out. I could tell he wasn't letting himself get too wrapped up. But I can also tell he feels different about you. You're the first woman he's brought home since Yolanda. Remember when he sent you the flowers at the firm?" she said as her smile returned. "He called me up and told me he was nervous about approaching you. Said he didn't think you would be interested in a common everyday person like him. But I told him to call you up. To give you a chance. And the night he called you, he phoned me afterwards and told me how relieved he was and how nice you were."

Betty softly bit the inside of her cheek to keep from saying, *Mrs. Jones you just don't know how happy I am to be with Evander. How I am already trying to decide if I should hyphenate my name. How I love this man so much it is scaring me.* But this was not the time, nor was it the place.

Six-month-old BreNushia's mother, Wa'Kanesha, arrived to pick her up while her friend sat outside in his pink and white Cutlass, which sounded like a dance floor on wheels.

"Nesha, I been meaning to ask you sumthin'," Mrs. Jones said. "Why you name that pretty red baby that crazy-ass name?"

Wa'Kanesha, who had obviously answered the question many times before, said, "Well, I wanted to name her after my best friend Brenda, but there's a lotta Brendas running around, so I named her BreNushia. I was going to name her BreNeissy, but I know a lotta Neissys too, and besides, I didn't want Aneissa Clark to think she had anything to do with my baby name. 'Cause she use to go with my baby's daddy in high school and stuff."

"Well, you damn sho won't have that problem with a name like BreNushia," Mrs. Jones said, and folded her thick arms tightly. "Giving that child a name she won't even be able to spell before she in high school. I bet you can't even spell it—can you!"

"Ah, excuse me," Wa'Kanesha said, and with the baby on her shoulder and her hand on her flexed hip she began, "My baby's name is spelled B-r-e capital N—"

"Shut up and get out there to that crazy boy making all that noise with that loud music. Make me sick!" Finishing the sentence, Mrs. Jones looked at Betty as her brow unfurled and her smile reappeared.

Betty had walked outside to play with Anna and Jake when Evander drove up, and for a split second she felt like a housewife who awaited her husband's return. After he hugged the kids again, Evander walked over to Betty and asked if she would like to take a walk to digest the meal. She nodded her head yes and he gave the package from the store to Anna to take inside while Jake tried to wrestle his uncle's leg.

As Evander and Betty left, they could still hear Bobby Jo's voice clear above all the others. "And then he told me dem his sister's drawers in the backseat! He must think I'm a fool! Cynthia's ass way bigger than mine!"

Evander walked Betty through his old neighborhood with pride. As they walked, he held her hand and occasionally sang songs he didn't know the words to and told her jokes he had heard that he felt would top Jacqui's. When they returned hours later to the Jones house, it seemed everyone had departed except the old men guzzling malt liquor, smoking reefers, and still playing dominoes in the backyard. Inside the house, Mrs. Jones was on the phone talking to a friend and watching Betty and Evander walk up the driveway through the blinds.

Before walking inside, Betty stood in place on the porch and said, "Vander. I just want to say thanks."

"For what?"

"For so many things. But mostly for getting me away from the office. I can't tell you how much better I feel not to be working today. It just occurred to me as we were walking that this was the first time I've not worked on a Saturday in about three years."

"You're welcome."

"But I really wanted to say thanks because you've shared so much of yourself with me today. No other man has ever done this for me, and it means a lot. I know you're serious." And then, looking into his eyes, she stepped closer and continued, "And so am I. I just want to say—" And then Betty was ready to finally say the words she felt deep inside when Evander covered her lips with a kiss that was as soft as candlelight.

"I love you too, Beep," he said with an understanding tone. "I love you too."

CHAPTER 11

‡

Monday, two days later

With a nervous tap of his pen on the oak credenza, Drew sat behind his desk, silent, absorbed and alone.

He gazed out the window of the office, which was a vast improvement over the first home of Andrew Patrick Staley and Associates. It was in the Millhopper area of Gainesville, which was the town's version of Park Avenue. While it was small, the sienna and burgundy office was tastefully decorated with artwork from Senegal, pampered plants, and Steven Scott Young prints. In the closet was a cot that Drew used on occasion when his days extended into nights and then mornings, a fully stocked nonalcoholic bar, and a small stereo that played continuous jazz.

As he watched the cars stop for the red light at the intersection of Thirty-ninth and Forty-third Street, Drew remembered the first time he took in the view. He remembered how he'd felt when the realtor told him the price, but he'd also known the location had an unseen benefit. Not only would it be easy for his potential clients to find him, he would also take pride in being at his desk before dawn and getting comments from other planners that they'd seen him after dusk as they'd taken their families out to dinner. No other African-American financial planner had survived beyond three years in Gainesville. Many thought it was because white prospects weren't trusting enough to give them large sums of money to invest, and black prospects invested elsewhere. Regardless of that, Drew's image in the window was a constant reminder to his colleagues that he had in fact survived and prospered.

Felicia had never liked him to go to work so early. Her biggest complaint about him had been the fact that she hated going to sleep alone and waking up by herself. But after several months, she understood that his firm was as much a part of him as she wished to be eventually.

After the initial rough spots of learning what each other liked and did not like, they became more than a couple. They walked and spoke alike, and appeared to be married in many ways. They had a connection that transcended a band of gold, although they both knew a church was in their future. When Drew was in the mood to take the leap, she always found reasons to say let's wait. When she wanted to say I do, Drew did not feel he was at a point to walk down the aisle. But marriage was never as much an issue with them as it was with their friends, because they knew one day they would be together and so they simply continued to enjoy each other for what it was worth.

Felicia took on the mantle of Mrs. Staley in many ways to assist Drew. She devoted each afternoon to riding around town with his mother to look for a house. She did the research, took notes, and often even took photos; then on the weekends she and Drew looked at selected homes together. Her search ended when she took him to a house that was painted eggshell white with a patchwork lawn in need of work.

"To be sure, this is not the house you want to look at," he asked with disbelieving eyes.

"Before we go in, just listen to me. Okay?" she asked. And then she allowed Drew to see the house through her eyes. Felicia proceeded to paint Drew a picture in his mind of a house with a vaulted ceiling and a crystal chandelier. She shared with him a home with Italian stained glass in the front door, hickory floors, and a kitchen with hanging pots over an island. A home that could be practical and beautiful. That could be both informal and elegant.

"Baby," he said, "I see where it could be improved. I love

the subdivision and all, but I'm not really interested in a fixer-upper. I just don't have the time or patience for it."

"I understand that. Trust me, I do. But," she said, and then looked at him, "I'll do it. I don't mind. I'm off early every day and I don't have anything to do on the weekends. I can make this work, Drew."

Drew looked at the bent mailbox held to its post with a single rusty nail, and the flower bed which was overrun with weeds, as the venerable owner of the property stuck his head out the door. "Why don't we do this?" he said as the man walked toward their car. "Why don't you just move in with me? If I get this place, I wouldn't need all of the room, and besides, I wouldn't want you to work here helping me with this and not live here."

Felicia returned his smile, reached down and squeezed his hand, and said, "Let's go look at the house. Okay?"

It took Drew three months to negotiate the price of the house, and Felicia another two months of working with subcontractors to get it up to move-in condition. But on Christmas eve the movers pulled into the driveway with only Drew's furniture. Felicia had told him a week earlier that she had decided not to give up her own house.

"Why?"

"Because I want it all," she'd replied. "I don't want half now and half later. When we get together, I want it all. Including the name."

On the night of the move with the clock ticking toward Christmas, Drew sat on an imported rug, exhausted from unpacking. He had just taken his bath, more to relieve his tired and aching muscles than anything else, when Felicia smiled at him from the island in the kitchen where she was chopping vegetables. "You know you're getting old, don't you?"

"I'm not getting old," he said as he looked at "Moneyline" on television. "What's that smell?"

"It's a surprise. I wanted the first meal here to be something different. You always say you like trying new dishes, so let's see how this grabs you."

Drew took a deep breath and released an old-man grunt as he lifted his achy body from the floor. "Whatever it is, it smells good. Are you broiling steaks?" he asked as he rubbed his football knees and moved toward the kitchen.

"No! Don't come in here!" she said with a smile and a knife pointed at him.

"I just want to get something to—"

"Shhh," she said with the knife still aimed in his direction, and blindly reached into the fridge for a can of Coke. "Here you are! Now, go back in the living room where you came from."

Taking the can with a smile, he said, "You don't scare me, you know. I can come in there if I want to. I just happen not to want to."

"Try me," she said slowly with a scowl on her lips and a twist of the knife in the air. "Just try me, *Mister* Man."

For their first dinner Drew and Felicia had roast beef covered with horseradish sauce surrounded by brown rice and English snow peas. The meal was complemented by pear and tarragon soup, and she served a red wine that was given to them as a Christmas gift from Peggy and Walter. For dessert there was a strawberry soufflé waiting in the oven. As she set his plate in front of him, Drew said, "Now, you know you're spoiling me with a meal like this. How am I supposed to go back to eating Boston Market after dining on something like this?"

"Be quiet," she said, barely above a whisper, as she scanned the table to make sure it was perfect. It was candlelit and she had used his special sterling silver and black china as well as the crystal wine glasses. Felicia had also used touches of garnish to make the dish as beautiful as it was appetizing, and in the background from the stereo was "Some Enchanted Evening" to hold the mood. "Just be quiet," she repeated, looking into his eyes, "and let's just enjoy the moment."

Drew reached across the table for her hand, and together they silently blessed the meal. As their eyes opened, they both looked at their hands in the middle of the table. Drew loved how soft her hands were, and as his thumb grazed the outer surface of her palm, he smiled and then looked at her over the blushing flicker of light as if everything else came in a distant second.

"Felicia? I'm not telling you this because of this meal. I'm not even saying it because of all the work you've done in this house. Actually, I really don't have a special reason to say what I am about to say at all." Then Drew looked into her dark brown eyes as he had never looked into them before and said softly, "I love you. And I just want you to know that." Then with a glance back at her hand, he repeated, "I love you."

Felicia stared at their hands as they held them firmly together in a connection that extended beyond the physical. "Drew, I've never told you this, and it never occurred to me until I was talking to my sister on the phone today. But you are the first man to send me flowers."

"Ohh, baby. I had no idea."

As she covered their joined hands with her free hand, she gazed at a spot just above his head and continued. "You are also the very first man to write me a poem. I know it sounds childish, but that means a lot to me." Then Felicia took a deep breath in and released it as she looked him in the eye. "But, Andrew, you are the only man . . ." And then her voice trailed off. Whatever it was she wanted to say, she could not.

"What, baby?" Drew asked, seeing the desire on her face to share whatever was in her heart.

Felicia had stared back at Drew, and whatever had been in her heart had not shown in her eyes, because her expression had been stoic. It had not been on her lips, because they had not moved. She'd sat the same and her impassive body language had given no clues as to what she'd wanted to say. But as Drew had asked her once again what it was she wanted to share, a single tear had found its way down her cheek.

While it had been a couple of months since her death, he often thought back to that warm Christmas eve. Not so much for the meal or the atmosphere. Not so much for the board game they'd played afterward when she'd beaten him for the first time at Monopoly. He didn't recall that evening for the way they'd played with high-powered water guns in the chilled waters of the pool or the way she'd made him laugh.

"Drew!" Felicia had screamed. "Boy, you know I can't swim, and if you drop me, I swear I'll kill ya!" She'd added, "Whatever you do, don't get my hair wet. You know we gotta go to church tomorrow." He did not recall that night for the way she'd looked after she reached her peak in the pool or how she'd felt when she pushed him away and dipped her hair in the water. That night was remembered for such simple words. Not the words she hadn't said, but the words she had. Words Felicia may have never thought twice about after saying them. When she'd looked at him over dinner and said, "Drew, let's just enjoy the moment."

He repeated the words aloud to himself over and over again. His shoulders slumped in his chair as he watched the traffic light turn green and he wished he could have understood fully what she'd so desperately tried to tell him. Now that she was gone, it was hard going back to Boston Market in so many ways. As the cars passed outside his window, the simple words stung like the winter's sun and were just as unforgettable.

The small TV in the corner of Drew's office played more for noise than anything else, and with a glance at his watch he clicked it off so he could concentrate on the solicitation of new business. Although he had received a call from the insurance underwriter informing him that the program he'd designed for Murphy, Renfro and Collins was partially approved, he felt uneasy about it. He had made several calls to Franklin Renfro regarding modifications, but the managing partner of the firm had not returned his calls, instead delegating the task to his administrative assistant. This was not an uncommon practice with people in his position, but knowing Renfro the way he did, Drew felt especially perturbed.

"Come in," Drew said in response to a knock at the door.

With a look inside before entering, Grace asked, "Why you got the door closed? I thought you were on an important call or something."

"Just thinking. Did they deliver lunch?"

"Got it right here," she said, and set the red and white Wing-A-Licious container on the edge of his desk. "So what are you back here thinking about, with the door closed no less?" she said, and took the first wing tip from the aluminum foil.

"Ah, they got this new thing now'days? It's called *asking* for a person's lunch before you start eating it?"

"Oh," she said between chews, "can I have some of your wings, Drewwww?"

"No," he said, and pulled the box closer to his side of the table as Peggy walked in.

"What are you all doing back here all huddled up? Dag, why didn't anyone tell me we had wings?" she said as she took one out and pulled the container back to the edge of the desk.

"Because *we* are not having wings. I'm having wings," Drew replied.

"Anyway," Peggy said, and sat in the leather chair across from him with her legs crossed. "Listen, Grace. What's up with you and old boy? You know? The football player?" She took a bite and looked at Drew with disdain. "Damn, Drew! Why don't you ever order spicy? These don't have any kick! I hate mild!"

Drew could only look at her and shake his head with a smile, as Grace said, "We're doing fine. We've been going out three weeks now, and so far he's been totally not what I expected."

"Grace? You dating a client?" Drew asked.

"Naw. Well, at least not yet," she said. "But possibly in the future. He's going to renegotiate this spring and he thinks they're going to give him a seven-figure deal. At least that's what his agent says. So if he gets it, I'll see if I can get him to invest a little with us."

"Seven figures. I like the sound of that," Peggy said.

"Tell me about it. But he's not what I expected at all," Grace said, and took another wing from the box. As soon as she did, Drew pulled it back to his side of the desk, which left a greasy skid mark. "When we first met, I thought he was just looking for a hootchie. You know, just a little bit of fun. But I didn't give it up and I think it threw his game off. Now he's cool. We have a lot of fun together."

"Do you all go out much?" Peggy asked, tugging the box

away from Drew and cleaning the spot with a tissue from his tissue box. "I mean dancing and all?"

"I know what you're getting at, and he's cool with it. I thought he just had a brown-sugar fantasy myself when he first spoke to me, but he's not like that at all. Deep inside Jason wants to be a brother. He grew up near South Central, you know. Actually, I don't think he's ever even dated a white girl."

"So you're dating Jason Riggs?" Drew asked. "Who plays for the Jaguars?"

"Damn, Drew, you work too much. They've been dating about a month. But tell me this," Peggy asked as she spread out her tissue and took three drumettes from the box. "This is your first time dating a white guy, right? How is it?"

"Actually, there's no difference. I thought there would be at first. I mean he's cute and got a butt just like a brother. But I won't lie, I saw the dollar signs at first. I saw all the brothers who left sisters after they made it and I thought, I'll string this white boy out and score one for the sisters, right? But then, well, after a while . . . I dunno."

"You falling in love, Grace? Not you. Not Mrs. A-White-Boy-Can't-Do-Nothing-But-Bring-Me-a-Brother!" Peggy laughed.

"See, that's the part I don't understand. No, I don't love him. Let me set that straight. I love the lifestyle, I love the cars and the attention. And hell, I'll admit it, I love the sex. But right now that's about it."

"Well, take it slow is all I can say," Drew replied, and looked at Peggy's tightly crossed legs. "You know, you shouldn't sit like that, Peg."

"Why?"

"Because it causes varicose veins."

"Child, please," she said, then looked back at Grace. "I've been crossing my legs since I don't know how long. My momma used to sit like this for years and . . ." And then she looked at her legs and back at Drew and slowly uncrossed them. "Grace, as I was going to say, forget all that other stuff, honey. What's happening in the bedroom? Is what they say about white guys true?"

"I don't know about white men, but as far as Jason is

concerned, the man is the bomb. He has no—and when I say no, I mean *no*—inhibitions, girl. And to me that's new. But you know what he does that just kills me every time? Whenever I sleep over, he always wakes me up with kisses on my face."

"Ohh, I love that," Peggy sighed. "Walter used to do that too. To me that is so romantic."

With a look up from his lunch, Drew said, "Kisses on the face, huh? I'll have to remember that one."

"I know!" Grace shouted like a teenager at a slumber party. "Know what else?" she said in a lower tone. "He always kisses right here," she said, and pointed to her chin. "And then again here," she said, pointing to both cheeks, "and the last two kisses he saves for my eyelids. There is *nothing*, and I mean *nothing*, like a soft kiss on the eyelids after making love the previous night."

"Well, if you all continue, remember one thing. Don't ever let him stop dating you. Men forget that after they got you. I must admit that for the most part, Walter and I still date. We just don't allow it to get old."

"You guys have been married how long?" Grace asked.

"Sixteen years in about three months. And I love him more now then I did when we got married." As she spoke, Drew glanced up from the memo he was reading. "I used to hear people talk about how they had kids and then the romance stopped, but with Walt it was never like that. I guess because he was married before or maybe because he's so much older. If anything, we fell deeper in love than ever before once we had Todd and Tray."

"Really?" Drew asked.

"Without a doubt. I think it's because we fell in love so slowly. It took forever for him to believe I loved him for him. That I didn't give a damn about his money and all. You know, because of his weight, he had very low self-esteem that you would never realize unless you knew him well. But he has worked hard on the weight. In fact, just this morning I looked at the scale," she said with a proud smile, "and he's less than three hundred for the first time in years. I know it means a lot to him to lose the weight, so I am happy for him. But you know," she said, looking through the wing tips for another drumette, "I didn't marry him for the way he would fit in a Speedo or for his money. I married him because I loved him. Point-blank."

"That's sweet. You know Mr. and Mrs. Shepard?" Drew asked as Grace sighed.

"No."

"Yes you do. Bill and Gladys Shepard? Live out on Seventeenth Street, next to that restaurant that's so raggedy you need to bring your own chair if you want to dine in?"

"I know the restaurant. The food there is hitting, but no, I don't know them," Peggy said as she ate another drumette and then stared at Drew's Coke.

"Don't even think about it," he said, and moved the can to the credenza. "You know Mr. and Mrs. Shepard, who had a son that got in an accident a few years ago?"

"I don't know any Mr. and Mrs. Shepard, Drew, damn!" She looked at Grace and laughed.

"Yes, you do. But anyway, Mr. Shepard had three strokes and a heart attack within the past three years. He's mean as hell, can't control his bowel movements, sleeps about four hours a night, can't walk without his walker and somebody watching him, blind in one eye, and on top of that, he tries to get physical with his wife. He even smacked her one time in front of me. But," Drew said, "although she complains about not sleeping, she'll tell you in a second, 'That's my husband. We've been married forty-five years and that's my husband.' Now, that's love. The words 'till death do us part' really meant something to her. That's the kinda love I wanted to have one day with Felicia," he said, and looked at the picture of them on his desk taken in the Cayman Islands.

"You'll find it, sweet pea. I know what you're going through. You remember how many trifling brothers I had to sort through to find this one. And when I met the old man I had no idea I would not only love him, but like him as much as I do. Now we're best friends. Can you imagine standing in front of God and saying to your very best friend, 'I will love you until the day I die'?"

After another sigh, Grace said, "I always like hearing you talk about Walt. It's nice to hear about a marriage that works every now and then."

"I feel blessed. Very blessed." Then looking at Drew, Peggy continued, "Drew, you know something? I never heard how you and Felicia met."

"Me either," Grace said, grabbing two more wings and settling in for the story.

"I thought I told both of you. I was working on that proposal for the city, and she worked in the clerical pool. I saw her that day and I never said anything. Later that day I saw her shopping in Ann Taylor with her friends. I just sorta walked by because she had her back turned and I waited to get something for dinner in the eatery before an appointment later that afternoon. So that same night, I'm in a club and she walks up behind me and tells me I should stop following her. We started talking and next thing I knew, it was three in the morning. She was a little aggressive at first, but later I thought it was cute."

"Meaning?" Grace asked, and flicked a small pile of bones wrapped in a tissue into the trash can.

"Well, she gave me her number on the back of a business card. She made the first move. I usually don't like that. But thinking back, if she had not, we may have never gotten together."

"So it was like fate, huh?" Grace said with another sigh in her voice. "You guys have fairy-tale stories."

With a stretch as he stood, he said, "Yeah, and in a way I guess it was just that." Then he opened the door to go to the rest room to wash his hands. As he walked down the hallway, he noticed a lady admiring the awards the firm had garnered on display in the reception area. "I'm sorry, ma'am, we didn't hear you walk in. Let me get the receptionist."

She was professionally dressed, average in height and size, and her hair was pinned up. She looked at Drew and said with a smile that made him weak, "Thanks."

Drew cracked the door to his office, where Grace and Peggy were laughing, and said, "Shhh, we have company in the front."

"Oh, I'm sorry," Grace said, and leaped up to greet the prospective client.

"Are you expecting anyone?" Drew asked Peggy as he returned to his side of the desk.

"No. Not until two."

"Umm, well, there's a sister in there."

"Real big eyes? Dark-skinned? Kinda long hair?"

"Yeah. You know her?"

"Sounds like it could be my two-o'clock. She must have gotten the times mixed up."

"Umm. She's cute," Drew said as he moved his mouse slowly along the pad and gazed into his computer screen.

"You think so?" Peggy said with an inquisitive smile. "I know for a fact that she's available."

Drew tightened his lips and shook his head with a not-interested gesture and then said, "I just got a letter that I need to meet with Felicia's attorney in a few weeks for a reading of her will."

"Really?"

"Yeah. I never knew she had a will. I didn't think she took the time to get one. I wonder what she had to disburse."

"Well, sometimes there could be small things like books or her clothes. Sometimes people just leave their last thoughts to their loved ones."

Grace opened the door and poked her head in. "All right, guys, break it up in here. Peg, you have a guest. A Miss Zelma McGrady?"

With a look at her watch, Peggy said, "Yep, that's her. She's an hour early," as Grace went back to the front of the office.

"Who is she again?" Drew asked. "Is she from Con-National?"

"Yes. She's the comptroller I've been telling you about. Con-Nat recruited her from a big-six firm in Manhattan and she's sharp. They use about ten firms for their benefits programs and they need a few minority contracts, so she's giving us a shot."

"How good are our chances?" he said, breaking eye contact with the monitor.

"Ahh, she's sitting out there an hour early, isn't she? And soon enough I want to introduce you to her. I think you'll really like her. Just your type. Petite, sophisticated, and intelligent."

Drew smiled. "Go take care of your customer, Peggy."

Drew sat in his office talking on the phone with a client in Jamaica, with his back to the door, taking notes. As he swiveled around toward his desk drawer for a Post-it note, he noticed Zelma standing in his doorway. "One second, Mr. Abracromibi," he said to the party on the phone, and with a smile he said, "Can I help you, madam?"

"Go ahead," she said, twirling her thick gold and silver Mont Blanc around her fire-engine red fingernails. "I'll wait."

"It may be a while."

"Don't worry, I have time." She smiled.

I don't have time to deal with this now. "Okay," he said with a smile, and went back to his conversation.

As he spoke, she walked into his office, sat in front of him, and looked at each certificate and degree on the wall. There was a photograph of him and several local celebrities as well as one of him and a U.S. senator. She also noticed the picture on his desk turned toward him. With a motion for his attention, she mouthed the words *May I?* as she reached for the lacquer frame.

Drew nodded his head with a respectful smile and then swiveled in his chair and looked again outside the window at the passing cars while he spoke to his client. Drew could see in the window's reflection that Zelma smiled at the photo of Drew and Felicia, and then placed it softly back on the desk in the spot from which she had removed it.

As he spoke of going to Washington, D.C., to lobby for a change in the tax codes regarding his industry, all he could think of was a delicate way to tell her to back off, that he did not want to get involved with anyone until he got over Felicia. He wanted to think of a way to tell her that although their relationship had at times been strained, she had left a void in his life, that since she had died, she was never far from his mind. Maybe it was the guilt of the last words on her lips being, "You're so selfish. Leave and don't come back here any damn more!" Whatever it was, the pain of life without Felicia was too deep for him to consider starting over before he could somehow close this door to his past.

After she looked at her watch, Zelma got Drew's attention with her smile and waved her business card in his direction. When he looked up, she left it on the desk and waved good-bye.

As the door closed, Drew reached for the gold-embossed card and noticed she was in fact the senior comptroller for the large conglomerate. He also noticed she had left just a wisp of her perfume on it, and on the back she had written her home, beeper and, cellular phone numbers with the words "I think you have a really nice smile. I'd love to see it again soon." *Damn! Here we go.*

CHAPTER 12

‡

Monday

Betty checked the time as she drove into the mall's parking lot. With a quick glance at the entrance she noticed Jacqui talking on the phone as she paced. She was over fifteen minutes late for their window-shopping excursion, partly due to office business and partly due to Jane. Jane was a secretary who had just received her wedding portraits, and as Betty had passed her desk, she'd had an urge to look through her cream and silver remembrance album from the wedding. When Betty had attended the ceremony alone, although love had been in the air, she'd been unaffected by it. Unlike the other single women, she had not stood in the crowd to catch the bouquet or make eyes at the single men as the newlyweds shared their first dance. But that was pre-Evander. Betty had looked at each photo as Jane narrated, and she'd thought of the possibilities.

"I'm sorry, girl," Betty said, walking toward Jacqui as she brushed wrinkles from her silk blouse and straightened the pleats in her wool skirt.

"One sec," Jacqui replied, cupping the phone closer to her ear. "Willie Mae? I took care of that. Are you all gonna need me to come in and help a little? Are you sure? All right, you call me if you have any problems. I'm only about fifteen minutes away, okay? And also get me the names and numbers of a few vegetable suppliers in the area. Have them on my desk and remind me to call them when I get in, okay? Thanks, honey. 'Bye." She put her cellular back in her purse and looked at Betty. "Where the hell have you been!"

"Girl, let me tell you," Betty said as they headed toward the entrance of the mall. "Renfro wanted to meet with me this morning. So I'm thinking it's about the partnership, right, because it's supposed to go down this week I think."

"Really. And it wasn't?" Jacqui asked, as they entered the mall.

"No, it wasn't, but in a way, it was better."

"Better than a partnership? Now, this I have to hear."

"Yeah," Betty said, excited. "I'm gonna sit second chair in this large lawsuit against North Florida General Hospital. It's a class action suit, worth more than eighty so far. They've already tendered an offer for ten, so it's going to be large."

"Yeah, that's nice, honey, but how is that better than a partnership? Do you get a cut of the reward or something?"

"First of all, it's not a reward, it's an award, and this is how it works. They never let an associate sit second chair in a case of this magnitude. Especially when the team is being lead by a senior partner," she said, leading Jacqui into Ann Taylor and admiring the suits without stopping the conversation. "Usually you go into a battle of this size with two or three partners leading the charge. Associates are only used on cases like this for the grunt work no one else wants. You see," she continued as they strolled the aisle, "I think my partnership is a done deal. I think they are giving me the second chair because by the time we go to court, it should already be official."

"That's good, that's really good," Jacqui said as she headed toward the designer skirts. "But you didn't answer my question. Of all these millions being bantered about, do you get a percentage for working on the case?" She looked at a price tag on the sleeve of a tweed blazer and tossed it down in disgust.

"No. No, I do not get a cut, today. But if I am a partner by the time the verdict is awarded, then yes, I'll do okay."

"And you really think they would make the partnership

official before the verdict? Isn't that literally taking money out of their own pockets?"

"I know where you're going and it doesn't work that way in this firm."

"Well, tell me this," Jacqui said as she declined a sales associate's offer for assistance as they left the store. "Could he have picked you for any other reason? What I mean is, have you checked to see if the judge is black or most of the defendants are black or the jury is going to be black or something?"

"Well, that's another reason why I was late getting here. I wanted to see who the players involved in the case were. The judge who was assigned the case is Travsky, but that's not really a big deal. I tried the Lopez case before him, but he's old school. He won't cut us any slack for that. The defendant's attorneys are all white and most of the women involved are white. So I tried to look at it through Renfro's eyes and it suddenly occurred to me. They are bringing in a high-profile jury consultant from the West Coast, and I guarantee you they are going to try to stock the jury with nothing but older black women."

"Why?"

"Well, they say black women are usually more anti-corporate-America and lean more toward the underdog in cases like this. I say sisters are just more humane. Then it made sense as to why he's giving me this shot. I mean, let's face it. Renfro has a lot riding on this, and I think he wants to cover all his bases. There's a move to allow Burt Collins to lead the firm since he has more trial experience. Most of the partners just think of Renfro as a pencil pusher with a law school sheepskin."

"Really," Jacqui said as her eyes followed a gentleman into a clothing store. "I thought he was the man around there."

"Please. Not hardly. I think that's why no one really said anything about the way his office is decorated or how he acts or anything. Until this situation with Jack, he was a nonfactor. He was just the person who made sure the firm ran efficiently. Everyone thinks Jack was grooming Burt to lead the firm anyway. Now all of a sudden Mister Nobody has become somebody. Nothing short of an act of God . . . or losing this case could leapfrog Collins into his position."

"So you're comfortable being the token?"

"I don't look at it like that at all. I know the only reason he picked me is because I'm black, but I don't have a problem with that because—"

"I hate to cut you off," Jacqui said, "but why is it we only say 'African-American' when white folks are around?"

"Child, I don't know, but like I was going to say, let's face it, if race was not an issue, with my record I would have been on the case anyway."

As the gentleman disappeared behind a rack of slacks, Jacqui cleared her throat, rubbed down the hairs on the nape of her neck, and said, "Well, it sounds good. Sounds like you're in a good position no matter what. But like I always say, watch your back in there. Don't take anybody for granted. You just never know where the arrow will come from in a place like that."

"Collins has been getting a little cozy with me, too, I noticed. I think he'd like me to complain about Renfro's attitudes and then he could move in with the threat of the NAACP or something. I know what he's up to, but I'm not gonna play that card."

"Betty, I don't see how you do it. Wait a minute!" Jacqui whispered. "Look at that one in the jeans."

"Girl?" Betty said, and looked at her friend. "That child's half your age!"

With a squint Jacqui said, "Oh. I gotta get my contact prescription changed. Although I still say he's gonna be fine as hell when he grows up. But like I was going to say, I don't see how in the world you put up with all of the politics and stuff around there. Don't you get tired of it? Don't you ever wish you were in business for yourself?"

"Not really. Starting a law firm has a lot of advantages, but liabilitywise it has a greater downside. I'm not ready to deal with that at this point."

"Well, when I grow up? I wanna be just like you."

Later, as they walked down the center of the mall, Jacqui eyed a gentleman in biker shorts at the pay phone. "You see, now, that's what I'm looking for in a man. You see them legs, that chest, and most of all, girl," she groaned, "that brother gotta have a U.S.D.A. card, 'cause I know he's packing nothing but meat."

"Girl, you're crazy."

Jacqui and Betty sat down in the café area of the eatery so Jacqui could have an unobstructed view of the brother in the biker shorts and tank top at the yogurt counter. "And he must wear a size-fourteen shoe," Jacqui continued.

"How can you tell? You can't even see his feet from here."

"Ahh, who's looking at feet?" Jacqui laughed. "Let me tell you another little something else I notice about men. If you're at a club and you see a guy who cannot dance, just can't catch the rhythm, do not, I repeat, do not sleep with him. Brother will be going off beat all night long. That's how old Harry was. Now, don't get me wrong. He was blessed physically, but he moved like Lawrence Welk or something, all off-beat. Can you imagine Lawrence having an orgasm? *Eeeeschhh.* And I get sick of saying, 'That's not iiiit.' Well, that was Harry. And to top it off, he always slept all over the bed. Just like a pair of open scissors. I mean spread out everywhere. Is it just me or doesn't it look nasty when a man is all flung out? I mean give me a little mystery, for goodness' sakes. I hit him about four o'clock one morning and said, 'Harry, Harry, wake up!' And he didn't move. So I yelled and said, 'Harry! Get up and get dressed!' So he jumped out of bed and grabbed his drawers and said, 'What! What! Somebody coming?' So I said, 'Hell no, fool. You just look stank! Put on some clothes or take your ass home!' "

"See now, you had me going for a second there, but then you had to start lying," Betty laughed. "I gotta get you to church with me sometime. Get some salvation in you."

"Ah, excuse me, Ms. Ann, but I go to church, thank you very much! I was just in—"

"Jacqui. Weddings and funerals don't count."

"Oh. Well, I was—"

"Jacqui? Don't start lying about going to church, honey. Like I said. Weddings and funerals do not count."

"Oh."

Betty gazed in the distance with a reflective smile on her face, then looked back at Jacqui and said, "Tell me something. Why do we do that? Why do we prejudge people as if they were livestock or something?"

"What do you mean?"

"Why do people reduce each other to such . . . to such menial terms?"

"What you mean is why do I say guys with big feet got big dicks and stuff, right?"

"No! Well, not only you. People in general. I mean it just gets a little old, you know? Men with long thick fingers got this kind. Fat men and white men got this kind. Skinny guys got this kind. I mean, where do you draw the line? It's like saying all black people are lazy and all Chinese are good at math. It's just stupid to me and I don't know if we should be buying in to it."

Jacqui's smile melted as she pondered her response. "I don't know about others, but I can speak for myself. I just don't give a fuck anymore. As far as—"

"I wasn't talking so much about you. I was just saying—"

"Since that mother left me, Betty, I just don't care. You know, I still wait for the phone to ring four years later? That makes no sense, since I've had the number changed three times since he left, but I do."

"Really?" Betty whispered. "I never knew."

After a pause, Jacqui said, "I never told you this, but I called his mom one time and asked her to give him a message for me. Actually, I just wanted to hear his voice again. I didn't expect him to call back. But he called me all right. Called in the middle of the day when he knew I would be at work and left me a message on the recorder that basically said stop fucking with him. To get over it." After licking her lips slowly, Jacqui said, "You wanna know why I have an unlisted number after all these years? I don't wanna wait for him to call me again. As long as it was listed, I knew if he wanted me, he could call information and get me at any moment. So I got it unpublished and what do I do? For some strange reason I still wait for the mother to call."

Betty wanted to say something comforting but was speechless as Jacqui continued. "Girl. I have never gone through anything like that in my life. When my granddaddy died at our house, as close as I was to him, it didn't hurt like losing Yancy. To this day when I hear a date I think about it in context to our relationship. Someone will say a year and I think, that was two years before I met him. Or that was the year he left."

"Hello, Miss Jordan," a lady who was a frequent visitor to Jacquetta's said in passing.

After Jacqui waved and smiled, she said, "You see, Betty, you know how it feels to be in love now. To be really and truly in love. I know you are not ready to admit it, but I can see it. But imagine if you were planning to marry Evander and one day you called, and the nigga just never called you back. Imagine if you called the bakery, his mom, his cellular, and beeped him to ask him about invitations to a wedding that was all his idea in the first place, and he never called you back. I never wanted to get married to him. Everybody talking about getting married to start a life. Hell, I had a life!" Jacqui shouted, then lowered her voice and narrowed her eyes. "But then this Negro just never said anything else to you again, ever. Never told you he was not interested, never told you if you had said something to upset him, never said he didn't like the way you looked, the way you fucked, the way you smelled. Just never said shit to you.

"Now, mind you," Jacqui continued, and leaned back on the two hind legs of her chair as her eyes reddened. "This is a man you wanted to spend the rest of your life with and thought you knew like the back of your hand. This is a man who held your hand for three nights after losing the baby. This is a man who would kiss you as you told him of not going full term twice and how you feared you would never be able to have a child. A man you would have died for in a second. I mean, given your life for. So you call and call and call and call, and you don't know if he's dead, alive, or nothing. I don't know how brothers can do that. After all that we had been through, it's as if he just left me on the side of the road half alive, half dead." She chuckled and looked away to avoid the tears.

Closing her eyes, Jacqui seemed to search for a word or phrase and then discovered it. "Remember that song by Stevie, and at the end he says, 'I wouldn't do that to a dog'?" As she squeezed her eyelids together to block the

pain, her voice weakened, but she obviously showed deter-
mination to finish the thought. "Well, I lay there bleeding
for almost two years with no closure, and that's how I felt.
After getting his call, I sent the ring to his mother, and you
know what? Four years later it still feels like I have it on."
She looked down at her barren ring finger and then stiffly
rubbed the inside of her palm with her thumb. "I still catch
myself feeling my finger, subconsciously hoping it's there.
So I decided at that very moment that I would never be left
alone again. Never. I know that's just crazy and I know
that's not healthy, but that's just me. I leave their ass before
they ever get the chance. Call it self-preservation. So now
to be completely honest, Betty, I don't care anymore. If I
reduce them down to dogs, so be it. Life's a bitch and then
you die. Let'um deal with it. I wanted a happy ending. But
that only happens in fairy tales, old movies, and bad
novels."

Silence reigned between them as kids ran by playing tag,
lovers kissed in front of the fountain in the center of the
food court, and a custodian swiftly scooped up little slivers
of wadded-up paper from the tile floor. "You know," she
concluded in a whisper as she looked at her nails, "he told
me he loved me. The night we lost Cayla, he held me so
close I could feel his heart thump and he told me he loved
me." And then Jacqui paused to swallow. "He told me that
he had never loved anyone as much as he loved me. Ain't
that something? He even told me that he didn't think he
could ever love anyone as much as he loved me. I mean, I
know men say stupid shit sometimes. But after a while, I
don't care who you are, you start believing them. Guess
what." She bit her lip as she looked at Betty. "He got married a year after we broke up. Not just dating again. Not
engaged. Married. One year later. But yet he told me he
loved me."

As the biker walked away, Jacqui sighed, cleared her
throat, and said with a smile, "Damn, I could've used me
some of that."

Betty returned Jacqui's smile. She always knew Yancy had
hurt her when he left just months after she lost the baby
prematurely. She knew how he'd gone through her money,

gotten one of their friends pregnant at the same time, and even pointed a gun at her one night when he'd had too much to drink. But she could never get her to talk about it. Betty wanted her to go to counseling, but Jacqui always refused, saying that white folks did that and she wouldn't give Yancy the satisfaction. But as they watched the biker leave, a part of her wanted to cry for her friend. Being strong, Betty said with a fake smile, "There will be other biker shorts, girl. Let's go."

They walked into another boutique and Betty saw an accessory that she knew would go perfectly with an outfit of hers. While she did not need another purse, she found it immoral to walk out of a mall without at least one shopping bag.

"Yeah, that's nice," Jacqui said.

"I like it too," Betty said without blinking. "Guess what. I'm gonna *let* you buy it for me. We'll call it my congratulatory gift from you for getting the big case."

"Thanks, heifer. I like the way you spend my money."

Jacqui walked toward the counter and handed the purse to the cashier. As she admired a few of the assorted earrings, she fished for a credit card. "Hey, Betty?"

"What?"

"What kinda credit does Evander have?"

"Pretty good, I guess. I mean he drives that Land Cruiser and has a nice house and all. But we never really talked about it. Why?"

"Run a credit check on that fool. I got a friend who could run it for free. All you need is his address and he can do it without the Social."

"I can't do that, it's illegal." Then Betty walked closer to Jacqui, "Why? Should I?"

Jacqui, who was preparing to sign the credit slip, looked at Betty as if she were purple with yellow polka dots on her face. "Child, most of these brothers now'days could not borrow a quarter for a glass of water if their mammy were on fire." The young black clerk behind the counter blurted out a laugh with Betty. "Ask her," Jacqui said, looking at the clerk. "Ask her how many brothers come in here and use a gold card. Damn a gold card, any card. Am I right or not?" she said, looking at the giggling teenager. "I'm serious. You remember that song, you gotta have a J-O-B if you wanna be with me? Forget that," she said quietly. "If he don't have a J-O-B, he just gotta walk on B-Y. Nowadays you gotta have a T-R-W if you want me to love ya. 'Cause it ain't nothing going on but the mortgage." Both the clerk and Betty laughed loudly now as another customer glanced over. "Come on, girl," Jacqui said, and grabbed her bag. "Let's get out of this place before they call security on both of us."

Walking out of the store, Jacqui caught the eye of another gentleman. He was tall, athletically cut, with a fair complexion and dressed in a denim shorts set. As they passed, he watched Jacqui intently, and she never looked in his direction. "I can't believe Renfro is giving you this opportunity with no strings attached," she said. "I know you are talented and know your stuff, but something is up with him."

Puzzled, Betty said, "Did you not see what was just looking at you?"

"Of course. I saw his married, yella ass," Jacqui said as she glanced at her watch.

"How you know he was married? You didn't even look up. He wasn't wearing a ring."

"Betty. Didn't you see the tan line on his finger?"

"Oh," Betty said, feeling stupefied. "But I didn't even see you look in his direction."

"Honey, all it took was a glance. I can smell a ring or a tan line a mile away. Now, as I was saying, I can't believe Renfro is doing this, no strings attached."

"He knows this can make my career. But with them it's all about money. Karl Marx once said a capitalist would sell you the rope to hang himself with, and that's Renfro. He's a racist, but he can count."

As they headed toward the exit, an obese man walked in front of them wearing a shirt stretched to the max and a quote on the back that said "Abortion Means Never Having to Say I Love You." Jacqui laughed. "That fat sum bitch don't even get coochie, yet he trust to tell me what to do with mine? Please."

A young man stepped up behind them as they walked,

and cleared his throat. "Excuse me, ladies, I was just notic-ing you all from across the way and I wanted to step up and say hi." The brother was wearing a suit that was clearly expensive with what appeared to be Italian shoes and ex-pensive jewelry. Unfortunately he also wore a Radio Shack name tag as well. He was a little on the short side, but he was impeccably groomed with S-shaped waves in his hair, and he appeared to have a nice body under his clothes. The first thing Betty did was look for a tan line. There wasn't one.

"Hello," Jacqui said, and then she glanced at the name tag, but apparently decided to hear his game as they walked before she dismissed him.

"So," he paused nervously, "how are you all doing?"

"We're fine," Jacqui said, trying to calm him down a little with her smile. "Just out here spending a little money before going back to work."

"So," he said, glancing at Betty, "what, ahh, what store do you all work in?"

"We don't exactly work here. But I guess we spend enough time out here to be employed, huh?" Betty said, laughing in Jacqui's direction.

"So, ahh, you all from around here or what?"

"Yeah," Betty said, and remembered the workload back at the office as she glanced at her watch and then at Jacqui.

"Yeah, honey," Jacqui said, "we need to go. Nice talking to you," as they walked faster.

"What y'all gonna do, just dis a brother like that?" he said, somehow gaining more confidence in himself and stop-ping in his tracks.

As they continued to walk, Betty said to Jacqui with a smile, "Now you know you wrong. Don't come crying to me when you want that clock radio on discount."

They could hear the little salesman, still standing in the spot where they'd left him, saying, "You all ain't shit! Black bitches!"

Jacqui turned around, but Betty grabbed her arm. "It's not worth it, child. We have to go."

"No, he did not go there! Childish punk!" Jacqui said. "We were nice to him and everything with his broke, midg-

ety ass. Besides, he raps like an old white boy anyway, trying to front like he's black. I bet you money he watched
'Seinfeld' instead of 'New York Undercover' anyway, with
his wanna-be white-boy self. You see? You see, that's why
I reduce their ass down to dawgs."

"Hey, I used to love 'Seinfeld,' " Betty said to avoid the
previous subject.

"Well, you can watch it 'cause you my girl," Jacqui replied as another young man walked by wearing tight
button-fly jeans. "Now, see that skinny brother there?"

"Jac, stop it!" Betty said, and laughed as she noticed her
friend looking at the obvious.

"Wait a minute," Jacqui said, grabbing Betty's arm and
slowing their pace as they were about to exit the mall. "Seriously, did you really watch 'Seinfeld' and that big doofus
Kramer, instead of Malik Yoba on 'New York Undercover'
with his fine-ass self?"

CHAPTER 13

‡

Tuesday, the next day

Betty unlocked the doors of Murphy, Renfro and Collins before the sun came up. Her arrival was earlier than usual, even for her. After she greeted the security officer, she walked toward her office with thoughts of her friend's past misfortune weighing heavily on her mind. She'd had another sleepless night, this time thinking about Jacqui, but she knew she had to tuck such thoughts away once her day started.

In her office she noticed the files she'd requested from Carol arranged in chronological order on top of her desk and filing cabinet. There were law journals left by her paralegal with Post-it notes indicating what pages she should turn to to find the relevant information, and her calendar had been cleared for the next six weeks. Carol had made sure Betty would have no distractions in the office, and since Evander had told her he would be going back to Orlando for a few days even though they had just returned, there would be no distractions outside the firm as well.

Carol said good morning at eight-thirty and brought Betty the interoffice mail, a cup of tea, and a Danish from the doughnut stand downstairs. Betty passed on the Danish, but lunged for the tea, clearly in her zone. Her office was strewn with documents. There were faxes in an unruly stack beside her trash can and documents to be scanned with pastel notes

attached to them. She had made several trips to the copy/
fax room and had already called and left messages for several of the attorneys in the firm who had previously re-
searched the case. Betty had medical records and depositions
on each of the over one hundred plaintiffs named in the suit
and on each doctor and medical team in attendance as well.
With the files spread in a controlled madness, Betty sat shoe-
less with her toes buried in the plush carpet, humming with
the radio.

She tried to uncover similarities thus far undetected by
the previous lawyers. A group of attorneys had worked on
the case for more than two years and had not made any
major progress, although there was certainly enough evidence to warrant a settlement from Amritrust Benefit Life,
who owned the hospital. Being an insurance company, ABL
did not want to have a lawsuit in a state in which they were
domiciled, nor did they care for the negative press. Jack
Murphy had spearheaded the charge and ABL had tendered
an offer of ten million dollars with a modest gag stipulation
weeks after it was announced that Murphy, Renfro and Collins would represent the victims. Feeling they had only
scratched the surface of a larger lawsuit, Jack had informed
the victims' representative of the pros and cons of the offer
and had been pleased when they'd decided to hold out for
a more equitable settlement.

Weeks before the turmoil in the firm, ABL legal representation had contacted the firm, and it was assumed yet another offer of settlement would be made. But after Jack
Murphy's heart attack, they would not reschedule a meeting
with Renfro.

Betty sat at her desk attempting to summarize the case in
her mind. A case that had been brought to light when the
sister of a patient who'd had a radical mastectomy had in-
cluded her experience in a newspaper column. In the article
she wrote of how people trust their physicians and the essence of the Hippocratic oath. The title of the article was
"First Do Harm?" She noted a case in which an elderly man
with sugar diabetes had finally taken his family's advice to
go through with the amputation, only to have the wrong
leg severed. She wrote of how a local lady had had a portion

of a sponge sown into her abdomen, and of course, she wrote about her sister, who'd had other options but had not been advised of them and had therefore opted for the mastectomy. When her family had questioned the doctor, he said he'd asked his assistant to discuss the matter with the patient and accepted full responsibility for her negligence in not doing so. After the article ran, several letters were sent to the newspaper detailing how other women in the city had had similar experiences at the same facility. The writer took the letters to a friend who worked for Murphy, Renfro and Collins, and within months over fifty women had come forward. After a year, the firm's investigators had uncovered over eighty women statewide with similar experiences and willing to take part in the class action suit.

While researching the information and scouring the files, Betty dreamed of the opening day of deliberations. Of walking out with Renfro after court each day to discuss a few bits of information with the media. Of appearing on statewide television, or maybe even "Burden of Proof," to discuss the merits of the case, without giving away too much inside information. Grandiose dreams of Renfro allowing her to give the summation and holding the jury spellbound, hanging on her every word. She knew such dreams had little chance of becoming a reality, but they were in vivid color. She could see herself holding the jury speechless as she said, "Ladies and gentlemen, Merriam-Webster describes *trust* as a charge or a duty imposed in faith or confidence as a condition of a relationship. That is the sheer definition of the word *trust*. What greater trust in a profession is there than the one between a doctor, with a pledge to first do no harm, and his or her patient?" She could imagine how it would feel to maintain eye contact with a male member of the jury and say, "Sir, this could be your wife or daughter." Attorney Betty Robinson imaged talking to the female jury members as if they were Jacqui and telling them how the hospital's "cupidity for profits had resulted in the loss of their womanhood."

No, she thought, and grabbed a notepad, already making notes to herself. "These moneygrubbing physicians butcher our womanhood," she wrote, "for increased profits." Betty knew such a statement, if she ever got a chance to deliver it, would be met by an objection from the opposing table, but who cared? The die would be cast. The opening statements would be in less than two months, and she was as anxious as if it were the next day.

"So you're getting into all this mess right away, honey?" Carol asked from the doorway of the office.

"Yeah, girl." Betty sat on the floor with a box of documents and peered up at Carol through her glasses. "Just like Murphy suspected, this hospital is doing some foul things, and I'm going to tie up these loose strings. This, 'it's just a coincidence' stuff ain't cutting it," she said, and removed her glasses to massage her temples. "I mean, how could this many women have unnecessary mastectomies over a ten-year period of time, and it be just a coincidence? I'm gonna talk to nurses, the anesthetic assistants—hell, I'll talk to the people who changed the linen if I have to. But I'm gonna uncover these jerks."

"Betty?" Carol said as she moved the files from a chair. "Have you ever worked with Renfro on a case before?"

"No. But I've worked on cases with other attorneys."

"I know. But you have run solo with them and that's fine. All of you associates try to get a little position when you work together. But when you work with a senior partner, especially one as insecure as Renfro, it's altogether different. It's just an unspoken rule that you do nothing without getting the okay from the senior partner. So are you gonna ask him before you talk to these people?"

"Of course I am," she replied, even though she'd originally had no plans to do so.

"Good. I'm not trying to tell you how to do your job, but I've seen a lot of associates come and go, and I know you have a bright future here. I hope you don't mind me butting in."

"Never. And thanks," Betty said. Then she caught her breath and smiled. "I mean it, Carol. Thanks for watching my back in this place."

"Honey, I have worked for a lot of associates and a few of the partners, too, and none of them can hold a candle to you. And I mean that. I just don't want you to get on the bad side of that idiot Renfro," she whispered. "So what do you need me to start on first?"

"Well, I need a few cases pulled up for me on West Law. And look up these topics on Nexus and sort them alphabetically. I've listed the West Law cases on that tablet for the paralegal. I also need you to call the attorneys on this sheet and set up a telephone conference for myself *and* Renfro with them after the seventeenth. Make sure it's after the seventeenth and make sure it's before ten o'clock. And then—"

"Wait, wait, wait a minute, honey," Carol said, frantically looking for something to write with.

"Lets go! Let's go! Let's go!" Betty said with a smile. And then as Carol left the room, Betty looked at the name she'd found in the file and debated whether she should clear each detail with Renfro.

Betty stood in line in the small cafeteria looking up at the menu on the wall, which had not changed since she had been with the firm. As she settled on her lunch she reached into the ice-filled chest, took out a bottled water, and paid the cashier.

As she turned, she saw a couple of associates chatting and a partner in the corner eating a banana and reading a magazine between chews. Then she noticed Kathy, who appeared to have just sat down and was putting her purse under her chair.

"May I?"

Kathy gave her a smile and nodded her head yes. Betty rarely had lunch in the cafeteria and had never sat with Renfro's secretary in the past. Usually she took her lunch to her office and worked while she ate, but since she and Renfro would be working closely for the next several weeks, she felt it was appropriate to get to know his assistant a little better.

There were a few awkward moments as both of the ladies felt each other out. And then Kathy mentioned a movie she and her husband had seen the previous night and she and Betty began to compare their favorites. Inside, Betty wanted to pick her brain to find out if she would be a partner, and

8

if not, why Renfro had selected her for the case, but as they
spoke of their favorite actors, those thoughts vanished.

"Well, this was enjoyable, Kathy." Betty smiled as she
wadded up her napkin and pushed her tray back. "One day
after we get finished with this case, maybe you, Carol and
I could catch a matinee. Although you know I have both
versions of 12 *Angry Men* on DVD."

"That would be a lot of fun. I'd like that a lot." And
then Kathy reapplied her lipstick with a mirror, cleaned any
possible remnants from her teeth with her tongue, and said,
"Miss Robinson. I've been wanting to tell you something for
a while."

Here goes, Betty thought.

"I know how most people here feel about Mr. Renfro.
Trust me when I say he can be a real pain you know where
sometimes. But he's smart and he's a very intelligent man.
I worked for a couple of firms before coming here. Actually," she digressed, "I wanted to be a lawyer myself, but
then, well, let's just say I chose the family route. But like I
was going to say. I know he seems to have this hard exterior,
but he's not like that at all. Deep inside, that is. I worked
here with him before the incident with his wife, and when
she was around I bet there was not a day when he didn't
come in with a guess-what-we-did-yesterday or guess-what-
we're-doing-this-weekend story. But after those kids did
what they did, and after she . . ." And then Kathy got quiet.
"Well, I guess you know what happened to her. He just
changed. I mean to be honest, he was always a little preju-
diced. Not just of blacks. One of the first things he asked
me when I interviewed was if I was part Asian. Actually I
am," she whispered, "but after that incident he became very
cold. Very crass. Especially toward black people."

"Tell me something," Betty asked. "Exactly how did he
get shot?"

After a pause Kathy said, "What I saw on the police report
was that she was working at this rally to raise money for a
housing project and these kids from the project followed her
home. Apparently they waited and then broke in the house
later that night. Renfro was working on a case with a couple
of associates, and in those days he would always work until

ten or eleven at night when he was in the midst of a trial. Well, they cut her up pretty bad and then shot her. When he walked in, he saw the body and then realized one of the kids was still in the house. The kid had a gun but ran for the door and down the stairs with Franklin chasing him. I guess the kid was scared and fired a shot at Franklin without even looking back. It hit him in the hip, destroyed his kidney, and bounced up into his chest, which is why he has the limp. The EMS had to do a tracheotomy on the spot so he would not drown in his own fluids."

Betty's breathing slowed as she learned that this man she had every reason not to like, and every reason to mistrust, was actually valiant. "I've heard stories about what happened. Someone even told me he got shot running away from the assailants."

"That's how rumors get started. Trust me, I've heard a few myself. But he never talks about it, and actually only a small handful of people here know what really happened." After a sip of her cola Kathy said, "I wouldn't have told you, but with you working so closely with him for the next few weeks, I thought you deserved to know. See, we all thought after he remarried he would change a little, but he hasn't. He's still bitter after all these years, and although I don't agree with a lot of what he does, I understand him."

Betty returned to her office with a new impression of Franklin Renfro and even more focused on the case. As she sat at her desk her two fingers lightly touched her lips as she would do when deep in thought, and her mind actively searched for unturned stones in the case. As a moot court case with relevance came to mind, she walked across the room to her law books, when she heard her secretary's voice on the speakerphone.

"Hello?" Betty said from across the room.

"Well, guess who just called."

"Don't tell me. Tell Jacqui I'm sorry I didn't get by there for lunch and that I will call her back in an hour."

"No, it wasn't Jacqui," Carol replied.

"Evander?"

"Strike two. It was your new *best* friend up on eighteen."

"New friend? What new—oh, you mean Kathy?"

"Yeah. She told me you were having a little *Waiting to Exhale* moment scheduled for your house after the trial is over."

"Yeah. It'll be fun," Betty laughed as she marked her spot in the law book with her finger. "Is that the only reason she called?"

"No. She said that all of the associates are supposed to be in the conference room at three-fifteen for some reason."

"Jeez. I'm busy," she said as she looked at the stacks of files yet to be opened. "Do you know what for?"

"No idea, and she didn't say. But I hate to tell you this. While you were at lunch, Jill Williams called me and told me that she was told by Mr. Collins that they made it official a couple of hours ago. They gave the partnership to Patterson. I'm so sorry, honey."

Betty slowly closed the book and sat on the arm of her couch as she continued to stare down at her phone.

"Are you okay in there?"

"Yeah. Yeah, I'm fine," she replied as she heard Jacqui's voice in her mind saying, *Don't trust them. It's a den of thieves.* Quietly she mumbled, "When they want to win a case, he picks me, but Patterson gets on the letterhead."

"Betty? Betty, are you okay? She told me that it came down to the two of you, if that's any consolation. But somehow he got the nod. Jill doesn't know why."

"I'm fine, Carol," she said as she plotted her next move in the firm. "I'm just fine."

Betty walked into the conference room at exactly 3:15 and it was packed. Renfro walked in at precisely 3:20, flanked by Collins, a partner by the name of Robert Stockton, and the newest addition to the partnership, R. Raymond Patterson.

Raymond glanced at Betty, and as she looked back at him he cowardly looked away. *Lord, I hope they're not bringing us in here to announce this fool is a partner.* And then Betty smiled as she refused to allow the wheels turning in her head to show in her eyes. It would be so easy to pull Renfro aside after the meeting and demand an explanation, but she was

thoroughly convinced that the way to advance in the firm
was to make herself immeasurably irreplaceable. Therefore
the case was even more important to her future with Murphy, Renfro and Collins. *They want to win the case, they choose
me,* she repeated. *Ain't that something?*

"G'afternoon everyone," Renfro said with a glum expression. "It is my sincere displeasure to give you this information." He did not have to say anything else as Betty's lower
jaw fell. With the blood draining from her face, she knew
this was the news she'd dreaded for the past two months,
and now she was forced to face it.

"At twelve-thirteen this afternoon our friend, our mentor,
our colleague, our leader, Jack Murphy, had a second heart
attack and left us." Renfro looked up at the ceiling as
Betty trembled.

"Jack, as you all know, was a man amongst men. I can
assure you, I will forever be a better person as a result of
working with him." Renfro continued to speak for about ten
minutes, telling stories of the struggles they'd had in building the firm and cases they'd worked on together. While
Betty didn't feel his sincerity, she was most distressed by
the fact he never spoke of the real Jack. The Jack who was
a great husband and caring father and a not-so-good fly
fisherman. He only spoke of his partner in the legal concern
and how they had won various cases.

Then Robert Stockton stood up to talk and he spoke for
a few minutes about how he and Jack had outfoxed an insurance company. Patterson then stood to tell how he'd
wanted to work with Jack on a particular case, but Jack had
told him that he did not need his expertise. "He told me,"
R. Raymond said, "you have a bright future with us and I
have confidence in your abilities to handle it alone." Then
a parade of attorneys stood to tell their Jack story, each
implying that the previous lawyer could not have known
him as well as he or she did. Like the others, Betty stood,
but not to give them a better story. Emotion was siphoned
from her face as she walked across the room toward the
door. After leaving the room, she walked quickly to the
elevator, still showing not a hint of her true sentiments.
When the doors opened, she felt the awkward tumble in her

chest as she felt faint and a little weak in her knees, but no tears fell. Betty leaned on the back of the elevator as she returned to the seventeenth floor of the Olsen Building, unnerved and alone.

In her office, Betty stepped over the files, sat behind her desk, and looked out the window she had gazed out so often before. Ironically, there was a dark cloud in the offing, casting a shadow as the forewarning of the approaching thunderstorm. Immediately she thought about calling Jacqui, but her fingers dialed Evander. She knew he said he was going to visit his mother, but she hoped he hadn't left yet.

"Hello, Eastside Bakery. Would you like to try our new chocolate twirlers today?"

"Hi, Val." As she spoke she surprised herself with the calmness of her voice. "I know he's supposed to be gone, but has Evander left for his mom's yet?"

"Oh hey, Betty, I think he has. Onc second."

"I have the phone, Val," Evander said on the other line. "Hey, baby, how are you? What's wrong?"

He can tell something is wrong? Without me even saying a word? God, I love this man. "We got the news this morning."

"Murphy?"

"Yes," she said softly.

"One second. Val?" Evander shouted away from the receiver of the phone. "Hey, Vally! Come here! Take care of this Kinko's order for Charlotte. I was going to do it before I left, okay? I got to run for a second. Betty," he said, taking control. "I'll be right there. You stay in your office. Lock your door and don't let the rest of those jerks see you like this, okay? Not even Carol. Hear me?"

"Okay," she said as meekly as a five-year-old being told not to open the door for strangers.

Prince Evander must have run every light between the bakery and the Olsen Building in his white stallion disguised as a sports utility vehicle.

"I'm here, baby. Open the door." As Betty unlocked the door, he walked in immediately and, without uttering a word, embraced her while gently rubbing the back of her neck. "It's gonna be okay," he said, and closed the door behind him.

Betty could feel tears in her eyes for the first time in years as she laid her head on Evander's chest.

"Let it out, baby. It'll feel better," he said in his slow, soothing, deep, southern voice. Enunciating each syllable, he repeated, "Betty? Let it all out."

"You should see them," she said, and took his handkerchief for her runny nose. "They're in there now with these long windy speeches trying to get in position for his parking space and shit. I hate to talk like that, but—but it just doesn't make any—it's just not right," she said, and buried her face in his neck. "The man deserved more than that." And then the tears came forth. The tears of loss, fear, rejection, acceptance, victory, defeat, death, love, and hate. They flowed for the past twenty years. Although the pain was deep inside, Evander and the tears were a small dose of relief for her years of heartache.

Evander held her face as she lowered her eyes and he kissed her softly. And then he eased off the desk and led her to the couch. Betty leaned into his chest as she sat and looked up at the ceiling. "I hate feeling like this. I know I'm supposed to be strong. But sometimes . . ."

"Beeper, it's okay to be weak at times. Even if you are an attorney. I mean we all have feelings."

"Remember how I told you about the accident?" As she spoke, she leaned into his chest and stared at the fluorescent light above. "I've wondered what I would be if it was not for that accident. How would my life be different? I don't know if I would be an attorney, because my mom never pushed me. I don't even remember her reading to me. But I know," she whispered, "I wouldn't be so screwed up emotionally."

"Baby," Evander said as he stroked her cheek with the back of his hand, "you've had some bad breaks, but I'm proud of you. I mean you deal with these people on a day-to-day basis and you hold your own. You're not screwed up. You're tough. Just watch what happens. In a few days I guarantee they'll announce that you will be the next partner. And that's proof that you're good at what you do. You're not screwed up at all."

Betty smiled, not wanting to deal with that travesty at this time. "Did I ever tell you what my mom did when the car hit us?"

"No, baby," he said, and relaxed into the couch with her body wrapped in his arms. "What happened?"

"Well," she said, with her eyes closed to travel back to that painful place in her past, "after the car hit us and sent us spinning, I remember waking up and looking at my step-daddy, and he was trying to get the car under control. And then I remember him looking out of his window." Betty fell silent for a moment but then gathered the courage to continue. "I remember looking out the window and seeing the truck driver's face before it hit our car. I could see him so clearly. If I live to be a hundred, I will see that fat man's face and his truck skidding into our car. And then POW!" she said as her body stiffened and eyes opened in fear. Vibrating like a pager, she said, "But right before it hit us, I remember my momma's hand pushing me back in my seat. Even though she was in front, she was trying to protect me in the backseat with a seat belt on and then . . ." The words died for Betty. "This is something I have never told anyone. Not even Jac. But about three years ago I got a call here at the firm. I asked who it was and they said, Darryl Robinson. So I'm thinking, I don't know any . . . And then the moment I pick up the phone I thought, naw, it couldn't be. So I say hello and sure enough, it was my dad."

"Really? After all those years."

"Yep. My daddy called me," Betty said with a smile. "I was so glad to hear his voice. For that split second I didn't care that he never came back to my momma and me. I didn't care that he was not a part of my life. I was just so happy to hear his voice. To feel like someone's little girl again. He told me how hard it had been for him to track me down. Said he had been looking for me for over a year. Asked me how I liked living in the South and then he told me why he had called. Said he wanted to get in contact with my momma to sign divorce papers because he was getting married."

"No one told him? After all those years? But wait a minute, I thought your momma remarried."

"Yeah. She did, and he said he never actually filed the divorce papers, but that's another story. My momma didn't have much family, and when he got my number from my aunt in New York, she just left me the honor of doing it. But before I could tell him, he started telling me how my momma was no good and how she drove him away and how he had written to me and she more than likely hid the letters. After I told him she was dead, he changed his tune a little, but before he hung up, guess what he did."

"I would hope he apologized, but I'm almost afraid to ask."

With a smile behind an uninterrupted stream of tears she said, "The man asked me if he could borrow a few dollars for a down payment on a house."

As he stroked her temple with the width of his thumb, Evander said with a sigh, "What an asshole. People can be so insensitive. But I'm glad you shared that with me. It's times like these that bring things like that to the surface. Death is never easy. I lost a close friend last year."

Betty blew her nose again into the handkerchief and said, "Baby, I'm sorry. You never told me that. Who was it?"

"Gary. A guy I knew back in the days when we were growing up in Orlando. He died last year unexpectedly, and it really messed me up. I ain't gonna lie. One day he was the epitome of life and the next he had full-blown AIDS and was dying. I was there with a few of his friends when he left. It really changed the way I live now. I have never told you this, but one of the things I admire most about you is the fact that you don't allow *money* to control your life. I once read that sometimes in life you have to sing like you don't need the tips. Laugh as if everyone gets the joke. Dance like nobody's watching, and," he said as he softly rubbed his thumb over her closed eyelid, "it must always come from the heart. And that's just one of the reasons I love you."

As Evander spoke, Betty had never felt as close to anyone than at that moment. If there were any doubts in her mind before, they were now washed away. Evander was the one.

"But there's something," Evander continued, "about losing someone close to you that will change your whole outlook on life. The sky is bluer and the grass is greener. Somehow, you sorta subconsciously want to suck every ounce out of life, out of everything you do. You work harder. Play harder. It even feels as if you *breathe* harder. I guess that's why I *try* to make love to you so passionately, Beep," he said, and took her chin as she opened her eyes and looked away. "Betty? Look at me." As she looked into his eyes, he continued. "Because you just never know when will be the last time you see someone you love. You know," Evander continued, "if Gary, if Murphy, had the opportunity to do so, would they wish they had worked a couple hours longer? I doubt it. They would probably wish they had spent more time with their family, more time working in their church, more time saying to that special person . . ."

He gently brought her face closer as Betty said, "I love you," to him for the first time.

She shook her head, unable to control the passion within any longer. "God, I love you so much, Evander," she said again, with tears clouding her voice.

"I love you, too, baby. You're my whole world," Evander said softly in her ear. "You're my everything."

Betty had never told anyone in her life she loved them. No one. She had always prevented people, and especially men, from getting close enough so that the utterance of such words was even a possibility. Now her defenses were weakened and her walls had melted. Finally she was ready to love, and to be loved.

They kissed with passion in Betty's office. As she turned her body around, they lay belly to belly and kissed with warmth on her couch. She ignored Carol's knock at her door as Evander said the words repeatedly into her ear and she replied in kind, feeling freer with each utterance. These were their first kisses after consummating their *I love yous.* These were the last passionate kisses they would ever share.

CHAPTER 14

✝

Friday

Of all the days Betty had worked in the firm, this was by far the toughest. Gardenias and dogwood blossoms sweetened the air with their essence as they prepared to kiss winter good-bye. Birds flew in arrow formation high above as they bid the state a fond farewell on their pilgrimage north. But as she sat at her desk dressed in black, Betty tried to think about Jacqui and her man problems or Evander, whom she was already missing, so she would not have to think about her mentor's funeral. She played the radio a little louder than usual and kept her door closed, which for her was very uncommon. Betty wanted to concentrate on the work at hand like the beam of a laser, because in hours the firm would be vacated in honor of Jack Murphy.

Before she dressed that morning she debated whether to bring another suit to change into after the services, because she imagined how depressing it would be to see everyone in black all day. As she drove into the garage, she decided to drive down to the executive parking area. And there it was. Renfro's extended-cab pickup in the first spot. The parking space that did not seem right without the mirror-black Mercedes SL600. spot. She could not figure out why it made her fingers grip the steering wheel until her knuckles lightened, but it did. After all, it was only a parking space. Just a few square feet of blacktop which, given the type of man Murphy was, he would not have had a problem with at all. But as she drove back up to the general parking area on the roof of the garage, she passed R. Raymond Patterson headed to his new spot, and yet another tear fell. For years she could not muster a drop, but once again a warm tear glistened down her face and over her lips. While she was hurt, the tears also cleaned the spaces deep within her soul.

The obsequies for Jonathan Alexander Murphy were stately, honorable, and well attended. All of the local officials and many statewide dignitaries were in the small cathedral to pay their respects. The governor relieved the lieutenant governor of such duties on that day and sat beside Agnes and the boys during the services. All of the partners of the firm sat with their spouses behind the elected officials and Jack Murphy's family. Instead of sitting alone, Betty elected to sit with a few members of the clerical staff who had decided to come by themselves.

From her seat in the back, Betty noticed the white marble pillars of the cathedral were encircled by fresh ivy. The coffin bearing his remains was covered with his favorite flower, white daisies. Above them was the boys' choir. Their voices blended in a tightly woven harmony as they sang sotto voce without visible direction. And then Betty noticed Agnes Murphy. Her veiled face looked tired yet strong. Sitting in the pew, she looked like the photo of Coretta Scott King in April of sixty-eight. Betty could tell by the look in her eyes that she wanted to be the rock for the rest of her family because she knew all eyes were on her. She knew what Jack would have wanted her to do. But deep inside, Betty felt she was just a step away from losing it altogether.

Looking at Agnes for the first time since Jack's death drove home for Betty just how dark and somber this loss was. She felt sorrow because she and Agnes had spoken often of the sacrifices the family had made to assist Jack in building what was now considered one of the top firms in the country. "We mortgaged the house, ate so many kidney beans I refuse to have them served in our home now, just to make ends meet," Agnes had told Betty. She'd spoken of how they'd been on the verge of divorce several times due to associated pressure, yet they were now enjoying the best years of their marriage and looked forward to spending the rest of their lives together.

Sitting directly behind the governor and Mrs. Murphy were Mr. and Mrs. Renfro. On that day Franklin Renfro appeared different to Betty. Usually she felt his mourning was a little disingenuous. But at that moment he appeared heavy-hearted. As Betty watched him, he never blinked, not even once. He did not look at who attended, nor did he appear concerned with who may or may not be watching him. Betty watched as his wife handed him a handkerchief and he did not respond. Then she nudged his elbow to get his attention. Betty wondered if the enormity of the job he'd wanted so badly had finally hit home. If it had sunk in that Jack Murphy would never again enter the doors of Murphy, Renfro and Collins. That he would never walk into the courtroom with his charm and automatically make the opposing attorneys quietly slouch in their seats. As he sat with his arm secure around his new wife, Betty imagined that he felt he had the tiger he had always wanted by the tail. But now he had no idea what to do with it.

After a few words of acknowledgment, "Ave Maria" was piped throughout the building as the attendees read Jack's obituary. And then from the front row, a young gentleman stood, breathed in deeply, and reached down to kiss his mother. He then proceeded to stand in front of his father's casket to give the eulogy. Betty listened as Jack and Agnes's youngest son, who was in his first year of law school, started by telling them a story. A story of how his father had taken him and his brothers fishing when he was in middle school. About stopping on the road to purchase a larger ice chest for the catch. And how Jack had eaten Happy Meals with them that night under the stars.

As the gathering laughed and shook their heads, Betty smiled as she thought about the first lesson she'd learned from the masterful counselor. She'd been leaving the courtroom after her first defeat in a case she felt she should have won. As he'd walked toward her, she'd felt herself tremble. But he'd highlighted every positive thing she'd done and then said, "Just tell them the story, Betty. Unlike the gobbledygook they teach you in law school, this is not rocket science. We make it tough, but it really isn't. They don't care about statues. They could give less than a tinker's damn about precedence. Just tell them the story," he'd said. "Just tell them a story." Obviously his son had listened well.

In the processional out of the church, the body was carried by a gathering of old men wearing white gloves who were colleagues at one time or another with Jack. As they walked in lockstep down the red carpet toward the awaiting hearse, the sounds of "Amazing Grace" permeated the air on the pipe organ. No, it was not a traditional Catholic song, but it was one of Jack's favorites. Agnes Murphy followed them as the others filed out in order of importance behind her. As she walked down the aisle, she made occasional eye contact with a few special friends of the family. Even in her most solemn hour, she attempted to encourage the others to keep a stiff upper lip. As she passed Betty, she gave her not only a glance, but a subtle smile. To Betty she was truly a special lady.

Betty covered her eyes on the bright and windy Floridian day as she walked down the steps of the cathedral. The winds carried the song of a lone kilted bagpipe player as he stood in front of the sleek white hearse. With each release of air from his dimpled cheeks, the pleading sounds emanating from the instrument were strained and mournful as he played "Danny Boy." To Betty, it did not seem like the type of song one would play on such an occasion, but it seemed apropos because if anything, Jonathan Alexander Murphy was an atypical attorney.

Monday, one week later

It had been another dull weekend without Evander. He had not been to Orlando for six months prior to the visit there with Betty, but this was the second weekend in a row he had made the trip, and this weekend had extended to Monday. The intuitive part of Betty said all was not well in their relationship, but the rational part of her pleaded for patience. As she put the documents back in the appropriate files after her daily 8:30 A.M. telephone meeting with Renfro, she considered for a moment driving down for a surprise visit, but with her workload, those thoughts soon faded.

Each day in Betty's meeting with the senior partner he wanted to know three things. What had she done on the case the previous day? What was she going to do that day? And what were her personal thoughts regarding the matter? Having never worked with Renfro, initially Betty felt uncomfortable with all of the attention. It was always said that while he did not have the courtroom presence of Jack Murphy, no one could question his attention to detail. Each Tuesday until the start of the proceedings he had Kathy block out five hours for all the attorneys assigned to the case to meet with him in the conference room. He asked that they each bring relevant files to their meeting. If a point was brought up he did not like hearing about, he wanted to see documentation. The unconventional way he prepared for the case agitated the other attorneys, but not Betty. The more she thought about it, the more she relished the opportunity to prove her worth as a litigator. While at times she felt she was tap-dancing for the blind, based on her record and her conversation with Mrs. Murphy, she knew this was still a golden opportunity.

That night as she walked down the hallway, Betty spoke to a couple of the office custodians and then she reached the door of Gregory Davis's office and noticed him busily at work. After a quick glance at her watch, she looked back and caught his eye.

"You still here?" Betty called out over the sound of the vacuum cleaners and buffers roaring up and down the long hallway.

"Yeah. What time is—" and then he noticed his watch. "Holy shit! It's nine-thirty. I had no idea it was this late."

"Oh well," Betty replied with a smile. "I'll see you back here in a couple of hours, I guess. Don't forget, we have that meeting with Renfro tomorrow morning."

"Forget? Why do you think I'm here now?" he said with a shout over the background cleaning noise. "You leaving?"

"Yeah. I've been in the library since about five. Sometimes I just need a change of scenery to concentrate."

"Well, if you let me get my stuff," he said, gesturing toward his briefcase, "I'll walk down with you."

"Sure."

Wearing a wrinkled JCPenney's suit, Gregory walked Betty to her parking space, carrying her box of homework. "I can't believe you take this much stuff home every night. You're something else. I just want you to know that," he said.

"Well, actually I don't take this much home each night. Just Mondays so I can prepare for my meeting with Renfro."

"Aren't those meetings a trip? Can you believe having a five-hour meeting on this one case each week? I mean I know it's a big case, but isn't that overkill? And also making us haul all those files up there?" Gregory loosened his tie and quickly placed his hand back under the box. "And what's the deal with that antiquated file system? Didn't that go out of style with Perry Mason and the Edsel? But then again," Gregory laughed, "so did his ties. And would you believe he calls me up every other day with all of these questions? As if he thinks I'm slacking off or something."

"Really?"

"Yeah. I worked with him on a couple of cases before. Neither of them went to court, but he was never like this. Never this . . . I don't know, I guess *uptight* is the word I'm looking for. I mean he's always been anal, but not like this."

"Well, maybe it's because there's no Jack in the office now."

Gregory smiled at Betty as he set the box down gently on the pavement beside her car. As he ran his hand through his conservatively cut brown hair he said, "You know, Betty, I don't know how to say this, but . . . how do you do it? I mean, how do you work with Renfro with his being like he . . . well, you know. If it were me, I don't think I could even continue to work here. I hate to ask this, but as a black person, how do you walk in that office of his?"

"It's tough. Very tough sometimes, but you deal with it. It's not like I just woke up black one morning. I mean, I came to this firm with goals in mind like everyone else, and if I allow Renfro to make me resign, then I've given him power over me I don't think anyone should have. So I bite my lip, overlook the small stuff, and do my job."

"Well, I would like to think that I would react that way. But I couldn't swear to it. On the other hand, we are not exactly cut from the same cloth. I mean, you came up with all of those facts that you introduced in the meeting last week," Gregory continued. "How the hospital doctors and insurance company connected. How could you have known to interview the guy in Northern California or about the sealed court records in Nevada?"

"Just going through all the files with a fresh eye and luck, I guess."

"Luck my a— Nothing," Gregory said with a smile. "I mean it. Betty, I leave this place and go home and work for another two or three hours each night just to try to keep up with you. I bet you I have not taken one Saturday or Sunday off since this case landed in my lap." And then leaning against her car he said, "Maybe I shouldn't be saying this, but I was more than a little jealous when I saw the role you were playing in this case. Initially I would bone up on my facts to try to show you up. Now I do it just to keep up. Like most of these guys here, I thought you were a little overrated. We thought you were getting powder-puff cases just to make you look good, as Murphy's girl. We thought that Askew case and especially that Lopez case were set up. I mean, there was no way an associate could pull that off alone. But after working with you . . ." Davis shook his head, running out of superlatives. "You know, if I had my act together half as much as you have yours, counselor . . ."

Betty unlocked her door.

"Listen," Gregory said, "I know it's been a long week and all, but could I invite you over to The Purple Porpoise for a quick drink and some oysters or something? I promise you, we will talk about anything *but* this case."

Betty declined, because while there was a thin line between business and pleasure, in her mind it was a defined line.

"Well, anyway, I'll see you tomorrow in the meeting," he said, walking away.

"Have a nice evening, Greg," Betty said with a smile still on her face as he headed off into the night.

After she arrived home, Betty immediately walked to her desk to make a few notations she had thought of while driving. Looking at her Caller ID box, she noticed a call from Orlando which was undoubtedly Evander. "Why is he still in Orlando?" she said aloud as she picked up the phone to listen to the message.

"How are you doing, baby? I've been calling you at the firm since about six and I kept getting your recorder. I wanted to let you know that I called Ferguson and asked if I could take a few more vacation days. Mom is having some problems with Shawn, and since college is not too far down the road, I'm taking him to visit a few schools in the area. Also she needs some help with a few things like fixing the sink and the door on the garage. So I'm just going to hang out here a few more days. I'm taking Shawn—or should I say Red Dawg—to the movies tonight, but I'll be back around eleven. I'll call you as soon as I get in. I love you."

As Betty hung up the phone, both the intuitive and rational sides of her wanted more answers. It was not adding up. But then as she pulled off her shoes and stockings she thought, *I should give him the benefit of the doubt. I'm just stressed about this case.*

After changing clothes, Betty went outside to get her homework for the night out of the car and noticed her neighbors pulling into their driveway. Like most of her new neighbors, they had come over and introduced themselves after she moved in, but she could not remember their names as she waved across the street. Then she picked up the box filled with files and carried it into the house, with Tickey scurrying at her heels.

Sitting in her office, Betty looked down at the files as she attempted to muster the courage to delve into them. Removing a single folder, she looked at the pages and they all looked the same. *I need a break,* she thought as she removed her glasses and did something she had not done in over a month. She signed onto the Internet.

```
DELTADREAM: Hello, guys, what's going on tonight!
CYNT4UZ: Hi, DeltaDream.
DAPHINESSSS: Hey, soror, long time no see from.
DELTADREAM: Working on a big project at work, you know,
    same old same old.
OMEGA OIL: It's me, baby, how are you? We are discussing
    the pros and cons of the welfare system. What's
    your position?
DELTADREAM: Let me just listen to you guys for a while.
```

Betty did not wish to engage in a profound debate right now. She had been absorbed in intelligent banter all day and preferred to take her mind away from things that were serious. The conversation continued and Betty was getting a little bored, so she decided to sign off and watch television until Evander called. And then out of nowhere she received a personal message on her screen.

```
DLASTROMEO: Hello, DeltaDream, how are you tonight?
DELTADREAM: How are you? It's been a long time. I remem-
    bered you telling me about your girlfriend.
DLASTROMEO: I'm impressed that you even remember. It's
    been over a month since we chatted.
DELTADREAM: Or longer. I very rarely come on-line any-
    more. But I remember the conversation because you
    don't often find intelligent life-forms on the infor-
    mation superhighway.
DLASTROMEO: I guess that's true. So how is Mr. Wonderful?
DELTADREAM: Jeez. Was I that bad? You sound like my best
    friend. She says that all the time. He's fine. Ac-
    tually I can't chat too long tonight because he
    should be calling in about 45 mins.
DLASTROMEO: I'll keep that in mind. So what do you do when
    you are not surfing the Internet and chatting
    with Romeos?
DELTADREAM: I work for a large corporation.
DLASTROMEO: How nice. Do you enjoy it?
DELTADREAM: It pays the bills.
```

Betty had heard about guys who used the Internet in search of women with deep pockets and deeper holes in their heads than in their hearts, so she decided not to tell him exactly what she did.

DLastRomeo: So what do you do for enjoyment?

DeltaDream: Enjoyment? What's that? I read.

DLastRomeo: No free time, huh? I can relate. Favorite authors?

DeltaDream: Favorite? Now that's a tough one. One of my favorites is Ntozake Sharige and of course my girl Zora. Although I enjoy commercial stuff like Grisham and McMillan as well.

DLastRomeo: At one time I never read fiction. I was always too busy. But mostly I read stuff like ''Why Should White Guys Have All the Fun'' by Reginald Lewis, ''The Art of War,'' Sun Tzu, and ''What Makes the Great Great,'' by this guy whose name escapes me.

DeltaDream: Dennis Kimbro, the brother is deep. I read him and Iyanla every morning.

DLastRomeo: You read books like those also?

DeltaDream: Yeah I'm a nerd. I just read, read, and read.

DLastRomeo: You sound like my girlfriend.

DeltaDream: Is this someone you have met since we last chatted?

DLastRomeo: Well actually no. I'm still not used to saying late girlfriend.

DeltaDream: I'm sorry to hear that. I remember you telling me about her before. Cancer took her if I am not mistaken. Right?

DLastRomeo: Yes, it was cancer and it was quick.

DeltaDream: Well I guess we must be thankful for small things. At least it was quick so she didn't suffer.

DLastRomeo: Yeah I've heard that and trust me I've looked for the silver lining. But I don't think that's it. I'm glad she didn't suffer, but I think we needed to bring closure to a number of things and we were never given that opportunity because it happened so fast. One day she was diagnosed and we learned that sometimes the word positive was not always a good thing. And then they

said the word we wanted to hear so badly. Remission.
Then a few months later we learned a new word. Metasta-
size. And then she was gone.

DELTADREAM: So it spread quickly?

DLASTROMEO: I think we just found out about it too late to
do anything. Want to know how she told me? She said
she had an illness and from the way she said it I knew
it was serious. So I asked what it was and was
there a cure. And then she said with a tear, which
was the first of many, cancer . . . and death.

DELTADREAM: It must have been tough for you guys.

DLASTROMEO: She was a hell of a lady. But yes it was tough.
I had never known anyone with the disease or even
someone who was chronically ill. I never knew how the
chemotherapy would physically change her body to
the point where sweets were no longer sweet and
steaks tasted bitter. In the bedroom we had problems from the very first day and I think it was because
she wanted to please me but felt guilty that she
may not be able to. But we just substituted cuddling
for that. I was never a cuddler before her but just
holding her close sometimes felt better than going
all the way. (I can't believe I am telling you all
of this.) We would go for X-rays and they would put
these red and blue marks on her forehead and shave
what little hair the chemo had not taken out. Then
she would go to work wearing sun hats. I didn't
want her to work but she needed that in her life. The
medication would leave her physically exhausted
at times. I used to drive by her house in the mornings
just to help her get dressed for work. But so much
had been taken away from her that she needed one aspect of her life to look and feel almost normal.
Then one day she overheard a couple of her co-work-
ers, one supposedly her friend, say they didn't
know why she continued to come to work looking like
that. After that, Felicia never confronted her
friend and she never went back to work again.

DELTADREAM: That's sad. People can be so cruel sometimes.

DLASTROMEO: Yeah I know, but she never got upset about it.

Or at least she never let me know if she was upset
about it. I wanted to go down there. At least call
her ''friend'' up but she said it wasn't a big
deal. She said she didn't want to go back because it
was upsetting the work flow in the office and she
could never get anything accomplished while there.
DELTADREAM: Sounds like you had something very special.
DLASTROMEO: Yeah, I know that now. That's why I haven't
dated. It wasn't a perfect love. I just wish I could
have appreciated more what we did have, when we had it.
But I guess that's normal after losing someone you
love.

**Betty and Drew both gazed at their screens for an endless
moment, neither knowing what to type next.**

DLASTROMEO: NEW SUBJECT! Tell me more about your friend.
DELTADREAM: Evander? Where do I start? I try to appreciate
each day. I feel fortunate to have him.

**As the words left her fingers, doubts bubbled in her mind
and she looked at the clock.**

DLASTROMEO: Well I assure you, love, Evander is more than
likely bending his knees every now and then
thanking God for you as well. You know, I hear a lot
of females out there crying about a decent black
man. But they exist. I have a young lady I work with
and she is always bragging about her husband to
the point where I think my office manager gets a little sick of it sometimes. But I am happy for her
just as I'm happy for you.
DELTADREAM: You are indeed the charmer. But I guess you
are told that often.

**They conversed until five minutes before Betty's expected
call, and Drew asked for permission to send her E-mail from
time to time. He added that he wanted to ask permission
first since Evander may find it and take it the wrong way.
Betty told him it would be okay and if he ever needed to**

talk to a friend, to drop her a line. More than anything she was impressed that he would ask for permission to correspond and felt that he was one of the few men on-line who had indeed earned his screen name.

Seconds after Betty signed off, the phone rang. "Hello?"

"How are you? Seems we've not talked in days."

"I know. It was a long day today." She wanted to ask him so many questions and she wanted to conceal her excitement at hearing his voice, but could not.

"I called I don't know how many times, but I never caught you in the office and I didn't want to leave a message. I know how busy you are with the case and all."

"I spent most of the day in the library and then—"

"Beep?"

"Yes?"

"I love you."

After a pause she said, "I love you too," with a smile that erased many of the doubts in her mind. "I miss you like I don't know what."

"I miss you too. It's just that when I came back down here I noticed all the work that needed to be done around the house, and Shawn is talking about not going to college. Momma just needs a man around here for little things every now and then. But you don't know how much I miss you. I know you're busy and all, but I am taking Shawn to visit a junior college about forty-five minutes away from Gainesville. Do you think you could swing down and have lunch with me? I know this is short notice."

"Baby, you know I would if I could. But we have that meeting I was telling you about with Renfro on Tuesdays, and I promised Carol I would take her to lunch downstairs. Actually we'll probably have to work while we eat because there is so much to do." Evander was momentarily silent as Betty said, "I'm sorry. I really would like to see you too."

"I know. Well, I should be back Thursday or Friday and we'll make up for lost time then. Okay?"

"Okay," Betty replied as she settled on her couch and Tickey lay on the floor beside her. "It's a date. We'll do something special when you get home."

CHAPTER 15

‡

Tuesday

"**What time is** it?" Drew asked Grace, who was typing a memo at her desk.

"A quarter to four and you have a four-o'clock with Morgan and Kline, or have you forgotten that too?"

"That's right. That is today, isn't it?" Drew said as he glanced at the calendar on his credenza.

"Peggy!" Grace yelled toward the back of the office. "Pick up line three. It's the dealership! Drew, I looked earlier, but I didn't see a file for this appointment. Do you need a new-prospect folder?"

"No, that's okay. This is personal business." It was the day of the reading of the will, and between helping Peggy with the Con-National proposal and putting the finishing touches on the Murphy, Renfro and Collins deal, the week had passed him by like a blip on a screen. Peggy had had several interviews with Con-National, and after she'd impressed them, Zelma had asked Drew to approach the board of directors regarding the advantages of giving one firm a bigger piece of their retirement fund to invest. Drew had spoken with Zelma several times on the phone prior to his presentation to the board, and although she had asked him out to happy hour, each time he had had an excuse not to accompany her. Not only had the Felicia wound not healed, he had never mixed business and pleasure, and he had no intention of breaking his self-imposed rule regarding such a potentially large client.

The first time he'd met Zelma in the lobby of his office, it had taken all his self-control not to ask her out. As they'd made eye contact, the tip of her tongue had slid seductively across the inside of her enticing lips. Without her uttering a word, Drew could tell she was aggressive even before she'd walked into his office and left her business card. He could see it in the way she'd stood self-assured and well polished. The way her shapely body had appeared immodest, even under the blue cashmere suit. Drew could see it in her eyes, which were bawdy while being consummately professional. Her entire being had said, "I can have you if I want you," while her tongue had had no need to say the words.

As he slipped a few files in his briefcase in the event he was not able to make it back, Drew's eyes rested on the picture of him and Felicia on his desk. He had tried to move it so many times before, but never had the strength to follow through. And then it occurred to him that the Felicia he loved would not want him to build a bunker of self-pity. The lady he'd given his heart to would encourage him to live his life to the fullest and not dwell in the past. With those thoughts, Drew slipped on his jacket, placed the framed portrait in his briefcase, snapped the brass locks closed, and turned off the light in his office.

Drew was heading for the door as Grace ended a call and said with her finger extended, still holding the phone receiver, "Ahh, excuse me, Drew! I know you in a rush, but you better tell Ms. *Thing* here something before I have to hurt her feelings."

"Who do you mean? Zelma?"

"Ahh, yeah. She called here yesterday and I told her I gave you her message. And now she just called again and asked, 'Did you give him the messages?' and I said yeah and she said just like this, 'Yeah, right.' Just like that, she said it. 'Yeah right.' She don't know me like that." Grace hung up the phone, put her hand on her hip, swiveled her neck while her extended finger made a tight circle in the air. "I'll hurt girlfriend's feelings. Who she think she is? You better talk to her, Drew."

With a smile Drew looked back as he opened the door. "I'll talk to her. Thanks for telling me."

As Drew put his car in reverse, he saw Peggy run out from the firm waving her hands.

Running up to his door, she asked, "Can you give me a ride down to the repair shop to pick up Walt's car?"

"I'm running late, but jump in," he replied, and cleared a space on the seat.

As she sat down, Peggy buckled up and caught her breath. "I appreciate this. That damn Four Hundred stays in the shop more than the Three Hundred does."

"That's what you all get for buying a Lex. You should have bought a Benz. I tried to tell you," Drew replied, and pulled out of the parking lot.

"So where are you off to, without a client folder? Sneaking out for a little golf, huh?" And then before he could answer she said, "How's Murphy, Renfro and Collins looking?"

"Well, I spoke to the underwriter last week and it looks like we should be ready to deliver the plan and make it all official, if not this week, by the middle of next week."

"Good," she replied, looking out the window and tapping her thumb nervously on her thigh.

"Why? Is everything okay?"

"Everything's fine," she said, still peering out the window, apparently deep in thought.

"Reason I ask is if you need an advance or something, you know—"

"Drew," Peggy said as she looked him in the eye and her thumb paused in its tapping, "I'm okay. I was just checking. Besides, you never answered my question. You got the golf clubs in the trunk?"

"I wish. Today is the day of the reading of the will, and I am not looking forward to it."

"Why not?"

"Peggy, from what I could see at the funeral, these people are dirt-poor," Drew said, putting on his sunglasses. "If she had something and left me anything, it would be too much as far as I'm concerned. I just don't want to walk in there looking like a gold digger or anything."

"Please. Whatever she left you, Drew, you would be disrespecting her memory not to take it. She loved you and she meant for you to have whatever is in the will."

"Thanks, I needed to hear that." And then Drew lowered his voice and said, "You wanna know what my biggest regret was about all of this? Other than never saying goodbye? I bought her a ring about a month after we met. Like I told you, I always knew she would be the one, but I just never found the right time to give it to her. And then there were times when I just didn't think the love was fifty-fifty. One night I remember we were watching this movie and I thought to myself, now would be a good time. So I went to my room and put it on my pinky finger. When I got back in the living room she asked me about a phone number she saw written on the back of a magazine, and within minutes we were arguing. Then I thought I would wait until I got the house and she moved in. Then I thought I would wait until things got a little better at the office. And then it was until we beat the cancer. Well, at the funeral, I kissed her on the forehead and placed the ring in the palm of her hand. Then Drew whispered, "I just guess we ran out of untils."

"That was very nice of you. But I know for a fact that she loved you just as much as you loved her. Trust me, it was always fifty-fifty."

Drew replied in monotone, "How do you know?"

"A woman can tell. I guess it's female intuition. I saw you holding hands. I saw her wiping spaghetti sauce off your face when you all had dinner at my house. Remember that morning she took you to the airport and I happened to be there dropping Walt off for a business trip? I never told you this, but after you all kissed and you walked down the corridor to board the plane, she stood there and watched the airplane take off. We noticed her looking at her watch as if she would be late going to work, but she stood there and watched that plane until it disappeared with her face against the glass like a child. Like a part of her was in that plane. That was when we knew for sure it was love."

Drew sat silent, turned up the radio, and then loosened

the knot in his gold silk tie. He remembered that day and how it had hurt him so much to leave Felicia for just three days. Turning the radio down, he said, "When I checked into the hotel in Chicago, I sat at the desk in the room that night and I knew I was in too deep. Peggy, I never had a woman who could move me the way Felicia could. So I took out one of the hotel envelopes from my desk, removed the petals off the flowers in the suite, and put them in the envelope." Drew rubbed his sweaty palm over the leather-wrapped gearshift and continued. "And then I took my spare house key from my briefcase and put it in the envelope with a yellow Post-it note that read, 'To you I give the key to my heart.' I mailed it that night, and when she opened the letter, she said she started crying at the mailbox. She liked that sort of stuff."

"That was so sweet. You know, when you want, you can be a regular ole Casanova."

"I don't know about that. It was just something about her that brought out the best in me. Once I noticed her trying to apply her makeup and do her hair before we went to see *Beloved*, and I watched from the hallway as she got more and more frustrated because her hair was thinning. She never liked wearing makeup before the illness and was never comfortable applying it. I walked up behind her and said, 'Felicia? Remember that song by Anita, "You Belong to Me"? Well you belong to me, baby. To me you're beautiful. More so now than ever. So sho cares what anyone else thinks? Drew swallowed and continued, "I told her, 'I love you for who you are.' And I think I hurt her feelings, because she started to cry so much we never made it to the theater."

Silence settled as Drew gathered his thoughts. "But the one moment together I will never forget, Peg, is when she was feeling weak from the chemo and the pain medication. When we initially spoke to her oncologist, he mentioned something they refer to in the medical industry as double effect. Basically it meant that you could take drugs for the pain and die faster or not take them and live longer in agony. We chose the former."

After Drew said the words, once again in his soul he questioned whether the decision they'd made had been right. "Anyway, one day I went by her house to see her. Her skin was a little pasty and she looked tired, and her hair by this time had really started falling out. We sat in the backyard on a lawn chair and this cardinal flew over to her bird feeder. She looked at it with a bag of birdseed in her lap and said, 'You know, Drew? God would not put it in that bird's heart to fly south for the winter if it did not exist.' So I said, 'What?' because by this time she would sometimes ramble, especially when she was weak and medicated. So she said it again. 'God would not put it in that bird's heart to fly south if it did not exist.' And then about a half hour later she said, 'Drew, you and I have made so many plans to be together, to have children, to have the type of love affair we both want. We have wanted this so badly.' And then she closed her eyes, leaned her head into my chest, and said, 'So God would not allow us to have these dreams if they were not out there for us, somewhere.' By this point I was about to lose it and then she said, 'I may not be there physically, Drew, but someway, somehow, we will find our south . . . together.' "

After a pause Peggy looked out her window, discretely wiped her lower eyelid, and said, "She was a special lady."

After dropping Peggy at the dealership, Drew glanced at his watch and noticed he was already ten minutes late. As he came to a stoplight, he was ejecting a CD when he heard her voice. It was so clear and distinctive he thought Felicia was in the seat beside him. "Felicia?"

"Drew, I loved you. Don't ever doubt that."

Drew's chest felt full as he gazed forward and said, "Baby, I'm so sorry I never said good-bye. I owed you that much. I love you so much."

"Drew," the voice repeated, "I loved you. Don't ever doubt that."

"Felicia? I miss you I . . . I . . . sometimes I can't breathe it seems. It's been ten weeks and I miss you just as much as I did the day you left. I try, but you're still there. I close my eyes, and I can feel you."

"Enjoy the moment, Drew. Just enjoy the moment." And

then as suddenly as the voice came, the light turned green and it went away.

The closest parking space to the front door was quite a distance away. The April sun bore down hot and Drew walked swiftly across the grass while trying his best not to sweat. Another glance at his watch showed that he was fifteen minutes late. As he stepped inside the overly air-conditioned building, he looked at the directory and caught the closing elevator before its doors met. Although he pressed four, the elevator lowered to the basement, and when the doors opened he saw a familiar face. It was Estella Neal. Felicia's mother. While she and her daughter were never close, Drew had visited their home several times, and before she was always cordial. But on this day when Drew greeted her, she barely said a word.

As the elevator ascended, Drew adjusted his cuffs and straightened his tie, wanting to say something to her to break the tension but not knowing what exactly to say. He wanted to express in a delicate way, "Mrs. Neal, I loved your daughter and I know she loved me. She wanted me to have whatever is up there, but I'll give it to you since she was your child." That was what he wanted to say, but all he could get out as the doors opened was, "Well, I guess this is our floor."

Drew saw those in the conference room smile as Estella walked in, and then they lost that expression as he entered behind her. A what-the-hell-is-he-doing-here look permeated the faces. Drew tilted his head with a smile to the family members he knew and sat close to the door behind the large oak table awaiting the attorney.

The lawyer's paralegal walked into the room, did a silent head count, disappeared back into his office, and then the portly attorney walked out. His hair was salt and pepper and his complexion appeared yellowed. He placed the files at the head of the table, then said, "I am so glad you all could make it here today. First and foremost, as you know, Felicia Neal was not a wealthy person. I should say she was not a wealthy person in material possessions, but she was wealthy in her kindness toward others."

And then he sat gingerly and said, "Let me first introduce myself. My name is Sid Rothstein. I met Felicia at our doctor's office about two months before she passed. And yes, I have cancer as well. Although she was at an advanced stage, I always noticed her trying to keep up the spirits of the other patients. One day we sat down and I shared a sandwich with her and told her what I did for a living. She told me she wanted to put together a will, and I told her I would do it under one condition. That she allow me to do it pro bono. We met several times, and the last time we got together, I visited her at the hospital a week before she left us." The rotund counselor closed his eyes briefly to conceal his pain as his assistant whispered something in his ear and took a piece of paper from him after a pat on the back for consolation.

"I will add," she said, "typically we do not wait this long to disburse the assets from a will, but that was Ms. Neal's decision. As I call off your name, please raise your hand and I will give you the package Ms. Neal has left you. After you have signed this document of receipt, you are free to go." Drew silently held his breath as the assistant said, "Mr. Andrew Patrick Staley?"

"Here," he said, embarrassed to be the first name called. Drew walked toward the front, intent on not making eye contact with anyone else in the room, signed the form, and was given a medium-sized box and a parchment envelope. While he considered it rude to just leave, under the circumstances he felt it best to do so.

As he sat in his car, Drew relaxed his tension-filled body in an attempt to slow the beating of his heart. He closed his eyes as he placed the articles he had received on the passenger seat and started to breathe deeply to gather his composure. He did not know if he was jittery due to the drama of the eyes upon him on the fourth floor, the items in the seat next to him, or the last page of the love story between him and Felicia being finally revealed. But as his pulse slowed, Drew opened his eyes and picked up the box. As he shook it like a Christmas gift, he could identify its contents. Felicia, who was a music buff, had left him a CD.

Backing his car out of the parking spot, Drew thought of Felicia's voice. How she would purr the lyrics to "I love you, I honestly love you," in his ear as they made love. After shifting the car into first gear, Drew managed to open the box and dump its contents on the seat. As the CD fell free, he shook the box to see if there was a note inside, but there wasn't one. Glancing over, he noticed which CD she had left him, and no note was necessary. She had bequeathed to her love her favorite CD. It was her favorite for a number of reason besides the fact that it was the first album her mother had allowed her to listen to as a child. It was the first album she'd learned all the words to by heart. He was the first singer whose *Right On* poster had made it on her wall. And it was the first album that made her not want to have green eyes like her friend Heather, because of the song "Ebony Eyes." The CD she'd left Drew filled him with emotion as he smelled it in the slight hope her scent would have remained. Its title was so appropriate for the moment, *Songs in the Key of Life*.

It was a beautiful day in North Central Florida with just a slight breeze in the air, but Drew was in pain as he drove his car down the highway. He had no idea where he was going, but he knew he could not go back to the firm, nor could he face the memories within the four walls of his home at this time. Driving made him feel closer to Felicia, as if she could see him through the clouds, as if he could touch her one last time. And then he cued up the CD and fast-forwarded to her favorite song. He, too, had always liked the song "As," because it spoke of a love that had no limitations. A love that would last for always. As the song played, Drew sang while his fingers rubbed the envelope she had left him. Her last words to him were inside, and he did not wish to read them on the road, so he turned and headed for their favorite restaurant. The Sovereign.

As he drove to the only spot they had affectionately called their own, he started to tremble as Stevie sang of physically dying, yet leaving a love that would last eternally. Drew shook his head slowly, inhaled to gain his composure, and missed Felicia just a little more.

*   *   *

"Mr. Staley, how are you! Long time no see. How have you been?"

Drew greeted the maître d' at the door with a gracious smile. He had not been in the restaurant for several months, and as he palmed the gentleman's hand with a bill, he was led to his favorite table.

As he sat at the table and spread the linen in his lap, he looked around the restaurant for familiar faces but did not see any. And then he looked at the pond outside the window. Even in the light of day, he could see the red flood lamp at its center, which brought back fond memories. He could see the flamingos nesting at the edge of the rippling waves. In the distance there was a couple having a picnic on the plush lawn. And then from behind him he heard a high-pitched sneeze. "Bless you," he said, and looked around. It was her. The attorney from the firm upstairs, Murphy, Renfro and Collins.

"Thank you," she said with a smile. Even with her fingers in a tepee gesture rubbing her nose, she looked stunning to Drew. She was sitting with an older lady with red hair, and it appeared to be a working lunch. Drew turned back around to stare once again at the lake. A part of him wanted to tell the young lady he had seen her previously upstairs in Murphy, Renfro and Collins, but he could not as he turned his attention back to Felicia. Then he took the parchment letter from his coat pocket and gently laid it on the cream cloth covering the table. In his heart he tried to guess the contents as a couple at another table laughed aloud, but he could not. *What words could she put together to tell me good-bye?* he wondered. *To describe what the relationship had meant to her?*

Then as he looked over the flicker of the candle flame, it was as if he saw her walking his way. She appeared as graceful as ever and sat at their table in the same chair she had sat in so many times before. Drew's lips curled into a smile as she gazed at him with an it's-going-to-be-all-right look. There were so many words Drew wanted to say to her but could not, so he just enjoyed her presence one last time. The young couple across from him laughed out loud and then said, "Sorry" to the others in the restaurant as Drew smiled at them and then back at the love he had lost. She was wearing a white halter top, which he had bought for her in Cancún, and the antique pearls she loved to wear. Her color had returned and her auburn hair danced over her eyebrows. And in her eyes was a look Drew had not seen since their first visit to the oncologist. In her hazel eyes there was a childlike glint, an excitement, that had always made him weak before. Drew leaned back in the padded chair and was diverted by the waitress taking his drink order. When his eyes returned to her chair, just as on the day she'd left this earth, he was once again alone.

Drew's ring finger slowly traced a valentine over the envelope in front of him. *So this is how it ends,* he thought, wanting to open it so badly, but scared to death to do so because when he read these last words he knew that would be the last note of their song. The couple blurted out yet another laugh and the young lady looked at the other patrons with her palm extended apologetically as Drew smiled at her and then felt the object inside the envelope. As he pressed more firmly, he could tell it was a key. When the waitress returned with his mineral water and asked if he would like to order lunch, Drew told her he wasn't ready yet. Instead he opened the envelope.

Dearest Andrew:

I'm certain you never knew I did this and I had no idea that I would do it until I had this dream and the next day I met the attorney who gave you this package. In case you're wondering, I'm returning the key to your heart. For some reason it never worked for me.

Drew, this is the toughest thing I have ever done in my life, but I could not leave this world without you knowing exactly how I felt. I lived a lie for so much of my life, I sometimes forgot what the truth was or how it felt.

Remember when I used to ride around looking for a house with your mother? Remember how you told me about the affair she had with the neighbor next door and how it made you feel? Well, on my rides with her we spent a lot of time talking about our feelings, and the more I got to know her, the more she would open up. She had tremendous feelings for your father. She adored him in so many ways. But she did not love him, as you well know. She lived a lie his entire life, and while she never said it, I think a part of her regretted never being honest with him. I must say, Drew, that I had feelings for you too. But I have never truly loved you. Not the way I wanted to love you. Not the way I pretended to love you. Not the way you deserved to be loved.

Why am I doing this? I could never tell you this face-to-face. I found the ring you bought me and I am so happy you never put me in a position to say no. There was one night I just knew you were going to ask me, and when you returned with it on your pinky, I did everything I could to push you away. Maybe I should have just told you then. As I dictate this to the nurse, I am thinking I should have had the guts to tell you all of this in person. In not doing so I guess I have failed you once again.

In a few minutes you will be coming up to visit me, so I should wrap this up now.

Drew, I must leave this world with a clear conscience. What we had was special. But I lived a lie. I can't allow myself to die with one.

Whatever it is you search for, my love, I hope you find it.

Until . . .
Felicia

After he finished reading the letter, Drew was bewildered. It appeared as though a veil had been dropped over his eyes as everything momentarily went black and he felt dizzy. He read it once again looking for a hidden meaning, but it only intensified the pain. His mouth was dry, although he did not think to drink from the water glass. All he wanted was air and to get out of the restaurant. Standing up wobbly-kneed, he took a bill from his wallet without looking at the denomination and left it on the table as the young attorney from upstairs asked with concern in her voice, "Excuse me, are you all right?" Drew looked at her and wanted to at least nod his head yes, but did not have the energy as he walked past his waitress and the maître d' out the door.

Once outside, he leaned on someone's car, feeling nauseated. His nostrils flared with emotion. He put his hands on his waist and walked toward his car in the distance as a patron of the restaurant looked at him and said something to her companion.

As Drew sat on the hot tan leather, he left the door of the car open. *How could she do this? She had a chance to leave me her last words, and this is what she did?*

Drew looked on the seat beside him and saw the orange and brown *Songs in the Key of Life* CD. *This can't be happening,* he thought. *This cannot be happening.* And then Drew turned on the ignition, ejected the CD from the stereo, popped it in the CD case, and placed it on the ground. As he put his car in reverse, he heard the plastic shatter and he drove away.

CHAPTER 16

‡

Thursday, two weeks later

Betty could close her eyes and see the pieces of the puzzle coming together in the case. Renfro had announced in their last meeting that another offer had been tendered for twenty-five million, but the partners felt they should hold out for a minium of fifty. He'd also indicated that he doubted the case would see the light of day in the courtroom. While he did not need to say the words, she knew part of the reason they expected the offer to double was because of the notes she'd followed up on in the file which had led her to the numerous cases that had been settled previously. Yet the hospital had taken no corrective measures to assure the acts would not occur again.

Betty opened her desk drawer for a pen and then removed her glasses as she noticed the three keys given to her by Evander. She had left them by mistake in the office, and as she picked them up they brought back fond memories. They took her to a time when she'd felt special. When she'd felt as if she was the only thing that mattered in his life. When he'd returned from Orlando and brought her lunch. The special date they had spoken of ended up being egg foo yung with plastic silverware on a beach towel on the floor of her office. He'd told Betty that since he had missed so much time from work and Mr. Ferguson was taking his family on vacation, he had to work a couple of double shifts.

Since she was putting in extra hours, Betty did not feel she was in a position to ask for more time, yet she missed his touch.

Then one night he made an impromtu visit around midnight, and after they had sex he immediately left, which was very uncommon for him. During the act, not once did he say *I love you*, not once did he look her in the eye. Hearing the front door open, she turned the large knob with the *H* on it in her shower as far right as it could go. Stepping inside the stall, Betty heard his truck's engine fade into the night, taking him with it. Leaning against the cold onyx tile, she heaved gasps of the dank air deep into her lungs. So many emotions begged to flow, yet she would not allow them. She was determined to be strong. But as hot steam covered the bathroom like a London fog, a tear fell. Betty slid down the tile, and as she sat on the floor with the water pelting her body, her forehead resting on her knees, she felt for the first time completely out of control. She had encountered her biggest fear. She loved this man. There was no denying it. But if he loved her, how could he do what he had just done? How could he take her body so savagely? How could he not say the words he had spoken to her before? How could he make her feel as if a part of her had been raped? Not physically, but a part of her that hurt so much more. This man whom she'd begged herself not to love had conquered her heart, and she was defenseless against anything he wanted to do to her.

A tap on the door pulled Betty from her trance.

"Wake up! I caught you daydreaming," Carol said as she stood in the doorway. "Hon, have I got the lowdown for you!" Betty smiled as Carol closed her door, beaming with fresh gossip. "But first you gotta swear this goes no farther than this room!" Before Betty could utter a word, Carol said, "I was just downstairs with Patsy. You know, Burt Collins's secretary? She told me that she couldn't stand working for the man and then she just started rattling off things about him. About how he treats his wife and all, which to me was irrelevant. So then I asked her what he thought about you. And guess what she said. She said she overheard Collins and Murphy discussing this case months ago when you were working on Lopez, and they picked you because they wanted you to deliver the summation. The strategy they're going to use is to allow Renfro or one of the other attorneys to go in there and fight with the opposition and then allow you to smile and be the good guy in the summation to the jury. So in answer to your question, darling, you got this case on your merit. It had nothing to do with color or anything else. They could have picked several of the other female attorneys here, but they chose you because you are the best and they know it!"

Betty smiled softly as thoughts of Evander churned in her mind and then said, "Thanks. I appreciate that."

As the phone rang Carol said, "I thought you would," and then exited the office to her desk. Over the speakerphone, she said, "Betty? Line two-oh-three."

Betty lunged for the phone. *Be Evander, be Evander, be Evander.* "Hello, this is Ms. Robinson."

"Hey, girl. That Negro called yet?"

"No," Betty said to Jacqui, "but actually I haven't thought about him all day."

"Whatever."

"Seriously. Girl, I have been too involved with this case to deal with him and his games."

"Uh-huh, like I said before. Whatever. I know you, Betty. You can't pull that on me," she said as she bit into what sounded like a piece of fruit. "So is he still in town?"

"Yes," Betty replied quietly as she walked over to close her office door. She then sat on her desk and eased off her shoes. "I called him yesterday and we talked for about five minutes, but he said he was too busy at work and that he would call me as soon as things slowed down a little. Well, he didn't call, so I phoned him last night at home, but he was talking to his mom. Before you start, yeah, I know. He said he would call me back and that's the last time I spoke to him."

"Umm. So you think he's got something else going on?"

"Jac, to be completely honest with you, I don't know. And I really don't care anymore. I mean we've had our fun and I've got too much going on in my life to allow this man to get inside my head right now. I just wish if he has changed his mind about all of this that he would at least have the balls to tell me."

"Betty, let me tell you something about men. They don't think like us, so no, if he didn't want a relationship, he would not just come out and tell you. See, men are just put together differently. I think deep inside they mean well, but they are all dogs, and I don't mean that in a negative way. They are just . . . different. And we keep expecting them to react like a woman with a penis, and that ain't gonna happen."

"I know, I know, I know," Betty said, wanting to change the subject as she looked down at her dangling feet. "So did you ever hear from that Harry guy?"

"No, and I don't plan on hearing from him either. Tell me something. And I need you to be honest with me, okay?"

"Yes, I do," Betty whispered as she closed her eyes and answered Jacqui's question before it was asked.

"Damn, you know me too well. Well, girl, if you really and truly love this man, and you feel it in your heart, what are you gonna do? What is it worth to you?"

"I don't know. That's the problem. I just don't know what I'm gonna do. I mean I sit here and for five minutes I think of ways to break it off and then the next ten minutes I think of ways to win him back."

"So you do think he has something on the side."

After a pause Betty replied with a long sigh, "Not really, I don't know. I mean the more I think about it, things started to change after I got this case. And I try to look at it from his point of view. I was hardly ever there during the Lopez case, and what do I do? I go out and get a bigger case."

"Betty? Don't do this."

"Do what?"

"Don't do what you're doing. Don't blame yourself for what this asshole is doing. I mean he knew you were an attorney from day one. You don't have a nine-to-five job, and cases like this one come with the territory. He knew what he was getting into, so if he's that petty, then he's got a problem, not you. But don't blame yourself for what this jerk is doing!"

"I'm not, Jac. Trust me, I'm not. But you do have to look

at both sides of the problem, and I think it takes two to tango. I mean it would be easy just to say he's a dog, but I believe there's more to it than that."

"Well, tell me this. Deep in your heart . . . do you really think—"

"I used to. Now I'm not so sure anymore."

"Used to what?"

Betty held her breath and then said, "Used to think he loved me."

"Damn, you do know me too well."

"I mean he acts the same . . . but different. Know what I mean? Seems like he's just going through the paces sometimes."

"Are you sure all of this changed when you got the case? Or was it after you told him you loved him?"

Betty gazed at the carpet, not wanting to answer the question. The question that had kept her awake the previous night.

"Well, anyway, girl, do you think it's worth salvaging? And if so, what are you willing to do to keep him?"

As Betty opened her mouth to answer, Carol said over the intercom, "Miss Robinson, Renfro on two-oh-four."

"Thanks, Carol. One second, okay?" Betty said as she eased from her desk and put on her shoes. "Jacqui? Dear, I got a call coming through. Can I call you back later?"

"You know where I'll be. But before you hang up. Could you just answer my question?"

Betty stood in front of the window and looked down on the people walking below as she said to her best friend, "I'll do whatever it takes to keep him. Okay?"

" 'Bye, sweetie."

Gathering her composure, Betty said, "Hello Mr. Renfro. How can I help you?"

"Yes, Robinson. I would like to discuss a few points with you on the case. Would you grab your files?"

Betty reached for the files in her bottom drawer as the case momentarily chased the thoughts of her love life from the forefront of her mind.

*   *   *

As Betty drove home with a box full of files to go through, she had a firm grasp on the case and felt that if the rumors were in fact true, she could not wait to give the summation. Stopping at a red light, she reached into her purse for her phone and dialed it without looking down. "Yes, this is Betty. Is Evander there? Thanks, I'll hold." As she held the phone to her ear she had no idea what she was going to say. But as he said hello the light turned green and she knew she had to say something. "So how are you?" she said in the driest tone she could muster.

"Fine. Beep, I'm sorry I didn't get a chance to call you back last night. I kinda fell asleep. I had to be in here this morning at four."

"Oh, that's fine." she droned. "So. How's your mom doing?"

"My mom? Oh, my mom's okay. Same old story. Jo running her crazy with those kids of hers and her sorry husband and also Shawn."

"Evander? We really need to talk."

"About . . ."

"About us."

"What about *us*?"

Betty did not want to get emotional. This was not a card she was going to give him the benefit of seeing. But she needed answers. "Evander, things have changed. And I know you know what I'm talking about. We hardly touch each other anymore. We never talk like we used to. I mean if there is someone else, Vander, trust me, you can tell me," she said with a smile in her voice and fear in her heart that he would do just that. "I'm a big girl. I can take it."

"Betty . . . Betty, if the truth be known, there is no one else in my life. I know things have changed and I can see that we don't act the same around each other either. I would be willing to say it's all my fault. But half the time I would call you and we would discuss the doctors in your lawsuit or we would discuss what Collins said or Renfro did, and while I want to be a part of all of that, in all honesty, Beep, I miss what *we* were. What *we* had the weeks before you got this case. Seems we grew so much closer after Lopez, and as soon as you got the big case . . ."

"We started growing apart," Betty whispered.

"Betty, there is no one else. I would never do that to you. My love has grown too deep and wide and I respect you too much to ever do that. You know, we have not really kissed since that day we were in your office? I mean, I always feel I am talking to the attorney and not the woman I fell in love with, and it's scary, especially after what happened with Yolanda. Her career sorta broke us up. Don't get me wrong, I know it's a package deal and I do love to hear about what you are doing at the firm. But, Beep, I love you."

"Evander, please don't say that if it's not true."

"Aww, Beep. Baby, you know I love you. But I'm sorry. I fell *in* love with *you*, not the attorney. The *you* that can't tell jokes to save your life. The *you* that always hides those stuffed animals under the bed when I come over. That's the Betty I miss, and since this is going to be a trial that will last at least six months, I guess subconsciously I was preparing not to see her for a while."

"Evander?"

"Yes?"

"I'm sorry. I know that's not what you are asking from me, but I should have been more conscientious of your feelings. I just get so wrapped up in my work, and since I have never . . . well, since I have never loved a man like I love you, it's hard for me to walk that tightrope sometimes. It seems the more of you you give, the more I need. Facing Amitrust or Midway is cake. Knowing how to love you . . . well, that's the part that's hard for me."

"I know, baby. This is new to both of us."

"Do me a favor? If you are ever feeling neglected again, please, just tell me? Okay?"

There was silence on the phone and then Evander said softly, "Thank you. And I love you too."

After another long conversation with Evander on the phone at home, Betty worked on the case until the early morning. As the clock struck one, she closed the last file, and returned it to the box from which it had come, and went on-line to check her E-mail.

She had been corresponding with the gentleman she knew only by the moniker DLastRomeo for several weeks and was fascinated by the fact that he, unlike most men on-line, never asked her for her phone number or tried to flirt with her. He seemed to actually enjoy conversing, and if something was important to her, he acted interested in it. As she signed on, she heard the computer say, "You've got mail," and a smile came to her face as she saw it was a letter from him.

 Hello, DeltaDream:

> Thanks for replying to my last letter so quickly. I just wanted to write to say it was refreshing to visit with you on-line. So often I notice that people have forgotten what a friend is as it relates to the opposite sex. I am glad to consider you a friend and it is my sincere hope that I can be a true friend to you as well.
>
> Today was a tough day for me. As I may have mentioned, I own a financial planning firm. I closed a deal with this law firm and found out today they were exercising their right of recession. That's when a company backs out of a contract.

Betty laughed for the first time in hours. *He still doesn't know I'm an attorney. How cute.*

> Well, they did not call me to tell me. They did not write me to tell me. They did it by fax at four-fifty on the tenth day. We were ten minutes from earning a substantial commission, and nine months of work went down the drain with a simple four-line faxed letter.
>
> Unfortunately in this state when that occurs you don't get a percentage or even a referral fee. You just get . . . well, I guess you catch my drift.
>
> So today I called to talk to the senior partner and he would not come to the phone. He just had his secretary tell me the firm was not interested and that they expected their check for the initial de-

posit to be returned within thirty days. The senior partner is a trip. If I told you how far this
idiot has advanced in this firm, you would never believe it.

"An idiot partner? Trust me, I can believe it," Betty said
aloud.

I called a few friends in my industry for advice
and found out he took the plan we spent so much time
working on to our competitor. In fact, he told the
other financial planner he wanted the exact same
program I had presented to him. They drew it up for
him in less than two hours and stole the commission
we had worked so hard for over the past nine months.
    I'm sorry to get so deep in this letter because I
usually contact you to keep my mind off work, and
I know I sound bitter. But to be honest, I have
been consumed by this situation. These are things
they don't teach you in business school. Well,
anyway . . .
    I appreciate your prayers, and yes, I have gotten
over the reading of the will. Yeah, it got to me,
but I must move on. I guess it is not for me to know
the whys of it at this point. I just trust that one
day I will.

Thinking of you . . .
Until . . .
Drew

In spite of the tone, Drew's letters always had a way of
brightening her day. This day in particular she needed to
hear from him. Betty wanted to reply immediately, but she
knew if she did, she would go into detail over either her
problems with Evander or her fears regarding the case, and
neither was an issue she wanted to revisit. So she turned
off her computer and desk lamp and went to bed.

CHAPTER 17

‡

Friday

Drew walked through the door of his home to find the answering machine winking at him. It had been over two weeks since the reading of the will, and he had spent his non-working hours on the golf course to keep the demons at bay. Unfortunately, he saw little improvement in his golf swing, and the whys were never far from his thoughts.

The third message was from Zelma. He had given her his home phone number to stop the friction in the office surrounding her calls. The more they talked—although he knew he should not have personal conversations with her—the more he became intrigued by her. She was even more intelligent, more driven, and more opinionated than he'd initially realized. Her postgraduate studies had been at Oxford, and she spoke three languages fluently. Even though they spoke after hours, Drew built a wall in their conversation and never divulged much of his personal life. And then one Friday night, the first Friday night he had not visited Felicia's graveside, he'd shared the intensity of his pain. He'd told Zelma how he'd felt blindsided by Felicia's letter and that there was a part of him he felt could never fully trust again.

Sitting on his couch, Drew clicked on the television, muted the sound, then picked up the phone and called Zelma. "Hello," he said when she answered, "What's up?"

"Nothing much. I just got this damn satellite dish installed, and now instead of surfing through forty channels of shit I don't wanna see, now I surf through two hundred and fifty. What are you up to?"

"Just got in. Had a couple of appointments cancel, so I took the sticks out and played a little golf," Drew said as he looked at Felicia's graduation portrait on the mantel over his fireplace.

"Good for you. You need to get out for some fresh air every now and then. We'll have to play together sometime. Maybe I can teach you a thing or two."

"Oh, it's like that, huh?" Drew said with a smile.

"Seriously. I'm a scratch golfer, you know. I have to be to compete with these white boys. After taking their money, for some reason they always take me more seriously in the office. Funny how that works."

"Umm." Drew walked in his kitchen and popped the top of a beer.

"The only problem with my work is you never develop true friends. I mean they invite you to golf and drinks, but you can never really let your hair down and all. Ya know?"

"Yeah, that can cause a problem at times. I remember how it was for me when I was in corporate America. I think I'm in a good position now, though. We never really have that problem, for obvious reasons."

"I always wondered why you just hired black women. Is that why? And why are they all so young?"

Returning to his couch and clicking off the TV, Drew said, "Well, Peggy's in her midforties, but I was never really worried about that. I just wanted the most qualified people, and that's what they were."

"My ex-fiancé's brother tried that. Hired three sisters and a brother in his paint company. It was just a small company and they robbed him blind."

"So you were engaged? How long ago?"

Zelma's normally assertive voice weakened as she said, "Last summer."

"May I ask what happened?"

"No!" And then after a pause he heard a smile in her voice as she said, "Yeah, I guess I can tell you. Although I must admit, I really don't like talking about it too much. To make a long story short, he and I met on a blind date. When I first saw him, I was not attracted to him at all. He was a little goofy sometimes. But he was nice and I had been in a relationship with this guy who was verbally abusive. Then from almost out of nowhere, I started having feelings for Vince—that was his name. Our relationship was the closest thing to magic I have ever experienced. In three months we were talking about a future together. Within six months I moved in with him. Within nine months he gave me a ring and we were planning a wedding, and then on my birthday we had this fight." She paused and continued over a sigh, "I can't believe I'm telling you this. But he put me out of the house . . . and it was raining that day. Well, I saw him about a month later and he was dating one of my friends who just happened to be white."

"Damn."

"Yeah, I know. It was messed up, and yeah, it stung a lot. Sometimes very smart women make very dumb decisions, and I made more than my share about men. But I will never make the same mistake again. You just try to get over it. Like the other night when you were talking about your girlfriend? Felicia? And I was telling you to stay strong? That's where that was coming from."

"Do you still love him? Deep inside?"

"I have feelings for him. He was my first mature love. I don't wish him any harm or anything, but do I love him? No, I don't. I mean, if he came back tomorrow, would I take him back? After what he did to me? Never."

"Seems you have healed very well."

"I don't know about very well, but I've healed. Now you tell me. If by chance Felicia was here today, after all that had happened to you, would you take her back?"

Walking in his living room, Drew stood front and center before Felicia's portrait and looked her in the eyes.

"The truth, Andrew. I know you *The Man* and all, but if you could, would you take her back?"

Holding the phone in place with his shoulder and folding his arms in slow motion, he said, "We didn't have a fairy-tale romance. We had good times. We had a lot of good times actually. When I think back on the relationship and the time we spent together, I guess I loved her a lot more than I even would like to admit now. You know," he said, staring into the eyes of the portrait, "when we first got together, I used to get up at six to get dressed for work. But whenever she slept over, I would get up at five-thirty, just so I could watch her sleep." It was the first time Drew had ever told that to anyone, and for a moment he regretted doing so. But there was something about saying the words that was cleansing. "Was our relationship magical? I don't think so, especially when you look at the last couple of years. Often, even before she was diagnosed, she would get jealous and accuse me of doing things. We would fight about the time I devoted to the relationship. I know I loved her. And in spite of the problems we had, she should not have done me the way she did." Drew reached for the portrait on the mantel, wiped off the glass, and then walked toward the hall closet, where he placed the picture on the top shelf and closed the door. "So to answer your question? No. No, if I knew what I know now, I would not take her back."

"Did someone come over?"

"No. Why you ask?"

"Just sounded like I heard a door close."

With a smile Drew said, "You did. In more ways than one, love. Tell me something? I have an idea that might be good for both of us. What if we go on a date. Not the kinda date where a kiss is expected or anything like that. Just two friends. Just a get-out-and-get-over-our-past kinda date."

With a smile in her voice Zelma said, "I think that would be nice. Why don't we go to see the Philharmonic. I think I could get us a couple of fantastic—"

"Wait a minute," Drew said, looking at his fireplace. "I'll plan this."

"Oh my goodness."

"Oh my goodness what?"

"Just the way you said that. We ain't going hunting or fishing or something southern, are we? I know how you southern boys are."

"Damn, you tried me that time."

"So how should I dress?"

"Very casual. As in shorts and sneakers."

"You have *got* to be kidding me. I haven't worn sneakers on a date since I was sixteen. And that was only because my momma made me."

"I kid you not. And I will pick you up tomorrow around noon. We'll make it an all-day thing. Okay?"

"That's no good."

"Why not?"

"You must not know many professional black women, Andrew. If you did, you'd know that Saturday is National Get Your Hair Done day. That's out."

"Do it earlier."

"You're serious, aren't you?"

"I'll meet you at your house tomorrow at four. What's the address?"

"Andrew Staley, if I have to reschedule my hair appointment for *youuuu*, believe me, this date better be the bomb."

As he drove up her driveway, Drew took a deep breath and looked in the mirror. While he had made the phone calls to arrange everything for their date, he had debated with himself about following through with this, but as she opened the door he knew he was doing the right thing. Her smile was different as she walked outside and the sun beamed on her chocolate brown skin. Although her hair was tied up in a wrap and she wore khaki shorts with a Karl Kani T-shirt and hiking boots, it was her smile that was the biggest difference in Zelma McGrady. It was not the smile of a senior comptroller. It was a smile that said, *Thank you for being a friend.*

"So," she said after getting into his car. "Where are we off to?"

Without breaking eye contact, Drew said, "You look . . . beautiful."

Zelma smiled as she checked him out as well. "Don't make me blush; besides you ain't looking too bad yourself, Mr. Staley. So tell me, where are we going? Tell me! Tell me! Tell me!"

"First do me a favor. Put your finger in your mouth."

"Put my what in my what?" she said, and tilted her head down. "See, I knew you were some kinda closet freak, Andrew!"

With a laugh Drew said, "Come on, just do it." When she did so and removed it quickly while staring at him suspiciously, he said, "Okay, now put it in the air."

"Oh, that's so cute," she said, catching on to what he was doing. "It's blowing, ah, thataway," she said, pointing to the left of her house. Drew put the car in reverse and they headed in the direction of the wind to start their date.

"You must excuse my wrap, but I couldn't squeeze another day out of this hair. I called Marcel and he'll see me tomorrow, so you're in luck."

Drew smiled as he put on his tortoiseshell Ray-Bans, and then he felt Zelma's full lips on his cheek.

"I just had to do that. Thanks for getting me out of the house and being so sweet. And besides, now all the pressure is off. We've kissed and now we can just enjoy our date. Right?"

"Right," Drew said, smiling more on the inside than he displayed on the outside.

"Tell me something," Drew said, and inserted a CD. "How often do you think about him?"

"Vince? All the time, that's all. But I'm getting better. It's been less than a year since we broke up, and you know, I used to cry every time I saw a green Camry like his. You know, there are a lotta green Camrys out there. I could just see her in it with her blond hair blowing out the window and him grinning and stuff, but I got over that. It takes time, but you'll get over what's-her-face too. I now look at the relationship and try to learn as much as I can from it. But to be honest . . . it still stings a little."

"If Felicia taught me anything, she reminded me of something my dad told me years ago. He told me you get what you got. I hate to say it, but people don't change. I saw a lot of things I did not necessarily like in her and I tried to overlook them. She was often selfish, mean-spirited, and downright nasty at times, but I tried to make her the woman I wanted her to be. Looking back now, maybe that's why she decided to hurt me the way she did. Maybe because I wanted her to change."

"That's not true. Andrew, I've listened to you talk about her, and I think she probably loved you more than you know, but what she did didn't make sense. She was bitter. Point-blank." Zelma spoke with her hands as if she were giving a presentation. "She was bitter because she got dealt a bad hand and decided to leave this world with a bang. I don't really know you that well, but from what I do know of you, I know you did not deserve to be treated like that."

Drew stared down the road and turned the volume down on the song "I'd Do Anything and Everything to Fall in Love." "Tell me something? Do you still see his face whenever you hear a love song? That's my biggest fear. Whenever I hear a love song . . . I'll always see her. She'll always be there."

After driving an hour, Drew slowed the car in the middle of the two-way road, and Zelma immediately looked back for traffic. "What are you doing?" she questioned with a smile of anticipation.

"This is where we will have our date."

Looking up and down the deserted stretch of highway, Zelma said, "On the side of a highway? There's nothing out here but trees and . . . See, I knew you were gonna take me on a country-boy date. You got moonshine back here or something, don't you?"

"Don't tell me," Drew said, turning off the road. "With that attitude you *must* be a New Yorker. Right?"

"Born in Jamaica, Queens, and you might not want to forget it. Hey, where are you going!" Zelma asked, laughing as they drove through an open gate down a bumpy path through the woods. "Andrew, where are we going! I'm serious! Wait a minute! Wasn't Ted Bundy from Florida?"

"You're sick," Drew said, laughing. "Just lean back, love, and enjoy the ride."

Drew continued driving for about a mile through the thicket until they reached a clearing with a large oak tree at its center. Beneath the oak was a picnic basket, and tied to the tree was a large brown and white mare.

"Oh no. Andrew, this is," she said, forming a circle with her lips, "too much. How did you get the horse out here? And what about the picnic basket? Are those fresh flowers on the ground beside it, and how did you know which direction the wind would be blowing, and how—"

"Zelma? Please hush," Drew said, looking at the expression on her face. "I just knew you had been putting in a lot of hours and so I wanted to get you away from the rat race and all. Give you time to just lie out under a tree and relax for a few hours and catch your breath. Is that okay?"

Looking Drew in the eyes, she leaned toward him and kissed him on the jaw. A pinky's width from his lips she said, "You really don't know how much this means to me."

"You're welcome." And then Drew took her hand and whispered, "I have only one request for today, okay? This is a date for two *friends*. Therefore, Vince and Felicia are not invited. Deal?"

"You know, Andrew, you are so amazing."

First Drew showed Zelma all the items he had packed for their day together. He had even brought the imported white seedless grapes and smoked Gouda cheese she'd mentioned in one of their conversations that she liked so much, and a bottle of her favorite white wine. Drew mounted the horse, then reached down and pulled her up in front of him. As they rode, she leaned into his chest a little more than she had to, and he squeezed her much closer than was necessary. The field was lush, the wind gently blew the tall stalks of grass, and the only sight on the horizon was a Winslow Homer–like burnt orange barn in the distance.

After the ride, Drew and Zelma returned to the clearing, ate lunch, and talked about their dreams, their ambitions, and their goals. Never did comments surrounding their past relationships come to the table, and it was not as difficult to keep the ghosts away as either of them had expected.

"You know what?" Zelma said from her place on the blanket as she ate grapes and looked up at the green leaves of the large, oak tree. "I have never done anything like this in my life. I mean where I grew up, you saw this as something people only do in movies." She paused and looked at Drew before adding, "That was the first time I rode a horse. Could you tell?"

"Yeah, and I got the fingernail marks in my wrist to prove it."

"Stop lying," she laughed. "Seriously, though, thanks for bringing me out here, and thanks for *not* telling me where we were going, because I would have most definitely thought of an excuse not to show up." She stopped chewing as she looked up at the clouds above. "You know what I miss most about a relationship?"

"What?"

"Having someone there. Not in a sexual way or necessarily at my house or what have you, because except for those few weeks with Vince, I have been on my own since I was seventeen. I mean not having someone to call and check in with if you are going to make it home late and all. Usually," she said, sliding a grape between her lips, "when we find out we have to work late at the office, everybody is complaining and running to the phone to rearrange their plans or contact sitters. You know what I do? I don't want to be left out, so sometimes I call my house just to check my messages. And sometimes I don't even have any damn messages," she said with a melancholy tone in her voice. "One time I had car trouble out on I-75 headed here from Atlanta. A fan belt or something, I think. It was past midnight and my cell was not working for some reason. I was about five miles from the next exit and I wasn't about to hitch a ride. So I walked to a hotel back at the last exit. By the time I got there, I was exhausted. I was sweaty and had broken both of my heels. My hair was standing on end, and of course, I get to the counter and the clerk who helped me asked what happened. When I told him, he said, 'Well, ma'am, here's a phone. Would you like to call someone to let them know you are okay?' He was just being nice, but, Drew, I almost lost it on the spot. I couldn't think of one . . . damn . . . person to call."

"It's tough," he said after a pause. "It's real tough at times. But it will make you appreciate the good times when they come along, I guess."

Zelma shook her head, looked at Drew, and said, "I'm

sorry. I don't know why I went there. I just wanted to say thanks for what you did for me today. I needed this."

"You're welcome. Well, we have a couple of hours left of sunlight," Drew said, looking up at the sky and inhaling the brisk air surrounding them. "What would you like to do?"

His mind immediately went to sex, but Zelma dug her toes into the soft grass, put the ball back in his court, and said, "No, you have done an okay job with this date-planning thing. I'll let you make the call."

"Let's go back to my place," Drew said before he could pull back the words. And then he softened it by adding, "I rented *Love Jones* from Blockbuster and I have to take it back tomorrow."

"Okay," Zelma said with a smile. "That sounds like a plan."

As they walked through the door, Drew went to his answering machine to check for messages. As he glanced from his kitchen to see Zelma admiring his decor, he was torn between offering her a glass of tea and a movie or a taste of wine in front of the fireplace. When she asked him about his music collection, he answered her question and thought, *It's the only way to get over her. It's the only way I can get on with my life.*

"I like your place, Drew. I never knew you were into both Biggie Smalls and acid jazz, and are those Annie Lee prints?"

"Yes," he said from the kitchen where he was pouring two glasses of wine. "I picked them up at an exhibit last year. Do you like?"

"Impressive. Your house looks warm. Not like a bachelor pad."

"Well, what were you expecting, bean bags and a big pool table in the living room or something?"

Zelma exclaimed, "Damn, Andrew, you have a screened-in pool? Man, I'm in the wrong line of work."

"This is for you," he said, walking up behind her with a glass of Chardonnay. Zelma turned toward him slowly, moved aside his hand holding the drink, and kissed him. This kiss was anything but a friendship kiss and was much more than anything they had shared before. When their lips parted he held the wineglass softly in his cupped hand between two fingers, and rocked it to a swirl before he blindly placed it on the end table. After a brief pause to heighten the moment, he then wrapped his arms around her and returned the kiss with passion.

"Andrew?" she said, breaking away a moment and looking into his eyes. "What about the movie?"

"Saw it before. They fall in love in the end," Drew said, and leaned her back to reclaim her lips. He felt Zelma shake as he moved his hands from her back, grazed her erect nipple, and then held her face gently.

As he did so, Zelma looked down and whispered, "Andrew, do you think you're ready for this? I mean, seriously. Let's not start something we can't finish. Do you really think you're ready to take this step?"

"Yes," he said, and kissed her sweetly on her forehead. "I want to be with you. I want to hold you. I want to be held by you." Then he grasped her face and looked back and forth at each of her eyes. "Zelma. Zelma, you have done more for me in the past couple of days than I thought anyone could do. I had so many doubts about myself, but you've helped me find something in me I thought was lost. Do you know how long it has been since I've even poured two glasses of wine? I know I'm ready for this. I just hope you are."

As she moved back from Drew, Zelma smiled, took off her shoes, and headed for the pool area. When she did so, Drew went into the kitchen to retrieve some items to make their encounter unforgettable. He and Felicia had made love in the same pool on many occasions, and if he was to weed her out of his mind, he was now convinced that this was the evening to take a giant step toward doing so.

Zelma bounced on her toes in the pool. Then the lights went out and the pool area was completely darkened. "Andrew," Zelma said with expectation in her voice as she heard the clinking of glass, "what are you up to?"

Drew stood silently at the head of the pool, watching Zelma as waves of expectation rushed through his body and moonlight cut across the water like a razor. From the silence came the rip of a match being struck and its accompanying blaze. The illumination pierced the darkness with a red flame which turned to orange, then to yellow, but remained blue at its base. Drew lit the tip of a candle and sheltered its burn by cupping his hand around it as he walked and set it at the pool's corner. He then repeated the action and set the next candle at the opposite end of the water. Feeling her eyes upon him, Drew paused and glanced back at his guest. As he smiled at her, his heart pumped faster and he could feel sensations inside that left goose bumps on his forearms. He moved to the head of the pool and brought the fire close to a large candle. Zelma watched him intently as he slowly brought the heat to the wick without breaking eye contact with her. Realizing what was missing to make the moment even more special, he abruptly walked away.

"Hey! Hey, Andrew! What's up! Where you going?" Zelma called.

There was silence in the house until music flowed from the speakers surrounding the pool like honey from its comb. Drew returned to the pool to find Zelma with her eyes closed. As he sang the lyrics to "Do Me Baby" Zelma opened her eyes and said, *"On se plaire fera moi?"*

"Cute, but I told you my college French was rusty."

Closing her eyes again, she said over the music, "I said, you *enjoy* torturing me like this, don't you?"

"Yes," he replied. "How can you tell?" And then Drew pulled out his belt and allowed his pants to settle at his feet. The clink of his buckle was heard as it hit the concrete, and Zelma looked at him as he pulled his shirt over his head, exposing his rippled stomach, and tossed it aside. While inside his excitement stirred, it was not shown on his face as he eased into the pool, never breaking eye contact with her. Drew swam toward the middle of the pool, and with every stroke he felt himself want her more. Wanting to hold her and stroke her and feel her caress over his body. He knew inside if this night was memorable, it could obliterate some of the haunting memories of the past.

"Damn, baby, damn," Zelma purred. "Andrew, what are you doing to me?"

As he got closer to her, Drew's head disappeared underwater.

"Andrew? What are you doing? Why are you under—"

And then Drew softly allowed his kiss to glide from the top of her foot up to her knee over her thigh until it rested at the center of her white silk panties. He could feel her tense body relax as he softly kissed her twice in the same spot and then slid his elongated kiss up to her navel and between her cleavage. His tongue followed the soft lines of her neck under her jaw and ended on her lips. He held her body close to his as the bitter months of confusion and frustration dissipated.

"Damn, baby, damn," Zelma repeated. "If that's the appetizer . . . Andrew, I don't know . . . if I could handle your main course. Andrew, why?" she said between gasps of air. "Why are you doing this . . . to me?"

"Zee, the night is just beginning. Tonight," he said, kissing her on the forehead, "any fantasy you have *ever* had, we can make come true." And then Drew leaned her head back into the dark blue shimmering waters and left evenly spaced kisses up her shoulder, inching his way toward her neck.

"Andrew, Andrew, Andrew," Zelma managed to say through clenched teeth.

"What, baby?"

"Bite me, baby. Bite me now," she said, and leaned her head to the side, "right there, baby."

Drew paused and smiled. "You'd like that, huh?"

"Oh God, I love that. Bite me, baby. Bite me hard, please, right there."

Drew held her close as their torsos kissed underwater and bit her firmly on the base of her neck. Zelma closed her eyes tightly and tried to make a sound, but none would come out. And then in one motion she managed to draw him still closer and wrapped her legs around his waist. Drew then brought her away from the edge and leaned her head toward the water. After she dipped her hair, Zelma gazed at him with an I'm-ready look in her eyes, but all he saw was Felicia and the way she'd looked their first night in the house.

Drew closed his eyes tightly and submerged his head to kiss Zelma's hardened nipples, but it was too late. His heart was pounding, and although he was in the pool, his mouth was so dry his tongue stuck to the roof. Zelma was only there physically; otherwise it was he and Felicia in the pool again. *I can't do this*, he thought. Drew's head came from the water and he held back. His breathing became labored and he could feel his excitement wilt.

"Andrew? Andrew, baby, what's wrong?"

He looked at her and shook his head. "I can't do it," he whispered. "I can't do this."

"Baby," she said, attempting to calm her breathing. "Andrew? Baby, I know it's hard, but this is the first step. Baby, you can do this. You know Rome wasn't built—"

"Getcha clothes." Drew lifted his nude body from the pool. "I'll give you a ride home," he said, leaving a trail of wet footprints from the pool to his living room.

CHAPTER 18

‡

Monday, three weeks later

Betty brought her head up from her files long enough to notice it was 10:15 A.M. and another morning had passed during which she had not spoken to her prince. The morning "I just called to say I love you" calls were fewer and much further in between as she reminded herself that he was subconsciously pulling away because of her obligations. *That's fine*, she thought as she scribbled notes on a legal pad regarding the case. Jury selection was scheduled to began in three days, and the trial the following week. *God knows I don't need the distractions now anyway.*

"Hello! I mean Ms. Robinson. May I help you?" she said after she grabbed the phone on the half ring.

"Girl, you got it bad!"

"Please, Jac. I knew it wasn't him."

"Ah, Betty? You didn't even give the phone a chance to ring. That was an *I hope this is Vander* answer if I ever heard one."

"Okay, okay, you got me," she said dropping her pen on the stack of files and sliding them from in front of her. "I don't know. I mean . . . I know why he's doing what he's doing and I can rationalize that until I'm blue in the face, but I still miss him." She grimaced. "Seems I need him more now that I have this case than I needed him before."

"When's the last time he sent you flowers? I never hear you mention that anymore."

"Don't ask."

"Betty, that reason he gave you a while back is BS and I trust you're not seriously trying to make sense out of it. I know you wanna believe it, and if you keep repeating it to yourself, you just might, but you don't just turn love on and off like that."

"I know, but like I said before, it also has to be fifty-fifty, and I haven't done my part."

"If that gets you through the night, go for it, but I'm telling you something's up with him. I can't put my finger on it, but something ain't right. How often you all doing it?"

"Don't ask."

"Well, honey, just like that song says, if you want to know if he loves you . . . it's in his kiss."

As Jacqui said the words, Betty thought of the encounter that had left her crying on the floor of her shower. With the phone held to her ear with her shoulder, she rolled her chair away from her desk, crossed her legs, and drummed her fingertips on her knee distractedly. She could feel the soft muscles around her mouth tense, ready to hold back her tears, as Jacqui said, "Betty? You there?"

After a protracted pause Jacqui continued, "Listen. Why don't I bring you some lunch? I can tell by your voice you're busy, and it ain't no use in trying to pry you out of that office today."

"Thanks, but that's okay. I brought lunch."

"Put it in the fridge. I'll see you around one."

"Jacqui? I understand what you're doing, but I'm okay. Seriously. I'm fine." And then as a gentleman stuck his head in her door, Betty froze and said, "Ah, Ms. Jordan? May I call you back around noon? Possibly we can pencil something in for this afternoon."

"Okay, sweetie, I know you got company, but I will see you *today* at lunch."

"Yes, that is confirmed. We'll speak then." Hanging up the phone, Betty said, "Mr. Renfro, how are you? May I help you?"

Walking in her office, he said, "Very impressive," as he looked at her awards.

Betty noticed an envelope cupped in his palm that he would occasionally pat against his thigh.

"So," he said, peering at a photo, "I see Jack introduced you to the governor."

"Well, sir, actually I clerked for Governor Todd when I worked in the SOB for two summers."

With a quizzical look he glanced at Betty and said, "The SO . . . oh, the Senate Office Building. Right. I never knew that. I never knew you clerked in Tallahassee. Well, I'll be damned," he said, and took a seat. "So you and the governor go way back, huh?"

He's getting just a little too excited about this, Betty thought as she watched him take a seat and rub his hand slowly over the ivory envelope in his lap. "He's a nice gentleman. Ambitious as heck," she said softly, "but he and his wife are as nice as can be."

"Well," Renfro continued in his awkward search for conversation, "he's in the GOP. Are you?"

"Sir? Is there something I can get for you?" Betty asked to put an end to the madness. "A file or anything for the meeting tomorrow?"

"No. No, I'm fine," he said, and stood up. "I was just down here and thought I would stop in to say hello."

As he departed, Betty leaned back, completely bemused. And then he looked back in the door and said, "Ah, Robinson? Do you have a couple of minutes?"

"Sir?"

"Do you have a moment? I would like to talk to you if you have the time. Let's go for a walk."

"You know, I've always loved the springtime," Renfro said as he opened the door to the parking garage and wheezed a lungful of air. As they walked out on the concrete slab, Betty listened intently to each of his words. "When we moved here from Wisconsin in the sixties, I had no idea I would even like it. I mean, I loved the snow," he said with a nervous stare around to see if anyone was watching them talk. "I loved getting up early to shovel my wife's car out and putting down the rock salt. Ahh, the smell of rock salt," he reminisced. "I bet you these guys in Florida never even heard of the stuff. To me it was enjoyable for some reason. Gave me time to plan my day. But here in the South, hell, it's summer year-round."

"Umm," Betty said as she noticed the tight grasp he had on the perspiration-stained envelope with the blurred blue ink.

"Yes, it's good down here in the South. But I miss the white stuff after all these years." And then Renfro looked at Betty and said, "Robinson, I've been wanting to talk to you for a few reasons." As they reached the end of the parking lot a soft breeze blew the fragrance from the potted flowering trees in their direction. Renfro looked down at the concrete bench, pulled out his handkerchief, spread it out, and gestured for Betty to sit beside him. As she did so, he said, "I've watched you work these last couple of weeks. As you know, before all this commotion started, I was so busy running the firm I didn't keep track of the associates. But I just wanted to tell you, you've got *it*. Whatever *it* is. You have *it*. I saw it in Murphy, Collins used to have it when he was in the firm more, and you have that same . . . that same stuff."

"Thank you, sir."

"I watched you jump into this case with both feet and you put us in an incredible position to negotiate. Not many partners, if the truth be known, could have done a better job."

While she wanted to ask, *Well, why didn't I get the partnership,* instead she said, "Thank you."

Renfro ran his liver-spotted fingers through his bristly blond crew cut and said, "Also, the reason I asked you out here is because . . ." Then he handed her the envelope. Betty opened it and then looked at him as she unfolded the document inside. As she read it Renfro said, "After talking to Collins and a number of the other partners, we felt it was the only practical thing to do. This way everyone walks away happy, and that is really the essence of mediation. Everyone should—"

"We settled for twenty-five million?"

The apologetic tone of Renfro's voice left as he said, "Yes. Yes we did, Robinson."

"But what happened to the previous offer? We were talking sixty just last week. Burt said we had a shot at sixty-five. Since we obtained even more new information."

"Those plans changed. Now, that's all I can say."

He sold those ladies out because he was too weak to take it to trial, Betty thought as tension knotted in her stomach. She lifted her chin to meet his icy gaze with a stare. "So *you* sold them out. Is that what you're saying, *sir*?"

Renfro stood up and said, "No, what I'm saying is the *partners* met and the *partners* decided what was right in this case for the parties involved. Now, I know you've worked hard on this matter," he said, gazing down at Betty. "But that's how it works sometimes. There are some things they don't teach you in law school. One of them is that the path of least resistance is at times the only practical path to take." And then Renfro turned to limp away and said, "Have those files on my desk by—"

"*Jack* . . . would never have done that!"

Renfro stopped, and as he turned slowly, Betty could hear the gravel under his leather soles. "What did you say?"

Betty stood up, picked up his handkerchief with her fingertips, and said, "Mr. Renfro, you and I both know that *Jack* would never have done that." As she handed him the swatch of white cloth, she continued, "Jack would have ensured that ABL would never have allowed what happened to occur again. Jack would have done the right thing regardless of the money. He would have put Alice Vincent on the stand to tell the court her story. How her husband left her and her three little children months after she lost her womanhood. He would have told them about Rachel Perry, who is still in therapy years after the fact. That is what *Jack* would have done. He would have ensured that there would never be another Alice or Rachel."

Renfro looked away with a half smile and mumbled, "You people kill me." And then he raised his voice to say, "You know, Ms. Robinson, you would have done a great job in front of that jury. I mean when those bla— I mean when that jury got to see you in action it would have been impressive."

As the words left his lips, Betty's heart sank as she thought, *You people, huh? So it was because of color.* Being the best had proven not to be enough. She was still seen as just a color. With alarm and anger rippling along her spine but not in her face, Betty stood tall.

"You know, you have a bright future in this firm. A *very* bright future."

"Sir, are you referring to a partnership? I want to clearly understand what you mean by a *very* bright future."

"Well, Robinson, what else could I mean? We did that search and you were one of the top people we came up with."

"Then why did the partnership go to Patterson?"

"Because our hand was forced. Jack put it in the contract when we recruited him from up north. Believe me when I say if I had my way, we would never have—"

"So when, sir. When will I get this partnership?"

"Well, actually, Robinson, now that this case is over, I can see it happening within the next six months."

Betty swallowed as the words she had wanted to hear for so long settled in her mind. She could for a brief moment picture her portrait hanging on the wall with the other partners in the reception area. She could feel the joy she would have relishing the moment with Evander and Jacqui and sharing with them that she was the first woman of color to achieve such a status in the history of the firm. She no longer had to depend on rumors, because now the senior partner had told her promotion was imminent. And then she thought of the ladies who had gone through the needless surgeries so that a group of attorneys could now celebrate the three million dollars they had earned for the firm.

With a polite smile she said, "Thank you, Mr. Renfro. I really appreciate the fact that you can see I have *earned* a partnership with Murphy, Renfro and Collins. But, sir, you can take that partnership and . . ."

"You told him to do what?"

Lying on the couch in Jacqui's office with her forearm over her eyes, Betty replied, "It's not funny, girl. For the first time in my life I'm unemployed."

"I'm sorry, Betty. I mean . . ." And then Jacqui burst out laughing again and said, "You really told him that? Those exact words? Even the part about him being a racist?"

"It's not funny, Jac."

Jacqui noticed her friend's blank expression and whirled her chair over to the couch. "Listen, Betty. I'm making a little fun of all of this, but you did the right thing."

"Jacqui," she replied as she opened her eyes and looked at her friend. "I just bought a house a couple of months ago. I have a car payment, Visa, Diners, student loans I'm *still* paying off, you name it."

"You have some savings, don't you?"

Betty sighed heavily, looked at the ceiling, and said, "Yeah. I have some retirement money plus the 401K at work, which I *don't* want to touch. But—"

"Girl, I have a little something set aside. We'll pull through this. Trust me when I say, you did the right thing."

"I know. But it's not supposed to be this way. When you follow the rules, attend law school, pay your bills, pay your taxes, go to church, it's not supposed to be like this. When all the girls were out partying in college, what was I doing? The right thing. When people were advancing to partnership all around me, what was I doing? The right thing. Well, look where the right thing has gotten me. I'm thirty-two, unemployed, and unmarried."

"Betty," Jacqui replied after a pause, "it's not fair, but you know something? Whoever said it was going to be fair? That it was even *supposed* to be fair? I got a headline for you: Life is not fair. Okay? I'm sorry to pass that bit of information on to you, but it's true." Jacqui rolled her chair back to her desk, and added, "But you just have to handle it the best you know how. What you did today took courage. Don't let fear steal that away from you. You may have made mistakes in your life; we all have. But this was not one of them. I never could stand Renfro. He has some nerve having that shit in his office you told me about."

"That was never a big deal to me."

"How could it not be a big deal? Just like you said, he is one of the biggest racists in this town. I would have gone up to that cracker and slapped his wrinkled-ass face. He got off easy dealing with you, believe me. You know he was just dangling another carrot in front of your face. What's up with this six months shit?"

"And if you had slapped him . . . what would that say about you?"

"Dammit, it would have said we were even. That's what it would have said."

"No, it would have put you on the same level as him. I never let that stuff get to me because I know who I am. Renfro can't define me based on my color."

"Whatever."

"I'm serious. If I let an insecure man like him tell me who I am, what does it say about me? I was watching TV the other night and they showed this movie about George Wallace." Betty sat up on the couch. "I remember the day he got shot. I remember being happy and my mom and stepfather calling people up on the phone and telling them. Almost like it was a reason to celebrate. I was just a kid and I can remember being happy he was lying there in a pool of blood with his wife covering him. So in the movie when he got shot, I tell you no lie, I was happy all over again. This man did more to hurt black people, not only in Selma and Montgomery but all over the world, than any man since Willie Lynch. But I had to check myself the more I thought about it. I had to ask myself, why was I happy?" Jacqui remained silent as Betty looked at her and said, "Did you know that until his death, this man had to live in constant pain? For almost thirty years he did not live a day without experiencing excruciating, agonizing pain. At the end he was bedridden, more than likely *wishing* he were dead. So as I was watching the movie, I thought to myself, if I'm happy because of what happened to him, at best I am on the same level as he was. And at worst, a lot lower. Girl, I couldn't give Renfro that kinda power over me. I told him what I had to tell him, but he can't make me hate him. We've come too far to sink that low."

Betty watched Jacqui's face crack a smile as she quietly shook her head. "We've come too far to sink that low, huh, I like that. Don't tell me, Jack Murphy."

"No," Betty said as the fear of unemployment sank in. "Me."

CHAPTER 19

‡

Monday

As he sat behind his desk, Drew could hear the swish of Peggy's panty hose as she headed down the corridor. Walking through his door, she stood in front of him with her weight on one foot as she tapped her burgundy sculptured nails on his desk.

With a quick glance down at her fingertips as he hung up the phone, Drew looked at her and asked, "What's up?"

"Drew, please tell me you didn't."

"Didn't what?" he asked, stalling for time.

"You know what I'm talking about, Drew. You went out with Zelma, didn't you."

Pushing his chair back from his desk, Drew wanted to avoid the conversation, but he could not lie to her. He wanted to tell her the Monday after his date but did not. Since it had been several weeks, he assumed it would never come up. "How did you find out?"

"Damn, Drew!" she said, and flopped down in the chair.

"Peggy, you never answered my question. What's up? What's going on?"

"Drew, I thought we had agreed that you were not going to do anything stupid like that. Did you sleep with her?"

"Damn, Peggy. First of all, you sound like I make a habit of dating clients. You know me better than that. Secondly, if it did go further, I wouldn't tell you. What's with you today?"

"Oh boy, you better tell me something!" she replied as she looked up. "This ain't got anything to do with being a gentleman. This is about money now. So what happened, did you screw her?"

"No!" Drew replied. "No, we did not sleep together. Do you feel better? Now tell me what's going on."

Peggy slammed a thick file on his desk, spilling white and yellow papers, and leaned over as she said, "I called her office a couple of times and she's been avoiding me the last few weeks. This morning she answered the phone by mistake or something and I asked her if she got my messages. She said yeah I got them, what can I do for you? And then I knew you slept with her."

"I told you we didn't go to bed!"

"Gaddamn, Drew! You should not have even gotten involved with her. Just so you know, I think she's blocked the deal. I hope you're satisfied!"

"Are you serious? But we spoke to the board and everything and they—"

"Drew, you don't know who you're dealing with. *She* put us in front of that board, and all it would take is a sneeze and we're out the door. I know you were good in the presentation and all, but trust me, if they have the comptroller telling them they should consider one of the other firms, we are out, like a scout, on a new route. Gaddamn, Drew!" she said, massaging her temples with one hand. "I just wish you would have told me, then I could have prepared for this."

Quietly Drew said, "I know. I'm sorry, but—"

"Drew!" she continued holding up her hand. "Please don't say it. Please don't use the thinking-with-the-wrong-head defense. If I hear another man say that shit, I'll throw up."

Drew sat wistfully and stared at his associate. "Peggy? What's going on with you and Walt?"

"What do you mean? *You* fucked up! I've worked on this damn thing for what? Six months? And we might just lose it over some nonsense!"

Over the loudspeaker in the phone Grace said, "Drew you have a call on one-oh-three."

"Take a message," he said without looking away from Peggy. "Tell me. What's happening? This isn't just about me and Zelma, is it?"

As she looked at Drew, he watched her eyes go from clear, to red, to wet. Folding her arms over her waist, she said, "It's Walt."

"What about him?"

"Can you believe that fat fuck cheating on *me?*"

"What? Walt?"

Peggy shook her head as she balled her fists. "I've known about it for some time, and I just tried to overlook it. Some ole hooker from his job. For three or four months he was always talking about Gwen. Gwen said this and Gwen said that. Well, *Gwen* is older than he is, and I thought, naw, he would never do that. He likes younger women and all. Well, about a month ago he asked if I had a problem with her calling him at home. What was I supposed to say, right? Then she would start calling later and later. Whenever I answered she would try to start some silly conversation, but I could see through her fake ass. I would hear him talking in the den to her and I could tell just by the way his fat ass would laugh that this was deeper than just friendship. I would be lying in bed I don't know how long while they talked about things they did in the fifties! Hell, I don't even remember the fifties. As soon as he would hang up and come to bed, this man, who would laugh and talk and joke with her for hours if he could, would just get in bed and say, 'Move over,' turn his fat ass back to me, and fall asleep." Peggy stared out the window with an expression on her face that said she had revealed more than she wanted to.

Drew stood up and walked around to her side of the desk. "I'm sorry, Peggy," he said quietly. "I really am."

"Don't be sorry," she said in a curt manner, "because you had nothing to do with *that* part." Reaching for a tissue on his desk, she said, "After that stuff with my ex-husband, I felt safe with Walt. That's why I only told you about the positive things, because I always suspected my ex-husband of cheating to the point that he said I finally drove him to actually do it. And that's also why I never said anything to Walt about his weight. The more he gained, the safer I felt. But then a month ago he starts taking step aerobics class and diet supplements. And never even told me about it. I found the canceled checks for his membership dues, and he said he was losing the weight for me. When I asked him directly why he was cheating, know what he said? Ass told me that she always made him *feel* handsome. Said she always complimented him. Hell, what he expect from me? I'm his wife. Not some office slut trying to get his wallet. So I was going to use the money from Con-National to put into my savings in the event I had to leave his ass. After losing Murphy, Renfro and Collins, I'm tapped out." With a look of desperation in her eyes she continued, "Drew, I really needed this case."

Drew's worst fear had been realized. He'd known his actions would affect him for more than one night, he just hadn't known it would be this soon. Standing, he closed the Con-National file, which was spread out on his desk. "Where are the rest of the files?"

"On Con-National? Grace has them. Why?"

"Don't worry about that. Go wash your face and put on some lipstick; we're going for a ride. Grace?" he said into the intercom in a controlling tone. "Pull the folders on Con-Nat and reschedule my one forty-five."

"Drew," Peggy cut in, "don't screw this up. Don't go over there acting like some jilted lover or something. That's going to only make things worse."

Reaching for his coat on the hook behind the door and shooting his cuffs before putting it on, Drew said, "Trust me, we will not come back empty-handed. You worked too hard for this one." As he walked out of his office, Drew mentally put together a strategy for their impromptu meeting. *I'll tell her she's above pettiness like this. There is no way we're losing both of these cases.*

"Drew," Grace said with a mouth full of granola. "You've also got a message in your box from that Ms. McGrady woman."

"What!" he said as he dropped his briefcase, laid the file on her desk, and lunged for his message box. "When did she call?" Drew asked as Peggy ran into the reception area.

"Five minutes ago. You were talking to Peggy. What's going on?"

Drew trotted back to his office as Peggy said, "Nothing, darling. It's a long story."

"Peggy? Are you okay?"

Peggy did not respond to Grace as she walked into Drew's office and closed the door. Drew was already on the phone when she entered.

"Peggy," he said, and cupped the receiver. "I need you to step out a second."

"Ahh, I know you're not serious, are you?" she said, and sat down. "I didn't start this—"

"Peggy, get out right now! I'll let you know what happened after I talk to her. Hello, Zelma?" he said, and changed the tone of his voice as Peggy grudgingly closed the door behind her. "How are you?"

Drew could hear Zelma telling someone to have a nice day, and then there was a pause. "How am I? How am I? Drew, don't go there, okay?"

"What do you mean?"

"I have not heard from you in weeks, Drew."

"Zelma, if memory serves me correctly, I tried to talk to you in the car on the way to your place and you didn't say a word. I called you twice the same night and *you* never returned the call. I was just giving you your space."

"Sure, Drew," she replied coldly. "But I didn't call you for that." As he listened to her speak, Drew took off his coat, allowing it to fall to the floor, and sat down to brace himself. "We had the meeting yesterday regarding the benefits packages. John Dukes phoned from London and told me he wanted to finally lay this issue to rest. That it was my call and I could use any firm I wanted in regards to this. I'll have you know, Drew, this is *never* a decision made by an individual. It's always made by committee, and I know they are going to scrutinize whomever I chose. So I told him I wanted to think about it overnight and get back with him today. Last night I did a lot of soul-searching, and this has absolutely nothing to do with personal stuff, Drew. But if I pick a minority firm . . . a *black* firm, it is going to send a message. A very clear message. See, I graduated from a black college, so I know what they are expecting from me. So," she said, and cleared her throat. "This morning I came in and told him it was really a no-brainer and that we could not find a better firm to handle our employee benefits packages than Staley and Associates."

Drew closed his eyes as he sat breathlessly.

"See, Drew, I know what you expected. Hell, I know what Dukes expected. But neither of you know me as well as you think. Trust me, no matter how fine and cute you were, I would not have given your firm the business if you guys were not the best. This ain't a black thing. Let me make that clear. It's a business thing. Now, was I pissed at first? Hell yeah, I was pissed. And for a split second I wanted to get you back where it hurt. Actually the reason I wanted to think about it overnight was because my knee-jerk reaction was to screw you and your firm. But the more I thought about it, the more I realized that if we had gone further, it would have just caused more problems."

With her voice lowering, Zelma said, "Although he's married, I'm really not over him. So everything happens for a reason, and our date happened for a reason. I had a good time," Zelma said with a smile in her voice. "I had a real good time, and although things did not end as expected, it let me know that what I am looking for is deeper than just the physical. Don't get me wrong, I wanted to be with you. Hell, I could have used some of you. But if we had gotten together, like I said, it would have just caused more problems."

Opening his eyes, Drew whispered, "Well, Zee. I had a good time as well. And you're right, everything does happen for a reason. Like I said, you made a part of me come alive. But I just could not go to the next level until I knew without a shadow of a doubt—"

"Drew! You don't have to explain. We both had a nice time and that's the important part. And now we both agree that it was for the best. So tell me, when would you like to start enrollment? And will the future disbursements from the investment portfolio come from—"

Taking a deep breath, Drew said, "Ms. McGrady? *You're* truly amazing."

CHAPTER 20

‡

Monday afternoon

The smell of the April showers was still fresh in the air and the sun beamed hot as kids played up and down the streets of Royalton Oaks. Trees spread their branches and were decorated with moss, green ivy, and an occasional bird as Betty sat on her veranda reviewing the résumé she and Jacqui had put together earlier that day. She had also gone through the names of the attorneys in her directory and decided upon three that she would like to work with, although Jacqui protested, saying she should start her own firm. But thoughts of starting a firm on the same day she had resigned from the only home she knew were a million miles away. With everything in her world moving so fast, she needed the security that an established firm could offer.

As she stirred a cup of half-eaten yogurt, she heard her neighbors across the street drive up. She noticed the father get out of the station wagon first and skip around to his wife's door. She watched as the kids spilled out the back doors clutching bottles and toys. And then Betty observed the mother carefully get out of the car and gently hold the newborn close after pulling the pink wrap over its head. As always, when she stood, she looked over at Betty and gave a courteous wave. Their yard, unlike most in the neighborhood, was adorned with hula hoops, a mini trampoline, and jump ropes instead of dogwood trees and azaleas. But the family seemed content with being atypical. They played hide-and-seek and the fox and the hound with their kids on the front lawn, gave an occasional pool party for the other neighborhood children, and each Sunday, like clockwork, they dressed in shades of brown and blue and headed off to mass together. As the last of the children made their way into the blue house, Betty picked up her cordless to call Evander.

The first time they spoke she was entranced by his voice as she talked to him while gazing at the flowers he sent. She thought of the lonely nights he would visit and the afternoon he raced to the firm to hold her hand. Now the romance was replaced with complacency after only a couple of months.

"Hey."

"Hey, what's wrong? You sound depressed."

"Nothing. Well . . ." And then Betty decided that she did not wish to revisit the pain and said, "I don't want to go into it. How was your day?"

"Busy, as always." As Evander spoke she could tell he was distracted with work. "But at least I get to sleep in tomorrow. Ferguson is working for me since he took a couple of extra vacation days."

"That's nice," Betty said dryly.

"Beep, are you sure you don't want to talk about whatever it is on your mind?"

"Positive."

"Well, when you're ready, you know I'm here. Okay?"

"What're you doing tonight?"

After a pause Evander said, "I need to make a delivery for Kevin in Jacksonville. Why? You wanna do something?"

"No. I was just curious."

"Are you sure? I'm just doing him a favor because he wanted to go out tonight."

With a sudden brainstorm, Betty's voice gained strength as she said, "No, honey, seriously, that's fine."

"Well, I should be back in town no later than eleven. Will you be up?"

"No, I think I'm going to crash tonight. I got a lot to do tomorrow."

"Oh well. I'll call you tomorrow morning . . . okay?"

"Sounds good. Good night." As Betty clicked off the phone with her thumb and hit speed dial with her pinky to call Jacqui, she knew exactly what her next move would be regarding Evander. "So what are you up to tonight? Going out?"

"Hey, girl," Jacqui said to Betty. "Yeah, Stefan called last night and wanted to know if I would like to go to a movie or something. What's up with you and *Vander*?"

"Just spoke to him. He's making a delivery for a friend in Jax."

"Umm. The old *delivery* lie, huh?"

"Here we go again," Betty sighed.

"Damn straight. Because he's doing something he ain't got no business doing, and I know it and you know it and you won't admit it."

"Okay, Jac. You're right, and yes, I know something may be wrong. I know he may be doing something or someone, but I need more proof before I can convict him."

"You still got that key to his house on your key ring? While he's out making *deliveries*, why don't you just make a visit? I bet you'll find something to convict him."

"Jac, not tonight, okay?" Betty said, feeling drained, weary, and lifeless. "Tonight, after the day I had, I need some attention. Tonight I don't feel like being Sherlock Holmes or Robert Stack. I just want . . . Never mind."

"Never mind what? And wait a minute. What do you mean by *more* evidence?"

"It's not important."

"Betty? You know I love you. And I know it's been a long day. But you are not telling me everything."

"What do you mean?"

"What have you found? Has he mentioned somebody's name? Have you found a receipt? What the hell is *more* evidence?"

"Well, I didn't think too much of it when he first did it, but about one o'clock one night when we were in Orlando, I suddenly woke up. He was sitting on the side of the bed, just sorta mumbling to himself. So I asked him what the problem was and he said nothing and apologized for waking me up. Well, a week or so later when we were at my place, he does the same thing. This time I was really curious and I kept pressing him as to what was wrong. Still, he said nothing, just that he had a lot on his mind, right? So then last week, same thing. So I got out the bed, turned on the light, and told him I needed him to come clean with me. Well, after badgering him for about thirty minutes, he finally told me—"

"He needed money, right?"

Betty sighed and said, "Yeah. Yeah, he needed some money, but first of all, it wasn't that much, and secondly, no, I did not offer to give it to him. But when he went there I sorta started questioning everything. I started thinking the only reason he wanted me was because of money. That all the flowers and special dinners were because he was setting me up for the kill. But he did not come out and ask me for it, he just said that he needed it and was trying to think of a way to get it so he could invest in the bakery. That has always been his dream. And I will admit, if he had said it a few months ago, I would have offered it."

"And you would have been a damn fool."

"Not give, Jacqui, *loaned* it to him."

"Let me tell you something girl. Three things you never do. Never ask a single woman if she has batteries, 'cause you know she ain't giving up the stash. Never ask a single man if he has any petroleum jelly . . . for the exact same reason. And never, and I mean absolutely never, ask anyone if they need to borrow money, because when it's time to pay you back, they give you the same old line. I didn't ask you for it . . . and you know the rest. What I'm trying to say is that it's deeper than just a few dollars. Be careful. I know you have feelings for the brother. But just keep your eyes open."

"Do you know how tired I am of keeping my eyes open? Of looking both ways? Of waiting," and then she paused before she whispered, "Until . . ."

"Betty, what you need to do—"

"Let me finish. I was sitting here on the porch and it occurred to me for the first time why I took that malpractice case so personally. Trust. It all boils down to pure and simple, unmitigated trust. What happened to those ladies was unforgivable. No dollar amount could replace what they've already lost. But I'm trusting this man with so much more.

Hell, I could replace money. A friend told me that some
wounds are never meant to heal and if Evander were to let
me down . . . Lets just say I can't live my life trying not to
be like my momma. Trying not to make the same mistakes
with men. She made some bad decisions but she also lived
life to the fullest. And to do that, sometimes you have to follow
your heart. Sometimes you have to let go . . . and trust."

"You done?"

"See I tell you a lot. Maybe too much sometimes. But it's
the small things. Yeah, he hinted that he wanted to borrow
some money, but this is the same man who also gave me
the keys to his heart."

After a moment of silence Jacqui repeated, "You done?"

"I still remember when it was raining one night and this
man started crying in my arms after we made love. He said
he started crying because after this girl named Yolanda, he
never knew he could fall . . . well, I remember things like
that. I remember him rushing to the office after Murphy
died just to be with me. When I was having serious doubts,
he held my hands and whispered, 'Betty, I love you, for
you . . . and not for what you do.' And he repeated it over
and over and over again. You're right. This is not about a
few dollars Jacqui. I've lived my entire life playing it safe.
Not taking chances. Not allowing men to get too close.
Why?" Betty relaxed in her plastic chaise longue as she
closed her eyes to finish her thought. "It's an oxymoron, but
I've come to the conclusion that I've been alone, because I
was so afraid of being left alone. And it's absurd and I'm
tired of living that way."

"Are you done?"

"Jacqui . . . yeah. Yes, I'm done."

"Trust is important. It just seems there are so few men
out there nowadays who deserve to be trusted. But . . . well
if you feel in your heart that he is the one, then maybe I'm
overreacting. In case you haven't noticed I can do that from
time to time. Hell, I know I got baggage and the oldest rule
in the book is never ask a woman without a man for advice
on how to keep one. All I can say is just . . . "

"I know. Just be careful."

"No Ms. Ann, and stop finishing my damn sentences. All I can say is . . . girl, I love you."

"Thank you. I needed to hear that." Clearing the lump from her throat Betty sat up in her chair and said, "New subject. I forgot to tell you I had the nicest letter last week waiting for me when I got home."

"Aww shit here we go again. Mr. Modem. Right?"

"Yeah. Drew's nice." Betty said, and smiled. "He sends me these wonderful poems, but he never makes advances. It's just sweet. That's all. He's romantic, like the men in the old black-and-white movies. The ones who would light two cigarettes in their mouth and hand one to the lady who was sitting at the bar crying. Sorta like Billy D in *Lady Sings the Blues*. I like that," Betty said, watching the father in the house next to hers walk out to adjust a sprinkler.

"I'm *touched*," Jacqui said sarcastically. "I've told you about meeting people on those computers. If he were worth a damn, he wouldn't be sitting in front of the computer typing poems to women he's never seen before. Besides, he probably married or got some disease or something and just doing this as a way to get off."

"Maybe, but I sit in front of the computer and type letters to him, so what does that make me?"

"You're different. I'm telling you something is wrong with this guy," Jacqui replied.

"But if he was trying to be more than a friend, why would he tell me about this woman whom he seemed to be getting closer to and his dead girlfriend?"

"Because he's sneaky. Does he tell you anything intimate?"

"Of course not."

"He hasn't gotten that far yet, but it's coming. Baby, let Momma explain this game to you. It's known by many experts in the field as—" Jacqui paused for effect "—as the oldest fuckin' game in the book!"

Betty laughed aloud, startling Tickey, who scampered through the glass door into the house.

"First of all," Jacqui said, "he ain't got nobody. Okay? He's hard up and just wants you to sweat him. Has he asked you what you do for a living?"

"No, he hasn't. And even if he had, I'm not that stupid. Besides, Jac," she continued as another two-income-household van passed. "Don't you sometimes feel like life is just passing you by? Like the whole world's been invited to a party you never got an invitation to? I know I do. Seems I am—" And then Betty corrected herself and said quietly, "It *seemed* I was the only one in the firm my age unmarried and unattached. I watch my neighbors over here, and she is in her late twenties with a house full of kids, and I've never seen the lady unhappy. Not that that's the life I want, it just seems I'm missing out on something."

"Honey, I understand that. But the answer is not on a computer."

"I'm not looking for it on a computer, and besides, you've never signed onto the Net. So how you know so much about it?"

"That's true, that's true. You have a point. But you know something? I've never had an autopsy; however, you won't see me standing in line for one of them either. I'm telling you he ain't got nobody. He most likely some pervert or something. Men lie like I don't know what sometimes. Just remember AMAD and it'll make life simipler: All Men Are Dogs. They just have different tail lengths."

"Sweetheart, you've got issues," Betty said with a giggle. "I don't think all guys are dogs. I think there are definitely some dogs out there, but I believe there's some good in Evander, and I think my *friend* on the computer is nice as well."

"See now, my date just pulled into the driveway, and I know he's a dawg, so that's the difference between you and me. Sometimes I even call him Amad by mistake. Look at him. He just knows he's getting some tonight, but he ain't. I bet he got a pocket fulla rubbersohmygoodness!" Jacqui said in a muffled tone.

"What!"

"Aww shyeet, he's wearing those black leather jeans."

"Leather? In Florida? In the spring?"

"I know it sounds crazy, but yes, girl. If you put those pants on a thousand men, nine hundred ninety-eight would look like a damn fool wearing them. But Amad, I mean Stefan and Eddie Murphy could pull it off," she said laughing. "I don't know, I might have to go to church with you this Sunday after all, because it might be a whole lotta sinning in my house tonight."

" 'Bye Jac."

"Hey before you go!"

"What?"

After a pause for the right words Jacqui said, "I know I've said a lot about the brother but, if deep in your heart you feel he's the one for you . . . well you know all I want is to see you happy. Do what you have to do to make it right, okay?"

"Thank you."

Betty smiled as she hung up the phone. But as the sun left the sky and she could see the neighbors sitting around their table preparing for dinner, loneliness returned. When she'd graduated, she could never see herself as anything but a power-wielding litigator. Yet on this night, she would have given anything to change places for an hour with the lady in the lace apron serving dinner.

Betty walked inside her house, triple-locked the doors, grabbed a box of raisins, and sat in front of her computer. She had not signed on for several days due to the caseload at work, but now that it was over she thought, *Another night on-line. Damn.* During her conversation with Evander she had decided to surprise him with a special evening, but the more she thought about it, the faster the idea had faded.

After she signed on, Betty's computer mailbox icon lit up, indicating she had mail, and a smile came to her face as she saw it was a letter from Drew that had been in her box since Saturday.

 Dear Betty:

> Sorry not to address you by your screen name, but for some reason, speaking to you directly makes me feel a little closer. I just got back home from a strange day and I need to write to sort out my feelings more so than anything else. Remember the young lady I told you I was debating about going out with? Well, if you noticed I haven't written

to you about her in a while, it's because I finally asked her out a couple of weeks ago. Actually we had a lot of fun until my hormones got in the way. As a gentleman I will just say it has been a while and I did not use good judgment. I brought her to my home, kinda got her excited, and could not finish what I had started.

As I was looking in her eyes, thoughts of Felicia flashed through my mind nonstop. And it was not just the good aspects of my relationship with her. It was also the bad, and I started seeing those same things in Zelma. They introduced themselves the same way to me, they were both a little overly aggressive, and they were both ready to make a move before we really knew each other.

I'm not the smartest man in the world, Betty, but I try not to make the same mistake twice. And looking at her that night, I saw myself walking down a familiar road.

As I drove her home, she was a little upset, and she had every right to be because I did start the encounter. I tried to make small talk and she would not say a word. Nothing at all. She just sat there staring ahead with her arms folded.

As I mentioned to you before, we lost the big account I had worked so hard on, so if we lose this one, I'll have to lay off Grace for a couple of weeks, which is something I have never done before. With the job market being the way it is here in Gainesville, there's a chance I may lose her to another company.

Don't get me wrong, Zelma is nice people. But I'm looking for something else. I am looking for someone I can fall in love with as a friend. The kind of woman I could one day look in the eye and say without a doubt, today I just married my best friend in this world. I'm aware that such a love may not exist and maybe I am too immature not to give up hope, but until I find it I will continue waiting . . .

Until . . .

Drew

Betty reread the word *Gainesville* several times. *He could have meant Gainesville, Georgia, or Gainesville, Texas.* Without stopping to think, she went into her kitchen, opened the phone book, and saw it in the financial consulting section.

Andrew Patrick Staley and Associates
Financial Planning, Annuities,
Life, Health, and Retirement Benefits

"Oh my God, Jac will never believe this one."

Betty sent Drew a quick reply, never mentioning she lived in the same city and only a couple of miles from his office. She told him not to give up on love and to listen to his heart. As soon as she sent the E-mail Betty signed off the Net, inhaled slowly and decided to follow Jacqui's advise. To do what she had to do to keep Evander in her life.

Standing on Evander's step, Betty peeked inside the glass in the door to make sure he had not returned early. She had parked her car down the block so as to not give him a clue she was there. The closer she got to his house, the more her stomach told her all was not well, but she did not care. Tomorrow she would pin him down as to what was going on. Tomorrow she would find out if her fears were valid. But tonight she needed his caress. She had followed the rules, and although she knew she might regret doing so, tonight she was prepared to break a few. Reaching in her purse, she used the key he had given her for the first time. As she walked inside dressed in only her overcoat and wearing the red pumps she had never worn for anyone except him, she set her brown bag of goodies on his coffee table. Inside it were strawberries, incense, candles, massage oils, and motion lotion. It felt so unusual being in his home without him there. Her first impulse was to do a little innocent snooping, but she resisted. With a quick look at the clock, she took out her Janet CD. She had always wanted to make love to "That's the Way Love Goes." Whenever she worked out, she would listen to Janet, and when the song came on she could see herself dressed as she was on that night, slowly dancing with Evander in the center of the room. And as they danced she would say the words softly in his ear.

Betty pictured herself dropping her coat to the floor and dancing nude with him fully dressed as she controlled his every moment with the grind in her hips. She would slowly disrobe him to the thick vibrating rhythms filling the air. And once he was undressed, she would lead him to the bathroom, where she would have the tub of hot water completely covered with Mexican long-stemmed rose petals, and surrounded by candles. The air would be kissed with the smell of incense, and cold enough for them to cuddle in front of his fireplace afterward as they would begin phase two of their night of romance. The fantasy was clear in Betty's mind as she looked at the clock and awaited his arrival.

Betty fell asleep on the carpet of the guest bedroom beside the stems from the flowers she had brought for their encounter together. The bubbles in the tub mixed with the rose petals had gone flat, the candles had burned to nothing, and the water was cold as Evander scrambled for his keys and opened the door a little before 3:00 A.M. As he entered the house, he did not notice the bag left on the coffee table, nor did he look into the darkness of the guest bedroom to see Betty lying on the carpet asleep. As entered his bedroom, his cellular phone rang.

"Hello? Hey what's up? No, it's cool. I'm glad you got the message. What's going on with you? Well, you know how Momma is. Always trying to make things out to be a lot more than they really are. No, not really. Naw, we're a long, long way from that, man. We're just kicking it."

Hearing Evander's voice, Betty awakened, wiped her mouth, gathered her bearings as to where she was, and then smiled trying to think of how she was going to surprise him. She blindly searched for the remote to the CD player so she could cue up Janet as soon as he was off the phone.

"No! I mean she's a nice girl and all, but no, I don't see it going in that direction. Yeah, she's an attorney. Cute as hell and she's making serious paper. Really. Well, you know me."

As Evander laughed, Betty's lips parted; she hoped this was another ghost from the shadows of her mind.

"Oh, I know she's making good money because I checked out her bank statement. I don't play," he laughed. "When I helped her move into this house in Royalton Oaks— Yeah, I know. She's the only black person I saw living out there. But I was in her files, man. I saw everything. You hear me? Bonds, stocks, CDs, the works! Man, I just don't care anymore. Listen to this. She's only thirty-two. Exactly. Check this out. I've been playing the game for a while looking for just the right moment. One night while we were lying in bed, I was broker than I don't know what, right? I noticed her purse right beside the bed. So I was putting my hand in it and— Naw, man, I wasn't looking for that. She don't carry any real money. No, I was looking for her Social Security card. Why? So I could apply for cards in her name, what else? So, as I was saying, I was fishing for the cards and stuff when I heard her wake up. I had to play it off, right? I sat up like I was half asleep and started running the game on her. Exactly, just like I did LaTonya. So she fell for it, and a couple of nights later she was begging me to take some money. I won't say how much, but let's say it was mid four figures. Serious. I told you it works, man.

"But it gets better. I found this twenty-thousand-dollar preapproved platinum application in her desk drawer. She gets so many I know she never even missed it. So in the meantime, I went back to Orlando the next weekend to spend a little time with Becky. I'll tell you about her later. But while I was there, I mailed off the application and got a PO box, and as soon as I get it, I'll do just like I did before. Cash advance the hell outta it. What? No, man, see, that's where you're lost. I know she's an attorney and all. But she is a woman first and foremost. This female adores me, man. I told her I needed some money to buy a piece of the bakery and she went for it. So I'll just tell her I made a mistake because I wanted to buy in so bad and planned to pay the card off before she ever knew about it. Trust me, she'll forgive me. See, she's feeling guilty about not being able to spend any time with me so I know she'll go for it. Yo. I even told her my cell phone and beeper was off so she would stop calling me in Orlando while I was with Becky. Now, don't get me wrong. I got feelings for her, man. No, I'm serious. I think she has a shot at *one* day being Mrs. Jones. But man, I gotta be me. You know?"

Betty heard Evander walk down the hallway and she waited for him to notice the lone brown bag sitting on the coffee table. "Yeah, man, you know I gotta get mine." She heard him walk a little faster to the bathroom, where he had to notice the tub of water covered with rose petals. Then she saw him turn around slowly and look into the darkened guest bedroom as he said, "Ahh, listen, man. I'm gonna have to call you back." As he clicked on the light he looked down at Betty looking up at him with only the flower stems and remote covering her nude torso.

"Evander?" she said, with disappointment spun so tight in her throat she could smell it, but refused to allow it to show on her face. "Can I just ask you one question? Can you just tell me, why?"

As she drove home, Betty sang loudly with Stevie and then repeated to herself, "You can't make me cry, Evander Jones. I won't give you that much power over me! You can't make me do it!" Sitting in her car, she blindly searched her purse for a poem Drew had sent her. As she pulled into her driveway she cut off her ignition and read it to herself.

Until rain falls from the heavens,
To an earth so barren and dry,
Until clouds form angels,
So high up in the sky.
Until kids cease to ask why.

Until yellow roses blossom
on snowcapped mountains,
Until moonlight shines all day.
Until August turns into winter,
And we bundle up, in May.

I've put my dreams off for so long
I get tired of hearing until.

I get so tired of not living today,
So tired of restraining my will.

Like a jazz song with no ending,
Or a sonnet without a break.
My life seems to be continuously leading
To that one word . . . wait.

I thought it was right,
In fact it felt great.
I now had my love,
No need to wait.
For love, for passion
My wait was now complete.
But now she is gone,
But now she is gone.

Must a tree wait?
Must a flower wait to bloom?
That's a bad analogy I make,
For they too must wait, that's true.

So I'll wait to find another,
This time I'll assert my will.
But she too will break my heart,
And again I'll wait until.

Until rain falls from the heavens,
To an earth so barren and dry,
Until clouds form angles,
So high up in the sky.
Until kids cease to ask why.

Looking out her window, Betty smiled with a newfound strength and said, "See that? *Vander*, you can't make me cry! You are not worth the salt in my tears! You are . . ." And then Betty saw her neighbors' darkened house with the Big Wheel behind the Chevy station wagon and she sat in her car and cried, alone.

CHAPTER 21

‡

Monday, one week later

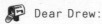 Dear Drew:

Today marks a week since it happened, and I appreciate the shoulder. The first couple of nights were hell. I don't think I had an idea how much this man had become a part of me. I went around the house and de-Evanderized it the day after the incident, and I thought doing that would make me feel better. I took a long ride in the country to clear my head and even wrote him a letter just to get the feelings out and never sent it to him. But none of that really helped.

I know I never told you what it was he actually said, but I haven't told Jacqui either. One thing he said to this person on the phone is that I offered to give him a few dollars, when in actuality I offered to *loan* him the money. This is something I could never tell Jac, because she is so jaded about love and men. Yes, I feel foolish now looking back, but I guess for a moment I thought if I did loan him the money, it would bring back the old Evander. I felt if he was happy career-wise I could stop waiting, as your poem says, Until . . .

I called a friend who works in the state's attorney's offices and they picked Evander up Friday from his job. My friend told me the officer called him and said Evander was crying like a baby in front of all the customers. I don't know why that didn't bring me joy, but it didn't. Then my friend told me that he doubted they could keep him in jail very long with the fraud charge, although he had priors I was not aware of. So he will be out to do what he did to me to someone else, more than likely tomorrow.

And then last night his mother calls me. She actually called the day after the incident and I never returned the call. When I saw her name on the Caller ID box I almost didn't answer the phone. But just before the answering machine picked up I grabbed it. Mrs. Jones was nice to me, so in spite of her son, I thought I at least owed her the benefit of allowing her to tell me what was on her mind.

She didn't do what I expected, which was to ask me to drop the charge. She just told me she was sorry for what happened. She adores her son and I guess he is a good son to her, and she told me more about his history with women. She said that if she had any idea he would pull the same scam on me, she would have told me. But she said she watched us together in Orlando and when she saw us kissing on her front porch she thought I could be the one that would allow him to heal some of the pain from the past.

Oh well, I did not mean to be so long-winded and I thank you for being there. It's almost 6:00 A.M. and I have an appointment to meet with a gentleman about employment at 9:00. As I mentioned, of the three I spoke to in brief last week, I enjoyed the conversation with his company the most, and I think if today's meeting goes well, I may decide to work with them. Say a prayer for me.

Until . . .
Betty

Betty looked at her watch and was happy to see that, just as planned, she was ten minutes early for her scheduled

interview with Latrobe & Fitzgerald. As she sat with the latest edition of *Time* in her lap, she wanted to look at the small things she could not determine in her research of the firm. What time the partners arrived, how the attorneys interacted with the clerical staff, and whether the firm was any more integrated than the one from which she had just resigned.

After talking to other attorneys, her decision to work with Latrobe & Fitzgerald was an easy one. They were an up-and-coming firm, and although they did not have the national presence of Murphy, Renfro and Collins, they were well respected in the state. She could ask for and likely receive a larger compensation package with firms in major cities such as Atlanta, but since she had just purchased a home, such a move was not practical.

Betty noticed the decor was not as opulent as Murphy, Renfro and Collins. There were no silver tea sets in the reception area, no aroma of potpourri in the air, and the firm was on the second floor in one of the less prestigious areas of town. But as she waited to speak to the senior partner, it did not matter to her. Of the three firms she had seen, this was the only one to indicate that not only would they give her a partnership within six months, they were willing to commit to doing so in writing, according to the managing partner, Charles Fitzgerald. He had advised Betty that only a meeting with the senior partner, Benjamin Latrobe, stood between her and a new beginning with Latrobe & Fitzgerald.

As she sat thumbing through the magazine, she thought about DLastRomeo and how tempted she was to casually drive by his office just to see if this man looked anything like she imagined in her mind. But she could not, for fear that seeing him would in some way ruin the relationship she had with the friend she so badly needed in her life.

Moments after Betty declined a cup of tea from the office receptionist, the senior partner walked into the waiting area. "Benjamin Latrobe," he said by way of introduction. "And you must be Betty Robinson."

"Good morning," she said as they shook hands, and then she reached down for her attaché case.

"Right this way, Ms. Robinson." As they walked down the corridor he said, "So sorry I'm late. It was one of those mornings."

"No problem," she said as she glanced into each of the opened offices they passed.

"Well, actually it is a problem. I'm a real stickler for promptness and here I go getting off on the wrong foot in our first interview."

They entered Mr. Latrobe's office and Betty was surprised to see it was twice the size of Jack Murphy's, decorated in redwood with classical music playing softly in the background. "May I get you a cappuccino?" he asked.

"Thanks," she said, "but no, thank you."

"Are you sure? We also have Jamaican Blue Mountain and tea."

"I'm sure," she said as she sat in front of his desk. "But I appreciate it." As he sat behind his desk Betty said, "Mr. Latrobe, there's a question I have been dying to ask. Are you related to the famous nineteenth-century architect, Benjamin Latrobe?"

Latrobe looked at her with surprise. "How did you know that name?"

Betty smiled. Her research had paid off. "I was just curious. I remember his work from a class I took in college, and since you are from the Northeast, I thought there might be a connection."

Laughing, he said loudly, "You're hired!" And then as his chuckles decreased he added, "You know, you are the first person to mention his name to me since I've been down here, and we've lived in Florida for going on forty years."

"Well, he did great work. You should be very proud."

"We are," he said, looking at Betty a little differently. "We are indeed." And then his eyebrows settled as he said, "Ms. Robinson, I've talked extensively to Mr. Fitzgerald about bringing you into the firm. I must say he is very enthusiastic about adding you, but I will be very up front with you. We are not in the practice of bringing in associates with the promise of *guaranteeing* in writing they will be a partner. Actually you would be the first." He paused to look again at Betty's résumé and smiled. "But I will hasten to add that rarely have we had the opportunity to bring in an attorney at your age with these credentials."

"Thank you."

Betty quietly watched as he once again reviewed her career on paper. He placed the lone piece of paper in the center of his immense desk and removed his gold-framed glasses. "Ms. Robinson, I will be candid with you if you don't mind."

"By all means."

"I was a good friend of Jack Murphy's. Although I did not know you, I had heard him mention a hotshot new attorney. I know the caliber of attorneys Jack attracted, so there is no doubt in my mind that if you were to join us, you could pick up the ball immediately and run with it. I must also say I spoke to Mr. Collins and Renfro. Collins was a little on the fence about you in some aspects, which I can understand. If I had invested six or seven years in an attorney only for her to practice elsewhere, I might not give her a ringing endorsement either. But let's face facts. Renfro, as you can imagine, was not on the fence at all. Now, I know Franklin. I have had him and both his former and new wife over to the house. He has his ways, and I have an idea of how it might have been for you to work with him. But I need to talk to you about that case. I know you are not at liberty to go into detail at this juncture, but I need to know more about why you resigned."

Betty did not answer immediately as the right response formed in her mind. And then as the senior partner leaned forward on his elbows she said, "First of all, Mr. Latrobe, I appreciate the fact that you would put this issue on the table. The sole reason I joined the firm was because of Jack Murphy. It was not because of money. It was not because of the prestige. It was because Jack was simply the lawyer I wanted to become. He spoke to our law school once," Betty continued, "about a case where he defended this lady and she needed what little money he won so badly he refused to subtract his fee. So instead she paid him in—"

"Campbell's soup," both attorneys said together.

"Once I was there when she brought him his lunch," Mr.

Latrobe said. "I think she did that every Wednesday until she died, even though Jack told her to stop."

"That's the attorney I aspired to be. I know making money for the firm is important. Don't get me wrong. But so is fighting for people who have been wronged."

Silence swelled and was broken as Mr. Latrobe said, "I can appreciate that, Ms. Robinson. But looking at your résumé, I noticed you also logged some serious pro bono hours."

"Yes I did, sir. When I was in college and the president of the Black Law Students Association, one of the things I preached to them was about never forgetting the small people who sometimes could not afford justice. People like a lady I defended earlier this year by the name of Consuela Lopez."

"I'm familiar with Mrs. Lopez," he said, and leaned back in his chair. "If the truth be known, I think she visited our firm for representation and we just did not have the resources to take the case. I read that Midway has decided not to appeal the verdict."

"Correct, sir. Here is a woman whom no one in our firm wanted to touch because of the particular situation surrounding the accident. But she deserved a voice, and I am very proud of the fact that her voice was heard."

"But our number one obligation, Ms. Robinson, is returning a profit to our partners. While that may sound boorish on the surface, it's reality. Once that is done, then we can do all of the other wonderful things to correct the ills of the world. I am not against pro bono work. I know we are all obligated to doing *some* of it. And yes, I, too, feel an obligation to give fair representation to all. We all do. But I can assure you when Jack started that firm he would not allow an associate to log this many hours. It's just not feasible, especially in today's economic climate."

Betty remained silent as the wheels spun in her head.

"Having said that, Ms. Robinson, I must tell you there is nothing that I can foresee which would prohibit our scheduling a time on Thursday to look at numbers. I already knew you would be an asset before we met this morning. And I have no problem with guaranteeing your partnership with a few minor stipulations regarding billable hours, et cetera. But I think if the numbers are in the ballpark, we can put together a compensation package for the partners to vote on Friday," he said, with a smile returning to his voice. "If all works out, we can have you become a part of our team on Monday morning."

Betty lowered her head thoughtfully and noticed she was still holding her keys. She saw that one of Evander's keys was still on the circular ring. Staring at the key, Betty said just above a whisper, "You know, sir, the day I drove to court for the verdict on that Lopez case I was scared to death. I could hardly sleep the night before. I knew no one expected me to pull it off." She returned her eyes to Mr. Latrobe as her voice gained confidence. "But I did. I won that case, and for one moment, the *system* worked. I know that sounds Pollyannish, but it made me proud. And it made me even happier to see Jack's face after I won. But you know something? After that case, all of my joy left. All aspects of my life were exactly where I wanted them to be, yet I could barely smile. I was not excited about my career as a litigator. But you know," she said, leaning back into the burgundy leather and rubbing her finger over the serrated edge of Evander's house key, "I'm excited now. I really am. Not because I'm joining you here at Latrobe & Fitzgerald. Because sitting here today . . . while talking to you . . . I've decided to establish my own firm."

As his smile disappeared Mr. Latrobe said, "Are you serious?"

Betty nodded her head. "Actually, Mr. Latrobe, I don't think I've ever been more serious in my life. I mean this is why I could not enjoy my success before. Because I knew I would have to put up with the normal office politics. I understand, but I didn't become an attorney to return a profit to the partners. And the only way I can avoid it would be to start my own firm."

"Ms. Robinson, may I ask you a simple question?" Benjamin Latrobe put on his glasses and leaned back in his chair. "How will you start a firm? I know you are an extremely bright woman, but are you aware of how difficult it is on this side of the desk?"

Looking him in the eye, she said, "I have no idea, sir. I have no idea how I will put this together and once again I'm scared to death. But for the first time I'm in control, and I think the risk is worth the reward."

Several minutes later Mr. Latrobe and Betty emerged from his office laughing and were greeted by Charles Fitzgerald. "Good Morning, Benny. Good Morning, Ms. Robinson. Sounds like you guys had a great meeting."

"Good morning," they both said as the laughter died away.

"So are we at a point were we can present something to the partners? This lady's not going to break us, is she, Benny?"

Betty smiled and looked at Mr. Latrobe as he said, "Well, Chuck, we'll talk." And then he looked at Betty and said, as they shook hands, "Betty, I think you are a fine woman. I was impressed after talking to Chuck about you, but even more so today. You've got guts. Most people are afraid to do what you are about to do. I can't tell you how many associates I have who I know would do well on their own. But they lack courage and that's why most people settle for mediocrity in life, because they're afraid to take a chance. I started this firm with Chuck thirty years ago, and no one thought we could do it. But you've got what my grand-mother in Tennessee called *gumption*. You'll do fine, and if you ever need me . . . you have my personal number. Call me."

"Thanks, Ben," she said, and then shook Mr. Fitzgerald's hand. "Thank you, too, sir. It was a pleasure."

"A what?" Mr. Fitzgerald said as he looked back at Mr. Latrobe. "What do you mean, what she's about to do?"

"Chuck, we'll talk. Betty, good luck," he said as Betty turned to walk away.

As she passed a trash can she tossed Evander's key into it as she heard Mr. Fitzgerald say, "But I thought it was a go. What happened?"

Betty sat in her home office in front of her computer making notes on her yellow legal pad. From the funds she had in her 401K investment portfolio and personal retirement, she could start her firm without the necessity of going further into debt. She had put together a list of fifty potential clients she had worked with or met while at Murphy, Renfro and Collins, and she had called her friend Agnes Murphy for sage advice. Everything looked so good as she glanced at the numbers on the pad she wondered aloud, "Why didn't I do this years ago?"

The phone rang, and as she blindly placed her hand on the receiver she looked at her Caller ID box and noticed the call's origination. Alachua County Corrections. As the phone rang for the second time Betty took her hand from the receiver. So much was happening that she did not want to revisit the event of the previous week. The phone rang for the third time as she stood and walked away, but on the fourth ring she lunged for it and answered. She was going to be strong and face her fear this time.

"Hello," she said with no emotion in her voice.

"Betty, thanks for answering. I know you know it's me, so please don't hang up." Betty remained quiet as he said, "This is my last quarter to make a phone call. I tried to call you at work today, but that bitch Carol lied and said you don't work there no more. Betty? Beep? I know I was wrong. I've thought about nothing else all weekend. I'm not calling you to forgive me, because I know it's too soon for that. And I know I don't deserve that. I just wanted to call to say . . ." And then he lowered his voice. "I love you. Beep? You there?"

Betty refused to give him the satisfaction of saying a word.

"You've got to believe me, baby. You even heard me tell Martin that when I was on the phone that night."

Quietly Betty said, "You said you had *feelings*, Evander. That we were just kicking it."

"Beep, it's the same thing. Men don't go around telling other men they're in love! Understand?" Betty held her tongue as he raised his voice. "Betty? Beep? Like I said, I know I was wrong. Looking back, I can see that now. But today I spoke to the PD's office because I couldn't afford an attorney. They sent this kid here who must be no more than twenty years old. His name is Karl. Karl Guillaume. But everyone in here calls him Karl Guilty because he never wins a case. Beep, I know I was wrong. I admit that, but I need a fair shake in court too. Just like anyone else. Betty? Are you there? Betty," he said after a pause, "I know you have friends in the court system and I know you can get me out of this mess. If you want me out of your life, although I think we can get over this, I'll leave. I made a mistake. Have you ever made a mistake? Honestly, Beep. I'll even pay you back the money on the gas card."

Betty closed her eyes and whispered, "What gas card?"

"Anyway, Betty . . . Beep, this is no place for me. You know I've never been in a place like this before. I mean I've been charged, but I was never booked. About an hour ago, Betty"— he paused as she heard tears thicken in his throat—"two or three guys came after me in the shower. They wanted to—"

"Two or three guys? You don't remember how many?"

"Okay, dammit! It was one, Beep. But damn, the brother was huge and he tried to take advantage of me. Someone tossed me this sawed-off mop handle and I hit him. Actually, I knocked the shit out of him, and they tell me as soon as the paperwork goes through, I'll be in lockdown. The only way I'm making this call is because a friend of mine works here. Betty, I know I was wrong, but you can't let them send me away for this. Beep, please!"

Betty leaned back in her chair and said softly, "Evander? Let me get this straight, because I want to be fair to you. You may not believe it, but I really do. You deserve that much because I know deep inside you're a sincere person. But what you did hurt me more than anything I can ever remember. So let me repeat what I believe you are saying. Okay?" Betty paused, remembering the time when she'd asked him in her bedroom, "Evander? Will it always be this good?"

"Okay here goes," she said. "You violated me, right?"

"Well, Beep, I wouldn't call it . . . well, yeah, I guess . . . yeah, I was wrong."

"Okay. And now you want *me* to get *you* out of jail for something you did to me?"

"Baby, please. See, actually, I found out they couldn't hold me on the first charge, but they can send me away for a criminal assault charge."

"I see."

"Betty? Please don't make a decision now. I know you

are a fair person and I know you are not vindictive. I know you are bigger than that. But please, baby, just think about it overnight. What I did was wrong and I'm prepared for the consequences, whatever they may be."

"Evander, as long as I've known you, I've known the very gentlemanly, kind side of you. And God only knows there are too many black men in jail today. But do you realize that in this entire conversation you have not once said the words . . . 'I'm sorry'?"

"Beep, I did. I said it when you picked up the phone. I'm sorry. See? I'll say it again. I'm sorry and I mean that from the bottom of my heart."

Softly Betty said, "When I sat in my car that night I tried to blame myself for what happened. I kept asking myself over and over again, what did I do wrong. Why couldn't I make you happy?" And then with a pause to gather her composure she said, "I tried to tell myself that it had to be fifty-fifty. That it took two to tango. But that night was the first night I could understand how abused women might feel. Monday night was the first night I truly understood how those women felt in the class action suit. When someone takes something away from you that even money could never replace. I also understood something my foster mother told me years ago. Sometimes in order to live, a little bit of you must die. That never made any sense to me . . . until that night. A part of me died on the floor of that room, Evander. But somehow I know it has made me stronger. It gave me the strength to make other changes in my life. So as I sat in my car thinking about you and all the good times we had . . . about the first time you sent me flowers and when you gave me the keys to your house . . . when I sat there thinking about the trip to Orlando, all I wanted to hear from you was an apology. All I wanted was for you to say, I'm sorry."

"Betty," he said contritely. "Again, baby, I was wrong. I'm sorry."

Betty smiled sadly and said, "You know, Vander? I thought that would make me feel better. I guess once again I was wrong about you. Good night."

CHAPTER 22

‡

Tuesday morning, one week later

 Dear Drew:

Thank you for making me smile at the beginning of
each day. Since I try to get up before the sun
rises, it's nice being able to read your letters
over a cup of tea. I know that is an odd way to start
a letter, but so often in life I think we take small
things for granted. I know I have in the past.
   In one of your letters a while back you were remi-
niscing about Felicia and what she meant to you. I
did not want to answer when you asked me, but the
more I thought about it, the more I realize Zelma
was right when she said Felicia loved you more than
you knew but could not face reality. Death is a terrible thing to have staring at you. I have often
wondered how I would handle being issued a death
sentence, and I can't truthfully say I would have
handled it any differently than she did. Think
about it. This young lady has waited her entire
life for happiness, for a man to send her roses, to
take her to vacation spots many people can only
dream of. And one word takes it all away. The word
''cancer'' turns her dream into one long
nightmare.

Deep inside, yes, I feel she loved you. So much
so she could never end a letter to you with complete
finality. She closed it by saying Until . . . because
she could not bear saying good-bye. A love like
that, Drew, would never hurt you intentionally.

If you love something, can you hurt it? My point
is, maybe it was just hard love. Maybe she did not
want to see you dwelling in the past. Possibly it
was a way for her to allow you to get over her death.

I've often thought of the story you told me about
the birds and finding your south together. Maybe
this was just a way to assist you in finding your
south.

I read a book recently where this lady was abused
by her husband who was a police officer. When she was
faced with no other viable options, she decided to
go into something similar to a witness protection
program for battered women. But to do so, she had
to change her name, move to another state, and
leave her old life. And it reminded me of something
someone once told me. Something I rarely thought
about until the past few weeks, and now I can't get
it out of my mind. A part of her had to die in order
for her to live again. Drew, maybe you had to suffer
that pain in order to be ready for love next time
around, because I am a firm believer that it's in
those moments when we do suffer that we discover
our truest character.

As I was driving home last night, the song ''Joy
Inside My Tears'' came on and I kept asking myself,
how could there have been joy inside the tears I
shed a few weeks ago for Evander? And then it became
clear to me. Before him, I thought I was emotionally impaired because of something that happened
to me early in my life. Now I know that is not the
case. I know I can love and I can feel loved. So I
guess to answer my own question, the lesson I have
learned from this experience is that what I've
worked so hard for my entire life is out there,
somewhere. And also that whatever we go through in

life . . . if finding our south is the outcome . . .
it's worth it all.

  Drew, I have no idea what tomorrow holds for me,
but for the first time in my life I am no longer
waiting . . .

Until . . .

Betty

Betty spent the rest of the day looking for discount furniture
for B.A. Robinson, attorney at law. She had secured a location to lease from a client who also promised to give her
his business in the future. Her former secretary, Carol, had
resigned and would join her the first day the firm opened.
When she'd gotten the call she'd thought it would be just
another *guess what is happening now in the firm* call. But Carol,
who was nearing the point when she would have secretarial
seniority, told her that working for O'Shaughnessy was not
the same. That his style of plodding through cases reminded
her of just how much she enjoyed working with Betty.

"Carol, I'm flattered, and God only knows I could use the
help. But I could never ask you to—"

"Then hire me."

"Carol, honey, it's not that simple."

"I know. But hire me anyway."

"But I don't have any—"

"Don't worry about it. If we can get a couple of juicy
cases, the money will come. You don't work in a town this
many years and not know anyone, so I think I can help you
there too. I was the third secretary Jack hired, and I remember a lot of things he did starting out. I know things have
changed, but I'll do whatever I can to help you build the
firm. Besides, I can't stand working there anymore."

Betty was speechless. Finally she asked, "Can you start
next Thursday?"

"Betty, I could start yesterday."

And then she'd received a call from Burt Collins, who'd
invited her to lunch. He'd indicated the partners had voted
him into the office of senior partner, and in that capacity he
wanted to meet with her personally to find out what had

happened and what, if anything, they could do to bring
her back.

Betty had ended the call by saying, "Thank you, sir, but
no, thank you."

As she sat at her desk, the fears of starting the firm dissipated. Agnes Murphy had put her in contact with a friend
who was unsatisfied with the attention his business had received since the death of Jack Murphy. Over lunch he'd
handed Betty a retainer check which allowed her to start
the firm without the necessity of depleting her 401K or other
personal assets. Feeling good, Betty took a break and reread
a letter from DLastRomeo.

Dear Betty:

I woke up early this morning to write you another
letter, only to find you had beaten me to the
punch . . . again. When you initially told me you
were starting a business I got the sense from your
letter that you were doing it because you did not
find a suitable company to work for and did not want
to leave town. But now I sense the reasons flow
deeper for you and I am excited about your future
as an entrepreneur. The fears you feel are only
normal. After the number of years I have been in
business I still have those fears. But those emotions are what push me and they will do the same
for you.

   The advice you gave me about Felicia was indeed
needed. It's difficult being a man and expressing
that side of you. I feel women in the office get a
little tired of it, and while I am not always successful, I try to keep my personal business out of
the firm. I talked to my mother about it, but she
just said that I needed to get over it and get on
with my life. So it's wonderful as a man to have a
friend with whom I can share all of the aspects of
my life. Betty, to me you are such a friend.

   Your last letter made me think about a number of

things, but what stands out the most is what you said about dying in order to live. I prayed and asked God more times than I will say, why? And what's the lesson in all of this? Where was my silver lining? Thank you for helping me to see a different viewpoint.

I don't know if I ever mentioned it, but Felicia had a passion for reading. I always read too, but my books were mostly motivational authors, as I mentioned to you in our first conversation. She would always try to get me to read novels, and I just never had time. I remember when everyone was talking about ''Exhale,'' and she went to a book signing and brought me an autographed copy. I never read it. They tell me she fell asleep on her last day on this earth reading ''If This World Were Mine.'' Kinda appropriate, huh? I finished reading that book for her and now I share that same passion for reading. Even in death, the woman continues to teach me how to live.

Remember I shared with you a few problems Walt and Peggy were going through? Peggy followed him to a hotel one day after work last week and she sat there watching him having sex with another woman through a crack in the curtains. I asked her why she would put herself through that and she just said she had to see it for herself. Don't ask me why she would endure such pain, but she is convinced it has helped her come to terms with it better.

Peggy moved out last night with the boys. She told Walt she loved him and always would. But she had lost her trust in him and felt it would never return.

Grace is still dating this guy who plays for the Jaguars. He had an off-season accident which I doubt will allow him to see much action next season. But as a result they're spending more time together and I would not be surprised if they're engaged in a couple of months.

Remember my friend Zelma? Well, she just got a

promotion and is now one of the vice presidents of Con-National. Unfortunately she is still alone as far as I know. Her ex-fiancé Vince came back into her life for about a month, although he's married, but could not deal with the money issue. So now she spends her weekends attending expensive tennis lessons and gourmet cooking classes, and she spends her nights dining and going to plays . . . alone.

Well, I must wrap this up because I am running late for a wedding. About a month ago I got a call from this lady who asked me what I thought about the prospects of her marrying this guy. Initially I was totally against it. But the more she talked, the more I sensed a side of her I had never heard before. She spoke of the love they had shared and how that love had endured through the years. She was married before, but the man, although he was a good guy, was never what she would call a friend. So now she is happy and I have given her my blessings. Today, in my parents' backyard, I will give my mother away in marriage to Mr. Douglass, and I've never seen her happier.

Love's a funny thing, isn't it?

Until . . .
Drew

CHAPTER 23

‡

Thursday, opening day of
Betty Ann Robinson, Esq.

"Hey, Girl. How are you this morning?" Jacqui asked.

"Fine," Betty said, sitting at her desk with the phone at her ear in an office in a relatively low-rent district. Her grand opening had consisted of a cake sent by Jacqui, plants from a group of secretaries at Murphy, Renfro and Collins, and over twenty phone calls before lunch. "Just sitting here wondering what to do with all this stuff in this tiny office. I've been so busy this morning I haven't even had time to fully unpack my stuff."

"We'll fix it up and it'll look good in no time."

"I hope so," she said, attempting to spin as she had so many times in her old office and then remembering her new chair would not do so. Looking over her shoulder, she said, "I sure miss my private bathroom and view and—"

"Forget the view. It's your sanity that's more important. I'll bring you a forty-ounce. That's what y'all drink on that side of town right? After a few shots you'll think you had your old office again."

"Shuddup."

"So what are you doing for lunch?"

"A phone conference with Mrs. Gaiting. She was one of my first clients at the firm and would like to continue giving me her business."

"Well, that's a start. So I guess the doors of Betty Robinson, Esquire, are officially open, huh?"

"I guess so," Betty said with a smile as she reviewed her receipts. "I guess this is all real."

"Well, the reason I asked you what you were doing at lunch is because," and then Jacqui said affectionately, "my *Stefan* is coming over for lunch and I wanted the two of you to meet."

"Ohh," Betty said, taking off her glasses and then crossing her legs and massaging the ball of her foot. "So it's my *Stefan* now. I haven't heard you talk like that since you were dating Yancy. Two grown folks playing you-hang-up-first on the phone, but I won't go there."

"Don't start," Jacqui said with a smile in her voice. "I mean so far he's looking like the real deal. We're going for a little weekend getaway to a bed-and-breakfast near Pensacola. And guess what. It will be our first time."

"First time for what?" Betty demanded, shocked as to what she could mean. "I know you don't mean the *first time* first time."

"Yes I do. I talk stuff and believe me, we came close, but like I said before, I wanted it to be special, so we're doing it the right way."

"Well, I'm proud of you. I really am. I mean so often we make the same mistakes with men over and over again. I'm glad you waited."

"I know. But tell me something. Have you ever noticed that as long as we've been together, as long as we've been friends—"

"We've never been happy at the same time, right?"

"Ain't that something? It's either you in a relationship and I'm on the outside asking how was it or vice-versa."

With a smile Betty said, "Oh well, no one said life was fair, right?"

"I guess not."

Changing the subject, Betty continued, "So tell me, is *he* cute?"

"Well, you know me. I'm not one to talk."

"Not one to talk? Are you kidding me? You better tell me something, girl."

"Like what? I mean he has a little hair on his chest and all and—"

"Hair on his chest, *bump* that! Tell me about the feet, girl . . . get to the feet! Inquiring minds want to—"

"Fourteen, double Ds, hands the size of baseball mitts, and child, that myth ain't no myth, if you must know. But seriously, he's really not my type at all. He's a geek with a pocket protector and everything. He's a Kappa, but he's not what you would call cute-cute."

"Damn. Most Kappas are pretty boys."

"I know. Leave it to me to find an ugly one, right?"

"So you got yourself an ugly Kappa man, huh?"

"Okay! Now, why you wanna go there? He ain't too bad-looking. He just ain't drop-dead or anything."

"Is he tall?"

"Yeah, he's just under six two and dark as an eight ball at midnight."

"Really? Is he, like, blue-black?"

"No, Stefan's purple-black. Child, when that Negro gets out the car, the oil light comes on, he so black. One night when I woke up, he was sitting across the room staring at me."

Laughing, Betty said, "That's cute. Just watching you sleep?"

"Cute my ass! I started yelling. When he looked at me, it looked like a train in a tunnel! But don't get me wrong, I'm not complaining. There's something that's so powerful about looking at rich, swarthy, dark, ebony steel, if you know what I mean." After clearing her throat, Jacqui called out, "Ah, Willie Mae. Bring me something to drink, please?"

"I know," Betty laughed. "A dark black man is a beautiful thing. That's the one thing I didn't like about Vander." As the words settled, the tension was thick until she added, "Well, let's just say that *stealing* thing wasn't too attractive either."

As she pulled into her driveway, Betty waved to her neighbors, who were playing dodgeball with the kids, and picked up a cup that had blown onto her property. As she returned to her car for her attaché, her mind immediately turned to

Drew. Deep inside she felt the desire, more than ever, to at least find out what he looked like, in spite of the threat to their friendship.

Walking through the door, Betty was greeted by Tickey. "Hey, sweetie," she cooed as she entered the code for her home alarm. Sorting her mail, she wondered how a man like Drew, who appeared to be so bright and strong, could be available. She wondered if he was gun-shy, and missing Felicia more than he seemed to share in his letters. *But then again, who knows?* she thought. *Maybe he is DLastRomeo.* Then Betty thought of the last man who was so kind and warm, and said aloud, "Yeah, right," as she tossed the mail on her dinner table.

After putting her purse on the couch and checking the answering machine, Betty went to her room, put on her Kobe Bryant Laker jersey, and then proceeded to her office. As she sat in front of the gray-blue computer screen, she thought, *I've got to get a life. Seems the entire world is off doing things.* She looked out the window. *Everybody out enjoying their lives and playing dodgeball with kids and I am sitting here in cyberworld. This is it. Tomorrow I call Compu-Line and cancel the service. I hate to lose a friend, but I need a life.* Then she turned on her computer, clicked her mouse, and discovered a letter from DLastRomeo.

  Dear Betty:

First and foremost I would like to apologize for the length of time it has taken for me to get back with you. I know it has been a couple of days and I counted three letters you had mailed me since. But if it is any consolation, I've thought of you continuously for the past 48 hours and I've really needed a little time to gather my thoughts.

This may take you by surprise, but I have been thinking of you in ways that are not purely related to friendship. To be perfectly honest, I originally had these thoughts a while ago after the Zelma fiasco, but I was confused as to whether they were based on my attraction to you or if it was a rebound situation. And since the situation with Evander occurred soon after, I felt it would be in bad taste to allow these thoughts to surface.

I did not wish to bring out these emotions until I understood them. Now I am sure, and I hope you do not change the way you feel about me as a friend due to the nature of this letter.

Betty, as you know, I had a tragic ending with Felicia. I never thought anything in this world could make me feel as bad as the pain of losing that woman. Afterwards I doubted myself in every aspect. I doubted if I was attractive enough, if I was man enough, if I was decent enough to meet and keep the kind of woman I wanted in my life. All of the self-confidence I had in myself from sports, from business, from public speaking, had all of a sudden gone down the drain.

But now I know I am ready because it occurred to me that after each day it's you I want to talk to if things went well. I rush home and turn on my computer before I undress sometimes, because it's you I turn to for solace. After thinking about what we have shared over the past several months, Betty, I find that it's you I look to as the soft place in my life to lean on when all the odds are against me.

I know you are a hardworking woman, although we really have never discussed what you do for a living, and what I am trying to say may be the last thing you want to hear. If it is, I'm sorry I have written these words because I would never want to lose what we have. But I would really like to know you better.

I know I am taking a gamble by sending you this letter. I am aware that the worst-case scenario may be your thinking I was just after you in a way that was not purely friendship. Actually the worst-case scenario may be that I never hear from you again. Well, Betty, a friend once told me something that I will never forget. She told me in a

letter, ''If the outcome is finding my south . . .
it's worth it all.''

Betty, I know you wrote me several letters over
the past few days that I never answered, and once
again, I'm sorry, but I had to be sure. Now I'm sure
that I would like to get to know you better. If the
feeling is the same, (352) 555-5896.

                                        Until . . .
                                           Drew

Betty read the letter with her hand over her mouth the
entire time, hardly able to believe he had written about feelings she wanted to share with him. And to top it off, she
now had his *unlisted* home phone number.

"So, let me get this straight, Betty," Jacqui said on the
phone. "This guy, on the Internet, who does not have a
girlfriend in the real world, and was dumped by a *dead*
woman, would like to talk to you—and you are actually
considering calling him?"

"Yes," Betty said slowly.

"Damn. Is that what sisters have come to? Okay. Now,
you have no idea *what* this guy looks like or anything?"

"Right."

"Okay. And for all you know, this guy could be some
serial killer or mass rapist working the Net."

"Jac, please," Betty said with a smile.

"No, I am serious. You should have him checked out or
something before you even consider calling him. I'm telling
you, you should watch a little bit of Montel. They have a
show on about these Internet fools just about every other
week. Get his last known address and I can have Stefan run
a background check on him. What if he has Caller ID or
something and he starts calling you?"

"I don't think so. This guy is nice. I mean he writes the
most wonderful letters, and from his description, he sounds
good-looking also."

"From *his* description. Check out what you said, girl.
From *his* description. What brother out there thinks he
ugly?" As Betty laughed, Jacqui continued. "I'm serious.

What brother out there don't think he's cuter than Denzel? Just ask any of them fools. I don't care how fat or skinny he is, he thinks he's three sit-ups and a bottle of Gatorade from dating Vanessa Williams."

"I know, I know. But," Betty said, and then her tone became serious, "I have my own business now. I have this beautiful home. I have the car and the lifestyle I have always dreamed of, and all I have to share it with is my cat. What's wrong with this picture? I mean I have had some serious, is-it-worth-it discussions with myself the last few days. I've sacrificed everything to be where I am now, and where am I? It has nothing to do with my biological clock. It's just that you work hard for a life. Okay, I've worked hard. Now, where is my life?"

"Honey, I understand. But if this man was half as nice-looking, half as intelligent, and half as romantic as you think he is, don't you think he would be off the market? You know how many women in this town would drop an ovary for a man like that? Honey, we are both in our thirties and the only thing left on the shelves are the half-priced scratch-and-dent men. They're the brothers who the other sisters done gone through and tossed away because they didn't fit, were too big, or too small, were the wrong color, or just did not catch their eye. Something is wrong with everything left on the shelves. It's not a matter of *if* something is wrong with him, it's a matter of finding *what* is wrong with him. It's tough looking at it in that context, but it's reality. If that Negro could conjugate a verb and count to five, child, he would be swept up like a dead cat on a Friday night in back of a Chinese food restaurant."

"Maybe," Betty said, smiling at the conversation and thinking the last thing she needed in her life at this time was another Evander. "Scratch-and-dent men, huh. Maybe you're right."

"Girl, you know I'm right. Now, let me give your number to Stefan's cousin. He works for Denny's, but he's a regional director or something. Stefan says he's nice-look—"

Giggling at Jacqui's contradiction, Betty said, "I appreciate that, Jac, but I need to hang up for now."

"Why? What's going on? Please tell me you are not ending a conversation with me to go on-line."

"Actually, I'm canceling the service tomorrow."

"Well, good for you."

After a pause she said, "Thanks. Now I gotta call Drew."

"Are you serious?"

"Night, Jac."

After getting off the phone with Jacqui, Betty went over to the computer and picked up the piece of paper with Drew's number on it. She sat on the oversized sofa in the living room while she pondered whether she could really go through with it. Was she prepared to deal with its contents once this Pandora's box was opened? She picked up the cordless phone beside her and dialed the number, even as she wondered, *What if Jacqui's right?* As she dialed the last digit, she knew inside that her life would in some way change as a result of doing this. Just like Alice, she was about to enter the looking glass.

"Hello. This is Drew."

Dayuummb, she thought as she listened to his answering machine. *This is how his voice sounds. So full, so rich.* Just like she expected.

"I'm presently not available, but your message is very important to me."

Damn, this man has so much sex appeal it comes through even on the answering machine.

"So at the sound of the tone—"

I can still hang up and he would never know I called—unless he has Caller ID.

"—leave your name and number—"

I hope I am doing the right thing; owww, I even like the way he says "number."

"—and I'll call you back."

Damn, I want my voice to sound right. I hope it doesn't crack. This'll be the man's first impression of me. I hope—

"Thanks, and have a nice day."

Oh my God, it's time. I'm not ready! I don't know what to, Beep.

"Ah, Drew. This is . . . this is Betty. I, umm, got your message and—"

"Betty?"

"Drew?"

"Hey, how are you?"

"Fine—and yourself?" Betty's heart beat like a jackhammer and she could feel her T-shirt move.

"I'm fine. One second. Let me turn this thing off."

Oh my God. It's really him. At least he can talk, so Jacqui was wrong about that.

"Okay, I'm back. I just came from dinner with Walt and Peggy. I told them I was not going to let them break up. Although they're separated, I think there's a chance."

"That was so nice of you."

"It was the least I could do for Peggy. She's my girl. But listen to me, I'm rambling on and on. I wanna talk about you. How are you, love? I can't believe I am actually talking to DeltaDream."

Their conversation lasted for hours and hours. They discussed everything from politics and what they would do if they were president, to the roles being taken by the current crop of top Hollywood black actresses. They shared childhood stories and favorite vacations, but the bulk of their time was spent talking of love. Not of their past loves, but the way it made them feel and what they missed most about it. For the first time they were communicating directly, and it flowed like the warm breeze that tossed pine needles against Betty's window.

"My goodness. Would you look at the time?"

"It's one-thirty. What time did I call you?" Betty asked.

"Ah, about nine. Remember I had just come in from dinner. I can't believe you are right here in Gainesville too. All this time we've been communicating and you were here in town. I was almost afraid to ask where you were, initially, because I didn't want to scare you off. Later I didn't want to know because I was sure you lived in western Afghanistan or something and I'd be crushed."

Flattered by the statement, Betty said, "I felt the same before you mentioned Gainesville in your letter. I'm just glad you can understand why I didn't tell you I was in town sooner."

"Are you kidding? Don't you watch Montel? Besides, as fast as both of our lives have been moving recently, love, I understand."

CHAPTER 24

‡

Friday

After saying good-bye to her secretary, Betty left the office with a genuine smile for the first time in weeks. Carol joked about the unexplained spring in her boss's step that day and the fact that she was singing aloud with the radio. When she looked at her quizzically, Betty said, "I'm just happy to be free. Nobody telling me what cases to take, no politics, just doing what I do best. Or should I say . . . what *we* do best."

Betty arrived at the meeting place where she had agreed to meet Drew ten minutes early. She did not want to play the fashionably late game, so being early was not of concern. "Turning over a new leaf this time. This time . . . it will be different."

Betty and Drew had arranged to meet at The Art House, which was a structure renovated by the city and used to display local works of art. It was a three-bedroom home, and as Betty walked inside, she looked to see if by chance Drew had arrived before her. From his description of himself, she knew he had not yet made it. The Art House was a little fuller than on most days, which meant there were a handful of people. A couple of blue-haired ladies holding hands for support, a few college kids, and the security guard slash custodian slash director of the establishment.

Oh well, I am early, Betty thought with a check of the art deco clock on the wall.

Drew sped down the highway toward The Art House. Looking at the clock in his car, he realized he had eight minutes to make the fifteen-minute trip. In the passenger seat was the file of a customer who had been given his name by Lisa of Murphy, Renfro and Collins. When he met with Mrs. Lopez, she spoke at length regarding her desire to protect her kids' financial future. He knew she was a good client, but she was the reason he was now late.

For Drew the day seemed to never pass. For the first time in a long time he was excited to meet someone and it felt good. He wanted to call her house just to hear her voice on the answering machine, but realized that in their four-hour conversation he had never thought to ask for her number.

With a smile on his face he turned on the radio and listened to Stevie. It was the first time he'd allowed himself to listen to him since the reading of the will. This time the words brought new meaning because they spoke of a love that would last through time, a love so strong it would last until the oceans covered the mountains. The song was not a tome of darkness but a beacon of light pulling him toward existence on another realm.

As he drove, Drew laughed out loud to himself. He had no idea whether Betty was overweight, a size two, fair complexioned or dark, but he smiled as he drove because it didn't matter to him in the least. And then on the side of the highway he saw an elderly lady beside a stalled car. Drew looked at the time as he sped toward the art gallery. He had seven minutes to save himself from making a bad first impression. As he drove, Drew looked in his rearview at the stalled car, which got smaller and smaller, and thought, *Somebody will help her. Hell, I don't know the first thing about cars.* And then Drew remembered his father. How he'd once worked on a car in the rain for a handicapped man while Drew and his friends waited in the car to go bowling. As he came to the red light at the intersection, Drew looked over his shoulder to see if he could see the lady, and he did. He could see her leaning against her car as the other motorists passed her by as well. And then Drew glanced at the clock, held the three roses he had bought for the occasion so they would not slide off his seat, did a U-turn, and said, "Betty, love, I hope you understand."

As Drew drove close to the car and parked, the lady's face lit up. "Thank you so much, son. I really appreciate it. I don't know what happened. I was just driving and I heard this loud noise which sounded like a shotgun blast. Blam! Blam! Blam! I stopped the car and got out to look at my tire. I would have tried to make it back home, but I was scared to drive on it like this. My husband used to tell me never drive on a flat, but this tire ain't really flat, see? So I didn't know what to do."

Drew looked down at the tire, which was still inflated but had lost most of its outer shell. The only thing he knew about a car was how to check the oil, replace the gas, and, thanks to his father, how to evaluate tires. "It's no problem, ma'am. Sometimes this happens with retreads. Do you have a spare?"

"I think so. I've never stopped on the side of the road." She headed toward the trunk. As she did, Drew glanced at his watch and heard her say, "Lord Jesus, would you look at all this stuff? I'm gonna have them churn get their mess out of my trunk. I don't keep my car like this!"

The trunk was packed to the rim with toys, clothing, canned meat, and shoe boxes filled with papers. After another quick time check, Drew rolled his sleeves above his elbows and said, "Ma'am, I don't mind helping you move some of that stuff out of the way."

"Are you sure, son?"

"Yes, ma'am," he said as he slid the items over just enough to get the tire out of the tire well. As he freed it, he noticed that it, too, needed air and that he was now five minutes late for his first impression.

Sitting in the museum, Betty took notice of the Darren Goodman display of artwork. His drawings of children's faces were so realistic they looked like black-and-white stills. Then a couple walked in with only their pinkies locked, swinging their hands back and forth in a way only lovers can. On the wall the clock reported that Drew was now fifteen minutes late. Betty was a little surprised because in their conversation he had mentioned how he took pride in always being on time. While they were meeting socially, nothing in his words had indicated that he was not the consummate professional.

"Chill, Betty, chill," she repeated to herself. "He could be in traffic or maybe his appointment ran a little late." Picking up her cell phone, she pressed speed dial so she could talk to Jacqui while she waited.

"Hello?"

"Yes . . . ah, did I call—" and then Betty realized her mistake.

"Hello? . . . Beep? Beep, is this you?"

Anger cinched her stomach tight as Betty figured out she had speed-dialed the wrong number, but she could not hang up.

"Listen, Beep . . . I know it's you. Thanks for calling me. I just want to let you know that I got out today. My momma put up the house and got me a real attorney and he thinks we can beat the charge."

Betty's hand trembled with anger, but then a calm of confidence came over her. She swallowed with difficulty, found her voice, and replied, "Evander? Let me just say that I'm okay with that. You hurt me, but guess what. It doesn't matter to me anymore."

Exhaling audibly, he said, "I knew all it would take is time, Beep. So what you're saying is that you would like to talk this thing over?"

"No. No, what I'm actually saying, is that I could give less than a damn about you doing time. What I am saying is you're petty, insignificant, shallow, and an ass. You played the role of a lifetime, but in actuality, Evander . . . it's *you* who got played. See, if I were like you, I would be upset right about now. But in actuality, Evander, I'm glad I called you . . . by accident . . . because you just gave me closure, which, as I look back, is the most you've ever given me. I once thought there could have been a little something for you in my heart, but there's not."

Before Evander could finish saying, "What are you—" she hung up. Betty sat with her cell phone bouncing in her lap with a big Kool-Aid smile on her face. But as she looked up at the clock, the smile disappeared.

"Drew, I'm so happy you stopped. I knew your daddy. God, he was a good-looking man. A good-looking man, you hear me? Had all that good curly hair and a silver cap on his front teeth. He used to sell my first husband tires back in the sixties. I remember he attended services at this church up on the hill. Had a woman pastor? Yeah, Mother Days Church. I remember it like it was yesterday."

Drew had removed the tire, and as he tightened the first nut on the spare he noticed he was drenched in sweat from the blazing hot sun.

"Son, do you need a towel to wipe off on? I think I got one in the trunk here somewhere."

"Ah, no ma'am," he said, flicking sweat from his brow and afraid of what she might return with. "I have one in my car. Thanks anyway."

The lady patted a tissue to her face and said, "Do you know these boys?" as a Ford Pinto which was covered with house paint and had a swinging crucifix on the rearview mirror pulled up behind them.

Drew looked over his shoulder and then at his watch. He was twenty-five minutes late. "No ma'am," he said, and continued to tighten the nuts.

Stepping out of the car, a brown-complexioned teenager with baggy jeans and a tight white tank top said, " 'Scuse me. How do we get to I-10?"

Drew continued to work but could hear the lady getting flustered as she tried to give directions. *Damn, Betty, don't leave. Why didn't I get her phone number?* Standing up with the crowbar in hand, Drew said, "Listen, man. You have to get on I-75 to hit 10. To get on 75, you have to—"

"What did he say to you?" demanded another teenager with distinct Hispanic features who was in the driver's seat. "This punk giving you lip, Carlos?"

"No. He was just telling me how to—"

"Shut up. You acting like a bitch again!" he said, glaring at the kid. "Now, we gonna do this or what, huh? We gonna make it happen this time or you gonna punk out!"

The elderly woman put her hand over her heart and rubbed it back and forth slowly. Quietly she repeated over and over words that were inaudible. "Ma'am, this is going to be okay," Drew said as he dropped the crowbar from his hand to seem less threatening.

As the metal hit the ground, the driver of the car whipped out his chrome handgun. "What the fuck was that!"

Carlos screamed, "Jesus! No! Put that shit away!"

"Listen, man. What do you want?" Drew asked in a composed voice. While the kid alternated pointing the gun at the old lady and Drew, his hand shook and a vivid look of fear glittered in his eyes.

Every time the steel pointed in the lady's direction, her body flinched with terror and the words crystalized into "LordJesusLordJesusLordJesus."

"What do you want, man? Nobody's going to be a hero today, okay? Just tell us what you want."

"I want your car keys, big man!" he said, looking at the Benz. "And I want your wallet and Grandma's purse!"

The first thought to cross Drew's mind as he reached into his pocket was, *It's insured.* As he grabbed his keys and threw them in the direction of the driver, the kid fired the gun, the old lady screamed, and Drew fell to the ground bleeding as Carlos followed orders to drive the Pinto while the other kid got behind the wheel of their new car.

The pinky-holding couple left the museum with the two old ladies. Soon it was only Betty, The Art House guardian, and the tick of the clock. As Betty walked out, the woman said, "Thanks for coming, ma'am. Have a nice day." Then she closed the door and slid the Closed sign into place, all in one motion. Betty's fears that something may have happened to Drew turned to frustration. Her excitement at meeting him for the first time and putting a face to the voice was now disillusionment with looking to find that special someone. As Evander's voice rang in her mind, Betty drove home hoping he would at least call, but in her heart not believing she would ever again hear from DLastRomeo.

Sunday

"Girl, what did I tell you about that nigga?" Jacqui said, fuming.

Betty lay on the couch in Jacqui's office and looked up at the light fixture.

"You didn't even know the man."

"You're right," Betty said like a child caught with her hand in the cookie jar.

As she sat and leaned forward on her desk with her weight firmly on her elbows, Jacqui refused to let up. "Now, just for a second, let's review what we do know about him. Or at least what he has *told* you about himself. He was head over heels in love with this female whose dying wish was to break his heart. He played with this sister's head and out of the grace of her heart she showed she was bigger than him and gave his company their business. And he graduated from a black college, yet he kissed up to some white man to make a sale? How am I doing so far?"

Betty said nothing.

"Now, to top it off, he invites you to this out-of-the-way—"

"It wasn't out of the way," Betty said quietly.

"Who gives a damn!" Jacqui exclaimed as she stood and walked over to Betty, who was still lying down and refused to make eye contact. "The man left you hanging, and if you are not pissed off about it, damn it, something must be wrong with you! Now, girl, this is hard to say, but I can't continue to follow up behind you when you make these bad decisions. From the day I met you, Betty, I've been cleaning up after you because I see what you could be. You know I love you, girl. Ain't no doubt about that. But I wish you'd learn to listen to me *sometimes* before this mess happens again. I know finding a man out there is tough, girl, but damn."

Betty turned her face away as Jacqui began pacing again.

"I don't care what you say, he could have called The Art House and left a message for you. He could have called you yesterday at home and said— I'll tell you why *Drew* didn't show up. It's because he's a liar. He lied about his looks, about his body or something. Push came to shove and he backed out instead of telling the truth. You probably shocked the hell out of him when you accepted his invitation and he couldn't get out of it. Otherwise, if he was halfway decent, he would have called. If something sounds too good . . . Think about it."

"I don't know. Maybe something came up."

"Yeah, right. Something came up and he couldn't call? And please tell me you didn't call that damn firm of his chasing after him."

Betty's eyes watered as she thought about being let down once again by a man. A man she believed in so dearly. "No, I didn't call him. But I don't think he has my number or even knows my last name."

"Betty. Please. Don't defend this jerk!"

Betty was silent, then rolled onto her stomach and aimlessly thumbed through the latest edition of *Ebony Magazine*. "Okay, okay. It's been two days. Let's just drop it," she said.

Taking a deep breath, Jacqui looked up at the TV and flipped to BET. "Listen," Jacqui said while watching the tube, "let's go get something to eat; we've been in this office all morning."

"I don't wanna," Betty said with the first glimpse of a smile she had mustered in days.

"Come on. Let's get some food in you and you'll feel better."

Standing slowly like a woman twice her age, Betty said, "Okay, let me put on my sneaks."

"Damn," Jacqui replied as she stood. "If you moving that slow now, can you imagine how you would have been in ten years with that firm, putting up with their nonsense?"

"I know," Betty said, standing in front of the mirror. "I actually look forward to Mondays again."

"Tell me about it," Jacqui said, looking at her in the mirror. "I remember all the office politics I had to deal with when I was in corporate America. Like when your boss comes and says, 'Ahh, Jordan. Let's get together on this project this afternoon.'"

"Yeah, and what he really means is, 'I don't have a clue, Ms. Jordan, but tell me what you know.'"

"Yeah, right. Or my favorite one. 'Listen, ahh, would you look this over tonight and give me your opinion tomorrow?' When they actually mean cancel your plans tonight because you don't have a fucking life and give me an in-depth report at nine o'clock sharp!"

"I know. I've been self-employed," Betty said, looking at her watch, "for seventy-nine hours and I already feel better."

With a smile at her friend, Jacqui said quietly, "And trust me, girl . . . it only gets better from here on."

As they walked out of the office Betty said, "Hey, I heard a great lawyer joke today!"

"Aw shyett, here we go."

Betty sat in a booth, awaiting Jacqui and their lunch. As always, Jacqui was filling in where needed while Willie Mae brought their food. "You can set it here," she said, moving a file out of the way. Betty tasted the soup and then decided that she should wait for Jacqui to join her, so she pushed the bowl away and placed a thick file on the table in front of her filled with old case summaries she had worked on for Murphy, Renfro and Collins. Betty put on her glasses and thumbed through the pages until she felt someone staring at her. Looking over her oval frames, she saw he wore shorts and his thighs were thick. And then her perusal moved up to his chest, which was wide, and then his eyes, which gazed back at her. And then he tipped his head politely, smiled, and walked away with a slightly confused look on his face.

What the . . . and then it occurred to Betty where she had seen him previously. *That's the guy I saw at the firm a few months ago,* she thought, leaning back in the booth. As her pulse rate increased, Jacqui walked up to the table.

"Did you see that brother standing here looking at you? Now, tell me he wasn't fine." Both ladies watched him as he walked outside, and got into his Honda Civic, and drove away. "What's wrong with you, girl?"

"Nothing," Betty lied as she closed her file. "Can you eat yet?"

"In one second, but don't let your soup get cold. I need

to balance out this register before Tequila gets off. She pays her baby-sitter tomorrow and she missed half of last week. I don't want her to approve a *loan* for herself."

Jacqui walked away as Betty reopened the file and noticed that one of the copies she had made of Drew's poem "Until . . ." was tucked inside it. She ran her fingers lightly over the print as if it were braille, then attempted to focus on the cases for possible future business. However, the more she tried, the more she failed. Her thoughts bounced from Evander to Drew. Why was it every time she was *so* sure about a man, she ended up being *so* wrong? As she sat looking at the legal-size pages, she decided that she would not call Drew's office the following day. It was time for a fresh start and a new beginning. This would be her first full week in the firm, and she looked forward to . . .

"Excuse me, but may I sit?" said a deep voice behind her.

Betty's head jerked around and her hand jostled the poem off the red and white checkerboard tablecloth. As it floated downward leaflike, he caught it with his fingertips inches before it would have hit the floor, glanced at it, and smiled as he handed it back to her. Then he sat and as he held his stomach and slightly grimaced said, "Have you ever had déjà vu?"

"I'm sorry. You didn't have to—"And then as Betty looked into his eyes she noticed it was the man who had watched her previously. But this time when she looked in his eyes, her heart stopped.

He sat there and said nothing. He stared at her, as if to memorize her every feature, and then once again looked into her eyes.

Dammit. See, I knew it. He too damn good-looking. I bet he's crazy or high or . . . Oh hell. "Ah, can I help you?" Betty said, and slid her hand into her purse under the table for her Mace. *You move the wrong way and I'll blind you.*

"I was detained."

"You were what?" she asked, placing her finger firmly on the trigger of the Mace. *Why is he telling me about his police record?*

"I was—" he reached down and painfully held up his

shirt, showing her a large bandage on his stomach
"—detained."

"Excuse me?" *Dammit. A freak. One more move and I swear . . .*

And then as he carefully lowered his shirt, he looked out-side and spoke to himself. "I don't believe this." Turning squarely toward Betty, he said, "I've seen you around town. The first time I saw you was a few months ago at Murphy, Renfro and Collins and I wanted to at least say hello . . . but I couldn't. I knew you looked familiar, which is why I was staring at you earlier, but since you had your hair done differently and you're dressed in sweats, I couldn't place you. But when I drove out of the parking lot, I saw the navy BMW and it all started to fall into place, although I had to come back inside to be certain. And then you dropped the poem."

"What are you talking about?"

After a swallow he said, "Betty, *love*, I was detained."

"How do you know my—" And then it sunk in with the subtlety of a ton of bricks. Betty's eyes widened. She wanted to scream, she wanted to laugh, she wanted to cry, but all she managed to do was say, "It's you? It's you, isn't it," even as she noticed Willie Mae walk back out with Jacqui's food, followed by Jacqui, whose mouth was slightly open. She tapped Willie Mae on the shoulder and motioned for her to take the food to another table. "I thought I had lost you forever."

Shaking his head, he said, "Betty, if only you knew."

Betty leaned back and gathered herself as she thought about the experience she had just gone through with Evander. With an assertive tone she said, "Seriously. Tell me. What happened?"

"Well, to make a long story short, I stopped to help this lady on the side of the road." He paused and looked at his trembling hand smoothing wrinkles out of the tablecloth. "These kids drove up, and well, we were carjacked, that's how I got the wound. But the entire time it was happening . . . the whole while I was in the emergency room . . ." And when their eyes met Betty skipped a breath as he said, "All I could think of was you. I saw your face.

Not your physical face but . . . your essence. And all I could think about was getting out of the hospital and waiting for your call."

"Umph-umm," Jacqui said, clearing her throat loudly at the table.

"Oh, I'm sorry," Betty said, looking at her for a split second, then turning to look at her guest. "Oh my God, I can't believe you went through that. I can't believe this is happening at all. Jacqui, this is Drew. Andrew . . . Patrick . . . Staley. Drew, this is my Jacqui."

"You have *got* to be kidding me," Jacqui said. "This is the guy? From the computer?" Neither of them said a word as Jacqui smiled and said, "Well, girl, handle your *business*," and walked away with Willie Mae.

"So could you by chance be my Betty?" he asked with a smile that highlighted a twinkle in his eyes that had previously been missing.

Betty returned the smile and replied, "Could you by chance be the man from my dream?"

Their fingers softly embraced somewhere in the middle of the table as their conversation picked up where it had ended previously on the phone. Drew mentioned the places where he had seen her and was surprised she remembered him from their brief encounter in the restaurant. As she felt the velvet edge of Drew's voice resonate within her, Betty noticed Jacqui occasionally in the background and laughed aloud with sheer happiness.

"I love your smile," Drew said, which then made her blush. In their conversation they talked about many things and Betty watched his eyes move. As they spoke she enjoyed the fact that she had no inhibition about allowing her feelings to show. While she had cautioned herself to be reserved when they met, those thoughts were melted by the warmth in his face and she felt she had finally found that soft place to lean.

Then in the midst of their conversation Drew stopped. Softly caressing her hands, he asked, "Have you ever met someone for the first time, and all you want to tell them is how much you've missed them?"

Betty's smile vanished as she said quietly, "Not until today."

The late lunch extended to dinner as the newly met couple watched the yellow and orange ball steal back its shards of light and kiss the spring sky good-bye, as it tiptoed away leaving everything in its path traced in saffron gold. Drew turned Betty's hand over and softly traced the M in her palm. With the white clouds on the horizon turning to shades of pink, Betty and Drew laughed and told stories, smiled, forgot, remembered, and looked forward. But never did they mention their past loves, nor did they mention their bad experiences, nor did their fingers separate from the middle of the table.

Until . . .